Fiction on a Stick

Stories by Writers from Minnesota

Fiction
on a Stick

Stories by Writers from Minnesota

Daniel Slager, Editor

MILKWEED EDITIONS

© 2008, Selection, Arrangement, and Introduction by Daniel Slager

(800) 520-6455

www.milkweed.org

Published 2008 by Milkweed Editions
Printed in Canada
Cover design by Brad Norr
Interior design by Connie Kuhnz, Bookmobile
The text of this book is set in Adobe Jenson Pro.

08 09 10 11 12 5 4 3 2 1
First Edition

Please turn to the back of the book for a list of the sustaining funders of Milkweed Editions.

Library of Congress Cataloging-in-Publication Data

Fiction on a stick : Stories by Writers from Minnesota / Daniel Slager, editor. — 1st ed.
    p.   cm.
    ISBN 978-1-57131-066-8 (pbk. : alk. paper)
    1. Minnesota—Fiction.   2. Short stories, American—Minnesota.   3. American fiction—Minnesota.   4. Short stories, American—21st century.   I. Slager, Daniel.
    PS571.M6F53 2008
    813'.54—dc22

2008042176

"Zamboni Blues" by Robert Voedisch originally appeared in *The Greensboro Review,* Spring 2004.
"The Prairie Town" by Éireann Lorsung originally appeared in *The Rake,* December 2007.

Fiction on a Stick
Stories by Writers from Minnesota

Introduction: Daniel Slager   vii

I. Heritage Square

"The Woodcutter," Sun Yung Shin   3
"The Prairie Town," Éireann Lorsung   13
"Norfolk, 1827," Shannon Gibney   19

II. Grandstand

"Hands," Kaethe Schwehn   33
"Assimilation," Sarah Stonich   40
"Red Cranes," Jacey Choy   55
"Nobody's Brother," Ann Bauer   68
"To Move a Tree," Diego Vázquez   82

III. Modern Living

"The Body Remembers," Diane Wilson   93
"Knowing," Josiah Titus   101
"Xanadu," Chrissy Kolaya   106
"The Rice Pickers," Linda LeGarde Grover   117
"Betty García," John Reimringer   145

IV. Midway

"Tandem," Steven Lang   165
"Sketchbook: Atmospheric Conditions," Anastasia Faunce   182
"Remains of Life," Kirk Wisland   192
"Zamboni Blues," Robert Voedisch   208
"The Broken Group," Ethan Rutherford   219
"The King of Marvin Gardens," Miriam Karmel   236

V. Progress Center

"Clean Laundry," Michael Walsh   247
"The Second Wife's Daughter," May Lee-Yang   262
"We Are Each the Seventh Generation," Marcie Rendon   280
"Knowing You in Snow," Dominic Saucedo   289
"Some Advice on Arranged Marriage," Pallavi Sharma Dixit   300

Introduction

Daniel Slager

The light-hearted title of this anthology commemorating Minnesota's one hundred and fiftieth anniversary as a state draws on one of the many symbols of our common identity, referencing the wide mix of homespun, original, and surprising foods served "on a stick" at the State Fair. Whether it is deep fried candy bars, bacon dipped in chocolate, or grilled corn on the cob, seemingly something for every taste imaginable—and some unimaginable— is available at the "Great Minnesota Get-together."

But our title also suggests a more grounded and democratic image of the state than its whimsical reference may first present. For if we see the Fair as an opportunity for people from all walks of life, from all corners of the state and beyond, to get together at one time, we also see this anthology as a similar celebration of the changing yet enduring face and personality of Minnesota. If the crowds filling Dan Patch Avenue every year show a different demographic—young and old, urban and rural—then *Fiction on a Stick* presents a heartwarming, diverse, and ultimately surprising literary portrait of the North Star State.

Divided into sections that suggest a walk through the fairgrounds, the twenty-four stories included—widely differing in tone and subject— together form the sort of journey we may make in a day or in a lifetime or in several lifetimes. "Heritage Square" honors the principle that at first there is the word—the recorded texts and stories that replay our beginnings.

"Grandstand" salutes the charismatic figures, heroes, mentors, and exemplars against which we measure ourselves and our communities. "Modern Living" wrestles with the compromises of living in a watershed period, dealing with the overlap of history and modernity. The stories in "Midway" suggest what comes after the carnival—picking up the pieces. And "Progress Center" looks ahead—as all these stories do in some way—catching glimpses of who we Minnesotans may become.

Putting this book together was a joy and an education. Our criteria were simple: we sought stories by emerging writers who live in Minnesota. As this introduction suggests, the combined effect of this sampling of distinctive voices is—and is not—the Minnesota that comes to mind around the country when one says the word. When we think of the people who have called this area home going back further into time than the state's history does, and when we measure that legacy against the current day's, we recognize that progress still needs to be made in terms of defining *Minnesota*. Covering a wide range of opinions drawn from an equally wide range of experiences and backgrounds, the writers in this anthology pose questions about our past and raise challenges to our current assumptions, even as they begin the work to build a sense of identity that all communities may one day be comfortable in sharing.

In the months preceding the annual return of the fair, rampant speculation takes place about the next creation to appear "on a stick." Similarly, as we read and treasure the stories in *Fiction on a Stick*, we draw inspiration for the future, with a clarified and empowering sense of our differences and commonalities—comfortable in the knowledge that whoever we become, we will be rubbing elbows and sharing stories.

Fiction on a Stick

Stories by Writers from Minnesota

Heritage Square

The Woodcutter
a retelling

Sun Yung Shin

Standing still, he received the clamor of the forest. The absence of other humans. All the green life speaking, vocalizing. Winged things and animals smaller than he hummed and sought prey, or moved with the anxiety of the hunted. Crickets. An occasional melancholy croak of a frog.

Perhaps even a tiger was about, fresh from tricking a halmoni into giving him her rice cakes. After those had been devoured, he demanded and ate each limb, one after another, until even her rolling torso became his afternoon meal.

The woodcutter's white cloth bag was full and heavy, the bark of the fallen and cut stack of wood scratching his back, imprinting his skin with the pattern of the tree's skin. Hard and rough, but no match for the sweet sing of the blade of his axe. Never had he cut himself, even as a boy, he was so careful. His mother told him that the Great King of Heaven had not given him a father but instead had given him his protection, which was far better, as a father might get drunk and beat his wife and son, or turn lazy and refuse to work, or gamble and spend money on prostitutes.

As he walked through the forest, down the mountain path, his foot slipped on a rock and he stumbled. As he scrambled to regain his footing, he stepped on a pine-needle cluster, and a few of its spikes stabbed the side of his bare foot.

—Aigo!

He sat and plucked out the needles. Clusters of the same littered the path, lazily, not needing to hide from predators. They looked like spirit creatures, like souls.

The green spikes had left three angry red marks on his flesh. He decided to veer off the path and soak his foot in a nearby pool whose water was clean and cool, shaded as it was by tall, somber faces of red-brown rock.

Suddenly, the bushes in front of him shook and a blur of brown shot toward him. It was a deer, a male. It came to a complete stop in front of him.

It looked as if it were wearing velvet. A prince. A young god of the forest. It spoke.

—There's a hunter after me! Would you hide me?

—I'll do better than that, friend deer. You go that way and I'll tell the hunter you went the other direction.

Before it bounded away, the deer spoke once more, turning back to the woodcutter.

—If you go to the pool at sunset, maidens will descend from Heaven to bathe. Steal the garments of one of the maidens and she will have to marry you. Hide her clothes. Whatever you do, never let her see them, no matter how she begs. Once she has three children, she will have too many to carry back with her to heaven and will be earthbound forever. Still, no matter how many children you produce together, keep the clothes beyond her sight. *Don't forget.*

He paused to imagine the unimaginable: a woman, a wife, young and beautiful, begging him for anything.

Begging. Naked.

Moments after the deer and all trace of its movement had disappeared, a hunter crashed through the trees. Red-faced and breathing heavily, he approached the woodcutter, who had not moved, lost in a vision.

—Did a deer just come through here?

—What?

—A deer. Did it—

—Yes, yes! He went that way just a minute ago!

The woodcutter pointed in the opposite direction and wore on his face an expression of supreme sincerity.

Without a word of thanks, the hunter ran past the woodcutter's outstretched palm.

...

It was something of a hike to the pool.

Once there, the woodcutter hid his wood cuttings at the base of a pine tree, cleared a brown slug the size of his index finger off of a flat rock behind some thick bushes, wiped his hand on the cool surface, laid himself down, and fell into a reverie.

In the ancient oak providing shade above him, the leaves fluttered in the wind, reminding the woodcutter of the laundry his omoni would hang behind the house.

As a boy, he had loved putting his cheek against the damp white cloth, feeling its warmth from the sun. He had a ritual. With his eyes closed, he checked the dryness and the softness of each piece of clothing. He knew the exact texture of every one of the items. After he had gone down the line, he reversed his steps, lying down in the shadow of each garment, placing his body so he would be exactly within its outer contours. This could only be done early or late in the day, as there was no shadow at high noon, or sometimes just a flicker, a thought of a shadow.

As he had gotten older, his clothes got larger, as did he, but his omoni's seemed to shrink. They seemed lonely with only his, her son's, for companionship. In person, she didn't seem to mind the lack of a husband, but to him, her son, her hanbok seemed terribly solitary.

His clothes looked feminine on the clothesline. Soft. Tender.

He was seventeen years old and a virgin.

The girls he grew up with were women now. When he walked by, even at a distance, it was as if he could smell their ripeness.

Seeing them made the base of his spine feel like it might dissolve, leaving him weak, unsteady.

Too many stories about vengeful fox demons.

His mother's favorite was the one about the dead virgin, buried by the side of the road.

A man was stumbling home one night after an evening of drinking. He stopped, pulled out his manhood, and pissed a long stream. It made a dark pool, then a river, in the dry dirt.

As he sighed with relief and satisfaction, a figure rose from the ground. It was a fox demon, the dead girl, the spurned girl, the untouched girl, whose bones had been pissed on by the unwitting man.

He ran, he spent his meager income on shamans, even Catholic priests, but he was tormented by the angry, unloved woman for the rest of his life. No living woman would touch him, as he was day and night followed by a phantasm with long black hair and a demonic gaze. He went completely mad and drowned himself in a well, but even in the afterlife the fox demon wouldn't let him go.

The sound of crickets.

It was evening. The air was cool, and the walls of rock seemed to emit a faint blue light. The white mist had begun to settle around the shoulders of the mountain.

Splashing, laughter.

Water droplets flung from arms as the maidens bathed.

Moonlight pooling in the hollows of her clavicle.

...

The woodcutter's legs were stiff. He groaned silently as he crept to the edge of the pool, where a small hill of fabric lay. Iridescent, finer than any mortal clothing, purple and blue like the wing of a dragonfly, or the back of a horned beetle. Sheer.

Still unnoticed, still in shadow, he reached for the cloth closest to his hand and quickly pulled it toward him.

As he pulled, the garment moved toward him like a stream of water, but his delight was interrupted by the whole hill of dresses sliding swiftly off the moving cloth and into the pool, without a sound.

But they heard, they saw.

Every one of them whipped her head toward the movement, toward their clothes slowly sinking beneath the surface of the mirrored water, and watched with horror as the woodcutter stood up, clutching a dress to his chest.

In the blink of an eye, the women captured their clothing and caught on to silvery ropes hanging from the sky, ropes that the woodcutter had not noticed until now. Not even taking the time to dress, the women were gone with a flick of their long black hair, still shedding droplets, which fell like pebbles, one or two hitting the woodcutter on his face, stinging.

The last maiden walked toward the man with deliberation, cutting through the pool as if it was air and not liquid. She made no attempt to cover her nakedness. She had no modesty or shame. As she rose out of the pool and took the last step toward the man, her body was completely dry, even her hair, which had wound its way back into a long braid, its end tapered like a paintbrush soaked in ink.

She stood before him.

Her hair appeared wet, soaked, but when he reached through the space between them and touched it, it was as dry as his. He had never touched a woman's hair.

She smelled like pine needles, like sap.

The man shivered, and with his left hand held the dress behind him, out of reach.

After that night, the woodcutter never went home again, as they lived in the forest, and lived well, even luxuriously, but in total isolation.

He left behind his role of woodcutter, his life as a boy.

He had become a handsome man, as if just by being with her he had absorbed her beauty, without draining any from her.

She seemed to grow more lovely with each passing year, never aging, never losing the moonlight that made her body glow with Heaven's blessing.

It was as if she, and what she brought with her, was made for his pleasure, for him alone.

Everything was provided for them—a house with ondol flooring, a table set with food each day, new garments and shoes every season.

They were happy, man and woman.

The surrounding woods, no longer in danger of being the victim of the man's axe, sang them to sleep every night.

The very trees protected their three children—two daughters and a son—from animals, the wind and rain, and bad fortune.

The man never gave a thought to his old mother. In fact, he forgot that he had ever had one, and that he had never met his father, and he began to talk as if he had been born in Heaven, like his beloved wife.

One day while the man was out taking a swim with his children, the woman was home alone.

She practiced her calligraphy, writing her name over and over again, each pass identical to the last.

White sheets written with fine black wings littered the floor around her, as if she were a tree that had shed its leaves.

She paused to glance out the window, a window that looked into a clearing.

A flash of brown—a deer, a buck, walked slowly across the field. It paused before entering the far boundary of the forest, then leaped in and disappeared, the heavy shade closing around the place where it had stood.

A memory.
A remembrance of a memory.
Laughing.
Wetness, then dry.
A hand reaching toward her neck, a flash of silk vanishing.
Nothing.

This life.

The wife began having nightmares.
As her husband was so bound to her, he began having the same nightmares.
They repeated themselves, the images. There was a king. A hunter. Eleven sisters sleeping in a row of beds, the twelfth bed empty, cold. A pair of slippers at the foot. Weeping. A silver rope. An old woman, stirring a fire, alone.

. . .

The man knew what he had to do.
He took out his old axe, which was rusty and dull.
He went to the market, stole a whetstone, brought it back home, and, at night, when his family was asleep, he sharpened his axe.

More dreams.
She woke up sometimes sobbing, her pillow wet, her face salty.

The man became elusive, often gone during the afternoon. When asked, he said he was making a surprise for the children, a novel plaything he had heard about as a child, something from China.
As he had no currency, he continued to steal.
With his axe, he slaughtered a farmer's single water buffalo.
He put its horns in his sack.
He stole fish from the market, cut out their bladders, made glue in a jar, laid it aside.

He cut down an oak. This would be the core.
He cut down a hickory. This would be the back.

...

He shaped the thing, in secret, missing meals.
The nightmares continued.
The wife woke with eyes red from sobbing.
The children noticed nothing, as by the time they woke she was fully composed, and had herself forgotten those terrors, those images, those fragments of memories.

It was finished, nearly.
—One thing, I need this last thing.

It was second best, but it would have to do.
He took his axe, now so sharp it sang as it did its work, and went out again.

He rinsed, disposed of the body, and brought the materials back home.
It was a shame. All he needed was the sinew from the back legs, but the whole animal, a horse, had to be sacrificed.

The bow was ready.

Suddenly the nightmares ceased, for both him and his wife.
Cheer had returned to their sleep.
Nevertheless, the thing was made, and it was better done than left undone.
The woodcutter, for the first time in his life, went hunting.

It took him almost a fortnight, but in the end, the deer looked at him, the arrow flew from the bow, and it was true. Through the heart.
The body of the deer dropped silently onto the mossy ground, its black eyes still open, staring upward, beyond the trees.

The woodcutter left the body where it lay, and left the bow and quiver of arrows at its feet.

When he approached his home, exhausted from being days on the hunt, he heard music.

As he stepped through the threshold, a figure pushed past him. He spun around to see his wife in the courtyard. She was wearing the dress, the dress he had stolen from her on that first evening.

He called her name, but she would not look at him.

She gathered one child in her left arm, one in her right, and their youngest, the baby boy, between her knees.

He ran toward her, fell to the ground, grasped clumsily at the hem of her gown, and begged her not to leave, not to do this, not to take their children with her, to stay with him, as he couldn't live without her.

He was ignored, as if he wasn't there at all.

He could not even get purchase on her clothes—the cloth was as water, running through his fingers, the fingers that were newly roughened with the work of making bow and arrows, of hunting for weeks.

A wooden bucket attached to a silver rope descended out of nowhere. She sat in the bucket, their three children firmly in her grasp, and, without a glance, ascended.

When out of his reach, his children looked down at him, as if with pity, and his oldest gave him a small wave, and then looked away.

Weeks passed. The man didn't eat, couldn't sleep for the nightmares.

He prayed.

He lit their house on fire and watched it burn to a black shadow.

He began to waste away, his eyes hollowed, he grew mad.

He started seeing nothing but whiteness, a moon glow, closing out the darkness in his mind. His limbs no longer felt cold but warm, as if coals had taken the place of his heart, warming his whole body.

The King of Heaven took pity on him, his mortal son-in-law, the one who failed, ultimately, to hide the King's daughter's clothes well enough.

He sent down a bucket, a bed really. The man didn't see the silver rope; he thought that it was his childhood bed, and he heard his mother singing him a lullaby. With the last movement he had available, he crawled toward the apparatus, made of shining hard wood, cut with the grain, the kind of wood he could never burn.

Now in heaven, she was happy to see him. She embraced him and kissed his ashen face. She laid him in a white bed, his children at his feet, and nursed him back to health and sanity.

Again, they had everything they needed.

Still, something ate at him, pulled at the back of his mind.

He dreamt of the face of a deer. Its horns grew and grew until they became a forest blocking out the sun.

Trapped behind the tangle of horns was a figure, an old woman.

His mother.

He remembered. He remembered her, how he had abandoned her without a thought, without a word.

Again, the Heavenly King gave the man his pity. He gave him a winged horse on which to travel down to earth, to greet his mother and ease both of their hearts.

His wife stood by the horse's harness and petted the white animal's strong neck. The man was ready. His wife spoke.

—Yobo, darling, remember—you must not get off the horse. If you put even one foot on the ground, Heaven will close to you forever, and we will be parted again, but this time for eternity.

The man nodded, having no intention of dismounting from the steed, eager to see that his mother was living well without him then return as quickly as possible.

He bent down to kiss his wife, then spurred on the horse, and they descended through the clouds at an impossible speed.

He grasped the reins as the wind clung to him like a heavy cloak.

As the horse landed, creating a cloud of dust, the man coughed and rubbed his eyes, trying to see.

As he laid his eyes on the shabby, one-room dwelling which had been his home for seventeen years, he felt pity for his mother, and for the boy he had been.

As the dust settled, he noticed something odd.

Above the doorway hung some contraption—no, it was a head, the head of a deer, still with its antlers. The eyes of the deer were glassy and wore a strange expression. A glint, perhaps of malevolence, or merely curiosity, or patience.

His mother, begging him to come inside and eat a meal with her. His refusal, her tearful entreaties, his refusal, her demand.
—At least eat this bowl of pumpkin soup—your favorite!
A nod,
the handing of the piping hot bowl, the young man's hands, soft from his regained luxurious life,
burned,
a curse,
the dropping of the hot soup onto the neck of the winged horse,
the cry of the horse, the rearing, the falling
of the man,
his back hitting the ground,
the horse's rapid ascent without its rider,
the man still in the dust, soup on his clothes,
the mother, wiping his hands
with the hem of her rough white shirt.

The passing of seasons.

The Prairie Town

Éireann Lorsung

She says, everything happens somewhere. Directs those eyes like light-house beams someplace west. Doesn't find what she needs. Looks at her feet. What she is out here: alone. It's not so bad.

When he landed he was only sixteen and piloting a light craft. One wing bent earthward and the old man slumping. Alone among planes of sand. Goggles to keep out the glare, met no one for hours by his watch. In three o'clock radiance he rested under a shelf of rock.

Finally, the watch full of sand. Moon rising on the white edge of dunes. He waited and walked in nighttime. Sliced the fleshy plants. Sap like meat.

There was a cord around his waist pulling him north, polish to keep his goggles black and clear, no one asking him who or what, or where the old man left his bones for animals to pick.

Like this, he walked out of the desert.

For the longest time it was a speck on the horizon, a cliché she would have lied and said she dreamt if anyone asked. No one was there to ask. One day it was a larger speck and then all of a sudden a boy her size. She sat under the azalea to wait, watched his knees pass by, stop a ways down the road. He could smell her where she hadn't washed, she thought. Both of them settled in to wait a while.

She hated to give away the secret: the boy had no eyes, only a pair of smokeblack glasses. His face was a dialect of stars reflecting. What if dust rose up? Out would come the cloth. The miniature bottle of polishing fluid. He walked like a ragtime piano. The little strings she wrapped around her fingers pulled toward him.

In between times she consoles herself with a battered *Oxford English*. The smell of leather, something like shaving cream, she imagines. When she picks up the book, she is touching something she's waited for. The pages sigh, or she does. Inside the dictionary everything is always the same as ever: a television, phonograph, or radio cabinet that stands on the floor; a desklike structure containing the keyboards, pedals, etc. of an organ; the control unit, oh, she thinks, the brain.

It's true her leg was missing. Sometimes when the uncle was awash in spirits he'd lead her out into barbed wilderness and wonder with her which direction it had gone. The new leg creaking. It had been a doll's leg, porcelain as a bathtub. Sometimes you just can't trust your own body not to run off, she thinks.

The boy has never seen it. Or anything. But he imagines the flexing muscles of the rabbit move like the ocean and in any case its smell is also salt. Under his insistent hand the rabbitbody moves uncomfortable. But it is so small. Part wants to open the sternum, feel the muscled valves pump and spray. That decision is permanent so he just waits, feels the animal know his danger, feels the heart-motor run: fast, faster. Smells the wet air.

At dinnertime the uncle brings a jar of olives out of the sack to put in the cupboard to take out for dinner when the aunt would come from the store to eat and the uncle's hand would stop scrabbling. Olives with pimento, small red peppers, the ninety-nine-cent jar. The cheap uncle. Doll's-leg cringes away from strap.

Chicken bone, kid glove, clock. Seven mason jars full of dust, another full of soot. Glass door of the drugstore. Crack down the street's center line. Yesterday's apple blossoms pressed flat as a kiss between pages of a leather-covered book. Yellow brick limestone slate roof thatch roof pavestone skipstone beggarman thief.

The uncle likes the smell of the ocean parts. Where he was in the army was full of ocean and the smell of ocean. He presses his nose to them. At night she puts them in their proper places. The uncle likes things out and messy. If they're put away just right he might not find them next time.

But sometimes the boy is there in the dark pretending to be a branch that moves air syrupslow out her window. The new leg asleep in its cradle next to her bed dreaming peaceful dreams—the branch or the boy scratches the pane and she lies still as last night's pan fish. If her sash is up he'll whistle—low—and make her look, give away her wakefulness, and then: can I know your name? in his brokenbottle voice. She whispers: ——

The azalea blooms. Some of its branches break. Sometimes the light in the house above the dining table tosses color onto the road. Sometimes he can hear the aunt laughing to the uncle. Sometimes he looks up into the trees. Feels her eyelashes close featherquick on cheek. Counts her blinks by the hour.

The bicycle in the garage has one flat tire and no brakes but it's cheerfully red. Basket waving tatters of a checkered bow. Left handlebar: rubber bulb of a horn shreds and peels. Over breakfast she tells the aunt she'll take hot lunch that day. Tells schoolteacher she's walking home, noon hour. Sits in the motey slant of windowshine, polishes that worn-out chrome as if there's no—tomorrow not even a thought.

Schoolteacher commands politeness, lifts it up on a platter of gold stars. Manners count. Rows of stars count. She counts them out loud for the class. Her glasses chain jingles as she moves, its fifty-four links glinting lively into the dark puff of hair. She counts on their manners, arm fat jiggling as the 14-carat tinkles above. Never counted on the two of them in next-door desks, passing notes on the rachis of a roseleaf. Rows, not roses, schoolteacher expounds.

She doesn't know how many stars they have, anyway: so many they can't be counted in numbers smaller than ∞.

Aren't the notes a promise. Don't they say I'll build you a house, with the vines on it you like. A hexagonal window. Little wires throwing sparks, a switch and a bare bulb, a built-in table, Murphy bed, two goose-down pillows, redchecked cloth, a pitcher and bowl for serving, three silver spoons and matching forks, an old knife and slab. Matching plates with apples painted on. A little garden down below. Promises growing up through the foundation. Linen sheets and a rope to hang you with.

Cusp of winter, she stands on a frozen lake and watches the world dilute. She was going crazy in the little room, the slabbody of the uncle in every corner like saltpork. White and unappetizing. The cold months hang over her head, a string of dried fish, and her body begins the process of living without her. Hair and shakes. What she's hungry for they haven't stored up in that house for quite some time.

When he is breathing in the alley sometimes he can feel the tips of his fingers glow blueblack and then he knows someone is there. In the perfect building of his mind he stands guard over the town. Eyes masked, all-seeing. Keep The Girl out of villainreach, swing her up on a magic rope, the sound of his cape. Then she passes him quiet as a ——. He hears the girl moving in his darkness, the smell of lilies-of-the-valley, her fear like a struck cat. Wants to go with her wherever she is hurrying.

He is a hard nut to crack. Next to her under schoolteacher's rigid gaze he slips loganberries, a rusted flange into her palm. She hopes. Hides his gifts under the mattress. In the house of the uncle she tries to be invisible but the little presents make her body take shape. He can't see her, makes her want to be seen.

Someone wonders where the uncle's voice is. Whether it is lying cutthroat in a gutter. She would answer in the paper tongue that house taught, the voice of the uncle is handmade lace along the pillow's edge. But this is not the uncle's story.

What it is: open bluegrass chords on mandolin, the slow fiddle's keening. Under the bleachers music wraps her like a shawl. Fringes touching her gooseskin. The taste of sweet tea. Shape of the window on her nightwalls, her right leg talking pretty to her left, hands clapping a double-time singsong with the red-sweater girls at school. Bird in the hand.

Walking along the curb, she notices violets beginning to poke through cracks. The shade of a police car. She remembers a matching tin one, its rubber wheels, carpet fuzz tangled in treads. When the boy comes out of the drugstore, she follows him. Alley to alley. Whether he can smell her or not he doesn't say, anything. She gathers her memories: railroad, dogwood, a mismatched deck of playing cards; tracks him into deep shade on meadow's edge, touches his back, watches his face change. Leaves lilacs and little dreams tossing in the wake of her sprintaway.

How many people can one girl, slightbuilt, weak in sports, easily distracted, plain grown pretty, love in one lifetime? What is it makes that sharpsweet first taste of soda bread, trace of wool on the tongue, and how to name what never belonged to her, never could? And who can love her? The touch of hand on skin like fine-thread cotton. Once things are fed and taken care of, every saucer proper in its proper place, who is going to name the way her arm muscles ache—what for?

A lot of things come in shapes with two edges. Hatchets. For example. The aunt is fond of saying her coming to live with them is a double-edged sword. She thinks, no, more like a cross to bear. What the sense would be of a blade with just one edge she doesn't know. You want to cut the person on the way out, just like on the way in.

After everyone is sleeping there is time to curl beneath the wood-shaving bench, listen for footsteps to the basement door, the trembling jars of relish and the girl brave among scraps of flaky pine. Or to run. She holds a thin spoon between her fingers, wonders what time the last light will pop into darkness, plans route after route through the midnight house.

At six in the morning something singing is in the bracken of his mind: it is no everyday. Fingers to the delicate tray of ear, glossy spectacles. Creaking out of the house, the boy with no eyes feels his way through the blossoming-unfamiliar garden. Radish bodies, potatoes budding tiny underground, the silk of dill new to flower. Tingles his palms. Leaves a blind dust on his shirt. Touches tomato leaves, feels aphids march battleward on fingernail. All new.

And if all this exists? Girl who speaks to the wolf-boy. Boy with pads of callus thick like two years on his feet. Tonight they can steal away in a red boat blue on the inside. And the sea and the boat and the bodies rocking. If she's never been on the water before, all right; if he doesn't know which way is north. They'll point toward shore.

Norfolk, 1827

Shannon Gibney

If there was no other way to leave, she would still leave. He could scowl at her from above his bowl of split pea soup, he could put a lock on her two-room cabin in the middle of the night, in desperation. She had been tiptoeing around the Scotts all her life, and as she sat down on her deflated bed to pull on James's work boots, she delighted in the thought that she would stomp the entire fifty miles to Norfolk, thrashing through brush, kicking away burrs and pinecones. She would get on that boat, no doubt about it, and Little George, Lani, Nolan, and Big George would too.

She had been to Norfolk only once before, as a child, when Daddy was sick. There had been an outbreak of the yellow fever, and Old Master Scott (then Young Master Scott) had sent for the best doctor in the county. She was only eight at the time, but she had been sent by James and Young Master Scott's son Henry to fetch Doc Lawrence, while Young Master Scott himself sat over Daddy day and night, feeding him liquids and keeping a steady stream of cold, wet cloths on his forehead. "I ain't never seen no White man hang over one of us like that," James told her on the carriage ride into town, which seemed interminable. She hushed him, even though he was ten years her superior, and he grimaced, then turned away out into the night. She had known even then that she would marry him, and that Daddy would die. Even if she and the family were set up with the nicest White man in six counties, they still had their bodies, broken by work and time.

"If I am going to die, it's going to be my own kind of death," she said, standing up. Lani cooed in the red-oak cradle James had carved for her. "It ain't going to be no White man's work killed me. It's going to be God's work." She smoothed her skirt and looked down at the worn, checkered pattern. "It's going to be *my* work." She smiled and stepped toward the small table by the window, on which she had stashed the bushels of tobacco, yards of dyed cotton, beads, and fine hand tools that she hoped to be able to carry with her on the boat, over the ocean, and into the Motherland, where they would build their new home. Big George had also managed to steal cheese, cured sausage, apples, and several bread loaves out from under Old Master Scott's careful and increasingly greedy eye in the kitchen. All this bounty was assembled in the modest table's center, and it was more treasure than she had ever seen in one place.

She walked over to Lani, crouched down, and began rocking the cradle. She looked at her small, chestnut brown hand resting on the cradle's edge and was shot six years back in an instant, when Nolan was inside an ordinary tub that Ms. Barnes had scavenged for them, and James's hand was on top of hers, resting easily, and they both knew—she knew that they both knew—that this day would come, the day when they alone would be responsible for any act they did or did not engage in, when a Black God's vengeance would trump any a White could mete out. She had never considered, however, that James might not be here with her now. And then she was shot back into her body just as quickly, and the pain came back, the sharp jab in her chest, the memory of his absence, the going on and on and on and on, and she stumbled out of her crouch, onto the floor with a thud. Lani was startled and looked up. The baby opened her eyes wider. Yasmine stared back at her daughter, the last person James had acknowledged before he passed on, and saw that she was disturbed, and about to cry. Yasmine gathered her weight and regained her balance, then reached out and wrapped Lani's small fingers around her index finger.

"Barely six more hours before we gone from this place, forever," she told her. Lani's clouded eyes instantly began to calm at the sound of her mother's voice. "All you need to do is sit pretty like you always do, and get ready to see some new country. Just so you don't get to worrying, here's what we going to do. Little George and Big George is going to leave early for church service, as Old Master always wants us to do on Saturdays. But instead of going to church, they'll hide in the tree stand up by the creek. Nolan will be with Miss Barnes in the kitchen, but as soon as she goes out to fetch the linens for washing, he'll run back here and wait for us. Now, you'll be under the Prayer Tree with Aunt Gertie, as usual. But soon as I see Miss Barnes head out the kitchen toward the backyard for the linen tubs, I'll grab you and head back here. As soon as we get Nolan, and pick up this pouch filled with our food and necessaries, we'll make for the tree stand and Little George and Big George, and then we're gone." She snapped her fingers, and Lani caught her breath. Yasmine leaned into her, so that their faces were almost touching. "It'll be as if we never were here at all," she said whispering. "Be like we were that river that used to run beside Old Master's property, then dried up to a creek, and then just dried up period." Lani's hold on her finger became lax. "Folks might say they remember the taste of that sweet water, can almost taste it on their tongues, but they never will taste it again, so they might as well get used to thirst." She could hear the sharp edge in her voice, and felt her back stiffen. She saw his old, withered hand on her breast, and she closed her eyes tightly, pulled her hands away from her daughter. "Go away," she told her mind. "Ain't got no use for you no more." Her voice quivered, but the image flew away just as fast as it had come, and she was back in the here and now, reaching toward Lani again, readying her for their own flight.

...

When the sun was just beginning to fall down from its perch, Yasmine carried the last bushels of wheat she had helped the field hands cut to the oxcart and walked into the dining room. Penny was already there, dusting imperceptible particles from the top of the bureau, the bookshelves, and the table. If there was one thing Old Master insisted on, it was a clean house; he could be like a woman in that way.

Upon hearing Yasmine's footfalls, Penny looked over her shoulder. "Afternoon, Mrs. Yasmine," she said, a shy grin spreading across her face. Penny was just thirteen and a half, and though her body still resembled a child's, there was something older in her neck and shoulders. Or perhaps it was her back, the way she held herself—upright, but just a little bit fatigued. Like she was already tired of this world, eager to step across whatever pain would last an instant into the gentle oblivion of the next. What Yasmine always thought when she was with the beautiful girl was that Lani would never grow up to know that feeling or have that wish. She would make sure of it.

"Afternoon, Penny," Yasmine answered back. She walked over to the girl and kissed her on her forehead, just below her head wrap. There was some perspiration there. Yasmine pursed her lips and tasted its bitter saltiness.

She wanted the taste and the sweat itself to be the only things she carried from this place that lasted, save her children.

Penny cocked her head and looked at Yasmine askance. "What you do that for?" she asked. She placed her right hand on the same hip. Mirth played at the corners of her mouth.

Yasmine walked past her to the bureau. She pulled out the polished maple case that contained all the silver given to Old Master's father, who was the first Quaker to start a plantation in Virginia. Old Master had told them the story so many times—usually when he was handing out their pittance of a salary every month. "He was a man before his time, my father," Old Master would say, his palsied left hand pointing at them, and shaking with his madness. "All the other White men wouldn't even call their workers workers. They called them slaves—because they *were* slaves! They didn't pay them anything for their labor, whipped them, mutilated some of them, even killed some. But my father would have none of that. He insisted on a more humane manner of dealing with his fellow men. He insisted that they have decent quarters, be fed properly, never be whipped or physically harmed in any way, even if they flagrantly disobeyed orders— and he even paid them! Can you imagine what it meant in the 1780s, to have Negroes in your possession in the state of Virginia, and to insist upon their humanity?" At this point, Old Master would invariably set an invasive stare on whoever was unfortunate enough to be next in line for payment, and they would flinch, and then look away. But Yasmine never did. She just stood there, and met him where he was. Once, in the middle of the story—the part about the things that the other White men did to their Negroes—she had interrupted him. "Did they rape their Negro women, too?" she asked evenly. His eyes screamed, and his left hand stopped shaking for an instant. Behind her, in the full line of hot, sweaty Negroes, someone coughed. Someone else shuffled their shoes, but mostly what she heard was the collective quiet of everyone holding their breaths. He grunted some kind of affirmation finally, then handed her her small pouch of coins.

"What? I can't give my niece a kiss from time to time?" Yasmine asked, lifting three spoons from their velvet casings.

"No, that ain't it," Penny said, turning to face her. "You know I appreciate anything you got to give me in the way of love. It's just that you ain't exactly a whole bundle of affection, usually."

Yasmine snickered. It was so easy to be with Penny—she would miss that. "Well, I ain't exactly got a lot to be affectionate about, usually." She scrubbed with the coarse rag vigorously at the first spoon. The silver caught a ray of sunlight, reflected it back in her eye, and her pupil smarted. Although it could sometimes hurt like this, she loved the sun, and couldn't wait to get out in it, moving with her boys and Lani, day in and day out.

Penny sucked her teeth. "You better watch your language, Mrs. You know God don't like ugly." She moved her dust rag to the gold-flecked frame that contained an oil painting of Old Master's father.

Yasmine snickered again, and raised an arm toward the picture. "See now, that's you all's problem—you think *that's* God."

Penny turned around and faced her, presumably to study her and see if she was being serious.

Yasmine picked up the next spoon, and let its coldness ripple up her spine. "That ain't God. In fact, neither that man nor his son ever had a conversation with God, or *His* son. But yet, they got every Negro up in this place thinking that they the very incarnation of all that's holy." She shook her head. "It's a shame. It's a shame what they done to us." She put down the last spoon and peered out the window. The light was just beginning to fade; she had better finish up in here, quick.

Penny looked at her aunt, befuddled. "There be plenty of worse places to make a home," she said. "And you ain't even have to go that far to find them, neither. Just head over to Master Kennedy's farm, and you find pregnant womens getting flogged nightly, and rations so strict they all but skin and bones up there. Plus, I think they'd just about fall over from the shock of it if they ever saw what a dollar looked like." Penny shook her head. "You heard what Master Kennedy told Old Master Scott last spring, right?"

Yasmine knew, but she turned her attention to the last few utensils at the bottom of the case.

"He told Master that he would whip any of us that wandered over to his place, even if we were family relations. He told him he didn't want to see his Coloreds getting any strange ideas in their heads about how they should be getting paid, how they should have nicer quarters and better food. He said that every time one of them comes back from visiting one of us, the whole plantation is agitated for weeks with everyone from the field hands to the house help complaining about unfair treatment and the like. He told Old Master that if it were up to him, he would have rounded up all the Scott people and shot them a long time ago. Said they tampering with nature, the way he's running things."

Yasmine closed the case with a thud, then pulled her shawl tighter around her shoulders. It would be cold tonight; she could feel it. She walked over to Penny and enclosed her in her arms. The intensity of the gesture surprised them both.

"Good night," Yasmine said, stepping away from her. She wished she could know, know for sure, that Penny would leave one day. She wished she could ask her to come along, but she knew better than to ask.

Penny's eyes were wet, and she searched Yasmine's. "Why you so . . . different tonight?" She took her aunt's hand. "Feel like you got something that you're keeping tight, right here." She brought her fist to her chest. "Like something got caught there, or caught you."

Yasmine knew she had to leave right then, or the entire story would come out of her, and then she would never be able to leave. "Ain't nothing caught me," she said, trying to laugh lightly. "Not about to let another thing take up root in my body." She smirked. "I'm done having babies, if that's what you hinting at. Bet you wish I had some fine man I was hiding on the side, so you and the girls had something to talk about."

Penny's face flushed, and she laughed in spite of herself. She slapped Yasmine's arm, playfully. "You just acting all crazy, as usual." She grabbed her dust rag harder and turned back to the picture frame. "I don't even know why anyone try with you—you just dead set on causing trouble."

Yasmine stepped into the doorway, trying to memorize the way Penny's spine curved deeply when she stretched toward items that were just out of reach. The sharp point of her nose in profile, the jut of her upper lip, which sometimes made her look stern, when she wasn't at all. Who would she end up being? Who *could* she end up being? Yasmine's eyes smarted, and she walked out of the doorway, into the living room, and out the front door, across the fields, to get Lani.

It was too cold. The first frost had come just a few weeks before, but long icicles hung down from tree branches in the night, and when they melted in the morning they left huge puddles of water that they sloshed through during the day, leaving a kind of coldness that they couldn't shake away because it clung to their socks, their shirts, even their undergarments. There was simply no way to get dry. Yasmine was just thankful that it was only a five-day journey to Norfolk, and that once they were there, they would have lodging at the home of one of the men she had met at the meeting last month. She hadn't liked or trusted most of the others in his group, but there was something about this man—a softness in his demeanor, perhaps?—that let her know he was a man who tried to do the right thing whenever possible, a man who saw that her children were every bit as much children as his.

"Ouch!"

Yasmine turned to see Little George clutching his left foot. She wiped the sweat from her brow and walked over to him. "Let me see," she said, bending down. "What happened?"

"Don't know," he said, pursing his lips. "Feel like I stepped on something—something with nettles."

Yasmine inched closer to him. She felt Lani stir on her back and hoped that they hadn't woken her.

Little George wiggled his foot out of his thin, torn leather boot, sucking his teeth. He shivered as the wind bellowed around them.

Yasmine sighed. The pad of his big toe was punctured, probably by a stinging nettle. It wasn't that they multiplied in December, so much as they had less lushness in which to remain covered. Plus they became more brittle in the cold, oftentimes making them even more painful and difficult to extract. There was an awful lot of blood for a wound so small, which told her that it must have gone deep. She wished they were someplace where they could stop and clean the wound so that it wouldn't get inflected, but it would be two more nights before they reached Norfolk. Little George would just have to hold on until then. Yasmine pressed the wound firmly with her thumbs.

Little George flinched at her touch. "Your hands freezing," he said, warming his own hands in his armpits.

She reached up to her head wrap and ripped a small piece of cloth off of the side. She tied the cloth around the cut, tight enough to stop the blood but loose enough so Little George could walk. "We can't stop," she told him. "We got nowhere to stop at."

Little George didn't meet her eyes. He lifted the shoe off the ground and carefully pulled it back on. "I know."

The wind kicked up sharply again, cutting at the tips of their ears. From his place beside Big George, Nolan whimpered and dove under the long brown wool of his older brother's overcoat, which hung down to his feet. It had been James' gift to him, on Big George's fifteenth birthday.

Yasmine stood up and got her bearings. They needed to head northeast for the rest of the day. Lani was restless now, and crying loudly. Like Nolan, she had no tolerance for the cold. Yasmine picked up her pack and stepped forward. "You shush now," she told her daughter. "We ain't got no time for such carrying on." This made Lani cry even harder. Yasmine felt her kicking her tiny feet into her back. That child could be so willful! Yasmine took another step. The harder Lani cried, the faster Yasmine walked.

The next morning, about a half hour after they set out, Yasmine noticed that she didn't hear the familiar trio of footfalls behind her. She turned and saw no one—not Big George, not Little George, not Nolan. Her breath caught in her windpipe. They had them, they finally had them! The last thing she would ever see before she left this Earth would be their faces. She tried to remember them: Big George's nascent triceps, his deliberate yet easy gait; Little George's intense stare, the way he could almost run you down with it; and Nolan's blubbery baby cheeks, which he was always filling with air at odd moments and then releasing in order to make disturbing sounds. Yasmine laughed in spite of herself. She picked up her skirts and began to run, back the way she had come, boots snapping twigs beneath her. White oak and beech trees blurred in her vision as she sped, and the hard shells of acorns pierced her soles more than once. The sun was just beginning to rise above everything, its rays slowly melting the frost that had come the night before. Yasmine could see her breath as she ran, hear Lani's faint cries on her back. An opossum stared her down as she hopped a fallen tree stump, as if daring her to come toward him. Yasmine stopped for a second, startled to see him in daytime but not frightened. "You get now," she said. But the beady eyes and whittled face just studied her harder. She stepped toward him, waving her hand. "Go on now. Get!" And he dove into the underbrush. Yasmine looked up and, suddenly, there the boys were, in a kind of oval around a big rock. Nolan was sitting on it with his eye sockets on his palms. There were streaks of tears all the way down his face, and his nose was running. Big George stood beside him, taller than she ever remembered him, his right hand on his little brother's shoulder. Big George's expression was stern, and as he looked up to see her, Yasmine thought she saw something akin to disdain in his eyes, but it disappeared just as quickly as she thought she had named it. Off to the right was Little George. He was not facing either of them but rather looked out into the deep darkness of the brush. He did not turn around to acknowledge Yasmine's approach.

She felt her heart slow as she came nearer to them, and her breath became more regular. "Boys!" she said. Only Big George met her eyes. "What are you doing?"

The top of a pine tree sawed near the sky, as the sky's air made it moan. Lani gurgled on her back, but the boys said nothing.

Yasmine reached out and grabbed Big George's forearm, and he flinched. "I asked you all a question, damn it! Now you best answer me. Here I was, thinking you all was with me, and then when I turn around and look, what do I see?" She pressed her face into Big George's and he backed up, unconsciously. Nolan looked up at both of them, crying.

"What do you think I see?" The pitch of her voice was rising. If James were here, he would tell her to step away for a moment to breathe, that he would handle it first, and then she could make her appeal, as long as she did it calmly. She had always hated that conversation with him, especially because she saw how much better the boys responded to his voice, his discipline, than hers.

"I saw dry nettles, I saw icicles falling off the tops of trees, I saw dead animals. But you know what I didn't see?"

Big George was staring at the ground. Tears kept streaming out of Nolan's baby eyes. Little George still hadn't turned around to even let her know that he was listening, or even cared.

Yasmine strode over to him, fastened her hand to his shoulder, and spun him around. "You look at me when I'm talking to you, boy!" she screamed.

His face was blank, completely empty. It was like the night sky before the stars came out, but more empty, somehow. Slowly, he focused his eyes on her face. She tried to see what he was keeping in them, what it was that had drawn them here, so far away from her, and not fearful of this distance at all, but there was still nothing. This enraged her further somehow, and before she knew what she was doing, she had reached up and slapped him across the face. Behind her, Big George and Nolan gasped, and the pine tree above kept on sawing back and forth, back and forth.

She had pushed Little George's chin farther from her with the slap, and he brought his palm up to caress his raw cheek, which was red from the stinging. When he looked back at her, he was not empty anymore— Yasmine recognized what filled his face, his arms, his pores. It was rage, barely contained below the surface.

Nolan ran up behind her and pulled at her skirt. "Mama, don't be mad at Your George, please. It was me, it was my fault we stopped. They didn't have nothing to do with it."

Yasmine turned slowly to face him. He was wiping away tears and snot with the back of his hand, sniffling all the while. He looked up at his mother, looked down at the ground, then looked back at her. "I . . ." His voice became smaller than she had heard it since he was a toddler. "I don't want to go there." He began to fiddle with his hands.

Yasmine had always said that she knew that Nolan had been here before; she didn't know whose he had been, she didn't know when, but he was definitely an old soul, and one who had known freedom.

"And . . ." Nolan looked askance, as if he was trying to parse out something far away. "I miss Daddy, too." Tears began to fall anew with these last words.

Yasmine sighed, and crouched down so that they were eyelevel. "We all miss Daddy, Nolan." She allowed herself to feel the truth of this statement for a short moment, then pushed it back down again, because she knew it could overwhelm her. "But that don't mean that we don't have to go."

"Go where?" Little George asked suddenly, venom infusing his words. "What you even know about where we going? Livingston said they all heathens over there anyway; that some jungle fever done killed most of the first settlers, and—"

Yasmine stood up and whipped around to face him. "Since when does Livingston say a thing worth repeating?" Livingston was Little George's agemate, who lived up the road. He could talk a wild streak about nothing until you swore you could feel your mind dulling in your skull.

Little George scowled. "You just mad cause his mama caught you and Old Master in—"

Yasmine was on him before she knew it. She would have slapped him again, twice as hard this time, if Big George hadn't come up behind her and held her back. "You *never* talk to me that way, you hear?"

"Easy," Big George told her softly. He was deliberately using his calm voice, she could hear it, and that eased some part of her to know that he, at least, was trying. "Easy, Ma. You know he don't know nothing. He's just a kid."

"And that is your saving grace, boy!" she hollered at Little George. "That you only eleven. Because if your father was here, he would be slapping you silly right now, and you know that's God's truth."

Finally, she saw some kind of recalcitrance on his face. Because he knew, she surmised, that she was right. There had not been much that James could do about so many things, but one thing he said that he always would do was raise his children—until, he said, he couldn't.

On Yasmine's back, Lani had begun to wail. She had new energy to spend on her tantrums, full of Yasmine's milk. Yasmine closed her eyes. *Just breathe, baby. Breathe.* It was times like these that he came to her—never in her dreams, where he might linger. "We got to go," she said, willing her voice to be level. "I ain't going to lie to you and tell you that it's going to perfect, but we got no other choice. We got to go *now.*"

Little George opened his mouth to say something, but Big George shushed him with one look. Nolan took her hand, and the two older boys set out in front, back the way she had come from.

When they arrived in Norfolk late the next day, the skies were clear and the temperature on the rise. Even Little George perked up when they entered the bustling port city, seeing the vast array of naval and timber stores, steam mills, tan yards, hotels, churches, bars, and even neighborhoods, dotted with expansive Georgian houses. Men with wide-brim hats and fuller bellies stood outside their storefronts hawking eastern white pine, passage to far and exotic places, and everlasting salvation in the pews of their worship halls.

"Mama," Little George whispered shyly in her ear. "How come you never said there's so many Coloreds here?"

Yasmine wished she could laugh at his excitement, seeing so many of their people in one place. She couldn't deny that it was something to see honey brown, chestnut, sallow yellow everywhere you turned. There was a certain kind of beauty to the way the mass of these bodies moved, sometimes across from other White bodies, but mostly behind them. There was a certain way that they ruptured the sterile, safe landscape that was so deliberately built and maintained, but in the end she had to conclude that it wasn't enough. There was still the fact that a six-year-old girl who walked beside them for a moment and smiled at Nolan was knocked down by the older White boy who was in her charge, for "watching them niggers, when you ought to be watching me." There was still the middle-aged woman who followed behind her madame, carrying her skirts over mud and ice, slipping on the bare soles of her feet as they crossed this unforgiving December ground, while her madame charged on in her polished leather boots, pristine petticoats, and dainty parasol. Yes, Yasmine mused, you could come to the city all you wanted, and expect its busyness, its hustle and bustle, to transform its inhabitants toward some higher form of being than this base system that had them all ensnared back in the countryside, where you could get away with God-knows-what because there was no one watching, and besides, you didn't have any attachment to the notion of yourself as civilized, which required city folk to bend their actions to at least somewhat fit their enlightened ideals. Yes, you could hope all you wanted that, somewhere in this country that God had forsaken, someone knew how to treat their fellow men and women, but it still wouldn't change what was staring you straight in the face.

Grandstand

Hands

Kaethe Schwehn

ELEANOR AND HARRIS: MAY 1943

The light comes down over a house in Minnesota. Secures itself at the corners. Stand in the garden. Feet in the furrows of absent snap peas. Here is the kitchen window in front of you. Both the setting sun pressing its orange fury across the glass and the mother's furrowed brow above the sink. She concentrates and does not see the sunset. She is peeling carrots or peeling the thin membrane off an egg still warm from hard boiling or she is opening a can of beets with a towel. She opens it above the sink because the jar is too full and because beet juice stains. The sunset watches her. Somewhere in India a man sleeps with tigers. White Bengal tigers licking their paws clean after a meal. She does not have the heart to suppose this. Or to imagine the sound of tiny golden bells on a thin blue silk cord. Or the person who would tie them around her naked waist. Or how her waist might come to be golden. Instead the front door opens and he unwinds a scarf from his neck though it is late spring. The whole body of her husband enters the kitchen at once. He pulls a chair from underneath the kitchen table and turns it so that he faces her. He sits heavily in the chair. Now she raises her chin and looks at the sunset. Now she leaves her task in the sink and turns to him with her hands raised, to show him the beet juice, to show him how there is nothing to be done.

ELEANOR: JUNE 1943

Things a mother waits for: the onions to come back in the sack with the daughter, the son to fetch the matches, the wick to catch, the meat to ready. If for one minute of the day I sit here to wait, then everything readies at once. Even the sun moves down and knits up in the lace drapes revealing how they are ready to be scrubbed. All I seem to manage of the trunk is the outside. Rubbing the outside with lemon oil until there is not a splinter and the emblem with her initials glows. You have six children and should not have a favorite. I do not love Ruth more but how could it be helped.

RUTH AND LEON: APRIL 1943

The stethoscope is cold but Leon's fingers prepare each patch of skin for the place where the instrument will press next. The white sheet begins below her hips and covers her legs to the ankles where the brown cotton socks begin, covering the two feet that rest in the steel stirrups. The heel of each sock is threadbare so the cold of the metal seeps in there, drawing goosebumps from her calves and thighs. The gown fastens at the neck, the breast, and the belly with blue cloth ties but he has undone the lowest tie so that he can move first his fingers then his stethoscope across her abdomen. Leon sits to her right side and behind him is a window and above it a clock. She thinks his fingers are too rough but it could be they are too tender and this is what makes her need to turn her head to the left and away from his concern. She studies the handles of the cabinets, the grain of wood, the three maroon jars holding cotton swabs, tongue depressors, Q-tips. He listens to the sounds her body makes and tucks his chin into his chest to hear better, frowning into the listening. Below the top edge of the sheet her right hand plucks a section of fabric between thumb and forefinger and twists it into a little ball, then releases it and plucks a different section. Well, he says and clears his throat so she will turn her head to face him. She has thick dark eyebrows and a thin beautiful nose. She has a scratch on her chin, red and angry.

Because he did not wear a mask to examine her, she could see the blue-black whiskers poking through the pores of his chin and when he finally touched her, when he put his fingers inside her, she watched the way his lips tightened and pursed with the effort, just as when he had been inside her before, squinting as though his keys had fallen to the bottom of a lake and he knew they could not be salvaged.

His right hand reaches across her body and finds the left tie of her gown. He pulls it back to her meridian where his left hand waits with the right tie and as he wraps them together he says well, it's just as you thought, and sees her nod from the corner of his eye, a sharp nod as he finishes the bow, pulling each side so that it is symmetrical. She shifts to the edge of the table and looks out the window, her shoulders slouching into her breasts, her knees pressed together, her feet swinging as if she were waiting to have her reflexes tested. Outside, the sky is lavender, a slim and wispy layer of cloud drifts just above the horizon, light gold on the fringes and a deep violet gray in the center, where it is thickest. Bare tree branches interrupt the sky from the lower corner of the frame, making the lavender more intense with their darkness. This is a delicate situation, he says. You're seventeen, he says, and Mary—well, there's Mary. You understand, he says. She nods. A flock of sparrows rises suddenly from the branches of the tree like a handful of pebbles thrown into the air. At the height of their arc, the sparrows pause collectively, black wing tips silhouetted against deep violet ash, before beginning their descent to earth.

LEON: SEPTEMBER 1943

The postmistress gave me a hell of a time. A hell of a time. A necklace shouldn't be sent in an envelope she said and why would you be writing to Ruthie Connor anyway. But I made her send it. I would have put my hand on her hand on the rubber stamp and forced it to the envelope if it had come to that.

RUTH: JANUARY 1944

The hands are folded in the lap. White hands with obvious veins but no rings. The empty white fingers of both hands. The hand props the head against the side of the train car. The bump of trestle and iron moves through her body. The constant chug of machine, the clatter of railroad ties in her teeth. The silos go by slowly enough. The draft of snow across the shunted fields moves in opposition to the train. Brown bare trees and her right hand moves to the back of her neck. Then both hands wander to the crown of her head. Undo the hat pins. Hat is set on the seat beside. A sprig of navy berries just above the brim. Starting to wilt, coming undone. Out of the front pocket of her camel coat the right hand pulls a metal tin that makes the thin sound of needles and the heavier sound of a thimble. The hands move clockwise and counterclockwise to open the tin. The left hand holds the smallest needle. The right hand pulls the thread across her lips. Twice because her lips enjoy it. The train makes the left hand shake so the right cannot make the thread go through. Somewhere, whole fields are planted with mines and white planks of wood are bursting into flames. Somewhere, men are slogging through salt water, icy rope wound around their hands. Her left hand moves the needle so that the sky is the backdrop for threading. Soft gray against navy. It will not go through. The left hand shakes because of the train and because of something outside the train. Either she is moving east or west. Either she has been there already or is presently arriving. Sea or lake, cottonwood or oak. The world is opening or it has shut. Both hands on the nape of her neck, both hands where the baby moves, both hands on her breasts.

RUTH AND ELEANOR: FEBRUARY 1944

Both hands are on the arm of the pump. Because she has no gloves the burn of cold in her fingers creeps into her wrists and up her forearms. There is an aluminum bucket below the head of the pump with an aluminum handle. When she pushes down on the handle she leans her entire body on it for weight. She rotates her left around the handle to lift it, pulling off a few of the last chips of green paint. The pump groans at its highest and lowest point. The joints loosen and she pumps faster. In the west, there is a swath of open sky at the horizon; a gray cloud sprawls endlessly above it. This sky turns from ash to light blue to a fine golden haze while she pumps. Around her neck, the silver cross on the silver chain swings into her breastbone with each movement. There is a turquoise bead in the center of the cross and this is what she feels bumping against her. In her right pocket there is another necklace. The snow begins slowly. Small flakes falling far apart from one another. It seems that no new flakes fall, that it is only the same few blown down from the sky and up from the ground at once, spinning around the base of the pump and gusting at chosen moments up through the bottom of her skirt, leaving pinpricks of cold around her calves.

Between the girl and the newly golden band of sky lies a patch of frozen grass. The grass cracked and broke under each step she took as she made her way from the house to the pump. At the edge of the yard is an oak tree; beyond it, a field of corn and beyond the field a set of train tracks. The water has begun to run into the bucket. Her hands are red and chafed and no longer feel like her hands but like part of the pump that moves things up and down though her shoulders ache and her knees crack as they bend and her stomach clenches to push and pull she continues and fluidly makes the water run and the sky brighten and the flakes dive against her cheeks until the bucket overflows and the frozen ground does not absorb the water and she cannot let go of the handle only watch as the water pours over the edge of the bucket, flowing around her brown shoes, around the tarnished eyelets and frayed laces until she is an island and she cannot move because to move would be to surrender two broken patches of grass below her shoes to the water to let the water envelop the space completely so she does not move until the older woman comes out from the house behind her, until the woman wraps a quilt around her shoulders, until she puts one hand over each hand on the pump, until the warmth makes it possible to let go.

When the hands release, the older woman takes the pail in her left hand and pulls the girl's body toward her with her right arm and the two turn around to face the house. Behind the house, the same gray cloud presses the same band of sky at the horizon, but this patch of sky holds the orange blinding of the sun and its leak of rose light stretching to the north and south. The girl squints against the brightness and the older woman guides her slowly to the back door. They step inside the back entry hall, a space just wide enough for two women. There are hooks lining the wall on the left and a neat row of shoes and boots below them. The older woman turns the girl's shoulders so that the girl faces her. They are the same height. The older woman pushes the door closed and in the sudden warmth uses both hands to wipe the stray hairs from the girl's face with both hands. The girl puts her right hand into the pocket of her skirt. This necklace has only one charm; it is heavy and intricately carved but she cannot wear it. She squeezes it and stares at her mother who does not speak but instead opens the back door again and lifts the pail and carries it into the kitchen. On the kitchen table, two pieces of cornbread have stopped steaming. In a pot of boiling water, a glass jar bobs, making soft clicks against the pot. The daughter stands in the hallway for another minute. Then she lets go of the necklace and with her right hand closes the back door. The mother opens a drawer and removes a spoon and two knives. The honey loosens inside the jar.

ELEANOR: NOVEMBER 1944

We left because it was best. We left the house and Ruth inside it because there are men who still will have her. I cleaned the curtains. I left her my beets.

Things a mother waits for: the udder to empty, the lather to foam, the face of the daughter to surface in the face of granddaughter. Caroline's face had risen into Ruth's. So we took Caroline and left.

RUTH: JANUARY 1945

The lanolin is thick and oily and gray, like margarine before the color is added. Her hands are red, darker red along the knuckles and the crease where the thumb and forefinger meet. She is sitting on a cushion in front of the fireplace and the fire reaches up into the darkness of the chimney just as high as it should. Her cheeks are hot and her chest and belly are hot but her back is cold and the house at her back is dark. In Minnesota it is difficult to ever have the entire body at exactly the right temperature; one part is always too hot and another just beginning to numb. She scoops the lanolin out of the tin with the fingers of her right hand and begins to rub it into the back of her left hand. The wind makes a high cooing sound below the front door although a braided rag rug has been pushed up against the crack to stop the winter air. Just inside the front door is an iron coatrack. It matches the poker set beside the fireplace. Along the tips of the pokers are bits of gray ash from yesterday's fire. Upstairs, there is a glass of water on the small table beside her bed. The white powder in the glass has not yet entirely dissolved though she stirred thirty times around the inside perimeter with one of the tortoiseshell pins her mother left behind. On the nightstand there is also a Bible and a round, white clock with a key to wind it in the back. She turns her left hand so the palm faces up and massages the fleshy pad below the thumb, moving her fingers the way he moved across her abdomen: slow circles that wind into spirals, creating a soft heat, like warm milk dabbed along the inside skin of the wrist. There are no baby bottles in the kitchen sink. They are wrapped in newspaper in a box with bibs and a little paper sack that holds the bolts for the high chair. There are no baby bottles in the kitchen. There is a piece of writing paper with her words upon it crumpled into a ball on the kitchen table, and beside it a fountain pen. She spreads both hands open until they ache and then holds them as close to the fire as she can bear. They shine. She pulls them away from the fire and rubs them together until the grease is absorbed. Then she stands and walks into the kitchen. She takes the ball of paper off the table and brings it back to the fire. To explain this, to explain cause or want or desire or must, words are not enough. And Caroline, her daughter, will remember smells; years from now that is all she will remember. She takes the poker from the iron rack and hooks the one log remaining in the fireplace, turning it so that its soft ashy belly shows. She scrapes at the log until the orange embers glow and places the paper on top. The edges of the paper blacken. The blackness shrinks back into flame.

Assimilation

Sarah Stonich

Veshko screws his ear closer to the television as the excited talk-show guest erupts in phrases that are obviously offensive and perhaps even obscene. Veshko looks from Tyrone, excited guest, to Jerry Springer, wondering when Jerry might take matters in hand, but he only stands mute in the aisle with his arms crossed, cradling his microphone the way some men cradle a bottle. Jimmy, the brother of Tyrone, shrugs at the camera, basking in the attention as the crowd hisses and shouts. There is some trouble having to do with the fat woman seated between the brothers, but Veshko can find neither "bonin'" nor "ho" in the Webster's pried open on his knee.

While watching television has only slightly improved Veshko's English, an abstract sense of his new country is clipping into focus.

Much livelier than those on *Ellen*, certainly more so than those on *Oprah*—many of Jerry's guests are distraught, angry, and often related. They argue using words Veshko cannot look up fast enough; full sentences slip past his ear as if greased.

Now they are trying to hit each other, these two brothers who have dressed in matching shirts for the occasion, but bald men in jackets emblazoned *SECURITY* press them back to their chairs. Tyrone and Jimmy glare at each other over the head of the woman, whose name is Anita. Anita is the color of a Sacher Torte, with great painted lips and metallic moons of eye shadow that shimmer like her outfit. Nowhere in his new home of Squaw Inlet, Minnesota, has Veshko seen women wear such abbreviated clothing. Anita's cleavage forms a holster of flesh deep enough to conceal a weapon. Ethnic Americans sometimes carry guns, Veshko knows, although the characters he has met on *The Cosby Show* would never. Or should he say would *not*?

There are no black people in this small Minnesota resort community, which makes Veshko suspect they must live in other places, like Chicago, where many talk shows are taped—a place he visited for several hours during his last layover at the airport of O'Hare, where Veshko saw many different sorts of people, many colors. Still, America seems less like the melting pot he'd imagined it would be and more like his own country, where people settle near their own and stick to their own. In America, immigrant groups even have villages tucked inside cities, such as Chinatown. This he has seen on cable reruns of *The Streets of San Francisco*, the program about two detectives, one handsome and young, and the other grandfatherly, with a nose resembling a penis. Veshko is amused by this program's portrayal of uncorrupt police.

Flipping pages he is pleased to recognize *ska*, a musical term he knows in English. Then his finger lands on what he is looking for, *skank*, which amid the many bleeps is the word Tyrone repeatedly shouts at the woman. He reads the entry and sighs, "Of course. A whore—a kurva." He puts the book down and rises from the sofa, crossing through the dining room into the kitchen, where his footsteps land on linoleum squares in sync in with the chant, *Jer-ry, Jer-ry*. Yellow-green, yellow-green. He opens the fridge and lifts a can of Budweiser from the door—a beverage that somehow shares an identity with the real Budweiser. The beer is as pale and subtle as the people of his new home.

He heaps cold meatballs and potato dumplings onto a plate, leftovers from his dinner at the Tuomala's. Since coming to Squaw Inlet, Veshko has dinner each Sunday with a different family, alternating between the two churches that sponsor him. St. Heikki's tiny congregation did not have the resources to get their own refugee, so they teamed with St. Birgitta's to pay Veshko's airfare and provide him a home. One Sunday Veshko has dinner with a family of Finns; the following week he is fed by Swedes. Oddly, the parishioners of both churches are so similar looking he can barely tell them apart. They seem to make no distinctions themselves and greet each other mildly, as if any history between them is forgotten, though they are only a few generations removed from brutality. Veshko has observed that in America the past can be just water under some bridge, as they say. Squaw

Inlet's citizens mingle peacefully and have many bumper-sticker sentiments in common—many are pro-life *and* pro-war. They share other similarities; the housewives, for example, seem to have an aversion to spice yet embrace salt. He reaches for the paprika just as the microwave beeps.

...

After his meal, Veshko returns to the couch, but *Jerry Springer* is over. He switches channels to a program about a small-town sheriff in a place called Mayberry where a woman named Aunt Bea is acting out matronly hysterics in black and white.

Veshko fiddles with the rabbit ears, but no color emerges. Assuming there must be some problem with the dish, he climbs to the second floor, then takes the rickety steps to the attic where he forces open a dormer window.

The satellite dish is anchored next to the chimney. He climbs out, clinging to the window sash, and immediately experiences a wave of vertigo that tugs from diaphragm to scrotum. He attempts to get better footing and, once secure, hunkers down, breathes, and looks out over the town. Spread before him is quite a view of the north part of the town. He can count seventy-seven houses, five bars, and three churches. There are two canoe outfitters, a bait shop, the IGA supermarket, three motels, the food co-op, post office, and a windowless library that looks like a power station. A new Pump & Munch sits directly across from the Holiday station on the piney road that leads south to the interstate that leads to the rest of America.

Just as the freeway sign promises, much of what a person needs in life can be found in Squaw Inlet—*Gas Food Lodging*. But if Veshko wanted to buy a parakeet, or see an ophthalmologist, he would have to travel thirty-seven miles to the first large town. He looks down to the T of the clothesline pole where the red bicycle leans, his only form of transportation.

Many roofs in Squaw Inlet have satellite dishes. Many yards have dogs, but the owners are either inside or gone, so that the animals pace yards fenced with metal mesh, or lie in hard hollows of dirt. The house next door has no dog, no dish, and a closed air, though Veshko knows his neighbor Pete is home because the back end of his Suburban sticks out from the garage not deep enough to house it. Pete works long days, and when he's not out tending sled dogs, inseminating cows, or stitching up one or the other after a wolf tears them, he sits in what he calls his rumpus room, reading

Larry McMurtry novels and drinking Dewar's from a coffee mug that says #1 *Dad*. Pete is divorced, and dislikes two things, one is his job. When Veshko politely asks how was his day, Pete sometimes makes a certain gesture, wriggling his fingers and saying, "Up to my elbows in cow, buddy, up to my *elbows*." Often he repeats himself for Veshko's benefit. After a particularly harsh day he might say, "Mud, shit, and blood, pal, *that* is how was my day. Mud, shit, and blood."

If Veshko peers past the trailer park and its slope of spangled poplars, he can squint across the expanse of the lake and the horizon of water, where, if he had binoculars, he might glimpse the province of Ontario. Balancing on his heels, Veshko feels the house shift minutely under him. Wind from the north scours his ears. He has taken in the highlights of Squaw Inlet, but has nearly forgotten his mission to check the satellite dish. The wires are connected and nothing appears to be broken, so he eases back through the window, shivering.

Downstairs he watches the screen as black and white switches abruptly to color the moment *The Andy Griffith Show* breaks for a commercial. "I understand," he says, understanding.

After the commercial, a new episode begins. Now not only is Aunt Bea afflicted with some brand of anguish, so too is Floyd the barber.

Ready to begin his practice, Veshko kneels near the coffee table, shrugs deeply, and shakes his arms like a swimmer before a competition. He rhythmically shakes his wrists and quickly rubs and squeezes each finger before setting his hands on the torso lying on the coffee table. He presses his palms to the sternum and begins.

He would prefer a living body, of course, but Jessica will have to do. It is no good for a masseur to let his hands forget their trade. Soon after Veshko moved into the tall yellow house, he and his good neighbor Pete made Jessica together. As they sewed and stuffed her, Pete pointed to the crotch and jokingly growled, "*Est ist verboten!*" and they discovered they had a language in common. While Pete's German is an old dialect learned from his grandmother, it is adequate.

Veshko is shamed by his own poor English, in spite of Pete's encouragement. Besides German and his own language, Veshko can speak a few Serb and Croat dialects, Italian, and some Polish. Pete knows some Finnish from his father, and he teaches Veshko words that are hills of vowels interrupted by the occasional brusque consonant. He learns a few unsavory phrases, mostly regarding sexual intercourse with one's mother or sister.

The German conversations become more fluent as empty Bud cans accumulate on the carpet of Mrs. Kubich.

...

Mrs. Kubich had abruptly passed on the week before Veshko came to Squaw Inlet. Stroked out, he was told, but since both church committees had planned he would live with her, the family offered the use of the house until they could settle the estate and sell. On the day of Veshko's arrival, the old woman's belongings were as they had been when she was removed by the ambulance—a load of delicates in the dryer and a saucepan in the sink. Veshko gently moved the support hose and cardigans and lavender sachets from enough drawers to put away his own things, then shut the doors of several rooms and settled in to live under the watchful stares of Mrs. Kubich's people. They gaze from gilt frames hung high on walls or set on bookshelves that hold no books—dozens of sepia eyes watch over as he practices his massage, eats, and sleeps. They are Slavic faces with wide cheekbones and high foreheads, and he doesn't much mind them, even feels an odd kinship, sometimes acknowledging them in no particular language at all.

Veshko has not placed any of his own family photographs out for display, assuming they would only elicit curiosity from his few well-meaning visitors.

He works over Jessica, kneading outward from imaginary ribs, his concentration breaking only when commercials blare and blast color into the dim room. The dummy, which Pete named, is fashioned from a leotard and several pairs of tights filled with flax seed. She has comically large breasts formed by bags of millet, with the knots centered to suggest nipples. As Pete sutured Jessica's torso, Veshko confessed that Jessica Simpson was not known in his home country. Pete only shrugged and told Veshko his own wife, The Ex, had small breasts. The Ex lives in Duluth with his two children, and her new husband, Needle Dick.

On the screen, Floyd the barber is now in full flummox. It turns out he has lost money Aunt Bea had entrusted him with. Aunt Bea won the money playing bingo, and feels guilt about gambling so has vowed to give her winnings to charity before her family finds out. But Floyd is weak and confesses to the men of Mayberry, who rally to help him. Floyd slumps dejectedly near an open cell in the sheriff's office. The police in this program don't even close the cell doors; they play checkers with their prisoners and serve them homemade meals with linen napkins.

Veshko repeats what the big-eared sheriff says to the troubled barber: "Now, think, Floyd, *think*. Where's the money?"

"*Sink*, Flood, *sink*. Veriz za mawney?"

"I uh uh . . .," Floyd hangs his head, "Oh, d-d-darn it, Andy!"

The other actors speak in slow drawls he mimics as he massages Jessica's calves and legs. She has no hands or feet. Veshko has considered filling pairs of Mrs. Kubich's gloves and socks with flax to make her whole. Seeds in Jessica's midsection make a faint *scritch* when he presses with his fists.

Aunt Bea's money is found and there are sly smiles all around, including a rodent like grin from Aunt Bea herself, who had known all along that her money had been misplaced. When the program is over, Veshko changes the station and flips Jessica face down for her second hour. Her spine is a length of plastic chain stitched into the back of the leotard. His hands move upward from imaginary coccyx to imaginary shoulder blades and to the wobbly neck and occipital ridge.

Nova has a special on dingoes.

At midnight Veshko turns off the lights and goes to his bed, where the sheets smell of bleach and dust.

. . .

Pastor Dan, the Swedish minister, was the first and so far the only person in Squaw Inlet to try to engage Veshko in a political conversation. At the counter of Pavola's Cafe, Veshko was deep in his textbook, conjugating verbs, and Pastor Dan was reading his newspaper. The pastor rattled his page, then poked it with a finger, asking Veshko, "In your opinion, Veshko, where do you think Slobodan Milošević should be buried?"

Opinion. He was almost certain he understood the meaning of the word. Rising from his stool and closing his English book, Veshko slowly enunciated each syllable of his response: "I have not an opinion in this matter." He smiled and left a tip for the young woman who'd brought his eggs and so much bad coffee. Once outside, he glanced back through the window to see Pastor Dan reach into his pocket and push several more coins across the counter to join Veshko's.

In the afternoon Veshko finds a package in his doorway. It's a video from Mrs. Jorge, the town librarian. There is a note, easy to translate. *I haven't seen this myself, but thought you might like it!* The video is *Welcome to Sarajevo.* The incongruity of the title puzzles him. A travelogue? From before the siege, surely. He will watch it once he's figured out what's wrong with the VCR.

Pete comes after work with a twelve pack and examines the machine, which turns out to be not broken. He demonstrates to Veshko how he need only switch the input cables, explaining that Mrs. Kubich must have let her grandchildren play Nintendo on the television. Pete begins to describe Nintendo but Veshko excitedly interjects, "I know this Nintendo! My nephews back home has it . . . *had* it." Veshko repeats, "I know this video game." He forgets *Welcome to Sarajevo* and goes to rummage through cupboards and closets, searching for the Nintendo, as if a child might leave such a thing behind.

. . .

On Saturday Pete takes Veshko fishing.

On a trailer coupled to the Suburban they pull an aluminum boat far out of town to a closed-up resort called Naledi, where, Pete explains, he once had a girl—in another life.

Veshko asks if he believes in . . . the word takes a minute—*reincarnation?*

He doesn't.

Pete expertly backs his boat trailer down to a narrow beach between two docks. Next to the dock is an old building for boats only, a water garage built on cribs. Pete takes a key hung under an eave and lets himself in. He comes out lugging an outboard motor.

"This is not trespassing?"

Pete snorts, "Hardly."

With the motor sputtering blue, they zoom from the dock and travel halfway across the lake at full speed. Veshko closes his eyes against the wind and feels his hair part, first one way then another. When the boat stops, it lowers itself like a big animal sitting. Veshko nearly asks Pete to do it again.

They reach an island Pete knows, one large enough to have its own inlets and bays. Skirting the shore, they turn into a narrow channel that leads to a marshy bay. Pete explains the water here will be choked with tall weeds by August, but for now, the bass swim under the boat in the new growth, begging to be caught.

Pete teaches him to cast. At first Veshko holds the rod too tightly, certain he will fling it from the boat, but after a while he is able to relax and the reel buzzes and the balsa-wood lure flies through the air. Veshko is a quick learner, and once he comprehends Pete's phrase *all in the wrist* and makes a few practice casts, he can throw his line and swat black flies at the same time.

He catches two fish, one resisting so wildly he expects some giant by the time it's pulled to the boat, but it is only a slender pike. Such fight in only an average fish, he marvels, asking Pete, "This is an American fish?"

"I guess. You don't fish back home?"

"Sometime, in rivers. Not like this."

Pete catches many perch and three bass too small to bother with.

They troll near the reeds for several hours, not saying much. Pete makes a few jokes about Veshko's fishing hat, borrowed from the closet of Mrs. Kubich, a straw cloche, at least freed of its silk flowers.

"I wouldn't wear that on the street, pal. . . ." Pete advises. "That faggot down at the B&B might just ask you out dancing."

"Faggot?"

"You know." Pete flops his wrist. "Homo."

"Ah, yes."

Pete offers some history of the area, telling of the fur-toting Voyageurs, tough little bastards who were not always French; some were native Indians, some Russians and Brits and even Bohunks like Veshko. "The lot of them were called Pork Eaters, mangeurs de lard, so probably there weren't many Jew paddlers."

He urges Veshko to guess what the leading cause of death among the Voyageur bastards was. Since Pete has described them paddling rapids and portaging for miles, shouldering loads weighing more than themselves, Veshko guesses drowning, and hernias.

"Nope. Constipation."

Since Veshko doesn't know the word, Pete pantomimes, scooting his bottom over the edge of his seat to grunt and clutch his stomach before falling dead against the oar.

. . .

By early evening the beers are warm, but taste better. Veshko discovers he can urinate off the bow while still fishing, simply by trapping the rod in his armpit.

"You got the hang of it now," Pete says to his back. "We call that double-poling."

Hoping for one last fish, they troll the entire way back to Naledi. Approaching the land so slowly like this makes it feel like a real voyage.

Veshko leans and watches the pines sway above the log cabins, and sees how late sun bounces from the lake to spray the resort windows with gem-colored reflections, making even the saddest little buildings glow.

In English, Veshko sighs, "This is one beautiful country, my friend."

Pete glances to where Veshko is looking and shrugs, "I'spose."

...

Veshko realizes the networks that broadcast talk shows knowingly exploit personal dramas and anguish to sell commercial slots. Such commercials have expanded his vocabulary to include pattern baldness, incontinence, vaginal dryness, and erectile dysfunction, as well as names of major pharmaceutical companies and the attending cornucopia of alarming side effects.

Still, he is drawn to the talk shows and has his favorite hosts. He knows instinctively not to trust small-eyed Doctor Phil, the propagandist, and half of the women on *The View*. He likes Ellen very much, an open-faced, seemingly humble person who Pete calls a carpet muncher.

Pete has suggested Veshko should get out more, away from the idiot box. He invites Veshko along to inseminations and sheep castrations.

Veshko politely declines, but takes the advice to heart. He packs lunches and takes long bicycle rides. He recognizes the roads Pete had steered them over to reach Naledi. One day he makes it the entire way. Though the bicycle is sturdy enough, the going seems more difficult the closer he gets to the resort. When he arrives, finally, Veshko realizes the tires have leaked, one nearly to flatness. Huffing, he shrugs out of his Spiderman backpack and soaked shirt. Down the hill from the lodge is a little beach where Veshko wades in to wash his face and underarms. Splashing in the shallows, he looks up at the few old buildings. Perhaps in one of them is a bicycle pump. He takes the key from the eave and opens the boathouse, where there are only boats and oars and cans of gas and a cupboard full of fishing gear.

Other buildings also have keys in their eaves—one is a garage with a rusty truck and snow plow. There are a number of tires leaning against a wall, but no pump to fill them. He eventually finds one in the shed nearest the road, hanging from the rafters next to an old red Schwinn with no seat.

After inflating his tires, Veshko goes back to the boathouse, where he borrows a rod. The two bass he catches from the dock are enough for a meal. He pierces his fish with long metal stakes, perhaps from a tent, and toasts them over a fire of smoking birch.

He settles on the warm sand and closes his eyes, only for a moment. But his sleep is so instant and deep the moment stretches to hours and he wakes to see the sun in a different place, feeling the tight scorch of sunburn across his brow.

Now he will have to hurry to get home before *The Price Is Right*, which Pete sometimes comes over to watch with him. Veshko carefully returns the few things he's used—the rod, the pliers he used to unhook the fish, the tackle jig. In the dark boathouse, he imagines a voice and freezes in mid step. It is only water muttering against the metal walls, speaking in the same caressing tone water everywhere does. Reluctantly, he backs out and locks the boathouse door.

Next time he will bring worms.

Once home, he abandons Jessica to massage his own calves and to spread butter across his pink shoulders. Veshko lowers his aching thighs to the couch cushions and is asleep before the anticlimax of *The Streets of San Francisco*. He doesn't hear Pete's tap on the door or his footsteps retreating.

. . .

By July, Veshko is stealing away to Naledi several times a week. He sometimes fishes from the dock, but more often he will liberate the wooden skiff from its slip in the boathouse and row nearly to the island—never landing, only skirting.

Pete ribs him about the new definition in his arms and legs, asks if he's training for the Tour de France.

"Only getting exercise," he lies.

By the end of August he knows the shoreline of Naledi and the islands well. A mile south is the Catholic summer convent, St. Gummarus. The bell that sounds for vespers is Veshko's cue to row back and pedal home, which places him on Mrs. Kubich's couch ten minutes before *The Price Is Right*.

. . .

A Saturday in September is set for the annual Swedish church supper. In the afternoon Veshko shaves and dresses with extra care. When Pete backs his Suburban into the driveway, Veshko is waiting with Jessica under one arm and his portable massage table under the other. Pete makes room in the back, moving ropes and harnesses and cylindrical metal coolers that hold semen. They strap the dummy upright into a seat, and Pete places mirrored sunglasses on her flat, drawn-on face. Veshko climbs into the cab, still vaguely uneasy in the vehicle which is the height of a military transport.

On the way to the church, Pete sings along to Willie Nelson, thumping the steering wheel to the tune of "Don't Get Around Much Anymore."

Heads turn when Veshko and Pete enter the church basement. Several young men hoot at the dummy, and there is a ripple of laughter when Veshko reaches to readjust her blond wig. They leave Jessica slumped on the stage and line up for the buffet. After perogi and wild rice hotdish, Veshko nervously gulps his coffee. While people pour sugar and some sort of powder into their cups, he climbs to the makeshift stage and unfolds his massage table. When he sees Pete nod, Veshko clears his throat and waits for Pastor Dan to join him. After the pastor introduces him, Veshko announces to the crowd that he would like to show the generous people of this good American village what was his profession back home.

The demonstration is the idea of Pete and Mrs. Jorge. When he and the Jorge family begin clapping, others join in a trickle.

As Veshko arranges Jessica's limbs, it is quiet enough to hear plastic spoons scrape Styrofoam. He begins by rubbing the dummy's lumpy calves and explaining the large muscle groups, base anatomy, and the many health benefits of massage. This is a speech he has written in English and practiced aloud several times while sitting in the borrowed boat.

He rubs and kneads while he talks, looking up at the crowd often. There are sniggers from the back of the room where several teens are gathered, but under Pete's glare those quickly cease. Veshko explains that many male athletes have sports massage, such as the Vikings that play American football for this very state. Veshko eases Jessica from the table and faces the crowd, offering, "I can do this to you. Who would like?"

The parishioners grow still. Men at the long tables are faceless in the shadows cast by their billed caps. Since he can read nothing on these male faces, he looks hopefully to the women of Squaw Inlet. As his eyes travel the crowd, girls giggle and women shake their heads or look suddenly to their hands. One old woman points at him and laughs out loud.

Only after it is apparent no one will volunteer, Pete steps up and bows brusquely to the crowd. There is relieved laughter as Pete approaches the table, peeling off his jacket. His face is red, as if he's swallowing something too large.

. . .

Back in his home, Veshko's spa was adjacent to the national gymnasium and natatorium. There, he'd directed seven masseurs, a hydrotherapist, a physical therapist, and a nurse specializing in sports injury. He thinks of these old colleagues while he identifies Pete's pressure points for the audience. The nurse, Magda, now teaches land-mine victims to balance on artificial legs and hold spoons in their hooks. One masseur, Goran, lives in Sarasota with a distant relative.

Paper casings for straws shoot across the tables where younger people are seated, and some women stand and begin to clear away dishes.

The fates of three of his coworkers—his friends—he does not know, and the rest are dead. Stepan. Vanja. Zdenek, Carl.

He is glad they will never know of this moment.

Pete coughs and turns his head away from the audience. "Hey, Buddy. Not so hard." Veshko eases his thumb from under Pete's scapula.

The crowd is the color of lake reeds, moving as stiffly, craning their necks in unison. Pete's name is wrapped in words of joking encouragement as Veshko finishes his upper back. When he kneads his way down either side of Pete's spine to his sacrum, guffaws ring.

Veshko shakes his head and mutters so only Pete can hear, "Fuck you people."

"Yeah," Pete whispers in agreement, "fuck 'em."

He suddenly hates each face in the church basement. Hates these people who have been so kind and giving to him.

"Fuck *you* as well." Veshko says to Pete. He backs quickly away from the massage table to face the parish, takes a short bow, and smiles, saying in his own language, "You are not my people."

. . .

He heads for home on foot.

After fleeing Sarajevo, Veshko spent a year looking after his brother's children in the country at the farm, the *majur* of his uncle. His days there were purposeful, taken up with finding fuel and growing enough food. At night he attended his orphaned nephews, whose dreams were perforated with city memories: bursts of smoke and people scurrying under the weight of water jugs, trying to avoid snipers. To add to the boys' confusion, they had been told that those lying in the streets were asleep. Veshko had been more forthright. Often he woke to cries from them as they lay in their beds, wet with urine and sweat. He would cradle their small skulls and rub their temples and foreheads, hoping to lull them to a sleep with better dreams. Veshko traded vegetables and well water for enough gasoline to run a small generator so that Gregor and Milan could have Nintendo. They could play a few hours each day, happily exiled into the screen.

Just when it seemed they might all go back, that things had settled in the city, he was contacted by the family of Veshko's dead sister-in-law. The nephews were taken from the farm with only a few days' notice so that this good family might promptly adopt the boys.

He'd returned to the city alone, but there was nothing left for him. The couple who'd taken his nephews emigrated to Canada, but Veshko was unable to determine what town or even what province they had gone to. He applied for emigration himself. Now he is here, in the United States of America.

...

Just as he arrives at the tall yellow house, Pete is pulling into his driveway.

When Veshko opens the porch door, Pete calls out, his voice gruff, "Hey!" pointing to the dummy sitting upright in the back seat.

Veshko shakes his head. "You made her. You keep."

...

He places the six pack of Bud within reach, opens a can, and crosses his ankles on the coffee table Jessica once occupied. He watches Jerry Springer. By the commercial he has gleaned the theme of the hour—mother-daughter team strippers. There is more breast shaking and cat calling than he is comfortable with, and he's about to turn the television off when he spies the boxed videotape wedged next to the console. He slips *Welcome to Sarajevo* into the machine, thinking he will be viewing tourist sites and vistas of that city as it was. Instead, it is a drama about foreign journalists who come to report on the siege. There are a few British and an American, holed up in a damaged hotel lobby, arguing and drinking between missions out to gather stories. The drama unfolds into a moral dilemma about whether or not one of them should rescue a young orphan from her current hell.

Laced through the film are bits of actual news footage; some he recognizes. One he does not shows a victim being helped from a bombed storefront— an elderly woman carried by two men whose arms form a chair under her bottom. She is in shock, looking down to where her foot sways loosely from bone and mangled flesh, the ankle destroyed.

Veshko stops the tape, rewinds it, and watches the bloody dance of the woman's foot in slow motion. He looks at her face. He plays the scene over. The only light in the house glows blue from the screen. More news footage shows heads of state and politicians making speeches about The Problem. When the face of Milošević appears on the screen, Veshko launches forward so that his knees burn upon meeting the carpet. He ejects the videotape and reaches around the set. The cord is yanked with such that force the television moves several inches.

"Opinion," he says, breathing hard. *Opinion.* "Yes. I know this word."

There are no lights on in the hall, so he moves by feel along the paneling to the foyer. Climbing, he counts the stairs to the second floor, and then to the attic, taking one breath for each riser. There are forty-two—his own number of years.

Once in the attic, he pries at the window, stubborn and swelled from a recent rain. He digs at the casement with his fingernails. Suddenly it is urgent he escape the stale air. He slams the cassette at the glass until the pane shatters. He reaches through and tugs the sash from the outside until it gives.

He climbs to the crest of the roof in three strides and disengages the satellite disc by kicking it from its mooring. It spins along the slope and bounces at the gutter to sail to the grass below. After hitting the lawn, it rolls a few yards, connecting with the Cyclone fence, where it dings to a halt.

A light comes on in Pete's kitchen. A curtain lifts, then drops. The light snaps off.

Vaguely aware of the blood running between his fingers, Veshko sits hard on the rough shingles. *Welcome to Sarajevo* is still in his hand, the cassette now cracked to expose its guts. He opens the plastic case like a book, and brown tape loops to pool in his lap.

Veshko pulls meter after meter of the tape, offering fistfuls to the wind. Tape billows, and he watches it flicker and reflect streaks of moonlight, fluttering farther lakeward—farther north—with each gust.

North. He thinks of Naledi—the quiet of the boathouse, where he will often sit in the rowboat that is neither red nor orange but somehow both, where light floats in on ripples and pricks through the corrugated tin skirting that has rusted like brown lace at the hem.

When he closes his eyes, he can imagine the slight motion of the boat and the lapping echo of water softly patting the hull. There is a small door on the lake side which offers Veshko the view of the outdoors as a room—a ceiling painted in blue daylight and clouds, with walls papered in trees. A room carpeted with water, like some Magritte painting.

The end of the videotape requires a firm tug. Freed from the reel it sails up and away—he cannot tell how far in the darkness. Surely it will tangle on a tree branch or fall to some road or yard, but Veshko chooses to imagine gravity defeated; that the tape might be carried high over Squaw Inlet, over the bays and winking whitecaps to Naledi—perhaps even farther—beyond the wild shore where begins yet another country.

Red Cranes

Jacey Choy

Yuki stared at her daughter as they worked in the garden. The radishes and turnips were starting to thicken and needed tedious attention. Jiro, her husband, and the hired hands were working in the rice paddies that framed her view of Mie, her daughter. It wasn't a large garden, but it was more than enough for their family. Yuki often gave much of the bounty to others, particularly the men in the fields.

Sweat dripped down Yuki's face despite the scarf wrapped around her head. The straw hat with its large brim shaded her face from the sun's brilliance but could not keep out the heat. Mie did not seem to mind. She was humming to herself as she worked, adjusting her hat when the heat bothered her, but never pausing. Yuki envied Mie's continence and wished she was sixteen all over again.

"Mie? How are you doing? If you get too hot, go in the house and get some water to drink. I don't want you to get sick from the heat," said Yuki.

"I'm fine, Mother. Don't worry about me." Mie looked up at Yuki and smiled. She took off her hat and shook her head.

"Keep your hat on, Mie. I don't want you to get burned. I'd rather you go into the house if you're too hot."

"Oh, Mother. My head feels so much cooler when I don't have to wear that hat."

Yuki watched Mie's hair fall around her shoulders and worried that Mie's beauty would make her life more complicated than it should be.

Young men already were visiting them. There weren't many young women like Mie around this part of Honshu, outside of Maebashi, and word spread quickly about her, despite the long distances between people out here. Yuki remembered when Mie was just a toddler, running out of the house into the garden, giggling and wearing nothing but a long shirt. I wish I could slow time down, thought Yuki.

Jiro walked slowly up the path from the fields, his bent head obscured by the brim of his hat.

"Yuki," called Jiro, "is lunch ready yet?"

Yuki looked toward Jiro as he called her name. She could see his tanned face under his hat; his eyes looked tired. He worked long hours, as most rice farmers did these days, but they were both thankful that there were plants to care for. Not so long ago the drought had dried up most of the plants, making rice scarce. The rice riots in the villages were often violent and unpredictable.

"Yes. Go on in and wash up. Mie and I will be in shortly. I put out the vegetables and meat, and I just need to get the rice and soup ready."

Jiro removed his hat and the cloth band tied around his forehead. Bending over, he untied his shoes, then set them in the shoe rack next to the door. He opened the door and shuffled over to the sink to wash his hands. Shaded by the aged cherry trees, the small house remained cool. Jiro wiped his hands on a towel and sat at the low table.

"Father," said Mie as she sat beside him, "how is the work going today? Do you think the plants will be ready to harvest in time? Do you have enough men to help you?"

Jiro turned to Mie and smiled. "Yes, yes, Mie, I think we will have a good crop this time. Kinshi and the others have been working hard . . . we can always use more help, but we're doing fine. I was going to tell you that I thought I heard some cranes early this morning, before the sun came up. I tried to find them, but I wasn't sure where their calls were coming from. They're so loud and resonant, so it's sometimes hard to tell. I was going to wake you, but I decided it wouldn't be worth it, especially if it wasn't a red crane."

"The red cranes! Father! Please wake me next time, even if you're not sure! I don't mind getting up that early, anyway." Red cranes were rare around this part of Japan, but Mie longed to see one. She imagined herself on the back of a red crane, flying high in the air.

"Oh, Mie," said Yuki, "all your talk of red cranes. Dreams, just dreams." Yuki picked up her chopsticks and shook her head.

"I know I sound foolish, but I'm so excited to see a red crane. I've been reading about them in one of your books, Mother, and I just wish I could actually see and hear one. Did you know that their nests usually contain only two eggs and can be found on the ground in marshy areas? And, most cranes are usually brown, gray, or white, so the red crane is unusual with its red feathers." Mie's eyes flashed with excitement as she talked.

"Well, Mie, if I hear any cranes, no matter what, I will come and get you." Jiro gazed at his daughter and then stood up from the table.

Mie and Yuki finished clearing the dishes of rice, namasu or pickled vegetables, and miso soup. Jiro had returned to the fields, leaving Mie and Yuki to spend some time in the house. Mie wanted to read her poetry anthology, the *Man'yoshu*, and practice her calligraphy. Because she lived in the country, she was unable to go to school like the girls who lived in Edo. They were closer to the priests and temples, where they could be taught how to read and write. But Yuki had learned how to read and write as a girl, and she worked hard with Mie every day to teach her what she knew. It was Mie's favorite part of her day, not only to learn how to read and write, but to interact so intimately with Yuki. She admired Yuki, a strong woman and a gentle mother.

Yuki walked over to Mie, drying her hands on a soft cloth. "Mother, what were your dreams when you were a girl? I know life was difficult, but did you ever think how things might be different for you? Did you dream you would be a wife and mother? Or did you have other dreams as well?"

Yuki turned to Mie. Dreams are for youth, she thought to herself. She had so many dreams when she was growing up, most that she dared not share with anyone. Life, for her, held so few choices. What should she say? She worried that if she told her the truth it might influence Mie in the wrong way. Women had a hard life if they chose not to marry and be a devoted wife and mother—and she wanted Mie to have a comfortable life.

"Well, when I was your age I had many dreams, as children do. One of my dreams was to fall in love and get married. I was lucky that one of my dreams came true . . . and that I met your father, who is a wonderful husband and father." Yuki worried that she didn't sound strong enough, sure enough about the path that her life took.

"Of course, Mother. But I mean, did you ever dream that you would be a famous puppeteer, or a rich merchant that traveled the oceans, or maybe a poet whose poems were written in the *Man'yoshu*? How about an artist that painted beautiful landscapes?"

Yuki laughed. "You have some wild ideas for a young girl. I suggest that you concentrate on your own reading and writing for now. You can work on your dreams later." Yuki shook her head and walked toward the kitchen. She felt like her own mother, discouraging Mie from carrying around her dreams. She wanted her daughter to have her dreams yet she didn't want her to grow up with unrealistic ideas and goals.

Mie continued reading, but when she heard her mother leave the room, Mie glanced up and stared out the window. She watched her father working in the fields, and the mountain, Fujisan, far in the background. Fujisan, a volcano said to have been created during an earthquake hundreds of years ago, was a sacred place filled with magic—or so many who had been there said. Mie dreamed of visiting Fujisan one day and climbing to its summit. She imagined herself at the peak and, like a red crane, flying into the sky. With these thoughts a peacefulness, a serenity, traveled through her. She closed her eyes and imagined the plum blossoms in the spring, their delicate fragrance. She imagined the Japanese maple trees in the autumn, deep purple and brown penetrating the landscape. She saw the snow in winter, covering the ground, the trees, and the bridge in the crisp air. Mie felt her heart soar and her mind drift.

Mie could not imagine living anywhere other than her parents' farm, yet she had so many dreams. She wanted to travel the countryside and meet new people. She wanted to live in Edo and learn about city life. She wanted to bring home books and writing to share with her parents. She wanted to try out different occupations and decide which one she liked best. Sometimes all her ideas came rushing through her all at once and she couldn't think straight. There was just too much to think about. And recently, young men had been coming to the farm to meet her. Laden with gifts, they spent time talking with Yuki and Jiro, while Mie sat and stared politely at them. There were a few other young girls, like Mie, around the countryside of Maebashi, but it seemed like many young men were looking for a wife.

Yuki stood in the doorway and watched Mie staring out of the window, seemingly lost in time. That Mie, thought Yuki, she could be anywhere right now.

"Mie? Mie? Did you hear what I just said? Are you finished reading? Did you get a chance to practice your calligraphy? I want to go back to the garden and finish the work we started this morning. The plants are young and tender and need a lot of care right now so they survive." Yuki sighed.

She knew that Mie would come out eventually and help her again; she just had to be patient. Youth was the time for thinking about life, before you got older and had to spend time *living* life—too tired to sit and just think about it anymore.

Yuki heard a quiet knock at the door.

"Hello? Hello?" Tall, for a Japanese man, with his dark hair tied up in a scarf, Kinshi was one of the young men they had hired to help in the fields. Kinshi came from a good family several miles away, and learned quickly and worked hard, but it was his positive demeanor that Yuki liked the most. Kinshi was willing to do anything that he was asked to do and often completed other jobs that he noticed half-finished. At only nineteen, Kinshi was already more reliable than the others.

"Yes, Kinshi? What can I do for you? Please come in," said Yuki.

"Is Mie here? I didn't see her after lunch and wondered if she was feeling well." Kinshi stepped into the doorway, removing his shoes.

Yuki smiled. "Thank you for inquiring, Kinshi. Mie is just fine. She is working on her studies right now and I'm not sure that she will return to the garden today."

"Would, would it be a bother if I talked with her? Is she too busy right now? I could come back later if she can't get away." Kinshi smiled broadly and cast his eyes toward the floor.

"Actually, yes, Kinshi. Please come back. Mie has a lot of work to do, but you can check in with her later this afternoon. Perhaps before you leave for the day." Yuki started walking toward the door, and Kinshi turned around to go outside.

"Thank you. I'll come by tomorrow. Please tell Mie I stopped." Kinshi closed the door gently behind him. Yuki watched him through the window and sighed. She'd liked Kinshi very much, right from the beginning. She remembered that first meeting under the cherry tree in the front yard. Mie came out of the house, looking for a book she had dropped. Jiro and Kinshi were sitting in the wooden chairs, sipping tea.

"Hello, Father. I'm sorry to interrupt you, but I was looking for a book that I misplaced out here. Have you seen it?" Mie was watching her father, but she noticed Kinshi in her peripheral vision. He was young and handsome, and she tried not to blush. She thought he was there to see her.

"Come back later, Mie. I'm discussing business with this young man right now. We can look for your book afterward." Jiro squinted up at Mie.

"Oh no," said Kinshi, "you can look for it now, if you'd like. I'm in no rush. In fact, may I help you look, also?" He stared at Mie until she lowered her eyelids.

"Nonsense," said Jiro, "let's finish this first. Mie, go back in the house." Jiro had hired Kinshi right away, and he came the next day—and every day after that. His father had died several years before and his mother was not well. Kinshi worked hard to support her.

Yuki walked quickly to Mie's room. "Mie? Kinshi was here to see you. I told him to come back later—it seemed you didn't want to be disturbed."

Mie glanced up from her book. "Oh, that's fine, Mother. I was just thinking about the red cranes. How about you? Have you seen many? They like marshy areas, you'd think they would like the rice fields."

Yuki sighed. She was both relieved and curious that Mie seemed uninterested in Kinshi—relieved because she wanted Mie to grow up more before deciding on a suitable husband, but curious because Mie was at the age when most girls were interested in boys, if only superficially.

"No, Mie, I haven't seen many red cranes. They are somewhat rare around here—really, around Japan. Maybe there was a time when there were more. I'm not sure why you're so interested in them. They're majestic birds, I agree, but I don't understand what draws you to them. Other birds are just as elusive as the red crane, you know. I'm going to go out to the garden now. Come and join me when you are finished." Yuki found her hat and changed out of her slippers. She tucked loose ends of her hair into her hat and walked out the door.

The sun was low in the sky and the wind had picked up. Jiro waved to Kinshi as he left to go home, then walked slowly toward the house. His eyes were drawn and framed in dark circles, and drops of sweat rolled down his face.

Jiro opened the door carefully and took off his hat. He stared at the small table in the main room with fruits, sweets, and some trinkets scattered on a tray.

"Yuki? What is all that on the table? Where did it come from?"

Yuki stepped into the room. "Well, let's see, Kinshi brought the tangerines, Yoshida sent a fan, Sano brought the sweets, and I'm not sure where the other things came from. It's hard to keep track." What else could she say? So many young men seemed interested in pursuing Mie—her beauty and innocence were quite a combination. As spread out as the farms were over the countryside, word still spread quickly about the young women who were close to the age for marrying. It was thoughtful for everyone to bring or send gifts, though it did seem like a bit too much. Most of all, Mie seemed uninterested in both the gifts and the people who sent them.

"What does Mie think about all of this?" Jiro changed into his house slippers and sat down carefully on a zabuton.

"Oh, Jiro. I don't know what is going on. Mie is not the least bit interested in any of her suitors, but it doesn't seem to dissuade them. They keep visiting or sending gifts. Perhaps she should say something—I don't know—what do you think?"

"Well, I think she should start showing some interest. After all, she is almost a young woman. Maybe if she would just pick one, the others would leave her alone." Jiro sighed.

"I'll talk to Mie. It's difficult to discuss this with her. She doesn't seem to take any of these men very seriously and manages to change the subject each time I bring it up. I don't want to pressure her, but I think that we should make some decisions." Yuki folded her hands in front of her and closed her eyes. She wished, on the one hand, that she could keep Mie a secret for just a few years longer—it would make life so much easier. Yet she knew that it was time to think about letting Mie marry and start a life of her own. A life separate from Yuki and Jiro.

Yuki found Mie in her room, practicing her calligraphy at the table, deep in concentration. Yuki stood at the door and watched her for a while until Mie finally looked up and saw Yuki.

"Mother, did you want me to do something for you? I'm almost finished with this sheet, if you can wait a few moments. Then I'll help you." Mie continued to write.

"I wanted to talk to you about something, Mie. I'll wait until you are finished. Come and get me when you are ready." Yuki turned around and started to leave.

"No, no, stay, Mother. I'm just about finished. Go ahead, I'm listening."

Yuki came into the room and sat down on a tatami mat. "Mie," she said softly, "what are we going to do about all of your suitors? I think you need to start thinking more seriously about them. Should we turn them all away? Are you interested in any of them—in getting married at all? What are we to do? Your father wants you to make a decision!"

"And you, Mother, what do you think?" Mie looked up at Yuki.

"I . . . I . . . agree with your father, of course." Yuki stared at the floor. She knew she couldn't look Mie straight in the eye.

Mie rinsed her brush and put it down. "Oh, Mother, I dislike having to discuss this subject again. Why can't we just leave things the way they are? We are meeting some nice young men, receiving some nice gifts, and no one is getting hurt."

"Mie, it's too hard to have men visiting every day. We all have many things that we have to get done in a day, and warding off suitors should not be one of them. Besides, you need to start thinking about choosing a mate. I was just about your age when your father and I met and got married."

Mie sighed. "Mother, you know how I feel. I'm not interested in any of the men and I'm not interested in getting married. Perhaps we could just tell all of them not to come anymore. Maybe then they would get the message."

Yuki thought for a moment. Caught again. She wanted to do exactly as Mie wished, but she worried that if they sent all of them away that Mie would never find a husband. She wanted Mie to have a good life, a happy life, and if she was not married, her life would be miserable. What opportunities did an unmarried girl have now? None that Yuki would want her daughter to pursue. "Mie, I'm not sure that is the answer. You know, you should be thinking about marriage even if you're not interested."

"Oh, Mother, we've had this conversation so many times now. I'll be fine without a suitor. I have so many dreams, and they do not include being married." Mie stood up and walked toward Yuki. "Can't we just leave things as they are for now, Mother?"

Yuki gave Mie a hug. "I just want you to have a happy life, free of struggles."

"Don't worry, Mother. I will. I just don't think I need to get married to find that happiness." Mie looked at Yuki. She knew that Yuki and Jiro had her best interests at heart, but Mie did not feel ready for marriage—if anyone was ever "ready." Mie wondered why she was so different from Yuki, but still, she couldn't imagine her mother not having at least one dream that didn't include, or preclude, being married. What was Mie to do? If she disobeyed her parents' wishes to find a suitable husband, she would shame them, and she couldn't bear that. But marriage before sixteen, or even seventeen, seemed too soon. Really, what did she know about being married?

Mie went into the kitchen to start cooking the rice. She knew that Jiro would want to eat dinner shortly. He liked to walk the fields after dinner and sit under the cherry tree before he went to bed. Grabbing some vegetables from the baskets, she set them in the sink to wash them. Then she felt a gust of cool air dance over her arm, and she walked to the door, opened it and searched the sky. She heard a distinctive bird call, but she wasn't sure what it was. Her heart raced with the thought of seeing a red crane. As the sun set, the sky was empty, with only cloud wisps dotting the horizon.

Mie watched her father standing in the fields, surveying the land. Yuki came up behind him and stood very close. Together they melted as one. The thought of her two parents becoming one parent made Mie smile. In some ways they were already like one. They were like two sides of one question—they each had their own opinion, but somehow they were still connected. She wondered if they were always like that or if they grew together over the years. It was a mystery to her how two strangers could love each other, live together, and somehow shape their lives as one.

Mie felt lucky that her parents weren't arranging her marriage yet. A few young women like herself were already promised to families and ready to begin new lives. She knew that her parents had been approached several times by respectable families. Her time was running out, and she knew one day soon she would have to make a decision. For now, though, she tried not to think about it. She wanted to do as her parents wished, yet she clearly had some desires of her own.

"Mie? Mie? What are you doing? You're not thinking about going to the fields now, are you?" Kinshi appeared from the side of the house. His head was wrapped in a white scarf and covered with a worn straw hat.

"Oh, hello, Kinshi. Are you still here? I thought you left to go home. I was starting to cook the rice and thought I heard a red crane. I came out to see if this was going to be my lucky day." Mie started to retreat into the safety of her home.

"Red crane? I hardly think so. You are some dreamer! I was going to visit the Tekona shrine later this evening and wanted to know if you were interested in coming with me. I wanted to pay respects to my father, make an offering, and pray. It's also a good excuse just to visit the shrine. When I walk through the sacred arch, I feel as though I was just sprinkled with magic powder that makes me feel strong and pure. I love the simple act of washing my hands and rinsing my mouth—it's like getting rid of all that's bad in my life. Then, seeing Fujisan in the distance, I feel my life is complete. Fujisan has that effect on me—it lifts my spirit. What do you say?" Kinshi came over and stood next to Mie.

The Tekona shrine. Mie loved going there at any time for any reason. She particularly enjoyed going with Yuki and Jiro to worship for rice planting and harvesting, although visiting the shrine for special occasions found it filled with worshipers. It was more pleasant when there weren't so many people around. She loved to close her eyes, stretch her arms out to her side, and listen to the silence. Mie did not really think of visiting the shrine for blessings and purification—more for inspiration. "Oh yes, I'd love to. Come and get me when you are ready." Mie returned to the house to finish making dinner. She ignored Kinshi, imagining herself deep in the landscape surrounded with Japanese maple trees, and Fujisan keeping vigil.

Kinshi stared after her. His eyelids lowered as he hung his head and walked toward the fields.

Yuki walked into the house and saw Mie drinking rice tea at the low table.

"How's dinner coming along? Do you need some help? Did you make some miso soup? I think your father really wants some soup for dinner. He said he hasn't been feeling quite himself recently." Yuki sat across from Mie and poured herself a cup of tea.

"Dinner is almost ready. I was just taking a short break. How was it in the fields today? Did you get a chance to talk with Father? Did everyone show up today?" Mie sipped her tea.

"Thank goodness! But there has been so much illness recently. We are lucky that we have been so healthy. And Kinshi, too. What would we do without him?" Yuki drank her tea quietly.

"Mother, I was wondering . . . how do two strangers decide to like each other and want to spend the rest of their lives together? It seems like such an odd idea, in a way. I mean, you and father didn't know each other when you got married. How do you know you want to be together? How do you know if you'll get along? How do you know if you can stand each other?"

Yuki laughed. "Well, Mie, you don't really know. You just make the commitment and hope that the bond develops. Usually good people, people with hearts that start deep inside of them, make it work. It's when one is good and one is bad that things could work out terribly. Your father . . . he is a good person, a good man. I knew that right away, and I knew we could make a life together." Yuki remembered the day her mother told her about Jiro.

Yuki was mending her kimono in the front room when her mother walked in and sat beside her. Yuki was sixteen or seventeen, just around Mie's age.

"Yuki, I have to tell you something. We have decided who you will marry. He comes from a good family, a respected family. The Tanakas say they come highly recommended. His name is Jiro; he is your age. We have sent word to his

*family that we are going to start the wedding plans. We are sure that you will
be happy."*

*What could Yuki say? That was the way it was done, the way it is still done. But
Yuki knew it didn't have to be that way, if she wasn't Japanese. She had read enough
books, imagined enough lives to know that life held choices. However, she knew she
wasn't strong enough to change her family's ways. She wasn't strong enough to cause
the pain, create the trouble. So she married Jiro. And she was lucky.*

"But, Mie, I would be deceiving you to tell you that it's always like
that. It's not. I am one of the lucky ones. Your father and I grew to love
and care about one another, but many others married and that didn't happen. Are you thinking about Kinshi? You know he would like to marry
you; he has already spoken to your father about this. But we wanted to
give you some time to consider the idea of marriage. We don't want to
force you into it."

"Kinshi? He's very nice, but I don't feel ready. Do you think that there
is something wrong with me, Mother? Why do my thoughts soar on the
wings of the red crane? Swim in the sea that is called life? Float on the edge
of my imagination?" Mie emptied her teacup and looked to Yuki for a reply.
Yuki stared back, wanting to shout out, no, you are not any different than
any other girl who has grown up wondering what life held in store for her.
But she couldn't. She couldn't give that affirmation to Mie just yet—but
could she ever?

...

It had been ten months since Jiro had passed away. Yuki rarely left the house.
The fields and the house, while functioning, were in need of serious attention. Yuki spent most of her day at Jiro's small shrine, making sure the candles
stayed lit and the food was fresh. Mie always found her kneeling in front of
the shrine, her head bowed. Mie felt the loss of her father as deeply as her
mother, or so she imagined. She remembered when Jiro first became ill.

*Mie had knocked softly on the door. "Mother? Are you all right? May I
come in?" Jiro had collapsed in the field seven days before, and Yuki had hardly
left his side. She had a bucket of cool water in which she dipped small cloths to
place on his forehead. His fever seemed to shift from hot to very hot, and he was
quite delirious.*

"Mother! Do you hear me?" Mie's voice had revealed her anxiety.

"Mie, yes, of course. Come in. . . ." Yuki's voice trailed off.

*Mie stepped quietly into the room. It was dark and the air felt heavy and
moist. She saw her mother hovering over her father, laying the wet cloths across*

*his forehead. Her father lay still in the bed, with a thick quilt loosely tucked in.
As she got closer, she noticed her father's skin, pink and puffy. His body was tense
and shivered just slightly. Her mother's body sagged under her kimono and made
her look smaller than she was.*

*"Is there anything I can do, Mother? Why don't you take a break now. I'll sit
with father and change the cloths. You should eat something, perhaps go outside."
Mie took her mother's hand gently.*

*"Mie, I don't want to leave him until his fever goes down. I'm worried; it's been
too many days now. His fever should be closer to normal. How long can he survive
like this?" Yuki sighed. She sat down and looked at Jiro. "Perhaps you could bring
me some rice and soup. I'll eat here while I watch him."*

*Mie stared at her mother. Her face was wan and thin, her eyes tired and
weary. "Okay, mother, I'll fix you something to eat. You need the strength. But
you also need some rest, too. Father needs someone to take care of him who is
healthy and strong." Mie walked slowly to the door and left the room.*

. . .

Yuki seemed to do the mourning for both of them; she rarely spoke to
Mie and cried often. Running the household became Mie's responsibility;
someone had to be sure that the boys worked in the fields and the chores
got done around the house. Yuki prayed often, although the Shinto priest
had only returned once since Jiro's funeral. Mie tried to get her to go to the
Tekona shrine to receive a blessing from the priests there, but Yuki feared
leaving Jiro's shrine.

"Mie? Mie? Are you here?" called Kinshi. He was standing at the front
door, looking through the doorway.

"Come in, Kinshi. I'm in the kitchen." Mie was grateful that Kinshi still
worked for them. He knew so much about the fields, having worked all
those years with Jiro. Mie knew that Kinshi could have found better paying
work elsewhere, but he wouldn't leave.

Kinshi took off his shoes and walked into the house. "Hi, Mie. I'm going
to go now. I did as much as I could in the fields. I'm hoping to hire one of
Sano's friends soon. There's so much work to be done, and without your father, it seems to take so much longer. How's your mother?" Kinshi brushed
back the hair from his face. Mie remembered when, not so long ago, he
would come bringing gifts for her. She smiled at him.

"Oh, Mother's the same. I guess it will be a while before she can accept
what happened. I worry about her health, though. She isn't taking care of

herself as she should and usually ignores my requests. How's Noriko and the baby? I wish I could see him now. He must be growing very fast."

Kinshi beamed. "Oh, baby Jiro is getting quite strong. He will be a strong and handsome young man some day, much like your father. But tell me, Mie, about yourself. How are you doing? It can't be easy for you, taking care of your mother, taking care of the farm and the fields. I hope you have time for yourself and your studies, now that your mother can't help you anymore. And, the red cranes. . . . Please, let me know if there is anything that I, or we, can do to help you. I know Noriko would come any time you want. We would like to have you come and visit us any time. Don't worry about notifying us first. Just come." Kinshi gazed sadly at Mie, his black eyes filling with tears.

"Thank you for all you have done, Kinshi. Mother and I appreciate your work and loyalty very much." Mie paused. "The red cranes are gone. I don't have time to think about such things. I don't even listen for their calls any more. And, my studies—well, my books are dusty and my brushes are stiff. I'm devoted to Mother now. How could I leave her while she is like this? Perhaps marriage is down the road, but perhaps not. Who would want to marry someone with her mother in such a sad way? I don't know, Kinshi, I just don't know. What I do know is that the farm and Mother need me and, for now, I have to accept this. This life."

Mie stared out in the fields and imagined Jiro working, bent over under his hat. She missed him very much. She could understand, but not imagine, the depth of Yuki's mourning. Is this what people have at the end of their lives? Sorrow, hurt, pain? If she ever married, would her life come to this also? Mie sighed.

Mie got ready to visit the Tekona shrine, her one refuge. She went every week when the priests were there; maybe receiving their blessings and purifications would have an effect on her life. After praying for Jiro, she would sit under the Japanese maples and gaze at Fujisan. Her dreams, like Fujisan, seemed just within her grasp. But she knew better now, that things didn't always seem the way that they looked. That life was what you made of it—not what just happened to you. Sometimes she wanted to grab Yuki by the shoulders and shake her, shouting at her to wake up. But she wondered if she would be shouting at the wrong person.

Mie found her cloak and wrapped it tightly around herself. She checked on Yuki and told her she was going to the shrine. Yuki nodded her head in recognition, but didn't look at her. Mie walked out of the house and looked straight ahead.

Nobody's Brother

Ann Bauer

Bo Robinson returned home in September of 1954 to find his mother dead.

He'd stayed for a year after the war ended to protect a skeleton Army unit that remained on the south side of the DMZ. Korea was eerily quiet during that time, like the halls of a school after everyone had gone home. Insects hummed in the hills. There was less to fear from North Korean civilians, who'd gone back to farming. But there were still men from both sides who resented the Americans.

Once, a seventeen-year-old boy who'd lost three brothers in the war had stormed the base. He was wearing tattered clothes, carrying a large gun, shouting rapidly—words that sounded like knives. Bo had tackled him easily, taking the gun away as if the boy were a puppy that had picked up an object he wasn't supposed to chew. Most days, though, Bo's responsibilities were few. He would walk the perimeter, perhaps lifting something into a truck for the officers who were being moved to Seoul. This reminded him of Detroit, the furniture store he'd left to come here. And his mother, alone now that both his father and brother were gone.

She worked at a department store on the Boulevard, helping people from General Motors find shoes that would ease the aches they got standing on the line. With one glance at the way a toe was gnarled, Eva Robinson could determine, for example, that a worker leaned to his left while tightening lug nuts. She could find a pair of brogans that had extra room in that space, or padding where it was needed.

She was still young: forty-nine to Bo's thirty-one. She'd lost her husband to a factory accident and her younger son to Rommel. After his military funeral—where rifles were fired over an empty, flag-draped casket—Eva had gone to the library to find out where her son's body lay. Her people came from Ghana, a tropical country of wild grasses and banana plantations; but Tunisia, where Rex had disappeared, was an arid place, full of people called Moslems who wore long robes and worshipped a man named Mohammed in place of Jesus Christ.

One afternoon in the summer of '54, she had just left the store and started across the street when a next-year's model Cadillac came around a corner and glided into her, a smooth motion that one witness later described as being like ballet. Eva's body flew backward thirty feet and landed against a bicycle rack. Blood soaked the springy hair that she kept pulled into a knot at the back of her head. By the time an ambulance arrived, she was dead and there was nothing to do but load her into the back with a sheet covering her face, close the doors, and take a report from the driver of the car—a young engineer who'd been sent out to test the dual four-barrel carburetors.

No one knew how to find Bo. He'd been overseas for so long: enlisting as the Korean war began in what his aunts and cousins knew was a misguided attempt to make up for his brother's death, then staying on even after the peace accords were signed. So they held her funeral without him on a Tuesday in late August, a scorching afternoon when the sun burned orange and seemed ready to melt the pavement.

There were few mourners; Eva's family was from Richmond, Virginia. But her dead husband's sisters did a respectable job. They made potato salad and had a tray of meats delivered from the Jewish deli on the corner. Some of Eva's co-workers from the shoe store came, as did two of her loyal customers. The Baptist minister spoke about her in his resonant bass voice, calling her a daughter, a sister, a mother, and a wife. These were, he said, the only things one need know about a good woman such as Eva Robinson. And her sisters-in-law nodded and wiped the sweat from the creases in their necks and said, "Amen."

By the time Bo arrived, on September 14, the house had settled into a dusty emptiness. He hadn't expected to find anyone at home—Eva would have been at work if she'd been alive—but after setting his duffel bag on the wooden floorboards of the porch, taking out the key he had carried with him on patrol for 1,083 Korean nights, and stepping inside, Bo could tell something was wrong. The shroud of quiet reminded him of the one he'd just left behind in Yonch'on. He walked soundlessly through the house, size fourteen feet making neat indentations in the nap of the hallway rug. He did not call for his mother, and when he left—turning off all the lights he'd flipped on, shutting the door gently, reaching into his pocket again for the key and locking the house behind him—he knew somewhere in the dark cavern of his soul that his mother was gone.

He walked down the broad sidewalk, duffel slung over his shoulder. Tree branches, heavy with leaves, rustled in the wind and cast tufted shadows on the concrete. The sun pulsed overhead, and for a moment, Bo felt dizzy. Then he saw a neighbor, a woman whose face he recognized though he could not recall her name, and she nodded, as if she were accustomed to seeing him, six-foot-five in Army greens, out for a walk every afternoon. He swallowed and the world slipped back into a form he recognized.

He went to the diner four blocks away where his father had taken him and his brother for breakfast on occasional Saturdays. Bo pushed open the door and saw that the vinyl booths and metal stools were exactly as he remembered. Behind the soda fountain, a spotless mirror shone.

"Sit wherever you like," said a woman, brushing by him with a tray, auburn hair caught in what looked like a nurse's hat on her head. Bo took a seat at the counter and stared straight ahead, into the mirror, watching the woman lean over a table, handing plates around, her hand unfurling each time, as if she were throwing a discus. He studied the menu. How long had it been? Three years? More? The prices were written in the same script he remembered from childhood, but where there once were 2s, there were now 4s and 5s. A meatloaf sandwich cost fifty-five cents! He marveled at this and felt in his pocket for the discharge money he'd been given, thirty-five dollars, which had seemed at the time a nearly unspendable fortune.

"Hey," said a soft voice at his shoulder. Bo turned to see a man with eggplant skin and pale eyes. "Ain't you Eva Robinson's boy?"

Bo nodded and held out his hand. When the man put his inside, it disappeared briefly while they shook.

"I was sorry to hear about your mama," he said. "She was a good woman, Eva was."

They were still locked at the hands, and even through the pain that went through him like lightning, Bo concentrated to keep from crushing the man's fingers. "Thank you," he whispered, his voice tight. But the man didn't seem to notice. He sat on the stool next to Bo's, leaning on the head of a worn cane with a polished wood handle.

"How'd they get a hold of you all the way over in Ko-rea?" he asked, eyes glittering like water. "I heard you was stayin' there, even though all the other boys done come home a long time ago."

Bo nodded and swallowed. "My term was over," he said. "I stayed on to help clean things up, but. . . ." He had caught sight of himself in the mirror on the opposite wall: his large head with the military buzz that was beginning to grow out into a mass of soft curls. He ran one hand over his head and grimaced.

Beside him, the man coughed. "Oh, sorry." Bo tried to smile. "Long trip. I'm . . . tired."

"Understandable. Specially for me. I served, too, y'know. In France." He nodded. Bo scanned the man's face, wondering if it was possible. Then he realized what this meant.

"You mean the first war?"

"Yup. 1918. Watched just about every boy I knew get blowed away. I was one o' maybe three that came back to this area without a arm or a leg missing. Don't know why. I just seemed to walk between the bullets. Like I had, I dunno, some sort of invisible cape on or somethin'. When I came back, everyone would ask how I did it, how I survived, and I had no. . . ."

"Can I get you gentlemen something?" The waitress had appeared in front of them, head cocked, left foot jiggling in a blocky padded shoe of which Bo's mother would have approved. He stared openly. She was the first woman he'd seen up close in over a year, and the palest one he'd ever seen in his life. Ordinarily, the girls on this side of GM headquarters were some shade of coffee. But this one: she was the pure white of summer clouds; her eyes sharply green; and her hair, now that she was close enough for him to see, glinted with threads of silver, though she couldn't have been more than twenty-four. "Is Arthur talking you to death?" she asked Bo.

"No, you're starvin' him to death," the old man said, grinning. Then he turned sober. "Meryl, this is Eva's boy, back from Ko-rea."

"Oh." The woman's foot stopped moving and she faced Bo so squarely, he turned on his stool out of respect. "I'm sorry about your mother. She was always very good to me." Her voice was strong but soft, the words ending in a throaty, foreign sound.

"Thank you." Already, Bo realized, it had gotten easier to talk about his mother's death—though he still had no idea when or how it had happened.

"What can I get you?" She spoke gently now.

Bo paused. For thirty-nine months, every day, people had fed him. He'd never had choices. He picked up the menu and turned it over in his huge hands.

"Get 'im a roast beef sandwich and some French fries. And don't be skimpy," Arthur said to Meryl. She looked at Bo, who nodded and said, "And a Coke?"

When she had whisked off to turn in her order, the men turned back toward the counter, and Arthur set his cane under his stool. "We discovered 'em, you know, French fries. That was one good thing that came outta that war."

"I don't know as anything good came out of mine." Bo heard himself say this, then realized it was true. He'd had a friend for a while, an odd, quiet boy from Minnesota who had loved being in Korea, mapping the flights of bombers. But that had ended when the boy was sent back home. Aside from Mickey, Bo's memory was filled only with the circle he walked, night after night, keeping watch. He didn't know what he was watching for, or what they were fighting for, either. Peace had come but nothing had changed. It was impossible to tell what they'd won.

When his lunch came, Bo ate and the man sat by his side—silent now, like a witness. The food settled into Bo's belly like pieces of a puzzle that had been missing. He ate every bite and threw his crumpled napkin on the plate, then signaled with two long fingers for the bill. Meryl, leaning over a little girl who had pigtails sprouting from every section of her head, only glowered. She mouthed the word, "Go," then smiled and waved, showing the pale underside of her arm and the line of numbers there, etched in green.

"She was in a war, too," Arthur said as he stood. "You take care, boy." Then he picked up his cane and stumped away.

Bo left the diner slowly, blinking in the midafternoon sun. He found a barber shop two blocks down and got a buzz cut, then took a bus to his aunt's house and climbed the front steps only to see her standing, framed in the cut-out of the flimsy screen door, staring at him. "I had a feeling," she said curtly, then reached up to hug him and held him fierce and tight. His bones ached with surprise; no one had touched him this way in years. He hugged her back, leaning down to bury his face in the velvety folds of her neck, and felt tears form at the corners of his eyes.

They sat at the table, cups of the morning's coffee—so bitter his aunt had cut it with condensed milk—on the oilcloth in front of them. "I'm sorry," the woman said, at least five times. "We wanted to find you, but none of us knew how." And Bo shook his head, again and again. "No matter," he said, though it was not at all what he meant.

"The house is yours," his aunt told him. "Everything is. Charley checked into it and the loan got forgiven long ago, back when your daddy was killed. GM mighta been responsible, so they sent a man out to tell your mama she wouldn't never have to worry about havin' a place to live." She put her small, plump hand on Bo's arm and it looked like a brown baby rabbit, hunched on the thick root of a tree. "You can go there while you decide what you're wantin' to do. Come join us for suppers. . . ."

Bo nodded. In the distance, the shift whistle blew with a hard sound that drifted and faded and broke apart. But when he left his aunt—kissing her on the check, tossing his Army duffel over one shoulder—and turned west into the glittering light of the waning sun, he couldn't go back to the house. In his mind, he pictured the way it had been earlier: still, empty, dead. He walked slowly, taking more than an hour to cover two miles. By the time he got back to the diner, the sky was murky, the horizon a strip of rose-hued gold that glimmered through the shadowy trees. Bo peered through the window; the diner was full now, and there were two waitresses in identical uniforms, crossing paths so they looked like twins involved in some complicated dance.

He opened the door and a bell jangled overhead but few people turned. Every stool was occupied, but there was a table near the back that had a hurried, recently-left look: soiled dishes, a half-full water glass, a dime and a nickel resting in a damp spot. Bo sat there and set his duffel on the chair opposite. As he lowered himself, fatigue washed over him and only the chair stopped his fall. He leaned against the wall and closed his eyes.

"You're back." Her accent had deepened with evening, the r like a low growl. Bo looked into Meryl's green eyes. Seated, he was level with her.

"I'm payin' this time." He patted his pocket. "The Army gave me money and it's burnin' a hole."

She didn't smile but stood, considering him. And then his memory blurred, becoming a mix of sensations: sweet carrots in the wine-colored juice of meat; the jagged stream of people leaving the diner; the scent of bleach and lime as someone mopped the linoleum; Meryl's soft hand on his back, supporting him as he rose from the chair.

He remembered their sex, too, as something distant. He was watching it from above, seeing them together, white on black, in her square bed. It had been nearly four years since he'd been with a woman. But Meryl was warm and she held him in soft arms that smelled like roses and cinnamon. And his body responded to her, like a machine, though his mind stayed apart.

Afterward, she slept with her head tucked into her chest, like a bird. And he lay on his back, staring upward at the low ceiling. As morning neared, he picked up her hand and ran one finger slowly across the green numbers tattooed on the underside of her arm. If he closed his eyes, he could feel nothing but her smooth white skin.

...

He went back to the furniture store for a time, but this made his life feel odd and empty. Living in his mother's abandoned house, driving the same delivery truck he'd used before the war, Bo could see no future. So he applied for a job at General Motors. There had been an unspoken moratorium on the hiring of black men, but GM made an exception because of Bo's strength and size. He would be useful on the end of the line when chassis became stuck and had to be worked free of the conveyor.

During the years Bo was in Korea, the unions had gone underground in response to McCarthyism. No one wanted to be labeled a Communist. But when Senator Joseph McCarthy was discredited early in '54, the American Federation of Labor and the Congress of Industrial Organizations began collaborating. By the time Bo was hired, the unions were strong again but split along racial lines. There had been several work stoppages among white employees protesting the advancement of Negroes. For the first six months on the job, Bo worked entirely alone.

It was loud inside the assembly room. He wore protective shells clamped over his ears and coveralls with a thirty-eight-inch inseam, special ordered from a clothier in Chicago. When the noon whistle blew, he took his lunch to a table along the wall in the room where the white men stomped and laughed and smoked. Negroes were not permitted to smoke inside because of their taste for mentholated cigarettes, which the crew foreman claimed poisoned the air.

One by one, the other black workers finished their lunches and went through a door onto the loading dock; Bo had smoked his last Salem with his morning coffee. He knew he could bum a cigarette from one of the other guys, but he hated doing that, plus it was January, a gray-white day with a fierce wind that blew across the city from Lake Erie. He stayed inside—warmed by the lunch in his belly and a paper cup of industrial-strength coffee from the company machine—leaning against the cinder blocks. He wished he read books, like Mickey, the air traffic controller from Minnesota. During the nights they'd walked the rubbly foothills of Korea, Mickey sometimes talked about the Westerns his mother sent. Now, Bo stared blankly at the opposite wall and tried to remember those stories: men who rode alone, met enemies, fought with valor, and went home to the warmth of waiting women. It sounded pleasant: bloody, quick, and clear.

"Hey, what're you starin' at, boy?" Bo focused and looked at the man who'd spoken, but didn't recognize him. He looked like all the other men at the table—grease-stained cheeks; ruddy skin; dark, slicked-back hair; Camels clamped in stubby fingers.

"Any reason you're hangin' around when all your brothers went outside to stink up the city?"

Bo said nothing. He knew if he rose, stretching to his full height, it would be an invitation. As a group, they might be inclined to fight. Any one of them alone, Bo knew, would avoid him at all cost. He fixed his eyes on the man who had spoken, keeping his gaze level and unblinking. Thirty seconds passed and the group fell silent. The man grunted loudly and stubbed out his cigarette. "Fuckin' nigger."

"What's that?" Bo heard it at the same time he was hit with a gust of icy wind. He turned to see the six men standing in a loose pack at the loading dock door. He knew immediately whose taunting voice he'd heard: the youngest on the crew at nineteen, Rodney was recklessly fearless and always looking for a fight. "What'd you call him?"

The men at the table began shifting, glancing at one another questioningly. Now, Bo stood. "Ain't nothin' Rodney. We should all go back to work."

"So you just gonna let him talk to you like that? Like you be some cotton-pickin' slave boy?" Rodney's voice was taunting, making Bo angry. He stood a couple feet from the group of young black men and they looked up at him, adolescent disgust shining from their eyes. Behind him, Bo heard one of the men at the table mutter, and the others began to laugh.

There was an instant in which the world went white. Then Bo was seeing the tents lined up in peaks against a pale orange sky, smoke rising from a fire. It wasn't a delusion. More like a life-size photograph that rose in front of him. He could smell the buttery skunk of gun oil—a scent not unlike the motor oil that clung to their clothes and the creases in their skin, but lighter. He ambled more than walked, put his hands on the shoulders of one of the men sitting at the table, he wasn't sure any more who'd spoken, so he chose one at random. When the man squawked and tried to shrug him off, Bo pressed down steadily.

"No one's goin' to talk to anyone like that any more. Right guys?" The man underneath his palms tipped his face to look at Bo, and there was pure hatred there. Far more than in war, where children strapped with guns blinked apologetically as they stumbled into the barracks, meaning to kill but beyond that intending no harm.

Bo let go, though there had been no response. He took three long strides toward the door, wanting only to leave, go back to the line where he would cover his ears and work in peace. But then he stopped. Still facing away, he said, "Come on. We're goin' now." He couldn't see them move, but he felt it. The six men fishtailing toward him, a small, swaggering army he'd never meant to collect. When he walked through the door and out into the hall, they followed.

He continued to work alone. But now, there were men always around him. After the incident in the break room, Rodney seemed to assume he was Bo's right-hand man. He referred to them once as "brothers," and Bo let him. But when Rodney bragged about how he'd impregnated a sixteen-year-old neighbor, Bo backed him against a wall and wouldn't let him go until he'd promised to marry her. Months after the wedding, Bo heard Rodney hit her sometimes and had girlfriends on the side. This was more evidence he didn't understand the ways of men and women.

Since the few nights he'd spent in Meryl's bed when he first came home, Bo had been with only two other women—both widows he'd met while subbing at the furniture store on weekends. He had never brought a girl to his mother's home, where he lived in a single bedroom, leaving the rest of the house exactly as it had been the day he walked through the door to find her gone. At thirty-five, Bo felt as if he'd skipped over the years when he was supposed to find his life. Now that opportunity had melted away.

"Don't be a fool," Arthur told him. "You're young. Go find some sweet young thing, get married, and have a boatload o' kids. Then you won't think so much; you'll be too busy just livin'."

Bo grinned. He and Arthur were at the diner, where they often met on Saturdays. At first, Bo had avoided the place, thinking Meryl wouldn't want to see him. But when they'd run into each other on the street one afternoon, three months after making love wordlessly on that first dark night, she'd picked at the lapel of his coat and asked why he didn't come in any more. He'd seen nothing but affection and pain in her dark eyes, so he went the following day.

"It don't work like that. Women don't think of me that way."

Arthur stared, eyes glittering, and planted the rubber tip of his cane so it made a perfect tripod with his feet. "Seems to me, boy, it's you who don't think o' yourself that way."

. . .

Over the next two years, Bo's house grew even emptier. The dust thickened and became damp until a layer of grime coated every stick of furniture—his brother's old desk and the rocking chair where his mother had sat listening to the radio. Every night when he went home, Bo passed these things and knew he should do something, perhaps throw them out or find out from the owner of the furniture store how to clean them. But he never did. Instead, he avoided the house in daylight.

As December of 1957 settled in, the sky began to darken earlier, going a muddy color by four-thirty in the afternoon. Still, Bo worked first shift and got off at three, so he had at least an hour to pass before he could move through the rooms downstairs without seeing. Often he would walk. If it was very cold, he might stop at one of the bars where black men gathered and sit alone at one end, drinking whisky from a short glass. On the twenty-fourth, he stepped into a place called Ike's and found Rodney buying drinks.

His wife had had a son, after two daughters: Rodney, Jr. Bo took a shot and a beer and, for once, joined the crowd of men who were gathered around. The talk was of babies, and of Jimmy Hoffa—a Detroit native who'd become head of the Teamsters.

"No way he's gonna work for us," someone said, and there were nods and grunts.

"He ain't supposed to," Bo said. The whisky had warmed him, making him more talkative. "Teamsters got nothin' to do with UAW."

"I meant *us*: brothers," the man said. He looked up at Bo calmly, the lenses in his wire-rimmed spectacles flashing in the yellow light. "Man's got the power right now, and if he wanted, he could. Help us out. Stead, he's just linin' his pockets."

Bo looked around. He knew Rodney and one or two of the others, but most of the men were strangers. Hardly brothers. Then a tray went around, another shot glass appeared in his hand, and Bo drank it all at once, putting down the beer and letting the whisky burn him. "So whaddya want from Hoffa?" His voice was starting to go sticky, but people rarely heard him speak, so no one noticed.

The man with the glasses reached out and took ahold of his forearm, holding it tightly despite the fact that he was so much smaller than Bo, he could barely get his fingers far enough around to grip. "Remember that kid who was killed last month on the line?"

Bo nodded. Everyone knew the story about the new man—a shy black boy just graduated from high school—who'd gotten tangled in the belt on the transmission line his third day on the job and strangled by his own sleeve as he tried to struggle free.

"There was a bunch of white guys standing around, just watchin'."

"You sure?" Bo tried to narrow his eyes, but the room had gone fuzzy and it felt like too much effort to squeeze his lids partway down without shutting them entirely. "I thought it was on shift change. No one else around."

"That's not what I heard." He paused.

A fourth shot had appeared in Bo's hand. Or was it a fifth? He downed it and swayed like a tree in a strong wind, still rooted to the ground but bending gently. If someone was there to see the accident, why hadn't that person stopped it? Thrown the switch to cut the line? Bo opened his mouth to ask, but the man spoke first.

"How long you been on the job?" he asked.

Bo thought back and counted carefully. It took him a full minute to answer. "Three years. A little more."

"In all that time, you got a raise? A promotion? You seen guys smaller and dumber than you get ahead only cause of the color of their skin?"

Bo had to admit, it was strange. The shift leader was a man with big sausage fingers who'd been painfully slow. When he was made a supervisor, the work speeded up simply because he wasn't there to delay it. But the man had gotten credit for devising more efficient methods, for somehow making Bo and the others work faster. He shook his head slowly.

The man in the shiny glasses looked up and grinned. He was older, perhaps fifty, but when he smiled his face took on a hopeful, youthful look that made Bo like him. "Egg-zactly. You got it, brother. You interested in comin' to a meeting? We could use a big, handsome guy like you—make those lazy white fucks take notice."

Underneath the hum of the men gathered in the room, Bo heard the faint chords of a song. He strained to separate the sounds, closed his eyes, concentrating hard. Then the music rose, briefly: *Fall on your knees!* he heard. *Oh, hear the angel voices.* He remembered his mother, long dead from a car driven by a white man who probably still worked at GM.

"Yeah." He heard his own voice against the receding notes and realized it sounded gruff rather than reluctant. Or drunk. He put more power into it. "Tell me where your meeting is and I'll try to be there."

The man, whose name was Dennis, had been smart enough to write everything down on the back of an envelope and stuff it in Bo's pocket. Walking home, his gait off by a fraction of a second, Bo fingered the paper. Once, he almost threw it away. Then he saw Meryl backing out of the front door of the diner, leaning over to lock the door with her key.

Bo stopped. He considered turning, taking the long way home, pretending he hadn't seen her. Instead, he stood still, darkness wrapped around him, snow drifting like tiny falling stars in front of his face. Meryl straightened and turned toward him. She smiled. Over the years she'd gained weight, but the softness somehow made her appear smaller. Everything about her was backward, he thought, including the hundreds of white strands twined through her hair that glinted in the light of the doorway, making her look even younger than when they had first met. He imagined her a plump nine-year-old taken from her parents, herded into a train car, and sent to work and starve slowly. She'd grown sick and weak and had been propped in a line when Allied soldiers arrived to liberate the camp, Arthur told him. There was no way to know for sure, but it probably led to the chambers.

He continued walking, stopping in front of Meryl. She reached up, without a word, to touch his face. Her hand was gloved, but he felt it and put an arm out to draw her in. "It's Christmas," she said into his coat.

"Yeah?" He had her trapped against his chest, pressing in from the outside because inside, something was shifting. Suddenly, he had more room to breathe. He needed the pressure of her body to be sure he would not fall.

"Just an observation." She laughed. "It's not my holiday, but I thought it might mean something to you."

Bo pictured the house when he was a boy, the tree that he and his brother had decorated with construction paper chains, his mother in an apron, bent over a ham in a dark, speckled roasting pan. His father sitting in the living room, smoking a pipe filled with something that smelled like cherries and clove. "Somethin'."

He took her to his house, and when they opened the door, he felt the emptiness of it, the way he had on the day he arrived home from Korea. An identical wave of fatigue washed over him. It was as if that afternoon were echoing through this cold night. He grabbed Meryl's arm roughly, and she flinched. "Sorry," he muttered. "I'm. . . ."

She waited. He closed his eyes and leaned against a wall.

"What are you?" she asked finally.

Bo groaned. "I got no fuckin' idea."

He felt her back away. "Don't talk to me that way," she said quietly. He looked into her eyes; they had grown hard. "I'm not some guy from your factory." Her accent thickened with anger. "Maybe I should go now."

"No." He stopped, confused. "No, I shouldn't talk like that. My mama would be angry, too." He rolled his head against the wall and it felt good, plaster meeting bone. "Stay with me. Okay?"

She stood, looking at him, for a few seconds. Then she took a step forward.

It was she who led him upstairs, fingers entwined in his so her hand was nearly lost inside. He undressed her slowly, setting aside the hat first, bobby pins protruding like porcupine quills. She shook her hair, which had grown long. And while she stretched, he reached in back of her to unzip the uniform she wore. The skin over her shoulders and rib cage had changed since he'd last been this close, becoming softer than anything he'd ever touched. Bo worried that his hands were rough, hurting her. But she arched her back and slipped her own hands underneath his heavy work jersey, lifting though she could not reach high enough to raise it over his head. He took it off himself and the cold air hit his chest, slicing through the haze. His eyes focused for the first time all night, and Meryl drew back.

"Are you sure?" she asked, pulling the sheet around her, preparing—Bo was nearly sure of this—to dress again and leave. He stood to turn out the light and returned to stand in front of her. She occupied the bed like an island, or a raft. He knelt and touched her cheek.

"Yeah, I'm sure," he said, kissing her in a way he'd never thought to before.

He would be thirty-seven years old on his next birthday. His first woman had been older, a neighborhood lady who took a shine to him when he was only eighteen. But he had never had an experience like this: it felt as if a fire were burning low and deep inside him. He moved slowly. They were locked together for what seemed like hours. Or days. And afterward, he slept.

On Christmas morning, they sat across the table from one another. Meryl had made coffee using a saucepan and a strainer, because the only percolator she could find was a metal carcass gummy with oil and dust. Bo drank, recalling the vapors that would rise up the stairs on Sunday mornings, along with the scent of bacon and their parents' voices, while he and his brother lay in bed, warm under the quilt, putting off the moment when they would have to throw back the covers, rise, and dress for church.

In halting language, he told her about the man who'd talked to him last night and produced the napkin with its scribblings: date, time, and place.

"You should go," she said simply.

"Why?" he muttered like a teenager, but he took her hand and it rose like a white spider inside his, fingertips dancing. "This ain't my fight."

"Yes." She flattened her palm against his. "It is all of you, together in this fight. That is the only way." She raised her face and her eyes were endless; he wondered if he could see whatever she was remembering if he looked far enough into them. "I know this to be true."

To Move a Tree

Diego Vázquez

I had spent enough time living in Duluth on Park Point to start recognizing the boats before they sailed under the lift bridge. Whether they were coming or going, I knew the names and the cargo they carried. My third year of living on the edge of the north shore, I discovered that there was truth in what I had heard. This was a good place to heal wounds, the ones that make life too hard to understand, the ones that keep scratching your heart, making you bleed for love in all that you do. Standing at my favorite stretch of sand about a mile from the lift bridge on the dunes, I saw a huge tree coming ashore.

The storms that had carried all sorts of underwater treasures to land had lasted for three days, but today was clear with sunshine everywhere, and the wind was a soft feather. Suddenly from out of the big bowl of clear water an enormous tree rolled onto the shore. It looked angry, hurt that it had been transported from whatever piece of land it had grown on for such a long time. But it also looked like it had spent a lot of time in the water—more days than the storm; maybe the storm had just released it from some other spot. I watched it for a long time, until it was finally beached enough that it wasn't going to float back out on the lake. I walked home knowing the tree would be there for a long time.

In my apartment, the phone was ringing. I answered before the voice mail got to it and heard my cousin Sandra. "Jimmy, you have to come home now. She's gone."

I live where glacial ice creates a new empire daily. After receiving the news that meant a return to Texas, I walked back to the stranded tree. I stood on the crest of a dune and watched the lake, the sky, the newly arrived tree, and wondered, "Where do I want to go when the ice melts?" I wash myself in the return of memory, rinsing the upstream of necessity, of the need to return; the essence of me began with this motion of returning. When I stood at this spot watching the lake break up from the winter ice, I was taken back to my grandmother's backyard, to the tree we transplanted when I was young. I liked that I could see a cardinal up here and that I could see one in the desert. My heart began the return to the breeding ground, the return to my birth. I decided I would fly back to El Paso the next day for Abuelita's funeral.

When I landed at the airport I realized that it had been more time than I could count since I'd seen the backyard, much less the tree. I had moved away at the end of the summer when we transplanted the tree. I had not started ninth grade in El Paso but instead went to California. And then the years had put me on the banks of Alaskan rivers; on a train to Narvik, Norway; and finally to the heart of the Midwest—Minnesota. I had never returned to El Paso before.

...

By the end of the day we had buried my grandmother. At the wake I discovered the tree had been growing well, had survived everything, even the death of my dear Abuelita. The leaves were bigger than I remembered. There was a sadness to the tree, but it was wide open with welcome. We were alone together. She was majestic in the backyard, towering over everything, the world safe right here with her.

The tree held firm in her new position. The three-bedroom house—one level spread wide, with an add-on porch that split the backyard into two sections—had crowded the place where the tree originally stood. The tree was too close to the porch roof, the rock wall, the chain-link fence, and the cactus. The other space in the backyard was larger and wide open, with enough room to move two or three trees and still add a garden. Although we never added a garden, a bench and a water fountain eventually joined the tree in its new location.

I took a seat now at the bench. We both remembered. She had a trunk that was sturdy, yet thin enough that I could wrap my arms around her. The bark was smooth, a light green cream. Even then, her branches were thick enough to hold anyone who climbed into her full leafy coverage, and enough foliage to hide anyone who wanted to be alone at night with the stars. When I had first moved into Abuelita's house, I spent countless hours in those strong branches, hidden from the rest of the world on warm desert nights.

On the day we moved the tree, we were happy. Before we started digging the new hole, Antonio, Abuelita's family helper, explained, "Nothing grows in mud. In dirt, yes, but never in mud. Mud is good for drying into bricks, stones, sidewalks, but not for trees. So we have to get the soil mixed up just right so that there will never be mud around this tree. Mud is what creates quicksand. You build houses with mud. Women make their faces pretty with mud. But you can't grow a tree in mud. So that's why we want to make this a good mixture to put around the tree, something that will keep it calm during the shock of the transplant." Antonio drove an old Chevy pickup truck with Chihuahua license plates. I was proud of that old truck, proud of Antonio and the way he went about his business. He was the painter, the landscaper, but most importantly the builder of children's toys from scrap metal, old wood, screws, nails, cardboard, glass, trinkets, and blown tires.

The location of the tree had bothered Abuelita from the day I was left with her. My mom, Abuelita's daughter-in-law, left town in search of a dream, leaving me kisses and a promise that she would send for me so very soon. My dad was Abuelita's second son, and he too was busy chasing dreams—although his were mostly dream-girls. He also made the same promise to return for me soon. But when we moved the tree I had lived for three years with Abuelita Hortencia and some other discarded cousins, there being an epidemic of dream chasers at that particular time in my family. I was the only boy in the house then. I would start ninth grade at the end of the summer.

Abuelita had been a doting mother. She loved giving her three daughters and two sons big birthday parties. Always a piñata, loaded with dulce de leche, tamarind, and any number of new beguiling candy from Juarez, would swing from the tree. And her children loved their parties—except for my dad, who stopped celebrating his birthday at thirteen, after three of the priests at the church suddenly disappeared. They had been reassigned overnight. Abuelita sang to us about how she loved all of her children, loved having children, and hated it when Abuelito Victor died.

She said that Abuelito Victor also loved life but died from too much rum and too much fun. She said he loved his pan dulce. I loved the sweet bread, too, but I knew Abuelito only through pictures, especially the one where he held me as a baby. Abuelita would whisper to me at night, kissing me good night, telling me so much about me reminded her of Abuelito Victor. I liked it when she said that to me.

. . .

Antonio had helped around the house as long as I could remember. There were times when Antonio stayed so late that he spent the night. I felt safe when I would wake early in the morning knowing that Antonio was in our house, seeing his truck with the Chihuahua plates parked in the driveway. My cousins Sandra and Olivia felt the same. Antonio laughed when he called them "las señoritas de Tejas," and they smiled with need.

Olivia and Sandra were twins, two years older than me, though when I was twelve years old they already looked like they were eighteen. Olivia would glide around as if she were a fashion model at the trendiest nightclub in town. And like a fashion model, Olivia never smiled. Sandra, though, would wear a dress for church only. We had recently started going to the early Sunday Mass. We would walk together as soon as I got home from delivering the Sunday morning newspapers, stopping at the bridge over a small, unnamed creek, that almost always had some water in it and talking about life. We never knew where the water came from. But Olivia always wore dresses, could not imagine going to any mass but the High Mass with the largest crowd of the day. She needed to be noticed in all the right places.

Flaco Smith and I were friends even before he started thinking about girls in that way. He was rough and tough with everybody but me. Too many people didn't understand why we were friends. We did have differences, but they hadn't been big enough yet. We knew something about the inside of each other and so we just liked each other. I knew how to read a book from beginning to end. Flaco insisted he only needed to read the first page, jump somewhere into the middle, read maybe a few pages in there, and then the last page. I could never convince him that he was missing out on so much that was good and important to a story. He asks, "Why, Jimmy? Like life, we have a first page, if we are lucky some of us get some inside pages, y, ya, basta, we hit the end. What goes beyond the end?" Nobody knew just when Flaco got stupid, but he really got stupid around girls.

. . .

When we moved the tree, according to Abuelita, it was still young enough to safely be transported. Though the tree was already big enough to block sunlight entering through the kitchen window, Sandra and I believed Abuelita that it was young enough to be moved from its birthplace yet old enough to survive the change. Olivia, pretending to be a grown-up, said of the tree, "It's ordinary and not worth the effort. Just a tree, no big deal, sweetie. No big deal."

On the day I told Abuelita that I would move the tree, she was joyful and hopeful. Sandra chimed in that she would help. We decided to start digging early the next morning, to have some cool hours before the sun woke up.

So at six a.m. on a Tuesday morning in the middle of summer, Abuelita, Antonio, Sandra, and I, stood staring at the tree. Antonio said we would have to dig the new hole first, and that it would be a long job. He was not wrong. When we started shoveling dirt we were quiet, so quiet that I could hear glamour-queen Olivia snoring through her bedroom window. Clank, dig, dirt. Dirt, dig, clank. Dirt, clank, dig. On and on. By nine o'clock in the morning we were halfway to where the tree needed to be and expected to have the hole completely dug by noon. Though the work made me feel like a prisoner, I was part way into a universe of unfulfilled expectations.

. . .

The first complication and delay was Antonio's being called away. We had no way to know when he would return, since he had to cross back into Juarez. If he was delayed, we would not know the reason. But for Antonio crossing back and forth was rarely a problem. He spoke often of his paperwork being in order. I was aware then that some form of paperwork was needed, but it was still a nebulous business to which I paid little attention. I didn't know of the free bridge, a recent addition to the border crossing that could make life easier. Lately, Antonio was more often than not using the new bridge. But that day he crossed on the old downtown bridge, and some form of migra sweep kept him away for most of the afternoon and most of the digging.

. . .

Quick to offer long, quiet answers on all manner of questions from me, Antonio was a man of dignity and kindness. When I asked about his family, he would slowly hunch his shoulders. Sorting through his memory made him look like he was trying to squeeze himself back into his heart. This man of sixty-seven years old looked like he was forty-seven. Antonio moved deliberately; when I worked with him I would never notice how suddenly he would leave to take care of something.

Abuelita came by while Antonio was gone, and began talking about the first time she came to El Paso. She was a girl from Santa Eulalia, a mining town in Chihuahua. I had assumed that she had crossed from Juarez into El Paso when she decided to come north. She told me otherwise. For the first time in my life I made a leap into the truth of adventure from those who came before me. She first crossed with three other people from her village, in the middle of the night through the open desert, west of El Paso, in the unnamed parts of New Mexico. At that time it was one of the safest routes because la migra rarely patrolled that area. For one thing, it was too far from the highway. And, too, if you were stranded in that desert in the middle of the day, there was no water. As she talked, none of her story sounded real to me. I couldn't imagine this woman, my grandmother, ever having to cross a desert in the middle of the night, much less doing anything illegal. Here she was telling me that she had never been documented, and that is why she never returned to Mexico. For the first time I understood her refusal to cross into Juarez, even just for a Sunday visit to the church over there that she always talked about. I understood her sadness, those days when she seemed to have trouble breathing, when she reached for a handkerchief and wiped her brow, then smiled to assure me that she was fine.

Abuelita was lucky on her first crossing. One of the girls that came with her had cousins in Las Cruces who picked them up on the highway. She lived in Las Cruces for a few years, then met my grandfather when he passed through while playing the piano with a small band that wanted to sound like an orchestra. It was not possible for the band to travel with a piano, so at gigs where no piano was available, Abuelito would sing backup. He was not a good singer. Abuelita said that fortunately he was also a baker, only traveling with the band so that he could earn enough money to return to El Paso and start his own bakery. When they met he was trying to sing a song whose words he had forgotten, and she laughed at him. The band played in El Paso for two weeks, and when they left town, Abuelita left with my grandfather.

They found their way back to El Paso, and he did start the bakery which was a success. They both stayed always on this side of the border. Abuelito was from Zacatecas. He used to say that even if he could go back, it was just too far to go. So Abuelito also never saw his hometown again after coming to Texas. As Abuelita spoke, I still could not imagine either one of my grandparents doing anything illegal. Through them I had learned what was good and what was bad. Their courage was much more than I could understand.

When Antonio returned from his long disappearance, he emptied fresh soil from the back of his pickup truck into three or four different wheelbarrow loads, delivering each to the side of the big new hole for the tree. I watched him, thinking back to earlier when he had shown me how to use the flat shovel on the side of the new hole. He said it was almost wide enough but there was still a lot of depth to uncover. I was shoveling and shoveling and then, *swoosh*, Antonio was gone. I looked inside the kitchen and saw him drinking coffee with Abuelita. Later the two of them came to the backyard, talking and pointing out different shrubs, bushes, and flowers. And I dug deeper.

Sandra too knew how to disappear. She was gone soon after starting with me in the morning. At lunchtime she arrived with tortillas and Coca Colas and water. I was hungry; I had earned this meal. Just as I stopped digging, Flaco came by, hungry of course. And in our house, of course he would be fed.

I drank water as I sat in the shade under the tree that was cataloging each of my movements. It would absorb this day into its rings. I knew somehow, even then, that I would not be around when the tree got old. But that I would want to come back to see it when I was Antonio's age, to wrap my arms around this tree that knew me as a child.

The hole around the tree began causing it to lean; we named it the leaning tree of El Paso. During Antonio's lesson on how to dig a hole, he had said that, when shoveling, it is easier to dig, scoop, and toss in a straight line than to twist around in any other direction. Any contortions were a waste of energy, and could be dangerous.

I was tired. I wasn't thirsty, because I just finished drinking a long stream of water from the hose. And the water wasn't even hot, because Abuelita had rolled up most of the hose in the shade. In my grogginess, I was surrounded by a thousand polka dots in mismatched roots. This made it difficult to cleanly dig, scoop, and toss. Though I was exhausted, I gave the shovel an extra push to make the dirt fly a little bit higher over that leaning tree. I twisted and shoveled to the side, almost flipping the dirt overhead, ignoring Antonio's warning. Dig, clank, twist, clunk, and *thud*. The shovel ricocheted off the branch and right onto my melon, knocking me out for a full count. It must've been pretty loud because everyone said they heard an unpleasant sound. By the time they got to me I was already opening my eyes to the big blur.

. . .

As I started to come to, I was having doubts about this tree, which did not seem worth the trouble. But at the end of the day, with the tree in the new hole, Abuelita was happy, Antonio looked sad, and I was beat. The twins were gone and Flaco Smith returned in time for the evening meal. He was moving to California and would not be going into ninth grade with me. We all stood around the tree, talking, as the night darkened and the ground closed around the tree. Abuelita said that someday she would put a bench next to the tree and maybe even a fountain. We listened to the noise of the city sirens, laughter of women walking down the street holding each other, the car radios of teens out on dates. We felt good about the work that we had done.

And the night folded over us, sweet and calm, the stars delicate pieces of distraction, beautiful, and unreachable. The tree held firm in its new home. Abuelita said we would have to water the tree in its new place every night for a long time. I had never heard her say anything like this before; we never watered anything, much less for a long time. Antonio explained that while he didn't know why the tree needed to be watered so much after being transplanted, he was certain that if we didn't do it the tree would not survive the transplant. And he asked, staring into the night sky, if we could stand to see such beauty as this die before us. . . . Now, could we?

I watched my twin cousins Sandra and Olivia standing around the tree, both of them very quiet. They too had been sprinkled with the magnificence of the desert stars. Flaco showed up then, but even he said nothing, just stared at the tree. I looked at the crowd of people who kept my heart busy with warm joy. I watched Antonio looking at the stars, Abuelita watering the tree, and I felt myself growing because of their beauty. I answered to my heart that, no, never would I want to see this beauty die.

When I returned to Park Point, I walked back to see the big tree beached during the storm, but it was gone.

Modern Living

The Body Remembers

Diane Wilson

The bell on the front gate rang late in the afternoon when Rene thought she was done for the day. She was standing in her back bedroom tucking clean sheets around the corners of the massage table when she heard the unmistakable clang of a late arrival. Moving to the front door with an armload of sheets, Rene saw a woman standing just inside the fence, looking around as if undecided whether she should come to the door. Her suit was creased from sitting, her shoes unused to soft grass.

While Rene waited, she threw the sheets in the closet and closed the door to her room. From his bed in the kitchen, Sunka stood on trembling legs and shook himself awake. He too had heard the bell, knew that it rang for him, summoned him from a deep dream of chasing rabbits.

Rene and Sunka stood at the door together, watching the woman's slow progress through the long front yard. Sunka's tail beat a steady rhythm against Rene's leg. Unaware that she was watched, the woman stopped to cup the face of a rose in her hand and sniff its sweet fragrance before moving on. She plucked a few silver leaves from the sage plant, crushed them with her fingers to release the scent, and held them to her face as she walked. She looked up as Rene stepped out of the front door.

The woman stopped and smiled. Her dark hair was pulled back in a long ponytail with streaks of gray near her temples, a loose strand waving across her round face. Pushing bangs away from her moist forehead, she held her hand above her eyes to cut the glare from the sun.

"Han koda," Rene said. "What can I do for you?"

"Han koda," the woman replied. "I'm Lyla Dubois. I don't have an appointment. I was at a conference in the Cities and a friend told me about you. My flight doesn't leave until tomorrow morning, so I took a chance and drove here."

Rene did not ask how she managed to find her house, tucked away at the end of an unmarked gravel road, deep in the woods on the Lower Sioux reservation. Generally her clients got lost the first time they had to find her. Lyla's friend must be someone who knew Rene.

There was something appealing about this woman. She stood patiently while Rene decided whether to invite her in. Despite her expensive suit, she did not assume that whatever power she held in the Cities meant anything out here. She simply waited while her heels sunk deeper in the soft grass, turning her head slightly as if drinking in the bright gold of the sunflowers.

Rene stepped forward with her right hand extended. "Welcome. This is Sunka, border patrol." At hearing his name, Sunka hobbled forward and sniffed Lyla's outstretched hand. She held it palm down, giving him time to investigate before scratching his ears. Another good sign.

Rene led her guest to the kitchen at the back of the house. Lyla sat next to the open window, running her hand over the uneven surface of the pine table, the old scars from years of hard use now polished to warm glow. White curtains softened the glare of the afternoon sun. Jars of dried herbs were lined up along the counter, with handwritten labels identifying each plant. A glass kettle on the stove was half-full of tea waiting to be warmed. A crocheted potholder scorched on one corner hung from a nearby hook.

"Where are you from?" Rene asked, turning on the stove.

"I was raised on Upper Sioux," Lyla said, a reservation not far from the Lower Sioux where Rene lived. "I moved to Montana when I got married." She explained that her work as the director of a health organization had brought her back to the Cities for a conference on diabetes.

"Do you like your work?" Rene asked.

"No. I mean, yes, I like what I do. It's the travel I get tired of. I have two young daughters who hide my suitcase when I'm home. My youngest told her teacher she comes from a broken home." Lyla laughed and rubbed her eyes.

"I met an old friend at the conference who told me that I didn't look well. I said, thanks, I'm just tired. She suggested I get in touch with you. Gave me directions and a map she drew on the back of a napkin."

For the past year, especially when she traveled, Lyla had begun waking at three a.m. The night before she lay in her hotel bed listening to the hum of the ice machine down the hall, waiting for the sun to come up. She thought of her oldest daughter, Amy, asleep in her bed a thousand miles away, the covers pulled up to her nose even on warm nights. Her youngest, Beth, slept with the blankets thrown half off the bed, arms flung wide, her brown hair missing a clump where she had experimented with scissors. Lyla remembered how her mother used to come in from a late shift at the casino and whisper to her, tell her how bright the stars shone that night, how she'd seen three deer on the drive home. Had she been dreaming of her mother when she woke? She could not remember.

That morning she stumbled through her speech, pausing occasionally when her thoughts seemed to evaporate. All those expectant eyes turned toward her, waiting to hear something that would inspire them to keep battling a disease that was epidemic in the Indian community.

"Ten years ago I would have set that audience on fire," Lyla said, leaning toward Rene. "People who knew me, like my friend, were waiting for that woman to reappear.

"Afterward, people avoided me. I could tell by the way some of them looked at me that they wondered if I was drinking. What else could be wrong with an Indian?" Lyla gave a short, humorless laugh.

She finished her speech, ignored the low-fat turkey wrap sandwich that seemed to be on the menu for every diabetes conference. When her friend pushed the napkin toward her with a crudely drawn map, she thanked her politely and shoved it in her suit pocket. How ridiculous to think she would drive that far for a massage, or as her friend had corrected her, for "bodywork." She may as well drive home, except there was no one at Upper Sioux she wanted to visit.

Driving back toward her hotel, she saw a sign for the highway exit that would take her toward Rene's house. Ridiculous, she repeated, setting her lips in a firm line. She needed to pack, finish a report, check her e-mail. The freeway was already heavy with afternoon traffic. Glare from the late August sun was reflected from too many cars jumping lanes at high speed, acres of concrete, and miles of blacktop shimmering in the heat. Strip malls gave way to hotels and superstores, with chain restaurants tucked between for convenience. Cutting across two lanes of traffic as car horns blared, Lyla nearly missed the exit. She hit her brakes hard to hold the curve as she headed south. What the hell, she thought, and punched the radio button to country western.

When she stopped two hours later at the end of a deserted road, she rolled down her window and took a deep breath. A light breeze carried the smell of summer: sweet grass warmed in the sun, the fresh scent of last night's rain. She looked at the tidy cabin flanked by cottonwoods and old, gnarled oaks. An enormous apple tree heavy with ripening fruit grew near the side of the house, a rope swing creaking softly as it swayed. Old-fashioned hollyhocks stood behind unruly shrub roses covered with pink flowers. Across the yard, she could see plump tomatoes trailing on straw mulch, silky tassels on tall cornstalks surrounded by squash vines and the few beans not yet picked. Containers on the steps leading to a purple front door held basil and lavender, self-heal, and feverfew. After a long moment while she weighed the risks of walking up to a stranger's house uninvited, Lyla opened the gate.

"So what brings you here," Rene asked, as she set two cups of swamp tea on the table.

"I don't really know," Lyla said. "I hate to say this since I just interrupted your afternoon, but I'm kind of surprised to be here." It was the fluorescent lights on my hands, she wanted to say, the smell of polyester bedspreads, the feeling of recirculated air against my skin. She looked at Sunka asleep on his bed. A child's drawing was taped to the refrigerator door. "I think I wanted to go home."

"I'm sure there's a reason why you're here," Rene said softly. "Sometimes the bodywork can help us discover what it is."

. . .

When Lyla finished her tea, Rene opened the door to the back room and invited her to enter. Half-closed blinds filtered the light, keeping the room cool. On a shelf near the window Rene kept a shell for smudge, a bundle of sage, tobacco, a handful of rocks, and two feathers. The air was scented with a hint of eucalyptus. After explaining to Lyla that she should remain lightly dressed and lie on her back beneath the sheet, Rene returned to the kitchen table.

Rene took a deep breath and closed her eyes. When she was a child, her grandmother used to cover her eyes with a wrinkled palm and then tap her sternum lightly to focus her attention. Here, she would say. Not here, and rapped the top of her head with a knuckle. If Rene came home furious after someone at school called her a squaw, her grandmother handed her a pair of garden clippers and pointed at the dead canes in the raspberry patch. "But

Kunśi, I need to talk!" She patted Rene's shoulder and said, work first. Rene
weeded and hoed and gathered with a fury, all of her pent-up anger vented
into the garden. Fed by so much electric energy, the hollyhocks grew ram-
rod straight; even the wayward indigo refused to bend. Her grandmother
told her that the lightning bugs looked forward to her visits. And then she
laughed.

On warm afternoons like this one, her grandmother would have walked
with her into the woods where it was cool. She showed her how to bury
her feet in sphagnum moss, how to trace the fine roots of wild ginger in the
fall. Pray first, she said, and never gather more than you need. They would
spend the evening washing the roots and patting them dry, spreading them
out in a single layer on wax paper. Before dinner, her grandmother would
hand Rene a tiny piece of ginger to chew. Making a face, Rene waited until
her grandmother turned away before spitting it into a napkin. One of the
jars on her counter was filled with dried ginger, the label written in her
grandmother's spider-fine handwriting.

When Rene left for college, her grandmother told her to study hard.
"Then you can come back and teach me," she said, turning toward the
garden.

The year before her grandmother passed away, Rene came home in the
backseat of her friend's car, her clothes packed in a single bag, holding a box
of papers on her lap. One of her clients at the shelter where she worked
had a daughter who used to sit on Rene's lap and draw while her mother
talked. One day Rene learned that her stepfather beat her to death while he
was drunk. After two days of not answering her phone, Rene's friend found
her in the yard behind her apartment, digging in the ground, her fingers
rimmed with dirt and dried blood.

Her grandmother said nothing when they drove up, simply turned and
walked back into the house. In Rene's old room her grandmother wrapped
her in white sheets that had dried outside on the clothesline, tucking the
ends tightly around her arms and legs, swaddling her entire body. At night
she burned Balm of Gilead while Rene slept. During the day Rene drank
tall cups of swamp tea while sitting in a chair in the backyard, listening to
the creek ripple over rocks on its way to the river. When Rene was stronger, her grandmother brought her to a sweat lodge where the stories were
leached from her skin, where they fell as drops on the ground. Later they
gathered wild greens, prepared corn for hominy, dried meat for wasana.
One morning when her grandmother was outside, Rene took the drawing

from her box and taped it to the refrigerator door. To Rene, Love Michelle. Before Rene left, her grandmother gave her a bundle of sweet grass from the garden. Find another way to help our people, she said. "You're not strong enough to carry these stories."

Her grandmother passed away a few months later, leaving her the house and the jars filled with medicine plants that she had so carefully gathered and dried. With the little bit of money Rene had left, she found a school that taught her how to care for the body. If she could not carry these stories, then she would release them, return them like caged birds to the sky where they belonged. An elder taught her how to draw from the energy she received in ceremony. Sometimes people tried to tell her how they hurt this leg or that arm. She held their words at a distance so they simply flowed away, not allowing anything to catch hold beneath her skin. Her touch was cool and dry, like the salamander she once caught in her grandmother's window well.

Before long, people passed the word that Rene had her grandmother's gift, only hers was in her fingers. She read bodies like Braille, found notes written in the tissue, whole chapters hiding in a single muscle. The more she worked, the fewer words she had left at the end of the day. They were pressed down, flattened by the energy she opened in tissue that had become hard and dry, calloused by pain, protected by the body's ability to divorce itself. Rene woke dormant cells with the warmth of her hands. She stirred sluggish blood by following the map within the body, calling energy with her energy.

At night she fell into bed, exhausted, her lean brown arms still humming. She dreamt of light streaming across the sky, falling from stars to the earth below. She held up her face as if it was raining. When she woke, Sunka snored from the foot of her bed, his warm scent a comfort to her. Sometimes when she needed to hear her own voice, she told Sunka stories while he slept. That same morning she had told Sunka that the earth would soon begin to pull the green back down to its roots, storing its energy for the coming spring. Pay attention to the crack between seasons, her grandmother had told her.

Opening the door quietly, Rene moved to the head of the table where Lyla waited, her long hair spread across the pillow.

"Don't you play music?" Lyla asked.

"No." Through the open window Rene could hear the victory song of birds raiding her garden, counting coup on the raspberries. She had been known to rush from the room to shoo deer from her lettuce.

With Lyla lying on her side, Rene stood with her feet well back from the table, using her body's weight to press her fingers firmly into Lyla's ribs. Her hands moved slowly forward, lengthening the tissue, testing for resistance in the layers beneath the skin. Sometimes Lyla moaned slightly as the pressure became intense. Rene eased up, searched for a less painful way to resolve the area. As the afternoon shadows lengthened in the yard, the quiet in the room deepened, closing down the world until nothing existed beyond this wordless communion between two bodies.

Rene probed the muscles on Lyla's strong back, sensing the strain from her job, her frequent travel, the long absence from home. Battle scars, she named them, the marks left by the weight of our lives. Lyla's shoulders curved forward, the familiar shape of a woman who holds a baby in her arms. Heavy, held far too long. Rene felt the weight in her own arms. She released her hands from Lyla's back.

"Where was your family in 1862?" Rene asked, referring to the war between the Dakota and white settlers that began at the Lower Sioux agency.

"On both sides," Lyla said. "Ending up together at Fort Snelling." After years of starvation and failed treaties, the Dakota were forced to choose sides during the war. Afterward, with the men imprisoned at Mankato, the women and children were marched one hundred and fifty miles to a concentration camp at Fort Snelling. In the years following the war, when the Dakota were forcibly removed to Crow Creek in South Dakota, hundreds of children died.

Rene had learned this history when she was in college, reading everything she could find. Determined to right all the wrongs of colonization, she graduated in Social Work and took a job at a domestic abuse shelter for Native women. When she tried to explain this history to her clients, they stared back at her, not caring, waiting until she said or did something that mattered, like finding them a safe place to sleep. Michelle's mother was different. She used to drink in Rene's words, her brown eyes large with wonder and dismay at her own history.

On one of their long walks in the woods, Rene's grandmother had shown her the old ferry landing by the Minnesota River, across from the Lower Sioux agency. Close your eyes, she said; and feel this place. It scares me, Kunśi, let's go home. Rene tucked her fingers in her grandmother's hand. Not yet, Takoźa, I want you to remember this feeling. A battle was fought here and many soldiers died. They still roam the land, they're angry, they want revenge. Learn to recognize them. Later I will show you how to protect yourself.

Moving her feet slightly to a new position, Rene felt the band that circled Lyla's back. This was the mark of a body guarding itself, pulling the chin down to the chest. She's lost sight of the sky, Rene thought, she sees only the ground in front of her feet. Dried leaves cling to the hem of a long skirt, pellets of hard snow swirl across brown grass. The child in her arm sleeps, no, the child is silent. Lyla's breathing deepened. "I'm cold," she said. The air in the room grew still.

Rene felt her body tighten as a familiar weight descended on her neck and shoulders. Every cell resisted, her muscles rebelled, her grandmother's voice rang in her ears. Here, she said, not here. Rene felt a small tug on her hair. Many times she had approached this place, only to be knocked back by the dark, by this black hole without spark or movement. Rene shifted her shoulders, turned her head, continued to push against the hard wall of the body's long history, reaching back long before she was born. She moved beyond the terrors of humanity's history and reached toward creation, where all of our pains, our sorrows, our undone lives are mended, restored to a state of innocence and hope. Rene felt a white spark surge up her arms, release from the top of her head. Lyla began to weep, quietly at first, and then her shoulders shook with great wracking spasms of grief. Her skin grew warm again and she fell asleep.

Later, after Lyla had left, saying she wanted to find her cousin at Upper Sioux, Rene sat on a stump in her backyard, throwing sticks on a small fire. The fireflies were beginning to wink in the tall weeds at the edge of the creek. She folded Michelle's drawing, its once bright colors now faded, and gently laid it in the fire. A flame licked the edge of the paper. It quickly burned to ash, became bright sparks rising toward the stars.

Knowing

Josiah Titus

We back out of our driveway and turn to the interstate. The city holds us in morning traffic and I flip aimlessly through radio channels. She holds her tumbler close to her face.

"This smells like fish oil."

I smile at her sense of sacrifice.

She says, "They told me I couldn't drink coffee, that it was better if I didn't, but look, all this tea and what difference did it make?"

I think about the difference and about the miles we have to drive. We are quiet as the traffic exhales us into the exurbs. As the freeway begins to twist into the mountains, we lose the radio channel and I opt for silence.

"It's still better that you don't drink coffee," I say.

"I don't know," she says.

. . .

We sink back into the car after lunch and she begins with *what ifs.* "What if we hadn't found out? What if we didn't know? What if we wait and try again? What if we don't tell my family? What if this really *is* just a visit?"

"We can do this," I say. "People do this all the time."

"What if we do tell my parents?" she says. "What then?"

I don't know what to say.

She says, "Can we go back from that?"

Past the first mountains, before the next, everything is dry and constant. The shades of earth shift to growing pools of dark as the sun slopes into the afternoon, and everything becomes a shadow.

After being quiet, she goes on.

"What if we can't do this?"

"I think we can do this."

"But what if we can't? What if we're wrong to think that we can?"

And then she is quiet again.

. . .

We are quickly into evening and through the desert. She turns on her reading lamp and opens her purse.

"I want us to stop somewhere," she says.

"We can stop."

"I don't want us to drive through the night."

I turn and can see the reflection of her legs and the lights of the dash in her window.

"We forgot about dinner," I say.

"I'm not hungry," she says.

"We should eat. You need to eat something."

"I want to find a motel."

"I can make it through the night. You sleep."

"I want us to stop."

She looks at me.

"I'm sorry," she says.

She reaches up and turns off her light. I look at the road ahead, at the reach of my high beams, and I am impressed. My headlights are steady and cavalier. I follow the bending white line to my right, keeping the car drifting close to its side.

"We can stop," I say.

"I want to stop for the night," she says.

"We will stop."

. . .

I wait outside and call her parents. I tell them not to expect us until the next night.

"No, everything's fine," I say.

I look at the front of our motel room, at our door and our window.

"It's cold here too," I say.

"We'll see you tomorrow," I say.

I put my phone in my pocket. The mountains behind me stretch across the dark sky. They are carved and arcing shadows. I should have told her parents about these mountains. It would have given them a sense of where we are, of the distance we've come.

...

Our room is kept and has the feel of someone's best efforts. I set our luggage on the end of the bed and turn the television on. She is spending too long in the bathroom.

I say, "Are you okay?" and I think she is crying.

"I'll be out in a minute," she says, and I can hear she is crying.

I get up from the bed.

I say, "I called your parents. I told them everything is okay."

She doesn't say anything.

I put my hand against the hollow door.

"Everything will be okay."

"No," she says. "I don't know."

...

Our room is quiet, but there is the light from the parking lot in our window and we are restless from being in the car.

She says, "Where are we?"

I turn and look across the room, at the window, at the light in the curtains.

"Somewhere past the mountains."

I think for a moment.

"We are halfway."

"I mean us," she says. "I mean, where are we?"

"I don't know. Is that really something for me to say?"

She reaches for me through the sheets and pulls at my arm.

She says, "This is not everything. There is more to life than this."

She pulls me through the sheets to her.

...

Awake early, we lay talking, tangled across the sheets.

"This isn't how I thought life would be," she says.

"No, you're right," I say, "but that's what everyone says. Life is never what anyone thinks it will be."

"What are we supposed to do?" she says.

She brushes across the hairs on my chest.

"I don't know."

"There was this tree when I was a girl. It was planted beneath a street lamp at the end of our block, where the park began."

She looks at me.

"This tree grew to envelop the lamp; it became a lamp inside of a tree. At night, when the lights came on, the tree would be filled with light."

I look down across the lines of our bodies, imagining this tree. I imagine a glowing tree watching over a quiet street and a little girl.

"It sounds beautiful," I say.

"It was peculiar," she says.

. . .

She goes to the car; I return our room keys and sign for the bill. I ask if there's a town where we could eat; there is, and I return to the car.

"There is a restaurant," I say.

"That would be fine," she says.

We turn away from the interstate and drive slowly into the town. It's not as small as I thought it would be. There are schools and churches. Blocks on end are lined with houses, and I have already seen more than one gas station.

"This is a nice town," she says. "It's how you imagine towns to be."

I find the restaurant and park the car. I leave the engine idling and look at her.

"We should tell your parents the truth," I say.

Her hands are folded in her lap.

"I'm a bad person," she says.

"You're not a bad person."

"I'm a very bad person. I think terrible things."

"We all think terrible things."

I turn off the car.

"You don't think terrible things," she says.

"I think terrible things all the time. We all think terrible things."

The keys are in my hand now and I open my door.

"Let's go in," I say. "Let's get something to go. We still have a long dis-tance to travel."

. . .

Inside and our turn, I say, "Coffee and a tea to go."

"No," she says, waving that off, "Not anymore. I'll have a coffee today."

She takes the scarf from around her neck and brings her hand to the back of my arm. I pull away and look at the man behind the counter.

The man says, "Two coffees?"

"No. A coffee and a tea."

"Tea's for you then, is it?"

I look at him and then at her. She is looking away.

"You order it," I say. "If this is what you want, you order it."

The man asks again, "Two coffees?"

"Yes," she says. "To go, please."

She reaches again for my arm.

"I'm sorry," she says.

"I'm sorry too," I say.

The man behind the counter is typing into the register and looking at me. He says, "There will always be tea."

Xanadu

Chrissy Kolaya

So twice five miles of fertile ground
With walls and towers were girdled round.

—Samuel Taylor Coleridge, "Kubla Khan"

This Carluto custom home is tucked away on the majestic seventeenth hole of the Esplanade golf course. Spaciousness and charm are standard in every Carluto custom home.

That's the kind of thing we memorized that summer, repeated over and over again every ten minutes as a new group of folks tramped through the house.

"Keep them on the runners," Mr. Carluto told us each morning before he opened the door to warmly welcome the first group of the day to his masterpiece. "And make sure they wear the goddamned footies!" Then he would shuffle to the foyer, his Italian loafers encased in cheap cloth covers, open the front door, and hold out his arm in a grand, sweeping gesture. "Welcome to the Xanadu!"

The other houses in the show were decorated by professionals, but Mr. Carluto's wife, Angela, had wanted to do the Xanadu herself. Like everyone in our town, the Carlutos were nouveau riche. Mrs. Carluto had her nails done every Thursday morning by the Vietnamese ladies at the mini mart and carried her bulk under swishy nylon workout suits. Mr. Carluto sported the quintessential gold chain and combated his advancing baldness with scalp massages, vitamins, and a steady regimen of Hail Marys.

The Xanadu was pink. "It's taupe," Mrs. Carluto insisted, but we all knew better. It was three stories of pink and white stucco, and as our crowning glory, every day at three when the crowds at the Home Parade would normally dwindle, they all flocked to the Xanadu to see the entire house locked down like a fortress. The doors and windows had been outfitted by Safety Shutters of Lisle. At the push of a button, metal shutters sprang into action, clattered to the bottom of the doors and windows, and locked, hermetically sealing the Xanadu with all of us inside, protecting it from rogue flying golf balls, prowlers, and the pricey leaking of air conditioning. Pete was the man they sent to push the button.

Pete was nineteen and newly dropped out of college. It had been Pete's idea to make the demo a once-a-day affair. He had the flair of a showman, and he was right. The crowds stuck around to see it. At three o'clock every afternoon, Mr. Carluto watched proudly as all of the other houses emptied and everyone headed to the Xanadu for Pete's demo.

Sometimes Pete helped Mr. Carluto, puttering around the yard. Aside from that, though, he had pretty much nothing to do all day. But he was paid by the hour, so he showed up, like us, at nine a.m. and drank Mr. Carluto's Diet Cokes until the show.

"Ladies! I'm on!" he would call out to us every day. "Lucy, are you coming to watch me work my magic?" he'd holler up the stairs. He did it because it embarrassed me. "She's a prude," Julia had told him, commandeering the introductions on Pete's first day.

I didn't feel like a prude. But I couldn't talk to Pete in the same way Julia and Alexa could. Each time I tried, I could feel the words stiffening in my throat. And every time he spoke to me, my face burned red against my will.

It was our first summer job. Alexa had arranged it for all of us. Her parents were friends of the Carlutos, and Mr. Carluto had told Alexa to pick her three most responsible friends. He hired us sight unseen. Me and Abby upstairs. Julia and Alexa down.

Abby and I liked to work upstairs. On the master-bedroom stereo, we played the Beatles' *White Album* or *Days of Future Passed* by the Moody Blues while the people mulled around downstairs. Abby knew all the speeches of the house by heart. She'd never even worked in the kitchen, and she could still do it better than Julia. At school, Abby had auditioned for every play, though she never got cast. Probably because of the acne that spotted her pretty, round face. Julia, with her blond hair and all-American, clear-skinned face, got cast instead. So Abby would volunteer to be the director's assistant or a crew member, and by the end of the play, she'd know the whole thing by heart. Sometimes on slow, dreary days at the Xanadu, she'd recite the lines. She knew *Arsenic and Old Lace*, *The Lion in Winter*, and *Anything Goes*, including the songs.

Julia and Alexa liked to work downstairs. "It's because they like to flirt with Pete," Abby said one day as we sat on the stairs waiting for the next tour group to finish making the rounds of the downstairs. Abby and I were green, Julia said. Inexperienced.

. . .

"Okay girls!" Mrs. Carluto had called out the morning of the Xanadu's unveiling, digging her fat, manicured hands deep into a cardboard box. It was the grand opening of the Home Parade, and the street outside was buzzing with anxious developers and interior decorators. "The shirts are here!" she announced, as if she were Karl Lagerfeld unveiling his fall collection. "We have three colors to choose from." She held them up. They were neon green, hot pink, and a horrible highlighter yellow. "Aren't they fabulous? You girls are going to look just precious!"

She had flipped one around excitedly to show us the back, where she'd had puffy, iron-on letters appliquéd. *Xanadu*, they read. Julia had chosen one two sizes too small, her new breasts pulling the buttons apart.

The Living Room and Foyer

Alexa was bossy, liked counting people off, then shutting the door in the face of unlucky number thirteen.

"But I'm with her!"

"Sorry," Alexa would say. But she wasn't. "Only twelve at a time."

The Xanadu was built and furnished by Carluto Enterprises and Associates Incorporated. This majestic home can be yours, including coordinating furnishings, for nine hundred and seventy thousand dollars.

Some of the men jotted the price down on their programs like they were going to sit down with Mr. Carluto and talk about picking one of these babies up some day. But the guys who jotted were always the guys in flip-flops whose wives wore cracked Lee Press-On Nails, and you could bet they weren't going to do any such thing.

The family room looks out over the Esplanade, an eighteen-hole champion-ship course. Distinctive mahogany floors give the room an ambiance reminiscent of an English manor home.

Alexa was from Romania. She had come over with her family in the seventh grade and learned English in one summer watching soap operas. Everything she said was dramatic.

"Oh my God in heaven. We are out of 7-Up."

But she had no trace of an accent.

The Kitchen

The kitchen is the heart of this home. The counter tiles, hand painted in Mexico, meld fashion and functionality.

"Guatemala, Julia!" Mr. Carluto called out in exasperation, passing through the kitchen with a Diet Coke in his hand.

Julia always wanted to work the kitchen because it was closest to Pete.

She had a loud voice, and even from upstairs we could hear her delivering the speech, different every time. She embellished a lot, answered every question, though she usually made up her responses.

Julia had started dating her first boyfriend three months ago—Chris Applegate. They had met when she was cast as the ingenue in the spring play. He was two years older and had the lead. Abby had been the one with the crush on him, but just like with the play, it was Julia who ended up with the good part. Abby got stuck being his buddy, but I guess it felt like a good enough substitute, because she smiled like she was going to crack her face in half any time he paid her a minute's worth of attention.

Julia didn't know it, but through the laundry chute in the master bedroom, we could hear everything they said in the kitchen. That's how I learned that she and Chris had done it.

"What's the most embarrassing thing that's ever happened to you?" Alexa's voice, throaty and full of anticipation, rose up through the laundry chute.

"Well, once?" Julia began. Through the chute she was barely a whisper. I leaned closer. "When we were doing it? We didn't have any—you know." They laughed. "So we wrapped it in cellophane."

Downstairs, Pete and Alexa erupted in laughter. Down the hall, I could hear Abby giving her speech to a crowd of housewives.

I was fifteen, the same as Julia, but the idea of doing it still seemed as impossible as it had at twelve when my parents left *Preparing for Adolescence* by Dr. James Dobson in my room. "Sex is something that happens between a man and a woman, Usually on a bed or a couch." I had pieced the rest together, and I couldn't imagine any of my friends doing that already.

I didn't tell Abby. Somehow the doing it had sealed something between Julia and Chris. It would mean the end of Abby and the dream I guessed she might still carry around in which Chris quit palling around with her and fell mightily in love.

The Master Bedroom

Opulence reigns in the master bath, featuring an imported Italian marble tub and vanity. The master bedroom replicates an authentic Hawaiian luau with a bamboo bed frame and a palm frond overhang.

Hanging over the bed in the master bedroom was an enormous photo of the Carlutos—Mr. Carluto, Mrs. Carluto, and their two fat and mean little boys. Mrs. Carluto had worked out a deal with the photographer whereby they plugged him in the Xanadu and he photographed them for free. He'd done a careful job with the picture. The whole garish family toned down in a pastel soft-focus lens.

The ladies with Coach bags always snickered to one another behind their hands, especially in the master bedroom. "Well my goodness," one of them said to her friend. "It's just like a whorehouse." But sometimes I thought they were laughing at Mrs. Carluto, plump and proud in her family portrait.

. . .

"Who's the cutest of all the girls?" The afternoon was slow and rainy, and Julia's voice rose up through the chute. I pictured her perched coyly on the kitchen counter, her finger working her dark hair in circles around it.

"In order of most to least." She explained the rules like she was teaching a class in this. "I'll take myself out cause it wouldn't be fair."

Abby had the day's sparse group of people now in the children's wing and was giving her speech when I heard Julia. Then Pete.

"Well," he said. "I guess Lucy. Then Alexa."

I held my breath for a moment, terrified they could hear me.

"Lucy? Over Alexa?" Julia asked.

"Lucy's cute."

I could hear Abby's tour group tromping down the stairs now, their loud footfalls on the staircase, my name hanging in the air like the answer to something I'd been wanting to know forever.

I thought about it all day, wondered where Julia would go on that list. Surely before me. But it felt good not to be at the bottom.

"Lucy." I said my own name out loud quietly, felt the shape of the sound on my tongue. I remembered the sound of Pete saying it, repeated it to myself over and over.

The Guest Suite and the Children's Wing

The spacious children's wing is mother's little helper. Cabinets featuring custom woodworking give each room bountiful storage space and a playful atmosphere.

Up until last year, Abby had been like a kid herself. That is, until Chris. It was sad, the way Abby watched him and Julia together. Like she was starting to realize that Julia had something she didn't and maybe never would.

The centerpiece of the guest suite is the distinctive skylight. Shower your visitors with warmth and natural light.

The big draw of the guest suite was privacy. "We had it *soundproofed*," a giggling Mrs. Carluto, full of innuendo, had confided to Abby one day.

That afternoon was slow. Outside, the sky hung gray around the windows and spattered drizzle against them. The groups were small—four or five at a time—old ladies mostly, with plastic handkerchiefs tied carefully over their permanent waves.

"What do you think about Pete?" Abby's voice was quiet, the last of our group creaking their way down the staircase.

"He's okay. Why?" I thought of the way he leaned over the counter in the kitchen, talking to Julia and Alexa.

"I don't know. I think he seems nice." Her voice trailed off at the end of the sentence as though, with a little prodding, she might change her mind abruptly. She fingered a bright green thread hanging from the bottom of her shirt.

...

Julia and Alexa were leaning over the dining-room table watching Pete through the bay window as he handed out fliers to the last group of the day. The tours never went through the dining room. A velvet rope hung in front of the doorway where the people lined up and craned their necks, looking left and right. Mrs. Carluto had decorated it to look like the dining room from *Gone with the Wind.*

Julia held a Diet Coke in her hand. Small drops of water ran down the side of the can and fell onto the glossy tabletop, making a small puddle, but Julia hadn't noticed.

"Hey you guys," Abby called out.

"Hey." They turned quickly, as though they'd been caught doing something sneaky.

I took a breath. "Abby and I were thinking. It's getting kind of boring giving the same speeches every day. How about if tomorrow you guys work upstairs, and Abby and I work downstairs. The upstairs speeches are shorter anyway."

"Well." Alexa thought for a minute, arms raised, working her hair into a thick ponytail. "Yeah. Okay."

"What?" Julia said, putting a quick smile on her face so as not to betray her annoyance at Alexa's defection. "Mmmm. I don't think so. I really don't think I could learn a whole new speech by tomorrow."

"That's okay." Abby said it so quickly that it must have been waiting on her tongue. "It's no big deal."

"Abby could help you learn them," I said. "I could help you."

Julia noticed the puddle on the table and ran her forearm over it. "Actually, we have some kind of important things to talk about with Pete. You understand."

It was a statement, not a question. I watched her as she spoke. We had almost the same small bodies, our bones long and slender, like the hollow bones of birds. But already she knew how to turn her body into an obstacle. How to place it quietly in our path in a way that wouldn't even allow Abby to feel angry.

I knew Abby would say it again. That it was okay. That she understood. But it wasn't okay. Julia understood why we were asking. She could guess at the reason.

Five minutes from now, at the Home Parade entrance, Chris would be waiting to pick her up in his car, the engine running. He'd lean over and open the door and in she'd go.

"We can hear you," I said suddenly. I hadn't expected to say it, and as I spoke, I could feel another part of me trying to stop myself. I put my fingertips on the table that shone like glass between us. "We can hear what you're talking about. All day. Through the laundry chute."

Julia looked at me calmly. She blinked once and said, "I know."

Alexa looked down and played with her watch. I thought for a moment.

"No you didn't," I said. "What about ranking everyone?"

Abby looked at me, confused.

"You didn't know we could hear that," I said, looking right at Julia.

A slow smile leaked over her face. "I knew you were listening. I just thought you could use a little boost. You know, to your self-esteem." She looked down at the table, then up again, smiling like a woman delivering a bag of charity groceries. "I was just trying to be nice."

As she said it, I felt my name erased from the air. I wasn't pretty. I wasn't prettier than anyone.

The next day, we didn't hear anything from the laundry chute. Just some whispering, which we assumed would be Julia explaining the events of the previous day to Pete.

The Garage

Saturdays were the big draw. That's when the men came. Weekdays, it was strictly stay-at-home wives. But on Saturdays and Sundays, they brought their husbands. And the husbands were the ones Mr. Carluto wanted to talk to.

Every Saturday, he'd watch from the window in the little office he'd set up in the garage as the lines formed in front of the houses. Or he'd pace the driveway, nervous if one of the houses looked like it was filling up faster than the Xanadu.

Mr. Carluto hated being called a builder. "Alexa! How many times I have to tell you? I'm a *developer*." He wore fat gold rings on his pinkies meant to send the message: *These hands haven't seen a bucket of concrete in years.*

In his garage office, he had laid out the plushest of AstroTurf and a big cherry desk with two soft leather chairs facing it. "This is where I'll reel them in, girls," he told us.

The office was his own doing. He hadn't let Mrs. Carluto get her hands on it. Here, he probably imagined leaning back in the dimpled desk chair, swiveling away from the couple for a moment, looking out the window as if to consider something, then turning back to the couple who, if things were going according to plan, would by now be breathless with anticipation, and telling them, "I think we can do that for you."

The Basement

The basement was off limits to the public, but it was decorated like the most perfect of rec rooms. All summer, Julia had been talking up the make-out parties she'd have if her house had a basement like that.

Mrs. Carluto kept the refrigerator stocked with diet soda. I was making a run for Abby and me when I heard him.

"What are you doing?"

Pete was sunk down into one of the pink-striped armchairs, his feet propped up on the coffee table.

"Just getting a soda," I said. "Abby wants one too." I held the can up as proof.

"Oh yeah? Well, why don't you get me one?" he said, leaning his head back and looking at me.

I put the two sodas into the crook in my arm and reached down for another. I set it on the counter that separated my half of the basement from his.

"Why don't you bring it over here?" he said, nodding his head once.

He was sitting in the darkest part of the room. He watched me as I closed the refrigerator door.

"Okay," I said. I wanted to seem casual, the way Julia and Alexa were.

But then he said, "Come on. I won't bite," and I knew I hadn't been successful.

"Ha. Ha." I had meant to laugh, but it came out as the actual words—*ha ha. Crap*, I thought.

I started to walk toward the armchair. The carpet was plush. Double the pad, Mr. Carluto said. Even in the off-limits basement. I could feel my feet sinking into the perfect carpet like quicksand. There was something almost crackling in the air that I had never felt before, and I thought—this is it. Something is going to happen. Only I didn't know what it would be, and I was terrified.

I stopped a foot from the chair, stretched my arm out, and tried to hand him the soda.

"Here you go," I said in a voice I hoped was jaunty and casual. He smiled. Reached out for the can, which had begun to sweat, and grabbed my wrist instead.

In one quick movement, he spun me around and onto the chair. Onto him.

I scrambled up, all limbs and the can flying, Pete laughing, calling out, "Lucy!"

"Lucy! Come on! I'm just goofing around. Why do you have to be so nervous around me?"

"I'm not nervous," I said, gathering up the sodas for me and Abby. "I just have to go."

"Lucy, what are you so jumpy about? Come on. I'm sorry." His tone was nice, like he really was sorry. And confused. "I'm just messing with you."

"I know," I said. "I know that." And I did. I tried to walk slowly up the stairs.

In the foyer, a group of retirees were struggling to bend over and put on their footies. Alexa wasn't helping. She was just standing there, tapping her foot.

Safety Shutters

When it came time for Pete's show, the house was empty of tour groups. Alexa hadn't let in the next one. From the window, I could see the line that stretched from the front door, down the long walkway and the pebbled driveway. They were queued up to watch Pete. He began his speech.

"She was like a deer caught in the headlights. What did she think I was going to do?" I had overheard him telling Julia.

"She's just—*inexperienced.*" Julia pronounced the word carefully, intending to convey its full and complete meaning.

"Oh," he had said, and I could imagine him smiling and nodding, "I catch your meaning."

With Safety Shutters, you're not only protecting your home, you're investing in it, he began.

It felt like Julia and Alexa and Pete spoke a secret language. What did it matter that I was inexperienced? What did any of that matter anyway? I just wanted to know how it was that Julia was so different from me and me so different from her. How she talked to Pete without her throat turning to stone.

Pete hadn't called upstairs to announce that he was going on. He'd just gone out the door and started the speech. I watched out the window of the master bedroom, the people drawn to him like a magnet. People in the street, headed the other way, stopped and came back to the Xanadu.

In the kitchen, Julia sat on the counter, her rear covering the bright, hand-painted Guatemalan tiles, and in the family room, Alexa studied her fingernails in the waning light.

The Xanadu was the only house that hadn't sold yet. The Emerald Palace two doors down, with its Wizard of Oz theme, had gone a week ago, contents included.

Selling the house wasn't the point, Mr. Carluto reminded us every morning before opening the doors. It was getting your name out there, and your style. Though that was precisely what I was afraid he'd done.

How would you like to thwart would-be intruders, protect your home from storm damage, and save money on heating and cooling? Do I hear some interest out there?

I half expected the crowd to call out *amens* to this preacher of safety, privacy, and frugality.

Mr. Carluto came out of his office and stood with his hands deep in his pockets in the foyer. He watched Pete working the crowd, smiling at the older ladies.

Ladies, how many times have you worried about burglars or Peeping Toms? With Safety Shutters, you'll say goodbye to anxiety and hello to privacy and security.

The shutters began their noisy descent. I could smell the plastic runners as the rooms grew slowly darker. We were sealed in together. The upstairs girls, the downstairs girls, Mr. Carluto.

Inside, the house was silent. Outside, its pink stucco glowed out into the sunshine. It was eighty degrees, and the people watching Pete's demo were standing in the sun holding hot dogs and gulping down the last of their sodas.

"You can't come in with that," Alexa had said to them before closing the door.

Pete's voice got quieter and quieter as the shutters descended, the house fortressed with all of us inside.

I wondered what their house looked like—Mr. and Mrs. Carluto's. I had always imagined them living here, and maybe they would if it didn't sell. Mr. Carluto would say they were eating their losses.

Mr. Carluto looked up at Abby and me at the top of the stairs.

"You girls. You're good girls. You learn the speeches. Abby, Jesus Christ, she probably knows more about this house than I do. It's a good-looking house," he said, though even he sounded unconvinced as he looked around. He sounded tired, spent. He hiked the waistband of his pants up over his stomach. "I hate these things," he said, looking down sadly at his Diet Coke. "Why can't Angela buy me some goddamned Coca Cola?"

We didn't know what to say. And, as we were only fifteen, we had that as an excuse, so we didn't say anything at all.

"You girls are good girls," he said again. Then he shuffled down the runner toward the stairs.

The clattering of the shutters slowed, and I heard the loud, solid click.

The Rice Pickers

Linda LeGarde Grover

Part I: Animoosh

The stranger showed up at the Lost Lake boat landing on opening day of the Mozhay Point Indian Reservation wild rice harvest and stood on the shore, next to his ricing car, a forest green sport utility Chrysler with a "Save Our Forests: No Logging" bumper sticker on the rear door, a Che Guevara decal on the front window, and a bicycle mounted upright on the roof. He was dressed for the occasion in an outfit that stood out in the crowd of rice pickers: a new-looking, many-pocketed North Face windbreaker with matching pants tucked into laced Gore-Tex high-tops, a spotless white mock-turtleneck sweater, and bicycle gloves. He'd chosen and donned it that morning thinking about durability and versatility, clothing suitable to wear for an outdoor event new to him, not realizing until he arrived at the landing the incompatibilities of North Face sporting style and the hard and muddy labor of the wild rice harvest. The Mozhay Point wild ricers were wearing jeans, sweatshirts, and tennis shoes; some had bandanas wrapped around their heads; several wore satin bar-style jackets ("Sanitary Harry's, Where You Can Eat Off the Floor," said one); two old men were tying string around the gathered ankles of their baggy work pants. A young man and woman carried an aluminum canoe past him without appearing to notice him standing there at all, until the young man turned around to quickly double take the stranger over, up and down, then away.

He smiled toothily, although uncertainly, holding out a small card, his Mozhay Point Indian Reservation ricing permit, to the people passing by, and asking, too loudly, "Excuse me; is anyone looking for a wild ricing partner?" There weren't any takers; everyone already had their partners, it appeared, or already knew someone else there who was looking.

Who was the stranger? Indians were pairing up right and left, meeting their cousins, pulling their boats to the shore, pushing off into the water, getting out on the lake. Everybody had a partner but the guy with the big Chrysler, the one in the conspicuous ricing outfit. As more people arrived at the landing he raised his voice, called into the void of response, "Is anyone here looking for a wild ricing partner?" No one answered, no one talked to him, although they were talking to each other, calling out *boozhoo boozhoo how you been* and asking what part of the lake was ready. Kidding around, teasing each other, nobody saying a word to the guy in the sporty ensemble.

But everybody noticed him.

"Looks like he lost the guy who was riding on top of his car."

"Must've been his ricing partner."

"What's he doing with that card?"

"Maybe he's gonna try to charge some rice!"

"Is somebody carding Indians? . . . Ay-y-y!"

Everybody was watching the stranger, but nobody looked at him. Everybody was as obviously and surreptitiously curious as Indians can appear, but of course nobody asked the stranger anything. Who was he? Was he an Indian? Was he a White guy, and if he was, how did he get the reservation ricing permit? Would it be proper to ask him where he was from and who his family was, what anybody knows are the polite things to ask an Indian? What to do?

The stranger swallowed, continued to show his teeth nervously to the group. Was there anyone in charge, he wondered. Should he ask if there was anywhere to rent a boat?

The ricers appeared to run out of jokes and whispers and started glancing toward an old woman sitting in a webbed lawn chair. As the oldest person at the boat landing (sideways glance), she would know what to do (sideways glance).

Beryl sighed. Ai, she had to do everything, it seemed. She had to come out on opening day, she had to point out what she had known for how many years of her ricing days, and how many years since that she didn't even go out on the lake anymore, where the pretty, light green places were out there, where the rice would be ready to pick. These younger people, making such a big deal about asking an elder if the rice was ready: what would they do if she told them to go home and figure it out, think and remember how they did it last year, and the year before. Before Noel died, the two of them were out there every year since before they got married, and anybody who bothered to pay attention and learn something could have seen how Noel looked out careful for the color of the rice stalks to get to just that point, like he'd learned it from watching people who'd started ricing long before him. But she had humored them, no point in being unkind, told them that today it would be time. And now here she was, up too early and wishing for her housecoat and television. She could have been home in her trailer, on the couch with her legs up and watching her morning programs; instead here she was with her tennies getting wet and muddy, sitting on a lawn chair that felt tippy and cut into the backs of her thighs, holding a styrofoam cup of bad coffee that was going to turn her plate brown for sure so she'd have to scrub it with bleach water tonight, with all these people expecting her to now do something about the strange man in the fancy jacket. Ai. It was always her. She pushed on the chair arms to get to her feet, groaning a little and waving away her nephew's arm. Standing, she leaned on the cane that Noel had used before he died, which sunk into the mud under her weight, annoying her further. She shuffle-clumped slowly toward the stranger, thinking how when she was a young woman, helping Noel push the rowboat out from the shore, she had hopped around like a robin. And climbed into the boat just easy, light and limber as a cat. A person doesn't appreciate that kind of thing until they get older.

She stood next to the stranger. "Hello, young man," she said in her soft mindemooye old woman voice that floated, lighter than air, to the lake, where it hovered, dropped into the water, and disappeared.

He stepped to face her directly, closely, blocking the lake. "Good morning!" Such a loud voice; he must be full of coffee. "I wonder if you could help me."

"... Oh, do you need help with something?"

"Yes! I'm new here, and I have a ricing permit."

Well, I can see that. "... Ohhhhhhh, that's nice."

"And I'm looking for an experienced partner to rice with."

"... Ohhhh ... so, where are you from?"

"Duluth. I just moved there from Red Wing. My name's Dag Bjornborg!" He reached out and seized her hand, shook it firmly. Arthritis flashed heat lightning into the joints of her first and second fingers. "What's yours?"

Sigh. Not his fault he didn't know how to act. ". . . Ohhhhh. That's a nice name. Who are your Mother and Dad?" Who named their kid after a dog?

"Well." The man in the eye-catching outfit was aware of the unstares of the crowd at the landing, and that most people near him, although looking around at the sky, the lake, inside their lunch sacks, were listening intently. "I don't know, actually. I was adopted and raised in southern Minnesota, and named after my grandfather, Dagfinn."

Beryl pictured a Mozhay Point rez dog, big and shaggy, humble and scrappy, swimming through the slough with the help of magical fins, perhaps a Nanaboozhoo trick.

"It's a Norwegian name, but my birth mother was from Mozhay Point. I'm an enrolled member of the band, here, but I've never wild riced before. I have a permit from the reservation business committee." He showed her the card.

He was a mixed blood, for sure, with those eyes and that hair, but now that Beryl took a good look she could see he looked like a lot of people she knew, especially some of those Dionnes. Who could his mother be? If the Ar-Bee-See gave him a ricing permit, he was a band member; if he was a band member, somebody over in the tribal building knew who his mother was. He probably didn't know how to ask. Not his fault. Was he a Brule? Not a LaForce, that was certain; not good-looking enough.

Beryl raised her chin, although not her voice, to address the entire group at the landing. "So, who doesn't have a ricing partner?" she asked.

Murmurs. Well, me and Jimminy are partners. I promised Rocky; he should be here pretty soon, him. My mom told me she was gonna be ricing with Baby Al this year.

"Tommy, find somebody who needs a partner, will you? Was Irene ricing today?"

"I think she's ricing with Butch but you know? Crystal was saying she might be going," somebody said.

"I saw her last night over at Harry's; she was talking about going out today."

"Ya, Crystal, she was talking about borrowing Michael's boat."

"Well, thank you very much!" Did he have to holler like that? "Where might I find Crystal?"

"Tommy, show him where to find Crystal, will you?" Beryl directed her nephew. "I'm gonna sit here a while and finish my coffee." She exchanged looks with another old woman and backed up against the lawn chair, grasping its plastic arms and shifting her weight from feet to backside, with a plop. "Mindemooye," she said, so softly that the crowd couldn't hear, "when are these young people going to learn to do some of these things for themselves?"

"Amanj, Beryl, my girl; who knows? Here, have a Fig Newton."

The crowd at the boat landing watched Tommy and the stranger drive down the dirt road and take the curve toward the LaForce family's allotment.

"I never seen a dog drive a car before," somebody commented, and the crowd laughed, except for Beryl. She was thinking.

. . .

This was too nice to use for a ricing truck, Tommy thought. Where was this guy thinking he would put his rice, if he got any? Everything inside was really clean; a bag of wild rice picked right out of the lake and dragged across the ground would get the seats and the carpets wet and muddy. The stranger didn't know to bring any plastic bags, or a tarp. He hoped Crystal was home at Beryl's; otherwise, Beryl would make Tommy rice with the stranger, he just knew it. Brooding, he almost forgot to tell the stranger which mailbox was Beryl's.

"Turn in right here; that's where she lives," he instructed.

The stranger braked and cut the wheel fast; the Chrysler squealed off the blacktop and onto the dirt driveway, cutting a neat crescent around the pink mailbox on a green-painted sawhorse twined with pink plastic roses. By dumb luck, he didn't hit the woman walking out to the road from Beryl's trailer. The Chrysler overshot the young woman, raising dust from the driveway. The stranger broke into a sweat. "Oh, God," he said.

She looked up and glared, shading her eyes.

Tommy stuck his head out of the window and asked, "Crystal, you going ricing today?"

She had a long, straight-legged stride and broad shoulders that swung with her steps, and was so short she stood on tiptoe to peer into the vehicle, gripping the door with both hands on the bottom of the window, where her chin rested. The front of her shirt and pants would carry the road dust from where she leaned her skinny body in its baggy clothes against the door;

she wouldn't bother to brush it off. She took a drag on her cigarette and coughed before she answered, "If I find a partner." Her peculiarly brown-blue eyes were narrow in her round face, and she looked tired.

"This is Dog, here, and he's looking for a partner with a boat."

"Pleased to meet you, Crystal!" Dag reached across Tommy and through the window to grab her hand firmly and pump, too hard, too fast, she thought, like that man visiting the tribal center from the state college, that recruiter.

"Hey, uh, pleased to meet you, too, uh . . . what was his name?"

"It's Dog," said Tommy. "So, you going ricing today, or what? Dog, here, is looking for an experienced ricing partner."

"That's me . . . ay-y-y!" answered Crystal, and the three laughed, Dag not sure why.

"I was gonna borrow Zho Wash's old rowboat; my mom said I could use it. And the knockers, too. And Michael's duckbill." She coughed again, craned her head inside the window to get a better look at Dag, narrowed her eyes further, and rasped, "Hey. He ever rice before?"

"I haven't done this before, but I sure would like to learn!"

Well, he seemed pretty wide awake, anyway. "You got coffee in there?"

"Coffee, and I've brought along some sandwiches from Duluth."

". . . ?"

"Subways."

"Anything else?"

"M&M cookies."

"Can I wear your sunglasses?"

"Uh, sure, you can wear them."

"You got any aspirin?"

"Painkillers, you mean? Sure; what kind would you like? I have Motrin, Bayer, some generic aspirin-free pain reliever. . . ."

"Well. All right. Let's go get the rowboat." Crystal opened the back door and hopped up to swing her backside into the rear seat, but she misjudged the distance. Her hip bounced against the seat and slammed her other side against the open door. Back on the ground, she kept her balance by throwing her arms wide, hit one against the door, muttered "shit," and climbed, more slowly on the second try, up to the seat. "Let's maajaa, Animoosh. Can I have a couple aspirin and some of that coffee?"

They backtracked toward Lost Lake and turned into another driveway, this one nearly covered by a sumac stand and marked by a large, rusting mailbox with "Joseph Washington" painted in peeling letters on the side. The driveway was a leaf-covered tunnel; at the end, the house looked closed up, abandoned, yet there were clothes clipped to a line hung from the house to a shed.

"Quiet in here; Michael must have took the dogs with him," said Tommy.

"Good thing," Crystal answered.

They found the rowboat behind the shed, the duckbill pole and knocker sticks under the porch. After moving the bicycle to inside the Chrysler, Dog and Tommy tied the pole and stick as well as the boat onto the roof rack. Crystal went back into the shed and came out carrying a pile of gunny sacks, which she set carefully on the ground while she helped herself to a dish towel from the clothesline and tied her hair into a turban. She looked more tired than before she'd had the coffee; the lines from her nose to the corners of her mouth were deeper than Aunt Beryl's, her face pale and puffy. Looks a little like death warmed over, thought Tommy. "You feeling all right, Crystal?"

She braced one arm against the back door and held the other, full of gunny sacks, to her chest as she coughed, nodding her head, yes.

The stranger looked concerned. "She's a pretty good ricer," Tommy whispered to him. "She just needs a partner."

. . .

Dag and Crystal had been out in the rowboat for nearly an hour, and Dag thought that Tommy was right, she seemed to know what to do. She had carried the burlap bags to the boat, set one in front of the seat, one on the seat, and the rest of the pile under the seats, carefully. She had helped push the boat down the launch, cautioning Dag not to kick the sacks under the seats with his heavy boots. She had told him how to pole from the back of the rowboat, pushing away with the duckbill while she bent the rice stalks over into the boat with the knockers, right knock-knock, left knock-knock, raining hulls onto the burlap bag on the floor in front of her. They worked well together, Dag thought, although she didn't seem much for conversation. She answered his comments about the weather, and the size of the lake, and what the weather had been like when he'd left Duluth, with "mmm's" and "mmmm-hmmm's"; other than that she hadn't said a word since they arrived at the landing except to give him directions. Dag finally had no choice but to be quiet and get used to working without conversation. He concentrated on pushing the boat forward smoothly with his pole, taking care to give Crystal time enough to bend and tap the stocks, right, knock-knock, left, knock-knock, before moving on, slowing when she slowed, speeding up when she did, matching his motions to hers. Physically, the work was as demanding as he had expected it to be; the technique was more difficult, but he enjoyed the rhythm of working with Crystal. Under her loose plaid shirt her body moved from side to side as her arms lifted, right knock-knock, left knock-knock, and her stately turbaned head moved gracefully as if to a tune, her straight back a metronome while her hips lifted slightly from the bench side to side, shoulders swaying, arms lifting right knock-knock, left knock-knock. Arms, shoulders, back, hips. Right knock-knock, left knock-knock. A steady rhythm of work broken only by Crystal's coughing attacks.

He tired before she did. "Crystal, do you think it's time for lunch?" She stopped and turned around to look at him through the too-big sunglasses, nodded, brushed insects and leaves from her arms and lap. Dag pulled up the pole and laid it carefully the length of the boat, then opened the cooler. "Would you like a Spicy Italian?" he asked politely.

After a fit of coughing rough enough to bend her nearly in half, with her arms crossed across her stomach, Crystal felt an appetite coming on. She cleared her throat, took two M&M cookies out of the bag, ate them without pausing, and took a couple of deep breaths. Better.

"My girlfriend went out with one once," she answered, feeling a little better now that her hangover was wearing off. "So, are you Italian, or what?"

After the silent morning it took Dag a second to catch on, then he laughed.

"I'm a member of the Mozhay Point Band of Chippewa."

"Yeah, but what else? Where are you from?"

"Well." How to begin? "I don't really know. I was born in Duluth, and right after I was born I went into a foster home, and then after a while I was adopted."

"Ohhhh, you were adopted out." One of many thousands, each with a sad and searching story.

"I was raised in Red Wing, and moved to Duluth last spring. My birth mother was from Mozhay Point. I don't know who she was, but I was put on the tribal rolls when I was born. I've never been to Mozhay Point before, though; I've never been north of Duluth until today."

"Ohhhhh." She didn't say anything more.

Dag and Crystal ate, Crystal smoked and coughed, and between coughs they sat in the rowboat listening to the sounds of boats being poled through the lake, through tall wild rice stalks, and rice pickers talking and laughing. "Whoa, whoa, whoa, look out, don't tip us over," a man's voice called softly, urgently. His partner, a woman, answered, "Just got to stand and stretch. Don't you worry, now; I never tipped anybody over yet." They laughed.

Crystal slid off the rowboat bench and rested her head against the cooler. She crossed her arms over her eyes and reclined under the sun, in the rowboat with Dag, surrounded by tall, pale green wild rice stalks. The stalks made a wall around them, and although they could hear other people talking and laughing on the lake, they couldn't see anything through the wall of rice. It was like a room without doors or windows, a green room, Dag thought, with a blue ceiling.

The people in the next boat left, the boat sliding through ripe rice with a swishing, rippling sound; then there was silence. Crystal's jaw and mouth slackened, loosened, then she swallowed and her mouth tightened and lifted at the corners into a near smile. Was she sleeping? Dag wondered. Should he ask? He took another Coke out of the cooler and turned from the girl, in order to not wake her with the sound of the can opening, and watched her sleep while he drank.

Crystal, Crystal. Who are you; who might you be? Who might I be? he thought.

She slid down from the cooler into a small, broad-shouldered puddle of hungover Indian girl on the bottom of the rowboat.

Where might our lives possibly have crossed, Crystal? Where might they cross yet? Her chest rose and fell as she breathed slowly and deeply; barely rising from her unbuttoned flannel shirt, her breasts, flattened in sleep, were two shallow mysteries of soft flesh covered by the lumpiness of a wrinkled, too-large brassiere and T-shirt. Watching her, Dag breathed with the rise and fall of Crystal's chest, succumbing to a rhythm that nearly pulled him into a sleep; then his head jerked. Up, wake up.

"Crystal?"

She turned onto her side, coughed twice in her sleep, and pulled her flannel shirt over her ear. Dag's sunglasses, scuba goggles on her small, wide face, were knocked crooked.

Crystal. You're short, like me. What does your mother look like; is she short, too? I was watching you while you worked; you have good arms, strong. Is that from ricing? Do you do other hard work, too? I look at you, and I look at the other Indians I see from up here, and it's pretty obvious that none of you think that I might belong here, too. I have my enrollment card for Mozhay Point Reservation; the reservation gave me a scholarship to go to college, they gave me a ricing permit when I applied for one. I'm legally enrolled; I probably have more Indian blood in me than some of the people at the boat landing who wouldn't talk to me. I don't know anything else, not about Indians or my parents, or anything else. When I look at you I can see how like the other people at the boat launch you are: you all know each other, and you know things about each other that you've known since you were born, some things you wish you didn't know about each other, probably, but you know who you are. And in your arrogance you just take that for granted. You don't even know your own arrogance; you don't know how lucky you are. To you I'm a stranger; you treat me as if I don't know some big secret that the rest of you do. You're right, I don't know it. If I knew it, I'd be like you.

Do you think that I don't care about how you and the rest of them looked me over? You looked at me, you looked at my car; you judged me on some standard that I know nothing about. Through no fault of my own.

I'm supposed to be thankful that I have been so lucky. I've heard that since I could understand what people were saying about me; I can remember sitting in a stroller, my mother pushing me down the street and stopping at a neighbor's yard. "He's so lucky," the neighbor said. "Just think of the life he would be living if it wasn't for you. When he is old enough to think about that, he will appreciate what you have done."

I do, I appreciate it; I realize that I have been lucky; I am thankful. Just look at my teeth; my mother took me to the dentist twice a year. I brushed them twice a day. I wore braces to fix an overbite. Look at them. They're whole and white and straight, the best set of any on the entire boat landing. When I got acne, my mother brought me to a dermatologist. When my clothes wore out, or when I outgrew them, or when they went out of style, I got new ones. When I outgrew my bike, I got a bigger one. When things needed fixing, they got fixed. I was a Cub Scout. When my mother took me shopping in Minneapolis for new school clothes, we'd drive past Indian Town on the way to the parking ramp, and I would see them, the real Indians is how I thought of them, sitting on the steps of apartment buildings, or wandering around as if they had all the time in the world, or sometimes drunk and staggering or even sleeping on the sidewalk, and I would look at their faces, hoping someone would look back, that someone would know me. That woman, are my eyes like hers, I would wonder, or that man, do my shoulders hang like his?

Are we related, Crystal-short-like-me? If we were, wouldn't we somehow be able to recognize one another, wouldn't there be some type of bond stronger than the circumstances of our absence from one another, strong enough that we would just know?

Crystal. How old are you? I never dated any Indian girls. How would I ever have met any, and where? At Hi-Y? DeMolay? And how could I have explained to my parents, to my friends, if I had wanted to take one of the Indian girls from downtown to the movies, to the prom?

"How about you, Crystal? Did you get to the prom?"

"Huh? Wegonen? What's that, Animoosh?" Crystal sat up.

"Sorry, I must have been thinking out loud. Is it time to get to work?"

"Sure, let's work. Anookii-daa. You want to try knocking for awhile?"

The rowboat rocked as Dag stood to change places with Crystal. She said, "Down, get down, don't stand in the boat." Dag knelt. "Ok, now you just crawl to the bench, here, and I'll step over you; I'm smaller than you, so the boat won't lean so much under me."

The changing of places was like a dance, Dag thought. We might be ballet dancers, or figure skaters, Crystal light as a bird and me ready to lift her to the sky. As she passed over his shoulder, the heady combination that made up Crystal became to Dag a body-heated breeze, moving air a fragrance of strength and thinness, muscles and fragility, an irresistible bouquet that turned his head so that her soft side, that part of Crystal below her armpit and on a level with her left breast, brushed Dag's face, which turned further, nearly making contact with that breast, so lightly that she appeared to not feel it at all. He stopped her with a hand at her waist, and with the other pulled off the sunglasses, placed them in his jacket pocket, pulled the turban off her head, grasped her hair and twisted, winding it twice around his fingers so that his hand was wrapped in hair and bound tightly against the back of her head, pulling. Crystal's face was tipped up toward Dag's, her eyes open wide and slanting, creases smoothed by the pressure of his hand pulling that tail of hair back and down. She stared, mouth open, one arm pinned against her ribs, the other holding her cigarette out to the side. Dag pulled her closer with one hand, thinking, she has a waist under that big shirt, touched by her slightness and softness. He pictured an unknown, mysterious Indian brave with long black hair and brown arms, hard and muscular, that held

Crystal's slenderness against a beaded belt buckle the size of a small plate; hawklike face nearly brutal in its pride and strength, its Indianness, crushing a nearly breathless, swooning, succumbing Crystal.

The generic Indian brave, who was Dag, closed his eyes and kissed Crystal, who had become an Indian princess, against an imaginary, impossibly brilliant pink and gold sunset.

She tasted like cigarettes and coffee, pickles and salami, and also ever so vaguely of a sweet vomit. Earth, the brave told himself, it was the taste of earth, and of ceremonial smoke. The princess was still, unmoving, transfixed in the moment, the timelessness and sheer beauty of smooth lips and wild hearts under an impressionist painting of sunset created by Mother Earth herself.

Crystal didn't move but waited, her lips rough and cool, her eyes wide open and slanting, looking right through Dag to take in the sky, the creases of her face smoothed by the pressure of his hand pulling her hair, and waited, waited for Dag to stop. She remembered her cigarette, held out to the side, probably ashing away into the water, and wished for a drag. "Ow, my hair," she said.

"That's the Indian boy in me," Dag said forcefully, manfully. He looked her in the eyes, ready to kiss her again, to kiss Crystal back into that nearly breathless, swooning, succumbing princess.

Crystal looked into Dag's eyes, then rolled hers. "Animoosh," she said, and looked back into the sky. And in that second he heard as clearly as if she'd said it aloud, "Not any Indians I know."

She didn't say, Do you think Indian men chase us around and grab us and pull us by the hair, do you think they do that? You, there, in the fancy nylon outfit; you, there, with the yuppie environmentalist big-bucks car, you think some Indian woman is going to follow you home when she reads your bumper stickers? Pretty impressive, advertising yourself with your car. How are sales? Do you think an Indian man would need to use that bogus kind of White-man love medicine? Who do you think you are, anyway? She didn't say any of those things. Dag wondered if she thought them, or if he did, himself.

Who, indeed. Who was he? And who was Crystal, this woman who was short like him, this woman who he saw now wore his face, if he hadn't had a dermatologist, and his overbite, if he hadn't had an orthodontist? In another life, would she have known him? In this life, what should she know, and what should he?

He let go of her hair. "You could be my sister."

"Christ." She sat, bent to paw through the pile of gunny sacks until she found the bottle. "Gawd." She unscrewed the cap, her cigarette still between her second and third fingers, and took a drink. "Here."

"No, thanks. Why would you bring that on the boat?"

"Keeps my stomach down; gets me through the day, Animoosh." She sipped, coughed, noticed her cigarette had burned down, pulled another out of her back pocket and lit it. "How about you? What gets you through the day? Granola? Cappucino? Your blond girlfriend? Is her name Tiffany? Kimberly? No, wait . . . is it Elise?"

"Close. It's Alexis."

Crystal snorted. "Good thing she's not here."

"I'm sorry, Crystal, I really am. And not just because of Alexis; I don't have any excuses. I'm sorry, and I promise that I won't do that again."

"And I'm not your sister. Jesus." Crystal took another sip. "What would ever make you say that? Jeez." She again offered the bottle to Dag.

"I said no thanks. What is that, gin? You'll make yourself sick."

"I don't drink gin; it'll rot your guts. This is vodka. On a full stomach. You don't get sick on that." She offered the bottle again. "Here. Come on, don't make me drink alone."

"I said no thanks." Dag stood again, at the back of the rowboat. "Let's go; I'll pole and you just keep knocking."

"Come on. Michael won't even know we drank it; he wouldn't care if he did. When he was drinking he used to hide bottles all over the place, just like his old man did; forgot where he put them, most of the time." She paused, pondering, and sipped. Cleared her throat. "He's probably dead, anyway," she added.

"Let's go, Crystal."

"Forget it, Animoosh. Quit your barking! You can't rice without some- body knocking, and I'm not gonna do it, and so you might as well just sit down." Crystal slid off the bench and lay again in the bottom of the boat, this time with her head on the empty gunny sacks. "I got a headache, I got a hangover, I feel like shit, I had to listen to you when I was trying to sleep. I had to borrow the goddamn boat, and the pole, and the knockers, I had to show you what to do. And now I'm gonna take a goddamn break here so you might as well get used to it and sit down." She got up on one elbow for another slug of vodka, coughed. "I mean it, Animoosh."

Dag sat. "What's an animoosh, is it something like Kimosabe? Like the Lone Ranger and Tonto?"

"It's a dog. Get it? Like your name? An animoosh is a dog. Where'd you get that name, anyway?"

"I was named after my grandfather. His full name is Dagfinn."

"Dog Fin? What is he, a Sioux?" Crystal laughed so hard that she hit her head on the side of the boat. "Ow."

"You're a comedian, all right. He's a Norwegian." I'll wait, he thought. I'll wait until she falls asleep, then I'll use the oars and try to row back. Which way is the landing?

The lake was nearly silent. Dag listened to the breeze moving and rice stalks rustling. Crystal took off her shoes, dug her forearm across the bridge of her nose, over her eyes. Her body twitched and jerked as she dove for sleep, grew slack, then stiff as she turned to her side, drew her knees into the fetal position, back curled and tight, elbows squeezed to ribs, hands up and supplicating in fists that held tight to the back collar of unconsciousness. She squinted against the white light of the sun that was a red heat back of her eyelids, her struggle catatonic. My sister in sleep, thought Dag. He bent to pick up the dish towel, draped it over her eyes. Her breath, and the heat that rose from her body, smelled stale and tired, restless. Cigarette smoke damp on a pair of unwashed jeans. Liquor bleeding through pores, absorbed into a too-big T-shirt and a limp flannel shirt. My sister, in sleep. My sister. In sleep. Crystal inhaled and exhaled deeply, painfully, her very diaphragm part of the struggle, forcing warm ricing-time air in, out, in, out, an ironclad lung. She frowned, squinted, farted. Muttered. Opened her eyes. "Who the fuck are you?" she asked, and fell back asleep.

He gave it two more minutes, timed on his watch. "Crystal?" he whispered, and reached for the oars, which were locked. Dag stood, balanced his weight with one foot on each side of the sleeping young woman. His shadow, cast across her eyes, blocked out the sun, and the red back of her eyelids shaded to a cool purple. Her dreams—those flights through long grass that waved in a still and windless vacuum, grasping her ankles with bladed and twining fingers as she ran, while the foul and ravenous breath of the Windigo behind her steamed and burned her back, causing her hair to fall out and into the cannibal's ravenous path—those dreams in Dag's shadow became an ice age, ten thousand years that she ran through a dark and frozen forest, barefoot on frost-covered rocks, slipping, startled awake, to see—

—Dag, who had shifted his weight to his right foot in order to unlock the oar, and who was now stumbling frantically, futilely, to right the rowboat.

"The rice! Jump! Save the rice!" Crystal shouted, as Dag's weight pulled the boat further to its side. And then Crystal took a deep breath as she, along with the cooler, Subway bag, bottle of vodka, the sacks, pole, knockers, and the rice slid into the lake after Dag, and the boat filled with water and sank.

Crystal surfaced, treading water. "Help!" she shouted, "Help!" She felt for the boat with her feet, found it, balanced and stood. She gasped, coughed, breathed. "Help!" she shouted again, "We tipped over!"

A man's voice called back, "Coming over, keep hollering, we'll find you!"

"Here . . . here, we're over here!" Where was Dag?

Dag kicked against the arms of lake weeds that pulled him down, down to the mud at the bottom of the lake. He pushed against their fluid and sinewy graspings with arms that became further entangled, then unable to move. I want to see the sun, he thought, before I die, and opened his eyes to find it, pale yellow and wavering through the lake surface, not too far above the dark watery green and black of weeds and rice. Alexis, he thought. If there is life after death, a thousand years from now I will tell you every day about the sun I saw through the lake, from the bottom of the lake, the sun the color of your hair, the sight and the thought of you the very last I had in this life.

When he stopped struggling, giving in to death, the weeds loosened their grasp, and he was able to stand with his feet on the slick mud of the lake bottom, and his face at the surface. He vomited water, slipped, and felt a hand pass across his left ear, across his face. "Right in back of you, I'm standing on the rowboat, Dag." He stood again, pushed with his feet toward the voice. Crystal grasped the neck of his shirt. "Hang on to me. Stand on the boat." Crystal was treading water, bobbing up and down on top of the sunken rowboat. "Somebody's coming, Dag." They locked wrists and alternated bobbing on top of the boat, pulling each other back when they slipped off, buoyant acrobats in an underwater stunt. "Here, we're over here," Crystal called each time the man's voice asked, "You see us yet?"

They were separated by the ricers, a burly young longhair and his father, who directed Crystal and Dag to each hold to one side of their canoe, then paddled them through the rice stalks and weeds back to shore. The old man and Dag were silent, one with the perspective of his years and the other with the exhaustion and perspective of his day. Crystal and the longhair, however, conversed. Briefly.

"Lake got all your rice, eh? How much did youse have?"

"Not so much. Good for next year's rice." She glared across the canoe at Dag.

"Hey, we'll have to make sure we remember that spot next year!" the longhair laughed. "Lots of good rice there!"

Silence from Crystal.

"How did you tip a rowboat over?" the longhair asked.

Silence from Crystal.

"It was my fault. I stood up to take the oars," said Dag.

Silence from the longhair, and a snort.

The old man spoke. "Hey, didn't Zho Wash do that, that one time? Tipped over the rowboat, all his rice went into the lake, remember that? Oh, was he mad!" The two men in the canoe began to tell all of the stories they could remember about people tipping their boats and losing their rice in the lake, each funnier to them than the last, by what Dag heard, but not a single one funny to him. Why in the world had he even come to Mozhay Point? What made him think he could rice? He had checked a video out of the county historical society's library, watched it done by people who were probably dead long before he was born, people who could possibly have been his grandparents, closely watching the faces of the man in the overalls and the woman in the housedress and straw hat as they glided in a canoe through the tall plants on the lake, the man poling, the woman tapping precious heads from ripened rice stalks into the boat, working in tandem expertly, effortlessly, with the practice of generations before them. Thought, this is where I come from, this is my home, this is the goodness and simplicity and the beauty of my home. My home.

Closer to shore, the lake became shallow enough for Dag and Crystal to let go of the canoe and walk onto the landing, where the crowd of people, cooking, eating, hoisting sacks of rice into their cars and trucks, began to ask what happened. Crystal, who still hadn't directed a word toward Dag since they were rescued by the men in the canoe, angrily answered, "Nothing," which caused laughter. She shook her head no to Tommy's offer of a ride back to Beryl's, and walked with that long, short-legged, fast stride away from Dag, past the Chrysler, away from the crowd, toward the road.

"Crystal. Crystal, wait." She slowed, her back to him. "Crystal, you saved my life."

"Why didn't you jump off the boat? Christ, we didn't just lose the rice, somebody's got to go back and try to get the boat out, try to find the oars, and the pole, and the knockers are probably gone, that's for sure. And my shoes. You already almost tipped it over once, didn't you learn anything? Christ, why didn't you jump off the boat?" She walked faster.

"I'm sorry, Crystal; I just didn't think. I haven't done this before."

"Forget it, just forget it." She kept walking.

"Crystal, I'm sorry. I'll help, and I'll buy you some new shoes."

"Just leave me alone." She was at the road, and needed to raise her voice. "Leave me alone!" Barefoot she walked down the road, away from Dag, with that long, short-legged stride.

The keys to the Chrysler were still zipped in his windbreaker pocket. Ignored, it seemed, by the crowd, he walked back toward the Chrysler, past the old woman in the lawn chair. Beryl turned her head to say directly to him, in her soft mindamooye voice that floated, lighter than air, "Young man."

And again, "Young man." *That soft mindamooye voice that floated, lighter than air, across Dag's face and chest, branding the moment into his memory and his heart, then into the sky over Mozhay Point, where it hovered and became the gentlest of rains.*

"Would you like to know who your mother is?"

Part II: Margie-enjiss

At the Mozhay Point Indian Reservation's early summer powwow in 1973, not that long before he became Margie's ricing partner and then fled to Minneapolis, Michael Washington danced in his father's moccasins. A folded blue bandanna, wrapped across his forehead and tied in back, held his hair in place and framed his face, which he had painted black with a narrow white stripe across the eyes. Michael's face looked fierce, predatory, super human; his feet appeared to not quite touch the dusty ground of the powwow circle. For the rest, he was dressed in his everyday street clothes: secondhand jeans, a graying T-shirt with a frayed neck, and a plaid cowboy shirt, pearl-covered snaps left unfastened, that after the next wash would be missing its elbows. Although he was not the only dancer dressed in both street clothes and powwow finery, the combination of his outfit with the face paint and perfect dancing was eye-catching. Spectators who watched from lawn chairs around the powwow circle turned their heads to watch Michael dance; dancers inside the circle followed the spectators' heads with their eyes; Michael didn't seem to notice. He danced as if he was alone in his mother's apartment, or in the woods outside his father's cabin at Sweetgrass, or in an empty powwow arena, his shoulders tracing figure eights through the air in the powwow circle, one rising as the other dipped, the beefiness he carried above the ribs balanced recklessly over his much smaller hips and legs; below, his father's beaded and ribbon-trimmed moccasins purposefully yet lightly, almost playfully, double stomped left-left-right-right on that eighth-inch of air between Michael and the ground.

"Who's *that?*" a young woman traditional dancer in beaded black velour asked her friend. From across the powwow circle they turned their heads to watch him dance, which caught the attention of the friend's brother, who was drumming and singing. With the hand not holding a drumstick he covered his heart; he batted his eyes at Michael, then at his sister, teasing her. Shooting him a dirty look, she brushed her friend's elbow with hers, and the girls concentrated on their dancing, ignoring both men.

Michael passed Margie and Theresa, who toe-heeled so carefully in their chunky clogs that the hand-tied fringe on the shawls they wore over their stylish peasant blouses and jeans barely swayed. From the fierceness of his black-and-white face he glanced down, amused by their dainty steps and small female feet in bulky shoes; his bashful and brilliant smile ricocheted from his mouth to the floor to Margie's rib cage, where it bounced and danced, as she had known it would if she ever saw him again, in a beat somewhere between that of her heart and the drum.

"It's Michael!" Theresa exclaimed to Margie. "Did you see that was Michael, in the face paint?"

Margie nodded, then pointed her lips slightly in the direction of Michael's back. "There he goes." In order to stay behind him so that she could watch him dance, she shortened her step; Theresa understood and matched her step to Margie's.

As the girls behind him watched, Michael raised his tobacco pouch. His feet pivoted *shuffle-ball-change;* the double stomp turned to a triple within a four-four beat, his shoulders and arms became wings, his chin jerked, and Michael shape-shifted into a raven. He danced in powerful near-flight; his stomp became a rush of wings, and as he broke tether from the ground a shifting pulse of electric azure blue from the sole of one beaded moccasin caught Margie's eye with every step change from left to right, lighting in his wake the path he broke for the dancers behind him. She tasted canned blueberries, and in a split second relived the afternoon last winter at Zho Wash's house. She took a deep breath. *Jiibik,* she thought. Magic.

A fancy dancer in scarlet satin bounded like a pursued deer into the space between Margie and Michael; with her hands on her hips she bounced on the balls of her feet; her shawl spread and spun, blocking Michael from

Margie's sight. When the dancer sprang back to the outside edge of the circle, Michael was gone, and Margie's eyes empty.

That was at the early summer powwow, a season after they met and a season before Michael fled down I-35 right in the middle of ricing, gone overnight it seemed, like the Lost Lake geese who flew south in autumn. He flew only as far south as Minneapolis, like a lot of people did from reservations up north, Indians on the road with a destination in mind, looking for work, for opportunity, for relatives who were homesick. To escape for a while. When their hearts' seasons changed they flew back home, in a migratory pattern that had come to seem as natural and inevitable as the patterns of birds.

Late summer into early fall is when wild rice, manoomin, ripens and is ready to harvest, its heads heavy and nodding on the green stalks that grow up out of Lost Lake, sometimes taller than a man's head. That ricing season following that late spring powwow, when his son had danced in his moccasins, Zho Wash decided he was too old to rice. "I'm not going out this year," he told Michael. "If you want rice you're gonna have to do it yourself, find yourself a ricing partner. Go see that Margie; her dad used to rice and she looks like a good worker. I'm too old for this stuff."

That was how Margie and Michael got to be ricing partners. Zho Wash drove them to the boat landing in his old Chevy truck that sounded like a helicopter, helped them unload his rowboat and duckbill, knockers, gunny sacks, and the lunch he had packed in a grocery bag for Michael and Margie. He pulled a crushed-looking straw hat from under the seat, his ricing hat, and offered it to Margie ("it'll keep the sun out of your eyes, my girl"), who said migwech, I'll take good care of it. At the landing, Zho Wash made a tobacco offering and said a prayer, helped Michael push the rowboat out onto the lake. "See youse later," he said, as Michael jumped into the boat, and went to sit at the campfire, where some older ladies were making coffee.

They worked well together, Michael and Margie. He poled with the duckbill, she sat in the middle of the boat and knocked rice hulls onto the gunny sack spread in front of her. They didn't speak; Margie listened to Michael hum his ricing song, then songs from the radio, and worked the rhythm of knocking rice left, knock-knock, right, knock-knock to the rhythm of his soft voice. A beautiful day, she thought. He finished "Blackbird," paused between songs.

"Mino giizhigad," she commented.

"Ay-yuh, onishishin," he answered. "It's a pretty day." He pulled the duck-bill up from the mud on the bottom of the lake, pushed it back down; she heard the swish and ripple of the boat moving through the water, and talk and laughter from other people out on the lake. "Good-bye, Ruby Tuesday; who could hang a name on you?" he sang under his breath.

A beautiful morning; I will remember this song, and the softness of the sunlight, and the breeze, light as sheer curtains blowing in an open win-dow. I will remember this morning with Michael, that today is a warm day, that the sky is a purely, deeply blue dome over Lost Lake, that I can almost feel Michael, can imagine that I am Michael, back of me, pushing the boat forward over the water, through rice stalks as tall as he is. Now his shadow cools me, as the boat moves away from the sun. If I turn around I will see him; his hair, getting damp as he gets warm from the work, working its way loose from the bandanna tied around his head. I can see him without even looking. I will always remember this.

"Are your arms getting sore?" Michael asked, and she realized that she had been sitting motionless while he had been poling the boat through a particularly thick and loaded stand of wild rice stalks.

"Gaawiin, I'm fine; just leaving some for the ducks." She concentrated on ricing: left, knock-knock, right, knock-knock. She ignored bugs lighting on her arms, wiped sweat from her face with her sleeves without breaking the rhythm of working with Michael.

Eventually, the hard work of ricing intruded on her body and on her thoughts. Margie's arms and shoulders began to tire, then to ache, and she ignored the pain as long as she could stand to, not wanting the memory she was making to be interrupted. She flexed her arms down, her shoulders up, as unobtrusively as she could, continued to match her work rhythm, left, knock-knock, right, knock-knock, to Michael poling with the duckbill, then her arms began to shake with fatigue, and she began to count to herself, right, knock-knock, left, knock-knock, to keep the rhythm. "Are you going to Scarborough fair? Parsley, sage, rosemary, and thyme," she hummed, and couldn't remember how the rest of the song went.

"Getting tired yet?" Michael asked.

"Gaawiin; well, no, just a little bit." She struggled, concentrated. "Remember me to one who lives there; she once was a true love of mine." Her knocking became uneven, ragged; the boat had turned, and they were moving almost directly toward the sun; light began to shoot jagged hot patterns in front of her left eye; she shook her head to clear it.

"Gi bakade, na? Want lunch?" he asked. "I'm getting pretty hungry; gotta stop for a while and eat."

Gratefully, she lay the knockers on the bottom of the boat and said, "Eya, wiisini daa."

They ate the pile of baloney and cheese sandwiches that Zho Wash had packed for them in a grocery bag, and shared the plastic jug of grape Kool-Aid. Margie looked out over the rice stalks growing from the lake, letting the wind cool her face, turned from Michael so that he wouldn't see how closely she watched him.

Michael lit a cigarette, asked Margie, "Hey, sagaswaa?"

"No; thanks, though." Margie didn't smoke. She stuffed wadded-up waxed paper from the sandwiches into the grocery bag. In Michael's shadow she inhaled his smoke along with the air of the beautiful day, sweet with rice, growing and green, smoky not only from the cigarette but also the burnt cedar from the smudging he had done that morning. She breathed in and out, in and out, until the elusive mystery of the day, of rice growing and green, cigarette smoke and smudged cedar, settled in her lungs and then on her face, throat, chest, and arms, on the places where her friends the little bottle spirits, the conjoined twins, usually lit when she drank, giving her company and courage.

"Got a puff?" she asked.

"You sure?" He sounded surprised. "You're not a smoker, are you?"

"Sometimes."

"You *sure*? Naw, you're not old enough to smoke yet."

His teasing was sunlight showering weightless flecks of yellow happiness in random, repeating patterns as seductive as the dance of the bottle spirits, on her arms, her face, her hair. She raised her face to speak directly, closely into his. "Sagaswaa, daga."

She took the cigarette from his offering hand, brushing his fingers with her own, and held it as Michael did, between her second and third fingers, filter end just inside her hand. She raised her hand to cover her mouth as she inhaled, cupped, as Michael did, faking a drag in order not to cough. She hated smoking. She handed the cigarette back to Michael, this time brushing her fingers accidentally, lightly, against the tender inside of his wrist. She leaned toward him, then knelt, fit her shoulders inside the half circle of his. She raised her face to look again directly, closely, into his. Curving one hand over the solid muscle between his shoulder and neck, she caressed and smoothed his lips with the other, cupped it under his jaw, brought her own face to his, closed her eyes. Her kiss was light; breathing with Michael, she felt as though the skin on their noses and cheeks had melted and merged into an intimate, cedar-scented sweetness.

Then Michael leaned backward, away from Margie, who opened her eyes. "I love you," she told him.

And Michael didn't answer. He looked up at the sky; his jaw shaded her eyes; she watched his pulse beat once, twice, on his neck. Once, twice again. And again.

His silence was sorrowful and pitying, louder than a shout of disgust, or ridicule, or laughter, longer than the years it must have taken for Zho Wash to carve and polish the rice knockers and wear them with his hands to the smoothness Margie felt when, to cover the glare and void of her exposure, she picked them up from the bottom of the boat and asked, "Think we've got enough rice? Or do you want to rice some more?" Her voice, usually breathy and low, sounded to her high pitched, tight, as though she were swallowing as she spoke.

"Let's go get this weighed," he answered, "see what we've got."

On the way back to the boat landing, she kept Zho Wash's hat pulled closely around the sides of her face and the back of her neck.

At the landing he told her to stay in the rowboat and stepped carefully out into knee-deep water to pull Margie and the rice to dry land. Zho Wash, Michael, and Margie bagged the damp, green rice in burlap sacks; Michael and Zho hung the sacks of the rice that they would sell on the hook over the rice buyer's scale, then loaded them onto his truck bed for the trip to his processing plant in Mesabi. Michael and Margie split the cash, twenty dollars each at fifty cents a pound for the eighty pounds they sold. Zho Wash and Michael loaded the rest, fifty pounds or so, into the back of Zho Wash's truck.

Zho and Michael dropped Margie at the end of her Aunt Beryl's driveway. As they drove away, Zho commented, "She's pretty quiet, Margie."

"Tired," Michael answered. "She isn't used to ricing."

Sometime not long afterward, Margie didn't know when, Michael left Sweetgrass. It was Beryl who told her that Zho Wash seemed to be living alone, again. "Big help he was with wild ricing, that Michael; leaves his dad with all that green rice to finish all by himself before it goes bad," the old woman commented. "Can't ever count on him for anything; you better stay from him. Lots of nice young men around Sweetgrass; have you ever met Mrs. Mino-geezhik's son, Punkin? Now, there's a nice young man: works hard, helps his mother, never gets into any trouble."

Margie knew that she should leave, herself; that she should go home, back to her family. She packed her clothes and said good-bye to Beryl, and began to walk toward Duluth. When she had gone perhaps a mile she was picked up by the rice buyer, who said he could take her as far as the gas station at the Dionne fork. At the gas station, she used the bathroom and bought a pack of gum from the nicest of the Dionne sisters, Dale Ann, who after returning from her Relocation Program distaster in Chicago, had been hired to clean and cashier. Then Margie began the walk back toward Sweetgrass and was picked up by one of the LaVirage brothers, who dropped her back at the end of Beryl's driveway. From there she cut through the woods to Zho Wash's cabin, which is where he found her the next morning, awake and exhausted, on the porch.

She had listened to the sounds of the old man waking at dawn: he had coughed, stretched and groaned, walked out the back door, stood silently. She heard him mumble his morning prayer, in Ojibwe, listened as he walked out into the woods to urinate. Back in the house he lit the woodstove and ran water. He rattled pots and pans on the stove burner; when he stirred them, the scraping sound of metal spoon on metal pot made her teeth ache.

Inside, the old man set a bowl of venison and oatmeal soup on the table. From another saucepan he poured coffee into a mug and stood for moment, sipping and thinking; through the front window he saw the bowed back of a young woman sitting on the stoop.

Margie turned to the sound of the front door opening and to the scorched smell of reheated coffee.

"Nice morning," said Zho Wash. "Would you like some coffee?"

"Do you know where Michael is?" Margie asked.

"Oh, I think it's Mishiimini-Oodena, where he was going."

"Where is that?"

"Mishiimini-Oodena, Apple Town! You know, Minneapolis? That's like a little joke, Mishiimini-Oodena. Apple-town, Minne-apple-is."

Margie tried to smile, and to laugh politely.

"Biindigen, Margie; come inside. Come in and have something to eat. Want some oatmeal soup?"

"I guess I'm not very hungry. It smells good, though." Tears ran down her cheeks to her jaw, dropped onto her sweatshirt. "Well, maybe."

Zho Wash's reheated coffee was thick and opaque. Because Margie was company, he opened a can of evaporated milk and poured a generous amount into each of their cups, stirring in several sugars. The cup he handed to Margie had grounds swirling in circles on the surface. She cried silently, watching their patterns.

"Have some soup, my girl. It's good for you; you'll feel better." He filled Lucy's favorite bowl from the pot. "Here, you eat. I'll just be outside. I'm going to be parching rice today, have to get that done." He left the girl at the table.

The soup was good, although a little thin. Zho Wash had boiled water and thrown in a handful of oatmeal and another of chopped dried venison, peppered it generously. Crying, she ate the bowlful and, crying, stood at the window to watch the old man.

In the front yard Zho Wash built a fire inside a circle of stones. From the shed behind the house he dragged an old iron kettle, which he set on top of four large stones within the circle, then from the lean-to by the back door he carried a gunny sack of green rice and a wooden paddle. He poured rice into the kettle and stirred; when steam stopped rising from the kettle, he tipped the parched rice onto a canvas tarp and began another batch. Margie had not seen wild rice being parched by hand before, and still crying, she watched Zho Wash repeat the task, and repeat it again, and again, always with an unhurried rhythm that oddly soothed her, and finally mesmerized her. She felt sleepy and decided to rest on the couch for a few minutes, to close her eyes, which felt dry and salty while at the same time continued to drip tears and tears. Crying, she slept until the next day.

When she woke, Zho Wash was not in the cabin. On the table he had left a note, "gone to town back pretty soon." Reading it, she blinked and squinted and realized that the discomfort was caused by her being temporarily out of tears. Cried out for the time being, she drank several cups of coffee and saw, through her red and scratchy eyes, that the corners of the cabin floor were grimy, the windows gray with dust and dried rain. She searched the cabin until she found a broom in the lean-to and began to sweep.

Margie told herself that she would stay just until things were cleaned up and straightened out, as a favor to Zho Wash. After that was done she would leave, she told herself, taking comfort in the magnitude of the task. She found a bucket in the shed, and a box of Fels-Naptha. Back of the door to the bedroom was a bag of rags. "I can just stay in the house; I don't even have to go outside, except to clean up the yard," she thought. Replenished by the coffee, her eyes dripped a fresh supply of tears into the bucket of soapy water.

Margie became a ghost, spending the days haunting the cabin while Zho Wash worked. After he had finished the season's rice and brought some to town to sell it, he began the next season's task, cutting wood pulp, which he sold in town, too. While he worked, and while he was gone, Margie straightened up the kitchen, washed the windows, sanded down the tabletop until it was soft as peach skin. Hunted for the old man's bottles, drank only what she needed from them, and re-hid them.

Zho Wash acted as if it was a natural thing, that silent young woman sleeping on his sofa, walking the floor of the cabin, leaving the imprint of her cleaning, weeping from time to time, drinking his liquor. He threw the bottles out into the woods when they were empty and didn't replace them. He let her work, and walk, and weep, alone every day until late afternoon; then they sat, the old man on the wooden chair and girl on the couch, and listened to the sounds of trees and birds and an occasional car outside the cabin. He picked strengthening plants from the swamp and brewed her tea, fed her sweet venison from a young deer he had shot and dressed just for her. Brought from the woods a snarl of sweetgrass, wet and fragrant, that he showed her how to braid, to coil and stitch into baskets.

He noticed that each day she cried a little less.

On a rainy afternoon in late fall, when the cabin had been cleaned until there was nothing left to clean and the furniture rearranged until it had repeated itself four times, she replaced the frayed ribbon trim on his moccasins with a new red ribbon he had bought her for her hair, then lay on the couch, where she fell asleep. She dreamed of flying over Lost Lake, over rice stalks growing a ripe light green up out of water that reflected the sky, the clouds, and Margie overhead; of Zho Wash below walking in the woods, the beaded wild roses on his moccasins scattering petals that took root and bloomed in his path. She awoke to the sound of tiny bells and looked out the window at a storm of ice crystals breaking themselves on the frozen ground outside the cabin. In a small area of sunlight caused by a break in the clouds above, glittering crystals bulleted from the sky, danced impetuously as they landed, prisms that seized the color of the sun and captured it in the yard outside the cabin, then shattered it against ground frozen hard. She watched the crystals heap and grow, listening to chime of tiny bells that had become menacingly assonant, and began to worry about Zho Wash. Would the truck skid on ice, slide off the road? Would he be hurt? The clouds covered over the sky, the sun set, the woods around the cabin darkened. Would the truck slide off the road? Would it skid, would he be hurt? She put two more pieces of wood in the stove and peeled potatoes that she put on to boil, opened cans of beans and corn. Set two plates, two forks, two coffee cups on the table. Would the truck skid on ice, would he slide off the road and be hurt? The truck cantered up the driveway.

"It's Zho Wash," she said aloud, and opened the door before he had walked up the steps.

"See how pretty it is outside?" he asked.

"It looks slippery. You could have gone off the road." So that he wouldn't see that she had been crying, she spoke toward the woods.

"Margie-enjiss, it's all right. It's all right, Margie; come out on the porch with me, and we'll watch the storm."

. . .

The afternoon Michael returned to Sweetgrass for a visit, Zho Wash was out in the woods and Margie was in the kitchen, smoothing a cloth over the scarred table that looked as old as the house, she thought, wondering if she should paint it. She heard the door open, turned.

"Michael." The pain was lightning that lit the room with a blue flash and burned flesh from her face and chest, exposing the rawness that was Margie inside. She rasped, "Biindigen, come in. I'm happy to see you."

"Margie." He had thought she was in Duluth.

When Zho returned, Margie met him at the door. "Zho, look who's here," she said, her voice a semi-pitch higher than usual. "It's Michael!"

They offered Michael raspberry tea, a comfortable place to sit near the woodstove, and shared their supper of commodity pork and macaroni and cheese. The cabin was tidy; she had hung new curtains, rearranged the furniture. Zho Wash had painted the walls, replaced the front stairs.

"Looks nice in here," Michael commented uneasily. What were they, honeymooners? Unnerved, he slept in the shed outside the kitchen, with the dogs. It became his bedroom whenever he visited.

She didn't rice the next season. The unusually hot and humid summer had swelled her hands and feet; her bony ankles that in winter Zho Wash had loved to hold in his hands and tap, cup, caress, were by the time the rice was ripe lost under the fluid that gravity pulled and held, water finding its own weight. Her abdomen was a melon held low to her body by wavy silver stripes of stretch marks; her round face reddened like a tomato even at light exertions, like hanging clothes on the line outside the cabin.

She would have the baby at the cabin, she told Zho Wash; she would not leave Sweetgrass. If she needed help, they would ask Beryl.

She slept on her back, more heavily at night, more soundly; she felt rested and cooled in the mornings, got up to fix breakfast. She washed dishes and made the bed, then chose one chore for the day, washing the floor or dusting or rearranging the dish cabinet, or doing a load of laundry in the wringer washer. During the hottest parts of the afternoons she rested, ready to get off her feet that were rising like bread dough. Lying on the bed with the pictures of Zho Wash's wives for company (one on the table by the bed, one on the wall; Mageet young and solemn, Lucy young and laughing), cooled by the fan he had bought at the hardware store in Mesabi and rigged to blow on her feet and legs, never on her face, which bothered her, she stretched her body nearly the entire length of the bed; mysteriously, she was taller lying down than she was standing up. In spite of the heat, and her size, and the swelling and pressure that gave her an occasional nosebleed, she slept lightly away when she lay down in the afternoons, her spine stretched straight and relaxed, the baby moving occasionally but content. She loved going to bed while it was light outside; she appreciated the bed's placement under the window, its cool sheets, the man-made breeze from the fan moving across her; the sounds of Zho Wash moving in the yard, the shed, or cutting wood, or cleaning and boiling roots in the kitchen soothed her. Sometimes when she awoke he was next to her, asleep; she never noticed when he lay down because he was so careful to not jar the bed or touch her. He respected hers and the baby's rest. His wide mouth smiled in sleep; he snored a light, old-man's snore from the back of his throat. One hand, darkened and roughened by sun and work, rested on the edge of her pillowcase.

The afternoon before the baby was born she woke Zho Wash by kissing that hand and then murmuring her dreams against his lips until he loved her, whispering the name he called her, Margie-enjiss. The next morning she awoke before dawn with the realization that her belly had not moved for hours; frightened, she walked out onto the stoop, where she began to pray. In the black sky overhead, stars sharp as glass glittered remotely; then, as the pink of sunrise faded their brilliance and sent them to their daytime sleep, the baby leapt so high that her nightgown rippled, and she went into labor.

At sunset Zho Wash heated broth on the woodstove for supper, put clean sheets on the bed, brewed tea; then they walked in the yard and in the woods around the cabin while they waited.

It was not a difficult birth; Margie eased her pains by sitting on the old man's lap, facing him, on a wooden kitchen chair, with her knees drawn up and her feet resting on the chair rungs. He held her with his stringy, muscular arms wrapped around and supporting her hips; she rested her head against his chest, just below his shoulder, and was quieted by the beat of his heart. Calmed, she breathed deeply through the pains, inhaling sweetness from the soft brown skin of his neck; as one pain began to grab her, ready to shake her by the hair, she opened her eyes and saw that he was rocking her almost imperceptibly, looking out the window at the trees outside the cabin, his lips moving as he prayed all but silently, his hair an un-earthly silver under the electric light bulb that hung from the ceiling. "Why, it's Zho," she thought, "it's Zho." She rested her face against the right side of his neck, her lips soft on the line of pale scars, tracks left by the bullet that found him when he was in Italy, during the war.

Crystal left Margie's body under her own force, fists first, hands crossed above her head. She arched her back, twisted, pushed with her tiny feet until she emerged. At first she was gray in color; Zho Wash loosened the cord from where it was wrapped around and around those crossed hands, and her color changed to lavender, then to a deep pink. The cord cut, and free of her mother, she looked coolly at Margie and Zho Wash with eyes the darkest of muddy azure. While Margie held her baby, wrapped as stiffly as a doll, Zho Wash unfolded a new, navy-blue bandanna and lay it on the bed. He placed on it a foil bag of Half and Half tobacco, an old silver dime, a beaded bracelet, and a ten-dollar bill, then tied the four corners together, opposite corners over opposite corners.

"For when she is named," he explained.

Margie nodded.

"Who will you ask to be her namesake?"

"I thought Aunt Beryl."

"And what will you call her?"

"Crystal Jo."

Betty García

John Reimringer

I

Betty García and I got together at a National Honor Society party during the autumn of my junior year of high school. Neither of us belonged there. A freshman, Betty had come to the party with an older cousin. I wouldn't be in the honor society until the end of the year myself, but I'd been invited by one of my track teammates. Nick lived on Summit Avenue and hung with a group of kids who looked like they'd just walked off a tennis court.

Before the party, I pulled on a striped, V-necked sweater and parted my hair neatly with water. Then I went downstairs to get my letter jacket off the coat tree. The old man and my brother, Jacky, were sitting on the couch watching Minnesota at Illinois.

"Joe College," the old man said. He nudged Jacky. "Where's Joe College going?"

"Some party on Summit," Jacky said. "Hey, Jimmy, you got real purty hair."

The old man grinned and pointed at me with a beer can. "They'll arrest you down there, boy. Bring us home some silverware."

. . .

Nick lived in a Tudor near the College of Saint Thomas, where Summit ran on either side of a wide parkway shaded by cottonwoods in the summer. Mr. Hawthorne answered the door. He had a golfer's tanned, lined face, a flat belly, and wore a forest green sweater with embroidered autumn leaves drifting across the front. "Straight back," he said. "Can I take your coat?" I shook my head, mumbled a *no thanks.*

The party was in the library, which jutted from the back of the house. A couple dozen kids were scattered on leather sofas and ottomans, talking and toying with swizzle sticks, heads and drinks cocked at careful angles. Ice clinked; Mickie Malone tossed her red hair and laughed.

"Hey, James." Nick left a circle of people by the fireplace. "Take off your coat and stay awhile. Didn't my dad let you in?" I left my jacket on and got a beer, then sat on the edge of a group of seniors talking about college visits and scholarship offers. I didn't know to be interested in that stuff yet, and when the talk turned to Homecoming dinners and the food at a new place on Nicollet Island, I got up to thumb through albums by the stereo: *Rocket to Russia. London Calling. My Aim Is True.* I didn't recognize any of them. On the stereo, a nasal-voiced singer said he used to be disgusted. A thin-shouldered, pinch-faced young man in nerd glasses stared at me from the last album cover. I had the urge to punch him.

Nearby, a Mexican girl in jeans and a maroon cowl-neck sweater stood looking up at the bookshelves. She wore her hair in a French braid, with silver hoops in her ears. I recognized Betty García, a freshman who'd been the team manager this fall when I ran cross-country. She felt me watching, glanced over and smiled, then looked back up at the books. I leaned against a set of Dickens. "Hi," I said.

"Hi, James." Her face was sharp, with a pointed chin and nose, intelligent eyes. Dark rouge highlighted her cheekbones. Her smile pulled at one corner of her mouth.

"Having a good time?" I said.

She glanced around. "I don't know any of these people. My cousin Linda brought me and then took off with this guy she likes. My Uncle Hank's strict."

I looked out a window. It was full dark outside. "You wanna take a walk?"

She studied me for a moment. "I could use a cigarette."

I got us beers and helped Betty into a navy blue wool coat, short and belted to show the curve of her hips. We walked toward the river. When Betty stopped to light up, I handed her a beer. She took a swig and offered me her cigarette. I shook my head.

"I forgot," she said. "You're a jock. How come you don't play football?"

We were walking again, the cigarette tracing an orange arc between us in the dark. "My old man won't let me," I said. "He says he doesn't want me and Jacky getting busted up in a game we'll never take past high school."

"Jacky's in my class," Betty said. "He cracks me up."

My brother was a charmer, all right. He'd lost his virginity in the seventh grade with a high-school girl who lived with her baby in public housing in Frogtown. Jacky would go over to her apartment after school, and the old man would stop on his way home from work and drag Jacky out of there. He didn't mind the sex but didn't want Jacky getting killed walking out of Frogtown at night. What bothered my father—us maybe getting hurt playing football—and what didn't—Jacky getting laid regularly at thirteen—never made any sense. When Jacky and I left for parties, the old man would say from the couch, "See if you can get your brother's cherry popped tonight, Jackyboy." I would duck my head, and Jacky would grin and punch me in the shoulder as we went out the door. "Everybody loves my brother," I said to Betty.

We passed the stone chapel near the corner of the Saint Paul Seminary, its Celtic cross rising against the starry sky, and stopped at the corner of Mississippi River Boulevard. The ground sloped to the river overlook, and the oak grove to our right rattled its dry leaves in the dark. In front of us, the granite pillar of the DAR World War I memorial ended in another cross; Father Phil had said in grade-school history that Saint Paul was a city of crosses and so you were never far from God here. In the west, beyond the cross, the skyscrapers of downtown Minneapolis winked and beckoned. We went to the overlook and sat on a bench. Betty talked about her family and her Uncle Hank, who was a labor lawyer, and told me that she was going to be a lawyer, too. Then she ground out her cigarette with the toe of her little black boot and said, "But I've been talking too much. What are you going to be?"

Father Phil had me thinking about the priesthood, but now was not the time. Instead, I kissed Betty. She drew away, then put her arms around my shoulders and kissed me back. Her breath was rough with beer, coppery with tobacco. It was a chill night, and we were alone at the overlook, and the moon sunk huge and orange over the skyscrapers, and the skyline and the moon together made it feel as if I'd never seen either of them before. Betty drew her feet up on the bench and curled against my chest, and we kissed until the night air chilled us, then headed back to Nick's. What was left of the year's first snow lay in shards along sidewalks and in the lee of north-facing houses. It looked like whitecaps in the moonlight. As we walked, I told Betty about the stars, because it was clear that she liked smart boys, and I outlined for her Orion, just risen in the east, but staggering, tilting north. "He's drunk tonight," I said. Betty stopped and turned her face up to mine, and we kissed again. We were in front of one of the big houses on

Summit now, and a woman, pausing at a window, watched us before draw-ing the curtains.

...

A week after Nick's party, I called Betty and asked her out.

"I can't date until I'm fifteen," she said. "But that's only three weeks. I'll see if you can come to my quinceañera." She paused. I could tell I was sup-posed to ask.

"What?"

"It's a Mexican debutante ball. There's Mass and dinner and a dance. Every night before my dad goes to the plant we practice waltzing, and I've been rehearsing my speech with Uncle Hank. I'll have all of my cousins and best friends, and a white dress and high-heeled shoes, and—oh, James, you don't want to hear me talk about all that." She paused again.

...

"The boy's going to a greaser hoedown," the old man said when Mom told him why I needed a suit. "Hey, don't look at me, I ain't prejudiced. Married your mom, didn't I, and her black Irish. 'Course, I didn't know that the first time I saw her walking down Selby, all blonde hair and hooters out to here." He raised his hands about a foot in front of his chest, shook them. "I thought I was bringing a good German girl home to my momma."

"With this skin and these eyes?" Mom touched her face, then shook her head, the corners of her eyes crinkling a bit. "I should've left that bottle of peroxide on the shelf at the drugstore."

"Can I have the suit?" I said. I'd heard all this before, but it meant the old man was in a good mood. If Mom hurried, we could buy the suit this afternoon before the stores closed. Tonight Dad would be at his taverns, and tomorrow he might say he'd changed his mind. Then Mom would light into him, and he would say he worked his ass off and wasn't a goddamned savings and loan, and I'd never get a suit.

The old man leaned back on the couch, his gut lifting before him, and pulled out his money clip, the one with the buffalo nickel inset in the back. He snapped off several crisp bills—he always insisted on new bills when he cashed his paycheck—and smiled as he handed them to Mom. "Buy the boy a good suit. Can't have them fancy-pants greasers looking down their brown noses at him. Get it? Brown noses! Haw-haw." I went for my jacket.

...

On our way home from Dayton's downtown store, with my new suit hanging in the back seat, Mom drove us by the Gossip Inn on University, a tavern wedged between a Vietnamese take-out place and a head shop. She slowed the car as we passed, and through the grated front window I saw my father's bulk at the bar. I glanced at Mom. "There's the money for a better suit," she said. I bit my lip. "Fine," Mom said. After another moment, she said, "At least don't take up for him," then she stepped on the gas and leaned forward to turn up the AM radio.

The Gossip's the kind of place that gets its windows shot out, where the guy on the next stool might carry a gun or a knife. And one night seven years ago, as my father sat at the bar, some men pulled a gun on him. They took him out back to the alley lot, where they beat him with a baseball bat. They took turns, the old man said later, passed the bat around like a grudge. After he heard the bat clatter into the bed of a pickup truck, after he heard footsteps and tires grind away over gravel, the old man pulled himself into his car and drove home. He drove by clinging to the steering wheel to hold himself up, while streetlights and the headlights of oncoming cars split and drew back together, half the world a dark pink haze because his right eye was filled with blood.

When the old man appeared at our back door, he was swaying, ready to topple, gravel from the parking lot ground into his swollen face and forearms. I was ten, sitting at the kitchen table eating a bowl of cereal before bed, and I screamed for Mom, only half-conscious that what was in the door was my father. Then Mom was there, holding the door open, reaching for him and drawing back, unsure where to find an unbroken place to support him. "They hurt me bad, Maura," he said.

He had broken ribs and a broken collarbone. The thick muscles of his upper back and his shoulders were a mass of bruises, and once, when he'd rolled his head from the protective cradle of his forearms to cry out, the bat had caught him just forward of the right temple, cracking the bone at the outer orbit of his eye. To this day, his vision is bad in that eye; he misses objects, movement, to his right.

But he refused to stay at the hospital for observation after the doctors set his breaks, and that summer he lay on the couch, using first his sick leave and then his vacation. Mom was working two jobs, so it fell on me to tend him, rubbing salve into his muscles and watching his back turn from blue and green to sickly yellow, shot with the purple of burst veins. It was hard to look at and harder to touch. I'd never been this near my father except when he taught Jacky and me how to wrestle. Up close, his skin was old and oily and darkened by years of working shirtless in our backyard, and there was a strong smell to him. My hands seemed delicate against his broad back and sloping shoulders, and it scared and thrilled me to know that some-one could beat him up. I thought the men from the bar might come to our house, and I rehearsed what I would do, how I would lock the door and run to where he kept his handgun. And when the men broke down the door, I would point the gun steadily at their leader. "If you take one more step, I will kill you," I'd say, and he would know I meant it.

My father didn't know how fiercely I meant to protect him. He bullied us from the couch, kept us all running to the kitchen for cigarettes and beer, changing the channel on the TV. He flew into rages, screaming and cursing if he were left alone in the living room, even if he woke by himself in the night. "Where the fuck is everybody? I could die down here while all you sleep," he would yell.

In the evenings, though, as I sat on the floor by the couch watching the Twins, he would tap my shoulder and point to the TV. "Look at that young Blyleven's big curve," he might say. "When it works, it's great, but when he hangs it, it's gone. Fucker'll give up a lot of home runs." That summer he point-ed out how fielders shifted depending on the batter, how the middle infielders called the pitch to first and third behind cupped hands. Watching boxing, an obscure middleweight match or a rerun of Ali and Frazier, he showed me how smart boxers adjusted to their opponents from round to round, how they used their thumbs and elbows in a clinch. One night he told me how sorry he was that he'd fucked up and couldn't get to my Little League games that summer. And when Mom tired of his slow convalescence and said that maybe she ought to find a man who could provide for his family, I stood next to the couch and cried out that I was sticking by him even if she wouldn't.

II

The quinceañera Mass started like a wedding with a procession of young couples in black tuxedos and purple satin dresses, followed by Betty in white, carrying an armful of roses that she laid at the feet of a statue of the Virgin. Later, the sandy-haired Irish priest gave a homily about Betty becoming a young woman. "In today's world, there are people, *feminists*, who object to telling a young girl to 'act like a lady,'" he said. "But those people, out there, are mistaken. *Ladies* respect God's gift of modesty . . ." He went on like that for a while. I worried Betty wouldn't want to make out with me again.

At the end of Mass, the priest led Betty by the elbow to the center of the altar, and she made a little speech, her chin in the air, her voice earnest and precise. "Standards are important," she recited, "but, if women have more opportunity to err in today's world, we also have more opportunity to lead, and we must make the most of it." Everyone applauded, led by the priest.

In the parish hall afterward, Betty hurried about, but she stopped long enough to introduce me to her parents. Her father was a short, barrel-chested older man with a broad grin—he'd started out as a line mechanic at the Ford plant, then been promoted to foreman, Betty had told me—and her mother was a tiny woman with quick, birdlike eyes and dyed-black hair. "I'm so pleased to meet you," Mrs. García said, glancing around my shoulder, then pulling Betty away to greet an aunt from Texas.

Mr. García shook my hand, then he introduced me to a big man who had come up beside him, Hank, the labor lawyer. Hank was huge for a Mexican—well over six feet and pushing three hundred pounds, I guessed. He had a big belly, but the vest of his three-piece suit was cut to hide it. The suit's charcoal-colored wool shone, and under it Hank wore a gray button-down shirt with a pink silk tie done up in a fancy knot. A matching handkerchief pointed out of his coat's breast pocket. I caught myself staring, but it wasn't at his size or the clothes—I had the feeling I knew him. Then I remembered: he umpired American Legion baseball. My family had had trouble with him; of course, with Dad in the stands and Jacky on the field, we had trouble with most umpires. Hank looked down at me, recognition dawning. He didn't offer his hand. "You're the quiet one," he said.

Mr. García told Hank I was a starter at shooting guard for Central and asked whether the team would be any good this year.

"We'll win some games," I said.

"You're starting," Hank said, "so it won't be five niggers on the court, for a change."

"No, sir," I said, surprised to hear a Mexican using that word.

"Fucking Roberto Duran," Hank said. There was liquor on his breath. "Letting that pussy Sugar Ray beat him. 'No mas!' Worst thing to happen to Panama since United Fruit."

"Sugar Ray was tearing him up, sir," I said. Dad had taken Jacky and me to a closed-circuit showing of the fight at the civic auditorium.

"The hell he was," Hank said.

Mr. García laughed. "Duran didn't know whether to shit or go blind, Hank. You said it yourself."

"He shouldn't have quit," I said, trying to ease things. The old man had been livid when Duran threw in the towel.

"The hell you know about quitting?" Hank said.

Mr. García grabbed his elbow and steered him away. "Hey, Hank," he said, then looked back over his shoulder. "You enjoy yourself tonight, James."

"Thank you, sir," I said. At dinner, seated with several of Betty's cousins who were around my age, I imagined kicking Hank in the knees—the best way to take a big man down, the old man said—or maybe just telling him he was a lousy umpire. The cousins were talking about Leonard-Duran, too; it seemed like every Mexican in Saint Paul was pissed at Duran for letting a black man beat him.

Dessert was cut from an ornate white cake topped with a Mexican doll in a little dress that matched Betty's. I was eating the icing off my piece when the band struck up. Betty walked out onto the dance floor in front of the head table, and one of her attendants brought her a chair. "Es tiempo de vivir," the band's singer wept while Betty's parents came out together, her mother carrying a pair of white high heels on a satin pillow. I sat up, noticed Hank watching me from a nearby table, and shifted my back to him. Betty had on flats, and her father knelt and removed them, then fitted a white pump onto the curve of her foot.

Lord.

Betty pointed the other foot, and I saw that her toenails were painted bright red under her hose. I glanced at Hank, but he was watching Betty.

She stood, twirled into her father's arms. The song ended, and the band shifted to a slow waltz. Betty danced with her father, her feet moving quickly and expertly in their new heels. The tempo picked up, and a slim, handsome Mexican boy cut in. I watched the familiar way she moved with him, the ease with which he held her, and felt jealous but told myself I was glad not to be at the center of attention. Betty danced with boys in tuxedos, uncles in suits. She was tiny in huge Hank's arms, and his face was the face of a father as they danced and talked. At last she stood in front of me, flushed with excitement. "Dance with me?"

We turned about the floor. "Having a good time?" she asked.

"Sure," I said. Her perfume wafted around us; she had dusky powder over her cheekbones, and red lips and nails. A gold cross with a diamond in the center that she'd been given at Mass hung in her cleavage, and I could feel the boning of a long brassiere under my hand at her waist. I imagined Betty dressing with her cousins: a cramped changing room in the basement of the church crowded with bawdy, black-haired girls. I imagined undoing Betty, laying her down on a big bed somewhere, all of those fancy clothes strewn about us. We neared Hank's table; he sat flat eyed, watching.

"Come meet my favorite uncle," Betty said, pulling me off the dance floor before I could tell her that I already had. She went on: "Hank's the only one in the family who doesn't expect me to get married right after high school."

Hank stood. "That's right," he said.

I stuck out my hand.

Hank took it, and I felt bones grind together. "Pleased to meet you, sir," I said.

Hank released my hand and turned to Betty. "And how *did* you two meet?"

"At that party of Nick's you had Linda take me to," Betty said.

Hank's eyebrows went up a little. "You a friend of Nick's?" he said to me.

"Yes, sir," I said. "We run the medley relay. I'm a half-miler."

Hank nodded. "That baton pass is tricky," he said. "I threw the javelin myself. 'Course, I was thinner then." He touched Betty's shoulder. "You have a good time tonight, Bettina," he said. "Make sure to dance with everyone."

He bent down, and Betty reached up on her tiptoes to kiss him on the cheek, then led me back to the dance floor. "Isn't Uncle Hank wonderful?" she said. "He's my mom's little brother—though he's not so little—and he understands me. He made Father Shannon give him that homily and helped me write my speech to go with it."

"That's great," I said. The song was already ending.

"Hank's right; I've got to dance with everyone," Betty said. "But there's a party after at my cousin's. We can be together there."

. . .

Betty's parents were already in their fifties—she was a late child—and their West Seventh bungalow was a very traditional Mexican home, every surface crowded with family photos and knickknacks and colorful plaster saints. There was a shrine to Our Lady of Guadalupe, and one to Betty's oldest brother, a Marine killed in the street fighting at Hue during the Tet Offensive. Betty was two when Gabriel died, but she claimed a memory of him: a man in a green uniform drinking beer with her father at the kitchen table. She had toddled in and sat at his feet, playing with the laces on his shiny black boots until her father swept her into his lap. Many of the photos on the living and dining room walls were black-and-whites of young Mexican men in US military uniforms dating back to World War II. "What a lousy way to be a part of this country," Betty said. "I'll work for my people like Hank does." There were pictures, too, of Betty's aunts and uncles when they were younger, including Hank in a Central High football jersey. He'd played tight end and been the hope of his family, and his eyes held the arrogance and fear of a young man expected to go places.

The centerpiece of one wall was a pair of framed prints of Jesus and Mary, heads tilted toward one another, chins and eyes upcast, intricate sacred hearts exposed on their chests. Betty and I stood looking at those prints one night after a date. Her father was working the night shift at Ford, and her mother had fed us Mexican sweet bread and coffee and gone to bed.

"Jesus," I said.

"What?" Betty stood in front of me, resting against my chest. I had my arms around her shoulders.

"We had statues like that in the hallways in grade school," I said. "In first grade, I thought holy people had their hearts outside their bodies, like dead animals in the street."

Betty stiffened. "I think they're beautiful," she said. "I love the little cross on top, and the way the roses loop around. I used to imagine my heart that way, a home for my soul."

"I used to want to be a priest," I said.

"Why?"

"Sex used to scare me." That was true, and it was easier than talking about my family.

Betty twisted in my arms. "It still scare you?"

"Nope," I said.

"Me either." We started kissing and lurched a little into the sideboard, and all of the holy medals and candleholders and china saints rattled.

. . .

I remember waking in the dark once, a Sunday before Christmas. I was in seventh grade, and Mom and Dad had yelled at each other until late the night before. I lay in bed dreading the tense ballet that would go on in the house all morning, the two of them tiptoeing around each other and we kids tiptoeing around them. On a Sunday morning, Mass might break the tension, but Mass was a sometimes thing in our house. More often than not, if anyone took us, it was our grandparents. My grandfather Otto, the old man's old man, would call Mom Saturday night and announce: "We're taking the kids to Mass tomorrow, Maura. Have 'em ready by 9:30."

On that morning, the fourth Sunday of Advent, with the Advent wreath my father had placed on the dining-room sideboard a month before dropping needles, its unused candles tilting now at odd angles, I decided to go to early Mass on my own. Maybe Father Phil would need an altar boy. In the dark, I dressed in my best Sunday clothes, even putting on a tie, tightening the knot before the mirror. When I went downstairs, I kept close to the wall where the steps were quieter. The old man would be sleeping on the couch, and I knew better than to wake him. I lifted my parka from the coat tree on the landing and wrestled into it. A few feet away, the TV hummed with a test pattern and my father snored, the coffee table littered with empty Grain Belt cans and an ashtray full of cigarette butts. The dead bolt squeaked when I turned the latch. Behind me, the snoring stopped. I dared a glance over my shoulder. The old man turned on his side and snorted, but didn't wake. The doorknob rattled under my hand, but I was ready to slip out when I heard a floorboard creak and was caught by the biceps in a hard grip.

The old man swung me back against the wall. He peered at me, his breath stale with beer and tobacco. "The hell time is it?" He shook me by the arm.

"I'm just going to early Mass."

He stared, puzzled, gripping my arm hard enough to bruise. I shivered, trying not to let fear make me look defiant, and noticed for the first time that his right eye had been skewed by the damage the baseball bat had done two years before. He shifted his hold, then shoved me toward the door. "Jesus, I'm raising a Holy Joe. Get the hell out of here."

The heavy wooden door caught me in the ear, and I scurried onto the porch. Halfway down the block, I stopped, looked back at our house. It was stinging cold out, and I rubbed at my ear with a mittened hand, then pulled my hood tighter. I wanted to be back in bed. But by now the old man would have the percolator going and be sitting in the dark in the living room brooding over the orange glow of a cigarette. I started walking again. I crossed the railroad overpass, face lowered against the north wind, then slipped on a frozen patch of sidewalk and looked up; ahead, the church's blocky red-brick bell tower and tiled roof rose among the morning trees.

. . .

But even for a boy who wanted to be a priest, purity was an easier thing to conceive of in seventh grade than now. I'd dated some before Betty, including a few heady but chaste weeks with a cheerleader named Susan Reading. But Betty was edgier than any girl I'd been with, and I found it alarming and attractive. For a month that winter, sidelined from basketball with a badly sprained ankle, I'd go to her house after school. Her parents both worked and her dad had moved to the swing shift, so we could squeeze in a couple of hours of heaven on the living-room couch between his leaving and Betty's mother coming home. Naked except for a taped ankle, I jumped whenever a car drove past, but Betty, the mechanic's daughter, laughed at me, swearing she could recognize the sound of her mom's car a block away.

One snowy February day, after we'd done all we would let ourselves do, we dressed and sat in the breakfast nook in the kitchen. It overlooked the backyard, where the ground underneath Mrs. García's bird feeder always attracted a big flock of pigeons to feed on the sunflower seeds spilled by finches and house sparrows. We were talking, holding hands across the table, when suddenly the pigeons lifted into the air as one and wheeled low over the chain-link fence at the edge of the yard. There was a *whump!* of brown feathers, and, where the pigeons had been, a hawk sat in the foot-deep snow, the pointed tip of a pigeon wing sticking out from beneath it. The hawk squatted for a while with glazed eyes, slowly shifting its legs like a man trying to keep his feet warm, then it hopped up onto the crust of the snow and began tearing at the pigeon, its hooked beak occasionally lifting the body half out of the hollow it had driven into the snow. After a few minutes, the snow and the hawk's brown-barred white chest were speckled with red, and feathers and bits of fluff blew about in the dusk. Betty moved over beside me. I put my arm around her, but she was absorbed by the scene in the yard. When a whorl of gray down that radiated from a crimson center floated up and settled on the hawk's back, she stood and busied herself putting her hair into a ponytail. "Fucking pigeons," she said.

"I love you," I said, and carried her back to the sofa.

. . .

We dated all that school year, and by summer we were fighting about birth control: I wanted to use the rhythm method, but Betty called that Vatican roulette and insisted on rubbers. Whatever I'd said, sex still scared me. In junior high, a couple of heavyset, middle-aged women from Birthright had visited our classroom, armed with films that proved birth control was both a sin and unreliable and that premarital sex led directly to the murder of unborn children. Our school nuns told us sexuality was a gift from God for married couples; as we prepared for confirmation they told us boys the Holy Spirit would make us soldiers of God, that if we were disciplined and strong, we'd be worthy of a girl dressed in blue and pure as the Virgin Mary. At the end of eighth grade, I had watched Susan Reading, always the nuns' favorite, crowned at a school Mass celebrating Mary, the Queen of May. Susan stood on the altar in a long, butter-yellow dress with a garland of daisies in her hair, and I dreamed that night of a virgin bride. Now, I worried that intercourse with Betty would leave her soiled in my eyes. But I couldn't tell her that, and so we argued.

In July, Betty went on a long car trip with her parents to visit her father's family in Pueblo, Colorado, the Texas panhandle, and Topeka, Kansas. She sent postcards of mountains, cactus, the world's longest grain elevator. This last, from Kansas, said: *I love you. I miss you. I hate Kansas, but I'm getting tan.* The next evening, when Betty came home, we drove slowly down Summit, hanging our elbows out the windows of the Plymouth, looking at the rich people's houses and remembering the night we'd gotten together. Betty picked out a favorite house on each block.

At the end of Summit, I parked in the overlook lot. We took a blanket from the trunk and followed the wooded ravine that cut through the bluff down to the Mississippi. "Bet no one's down here tonight," Betty said. There was a patch of sand beach at the bottom, a hollow in the bulge of the bluff with the ashes of a bonfire in front of it, charred driftwood and beer cans, a half-buried wine bottle. Kids came down here to party and scratch their names into the soft stone, but Betty was right and we had it to ourselves. We spread the blanket in the hollow and sat looking out on the river. It was a dry summer, and the water was low, and you could see the gravel shelving out under the ripples for a long way. Betty and I hadn't seen each other for three weeks, and we sat there feeling the summer heat coming off our bodies. Betty's brown limbs were lean and dark in the night. I reached for her, and we rolled together on the blanket, pushing off each other's clothes. She'd tanned in a bikini every day of the trip, leaving white triangles over her breasts and belly.

The rumble of a jet rising from the airport broke the still sounds of our breathing and the river. Betty reached across me and fumbled for her cutoffs. "I found rubbers in the room my uncle from Colorado stays in when he visits Abuelita."

"They only work half the time," I said.

"Bullshit," Betty said. "Those numbers they gave us in Catholic school are propaganda." She stopped and stared at me, and I felt the way I had when, drunk after a skating party that winter, she'd dared me into racing across an unfamiliar lake in the dark. I remembered the slice of our skates, the way the wind forced tears from our eyes as we squinted ahead for the blackness that would be open water, the feeling of uncontrolled speed.

Betty tore open the wrapper, wiggled the milky latex circle at me.
I took it. Swallows darted over the river from the cliff face behind us.

III

That winter, Betty stayed Saturday nights with her grandmother on the
West Side. We weren't supposed to see each other those nights, but I would
cross the river about ten, and Betty and I would crawl into the backseat
of Mom's car with a blanket from the trunk, fumbling under heavy winter
clothes until after midnight, the lovemaking better for the cramped quarters
and the cold. Then her grandmother, worried by our late nights in the car,
told her we could go upstairs, but to be careful.

Abuelita came from a different world, from turn-of-the-century Mexico.
She had still been a little girl when revolution drove her family from its
ranch; Betty told me her grandmother remembered lanterns, wagons, and
muffled voices, carefully packed heirlooms that were stolen at the border.
In America, in reduced circumstances, she married at sixteen and had a
dozen children. She never learned English, living entirely in the Spanish-
speaking world of Saint Paul's Lower West Side, doing all of her shopping
on Concord Street. When she talked with Betty at her kitchen table before
bed, she included me by occasionally waving a finger in my direction and
laughing. The staircase in her house was tall and narrow, and she slept in
the front room downstairs.

Upstairs, Betty and I made love. Sometimes we dozed afterward—I had
no set time to be home—and sometimes I would wake and sit by the lace-
curtained window, parting it slightly to look out over the chain-link fences
and alleyways of the snowy neighborhood, where Christmas lights were left
up until March for the cheer they brought in the long winter, red and green
and blue against the snow.

Saint Paul white nights. A foot of snow on the ground, a blanket of
low clouds, the world between bathed in milky light. Nights bright enough
for trees to throw shadows. The snow on garage roofs lay in long folds arranged by the wind. On the houses, bare shingles marked thin spots in the
insulation. There was a gray fox hunting the backyards of the West Side
that winter, taking cats and rabbits; the neighbors said that likely it had
come into town along the river. I spotted it from the bedroom window one
night, flowing over a low fence like a ghost that left footprints in the fresh
snow. Behind me, Betty lay under the quilt, hair spread about her face. All
was still save for the metallic tapping of a radiator and the wind that made

itself known more as a rising and falling pressure in the ears than a sound. The house breathed slow and deep, drafts moving about the window sashes and frames; cold from the window glass washed my face, rested a chill hand on my chest. Betty snored lightly. I tipped the chair against the radiator and, with a teenager's false nostalgia, dreamed warm dreams of someday buying this house for Betty, of our children in the sunlit backyard struggling to do pull-ups on the clothesline poles or running to show us four-leaf clovers they'd found.

...

I started at shooting guard again that basketball season, and we won the city-league title. Hank came to every game. He threw a party for Betty and me after the season ended. It was the first time I'd been at his house. He lived in a rambling one-story rancher on Mississippi River Boulevard, above Hidden Falls Park. The wide picture window in his living room looked out over a long, sloping, winter-browned lawn to the Mississippi River gorge and the old stone of Fort Snelling. The party was a kegger, and Hank pretty much stayed out of the way after making sure we knew enough not to bother the neighbors. Hank's daughter Tina flirted with me all night. She wasn't as smart as Betty, but she favored lots of makeup and low-cut shirts with push-up bras, and she was pretty hard to ignore. Around midnight, Betty tired of this and pulled me outside for a talk. I protested that I'd done my best to stay away from Tina, and Betty and I ended up in my car. We were making love when someone knocked on the fogged-up driver's side window. "Go away," I said. The knock came again louder, the heavy thuds of the meaty side of a man's fist. I cracked the window.

"Get out," Hank said.

We scurried into our clothes, and Betty followed me from the backseat, smoothing the front of her shirt.

"Inside," Hank said to Betty. She was spending the night with Tina.

"Uncle Hank—" she said, holding on to my arm.

"I just want to talk to him," Hank said. "You go inside now."

After Betty left, Hank reached into the backseat and picked up the wine bottle nested in the blanket there. He sniffed it, frowned, and took a sip. "Jesus, kid," he said. "My niece should be drinking better."

I laughed weakly. Hank leaned on the car, scratched his neck. "I have a dozen brothers and sisters in this town," he said. "Cousins. In-laws. Last family reunion, we had over three hundred people. So I move to Wonder

Bread Highland Park for the room and the view"—his hand swept out, taking in the darkness of the gorge, the lights at the fort—"and, of course, I've got people coming and going all the time. Then I introduce myself to one of my new neighbors, and the first thing he says is: 'So how many families are living in that house, anyway?' Beautiful autumn day, sky so blue you could fall into it forever, and I stand there thinking about using his head for a posthole digger. But that's what they'd expect, see? I always tell my kids: You have to dress better than the gringos, or they'll call you a dirty Mexican. You have to be smarter and more polite. So I smile with my big white teeth, and I say, 'I'm blessed with ten fine children.' The next weekend, I invite him over for barbecue."

"That's some story," I said, not quite following.

"I'm not done," Hank said. He leaned his face down into mine. "The point is, I don't need you in a parked car in front of *my* house with *my* niece after I've thrown a party for you." He brought his big hand up and slapped me on the cheek, just hard enough to sting, no harder. "Understand?"

"Yes, sir," I said. "I'm sorry, sir."

Hank nodded slowly. "I believe you are." He poured the rest of the wine out onto the street. "Go on home now. Don't get stopped."

He lumbered up his long drive, whistling and flipping the wine bottle in the air. I leaned my head back on the roof of the car. High clouds brushed the stars. It was a soft winter night with the smell of stirring soil in the air that tells you spring's coming.

...

A month later, Betty told me she was pregnant. We were alone at her parents' house on a day off from school that we'd looked forward to as a chance to make love in her bed. Thin spring sunlight filled the house, and when I went to use the bathroom I glanced into Betty's room at the high cottage bed with its white eyelet comforter and frilled pillows and stuffed animals, and I was angry that we could not be entwined in all that light and warmth. Instead, we sat in the breakfast nook at the back of the kitchen talking in circles, always coming back to the one fact that wouldn't change.

After a while, we went into the living room and argued on the couch. Betty said something about "looking into options" that I wouldn't hear. Before her parents came home from work, she kissed me good-bye at the front door, a distant embrace.

The rest of the week we talked around the pregnancy on the phone. I was useless in school, distracted at track. There'd been an April snowstorm, but the team practiced despite the weather, our thighs aching from the effort of running in snow, lungs burning from the cold. I threw up one night after practice, retching on all fours beside a shrunken, exhaust-blackened drift of snow near my car on Marshall Avenue while my friends laughed and lobbed snowballs at me. None of them knew that my life, which had just opened up with baseball and history scholarships to the College of Saint Thomas, was constricting around Betty's womb. Finally, on Saturday morning, listening for Mom's step on the stairs, I called Birthright and talked urgently in a low voice. The volunteer told me that my girlfriend needed to call, that we would want to come in. She said I was doing the right thing, sticking by my girlfriend and our baby. God had a plan He would reveal to us in time.

That night, in the car on the way to a Mexican wedding dance at the state fairgrounds, I told Betty about Birthright—that I was ready to do the honorable thing.

"I am *not* going to those people." Betty bit off the words, and I felt her close into herself on the other side of the car, saw her small, thin hand tighten on the door handle, as if she meant to leap from the car at the next stoplight.

We danced all evening, clinging to each other during the slow ones without talking. After the last set, we sat alone at the corner of a long table, drinking warm beer out of plastic cups. The band was packing up; a few scattered groups of people remained in the hall, talking in low, end-of-the-evening voices. We were soaked with sweat, and the emptying hall was suddenly cold.

Hank wandered by looking for his coat. His pinstriped vest was open, his tie loosened, and sweat stained the chest and armpits of his burgundy button-down shirt. "You two still here?" he said. But when he saw our faces, he swung his leg over a chair and sat down on it backward, arms crossed on the metal backrest. "What's going on?"

"I'm pregnant," Betty said.

"Jesus," I said, "that made it real."

Hank gave me a hard look, then turned on Betty. "Goddamn, I thought you were smarter than this."

"Hank." Betty's voice was pleading in a way I'd never heard.

"My sister didn't raise you to act like a whore," Hank said.

Betty's head jerked back, and I started to my feet. "How many kids did you mean to have?" I snapped at Hank.

He faced me full on and half rose himself, face dark with anger. "Sit down," he said. "I'm gonna forget you said that."

Betty began crying, twisting her purse strap. "Please, James—"

I forced myself to sit. "Look, I'm graduating," I said, suddenly desperate to fix things for them both. "My old man'll get me a union job."

Hank ignored me. "What are *you* going to do?" he said to Betty. "Look at me."

The lenses of her glasses were splashed with tears. "But I want to be a lawyer."

"I'll put you through law school," I said quickly. Neither of them heard.

"I'll tell you what you do," Hank said. "You get an abortion. I'll pay."

"I've got the money," I said. I didn't want Betty getting an abortion.

"My niece's honor is out of your hands." Hank flicked me a glance, then said to Betty, "This is one helluva thing you've gotten yourself into."

I tried again to argue that I could support Betty and a baby, but my words trailed off under Hank's cold gaze. Betty stared at her hands in her lap.

"Maybe we should talk to a priest," I said, playing my last card.

Hank laughed aloud at that. "Like who? Father Shannon?"

"Father Phil," I said. "He's been friends with my family for years."

Hank rested a hand on his thigh and squinted at me in a way that made my stupidity quite clear. "And what's he going to do?" he asked. "Last I heard, there weren't any special dispensations to end a pregnancy."

Beside Hank, Betty started to say something, then shook her head. "Please," she said. "I can't stand to think about it anymore tonight."

In the end, Hank walked with us out to Mom's Plymouth. There were only a few vehicles left in the lot. It was a blustery Minnesota spring night, a wind from Canada spitting snow, and we all stood there shivering and rubbing our arms. "You make a decision, Betty," Hank said. "Fast. Or this time next year there won't be any dances." Betty nodded, face pale around her red lipstick in the glare of the streetlight. At that moment, I hated the stickiness of her lips, the way women packaged their sexuality and used it. Hank put a hand on my shoulder. "I respect what you're going through, son."

I jerked away from him.

It started to sleet; ice crystals flickered in the street lamp's halo. Hank left us and walked across the lot to his truck, hunched and stumbling into the weather.

Midway

Tandem

Steven Lang

Lost somewhere in the middle of leafy, leisurely Otter Tail County sits Rush Lake, one of the smaller, lesser-known of the ten thousand or so we have to choose from here in Minnesota. In late August, lighthearted Otter Tail vacationers can overindulge in lighthearted vacation fare; in roadside stands selling fresh sweet corn, squash, green apples, and homemade pies; in main street dime stores selling arrowheads, rubber tomahawks, plastic Paul Bunyans and other north-woods trinkets; in guided fishing outings and canoe trips down small rivers and across chains of pristine lakes. Year by year, savvy local business owners get to know returning families, keeping mental inventories, noting changes, well aware that a few pleasantries go a long way. *Well, look who's back! My, you've grown! How's the missus?*

One August day nearly twenty years ago, my father and I, just the two of us this time, made the four-hour trip by car from Saint Paul north to Rush Lake. My father had reserved the same two-bedroom cabin at the Four Seasons Resort that we had rented the previous August, the August before that, and for every August I could remember before that. When we finally reached the Four Seasons Resort late that day, my father pulled our aging Volvo straight into its usual spot next to cabin number three. I was amazed at how little ever changed there, each of the seven cabins still the color of moss and still in need of paint, the resort owner's yellow Ford Bronco still rusting away under the carport, the miserable gazebo near the lakeshore more a patchwork of lattice than anything. It seemed even the grass refused to grow. That shabby sameness was what my father loved about Four Seasons Resort, besides the reasonable rates. It was what he called the *flavor of the place*. It meant something to him that the lodge owner wore sandals over white athletic socks, that the bicycles were rented on the honor system, that the families with Cadillacs and Lincolns were at lodges on the other side of the lake—the side with the sandy, groomed beaches and no weeds.

"Like we never left," my father said as the car engine sputtered to a stop. We got out of the car, stretched our legs, and breathed in the cool northern air. We wandered over to the main lodge slowly, as if laziness were a county mandate. The lodge, built in the nineteen forties, was a rough-hewn, two-story log cabin, decades newer than the shantylike cabins surrounding it, but aged by Minnesota's subzero winters and hot, humid summers. The logs oozed sap from every knot, and the fractured fieldstone chimney leaned precariously toward the lake. With its neon signs and *Four Seasons Resort* painted across the logs in bright yellow, the lodge was as boisterous as the cabins were muted. Stuffed inside the old log walls were a bar and grill, a liquor and convenience store, and a bait shop, as well as a home for the resort owner, Marty, and his daughter, Josie, a girl my age, then thirteen. As we stepped through the front door, my father could have said it again: *Like we never left*. The same baseball game played on the black-and-white television; the same forty-five-rpm spun in the jukebox; the same hamburger burned on the grill.

"*There* they are! Hot enough for you, Larry?" Marty kidded my father, wiping his brow in jest. The last week of August in northern Minnesota, with its forty-degree mornings, damp air, and bleak, cloudless skies, was only summer by the calendar.

"Hot?" My father shivered back at him. "Feels like we're in Winnipeg."

"Winnipeg? Raining up there, TV's saying. Just the two of you this year?"

"Raining, huh?" My father scratched his chin. "Well, let's get our key. We're only here for the weekend. Better get the car unpacked."

I stood by the jukebox. All the same feel-good songs I remembered: Conway Twitty, Crystal Gayle, Charlie Daniels, Olivia Newton John, The Gatlin Brothers. Still twenty-five cents a song, five for a dollar. I had grown up visiting this place each year of my life, and nothing here had ever changed. Now, I needed this sameness. I needed to know that there were people and places and things that did not change. I thought about Josie. I hoped that she would be the same Josie I had always known. There was something I hoped to tell her—something I had not been able to tell anyone else.

Marty got our key and my father signed the register. "Supposed to warm up tomorrow," Marty said. As we headed out the door, I glanced back at Marty, who turned away, tugging at the ties of his apron.

. . .

I was up early the next morning. I had the cabin to myself as my father slept behind his closed bedroom door. The tiny cabin had a small living room with a green love seat, a matching recliner, and a little black-and-white TV on a plastic stand. An old dial telephone sat on a round end table. The cubbyhole of a kitchen had a wide porcelain sink in front of a small square window facing the lake. Near the front door sat a rickety kitchen table with red plastic place mats and four yellow metal chairs.

I tried to imagine enduring a winter here as I zipped up my jacket, preparing to go out and fish from the small wooden dock. I took my fishing rod from the closet by the refrigerator and grabbed my tackle box, which I had organized and reorganized for weeks in advance. I reached into the refrigerator for the small container of earthworms I had dug from our garden at home. A full bottle of vodka sat in its usual place in the refrigerator door.

. . .

Perch and sunfish were the only kind of fish I had ever pulled out of Rush Lake, but with my new ultralight fishing rod and reel, a Daiwa Minicast my mother had given me the previous Christmas, I hoped that catching the wiggly half pounders would be more fun. Yet secretly, on my own, I had re-strung the reel with high-test filament, hoping to land a northern, a walleye, or the almost mythical muskellunge, a fish I now know would have yanked that rod right out of my hands had I been unlucky enough to hook one.

The air was cool and the dew in the grass soaked my shoes as I walked down to the shore. The water was high, nearly level with the ancient wooden dock. I assembled the rod, which I had practiced doing many times, tied a hook onto the thick line, and added a small bobber. I pulled a worm from the plastic container and worked it onto the hook, feeding the hook straight through the worm's body lengthwise just as I had seen on a TV fishing show. I took a deep breath, swung the pole back, and cast out. The bait landed a few yards past the weeds, sending ripples across the calm morning water.

"I'll bet you don't catch a thing!" A girl's voice from behind me echoed across the lake. I turned to see Josie—a somewhat older, taller Josie than the one I remembered from the year before, her red hair longer, her features more precisely drawn. I might have thought she was Josie's older sister, had there been one. She strode down the dock toward me, her now-lanky legs not entirely under her control. The warped boards of the dock creaked and slapped the surface of the water.

"You're scaring the fish away, Josie," I said.

She stopped beside me, kicking the toe of her left shoe between the slats of wood. "The fish? They'll come back."

I tugged on the line a little, then reeled in to recast. "You're up kind of early, aren't you Josie?"

"Not really. I saw your car. The blue station wagon. What kind of car is that again?"

"A Volvo."

"A Volvo. I thought it was darker blue than that. Did you get it painted?"

"No, got a new one."

"Oh. No one has Volvos up here. They look weird."

"Lots of people have them in Saint Paul. They're supposed to be safe or something."

"Safe?" She tilted her head, squinting at me.

"In an accident," I said. I looked closely at her eyes. She seemed to be wearing a small amount of mascara, something I had never seen her do. "So, you think I won't catch anything, huh?"

"Well, what are you fishing with?" She peered into the water.

I reeled in and pulled the bait up to the dock. "Worms."

"Worms? You need better bait than that." She tugged at my arm. "Come on, Eddie, follow me."

I set the pole on the dock, and she led me up to the lodge. As we neared the back door, I noticed five or six bicycles lined up on a rusty bike rack. One of them was built-for-two—a bright, metallic blue Schwinn with a pink wicker basket on the handlebars. I had never seen one like it before.

"Is that a new bike?" I asked her.

"Yep. It's called a *tandem*. My dad picked it out for the lodge. But the basket was my idea."

"I like it. The bike, I mean."

"Thanks. I think it's about time we get something new around here."

I wondered if I had been wrong, if things here really could change.

The lights were still off inside the lodge as Josie led me to where the live bait was kept. "Look," she said, pointing into a small, gurgling tank. "Minnows. We just got this tank, too. Isn't it cool? I've been waiting to show it to you."

"Really?" At home in Saint Paul, I had always imagined Josie busy fishing, helping her father, doing her homework, or just watching TV—anything but thinking about me. "We almost didn't come up this year," I said.

Josie glanced quickly at me, then turned to reach for a small green net that hung from a nail on the wall. She scooped up a few of the minnows and put them in a foam container along with a little of the tank water. "These minnows are guaranteed to catch a keeper."

"Really?"

"You'll see."

We headed back down to the dock. "Get rid of that worm," she told me. She poured a minnow into her hand, letting the water run through her fingers. "Here's a nice one. Careful. Don't drop it. You have to bait the hook 'cause you're the boy." She set the container down and put her hands on her hips, watching as I held the wriggling minnow in my cupped hand.

"I don't know how to bait a minnow," I said.

"Stick the hook through the mouth, then twist it so the barb comes out its stomach. It won't live long that way, but it won't fall off when you cast out. And it hides the hook from the fish. They never see what's coming until it's too late."

I slid the hook into the minnow's mouth, then curled the barb into its belly, popping it through the white flesh.

"Pretty good for a first time," Josie said. "Now raise that bobber a little."

I slid the bobber slowly up the line until Josie nodded. Then I cast out, just past the tall weeds, and we waited.

"This won't take long." Josie crossed her arms. "Hope that line is tough."

Just as I was about to mention the high-test filament, the bobber dove deep and fast into the water, nearly bending the rod in half. I tightened my grip on the pole as it thrashed and jerked.

"Whoa!" Josie took a step back. "That's a big one."

"It's just the pole," I said. "It bends easy."

"We'll see," she said. "The hook is set for sure. Let some line out for a second."

I released line, then brought it back tight.

"Now," Josie said, "reel it in!"

I pulled straight back on the pole, then eased it forward, reeling in as fast as I could. I repeated this motion over and over, just as I had seen on that same TV fishing show.

As the fish came into view, Josie yelled, "It's a *northern!*"

"A *northern?*" I blushed at my own excitement—an exuberance that belonged, I felt, to a much younger boy.

"You know, a *northern pike.* A real game fish. Don't worry, they're in season. We're gonna need a net, or you'll break that line for sure."

Before I could tell her about the high-test filament, she ran back up to the lodge. I had to keep the fish busy, letting out a little line, slowly reeling in again as the fish fought me in a zigzag pattern. Its scales flashed in the sunlight each time it neared the surface. Josie returned quickly, bounding down the dock once again, this time carrying a long aluminum net in one hand and a white plastic cooler in the other.

"Move over," she said.

I stepped to one side. Josie knelt down at the end of the dock. "Reel in a little more. Easy." She dipped the net into the water. "Easy. Here he comes." As the northern sliced across the surface, still far out of my control, Josie thrust the net forward and snared the fish with one quick sweep. "Got it!" She stood up, raising the netted fish for me to see.

"It's big." I wanted to say *huge*, but guarded against the return of that boyish zeal.

Josie opened the cooler and dropped the flailing fish inside. She rinsed her hands in the lake water and dried them on her dark blue jeans. "I'd say it's a four pounder. That's pretty good."

"Four *pounds?*" I slipped up again. "I can't wait until my dad sees this."

"Let's go show it to him."

I closed the lid of the cooler. "He won't be up for a while. Let's just keep it in the cooler for now."

"Okay. But you need to put some water in there." She pulled her long red hair back and held it in a ponytail. "It's supposed to get hot today. Like eighty."

"Really?"

"Really. My dad said a big warm front's moving north. It won't get warm like this again till next year." She let her hair fall. "Maybe we can swim later. Want to?"

"There's too many weeds," I said.

"Not in the lake, in the pool."

"Oh. Maybe. I guess. If it's going to be eighty."

"It is." She smiled. "*And* we just got a new diving board."

. . .

The sun gained strength by the hour, and by noon I was forced to shed the warm clothes I had worn that morning in favor of swimming trunks and a T-shirt. I spent most of the day on the dock, pulling in my usual perch and sunfish, tossing them back, probably catching a few of the same little fish twice. I didn't manage to catch another northern or any other big fish, but I already had my keeper.

Late that afternoon, my dad filleted the northern, breaded the fillets, and panfried them. I invited Josie, who brought potatoes and fresh green beans from the lodge. The three of us ate together at our cabin's tiny kitchen table.

"This was some fish, Ed," my father said as he finished his last bite. "I knew you had angler in you. You're lucky. I never learned to fish as a kid."

I looked over to Josie. "Well, I had a little help," I said.

"It was no big deal." Josie looked at me. It appeared that she had washed off the mascara. "I fish here all the time," she said, "so I know what works and what doesn't."

My father smiled at Josie. "She's a great little lake, isn't she?"

"Well, I think so," Josie said, looking down at her plate.

"That's what Mom used to say, right Dad?" I passed my hand through the air, palm forward, the way my mother would have. "She's a great little lake."

The smile was gone. My father stood up, picked up his plate, and set it in the sink. Josie picked at her food. I set my fork down and traced the edges of the plastic place mat with my thumbs.

My father stared out the kitchen window for a few seconds, then said, "Let's go over to the lodge. We'll see what your dad's up to, Josie."

"Probably just watching TV," she said.

We left our plates at the table. The three of us walked to the lodge without another word between us.

. . .

When we entered the lodge, Marty called out as soon as he saw me. "Eddie! I heard you caught Moby Dick out there this morning!"

"A real fisherman," my dad said, taking a seat at the bar. "I guess you weren't kidding about the heat after all, Marty. What did it get up to today?"

"Eighty-three. Still eighty out there. You guys must have brought the heat up from the Cities with you."

My father pointed at the beer tap and nodded. "We wanted to leave the Cities behind," he said.

Marty set a coaster on the bar. Josie walked to the back room. "That fish was more like Jaws than Moby Dick," she said, returning with a small bag, a diving mask, and fins. "I can't believe that line didn't snap."

I realized then that I would never reveal the high-test filament. "Just lucky, I guess."

"*Very* lucky," she said. "Well, are you ready to swim?"

"Now? I thought you weren't supposed to swim right after you eat," I said.

"I always do. But if you want, you can just watch me dive off the new diving board. I've got lots of different dives down perfect."

"All right." I turned to my father. "Dad, I'm going to the pool, okay?"

He was looking up at a car race on TV as Marty set a glass of beer in front of him. "The pool," he said. "Yeah, okay."

"Josie, no back flips," Marty warned her. "You'll hit your head."

"Fine."

. . . .

The swimming pool was as rough and cracked as a cement pool that still held water could be. It wasn't big, but it had a deep end, probably eight or nine feet deep, where the new diving board was installed. Josie set her fins and mask on one of the reclining deck chairs and walked into the wooden bathhouse. She came out a minute later wearing a white, one-piece swimsuit and orange flip-flops.

"I just got this suit. How do you like it?" Josie held her arms out, twisting her thin body at the waist.

I turned to concentrate on a leaf floating in the water. "It's nice."

"I got it up in Fargo. We go there when I visit my mom. You probably know, my parents are divorced."

I kept my eye on the leaf.

Josie headed straight for the board and stepped out of the flip-flops. She climbed up and walked out to the end. She turned around and balanced on her toes at the end of the board, preparing for a back flip. With a sudden surge, she sprung up and arced gracefully backward, slipping headfirst into the water with less of a splash than when she netted the northern.

She touched the bottom of the pool, spun her legs around, and shot quickly to the surface. "It's gonna rain," she said, as she paddled to the edge of the pool. She was right. It was getting dark to the north and west. I could see storm clouds on the horizon across the highway. "You can see the sky better when you're upside down. You should try a back flip. It's fun."

"I can't do back flips," I said. "I have a bad back."

"A *what?*" Her mouth hung open in disbelief as she climbed from the pool. "You're how old? Thirteen? You can't have a bad back yet. That's just an excuse because you're scared to try it."

"Sorry. No back flips. Can't do it."

"Your loss." She shrugged her shoulders and stepped onto the diving board again. She strode the length of the board and stood facing me this time. "I begged my dad for this board all last year. He finally gave in. I think it's an *amenity*. An *amenity* we can't do without. What's a pool without a diving board? Watch this one." She waved me over. "Get right up here so you can see this." She bounced three times on the end of the board, launched herself into the air, then curled up in a tight ball as she plunged into the water. I tried to duck the splash, but it drenched me. Josie came up laughing. "Sweet! You're soaked!" Josie dipped her head back into the water to straighten her long hair. "You might as well jump in the pool now. You can't get any wetter."

I was about to jump in when thunder rumbled in the distance, ominous and low. The clouds were restless. A faraway flash of lightning struck, and a few seconds later, more thunder. Josie quickly pulled herself out of the water. "Not good," she said, looking out over the highway. Water dripped from her face and hair onto her shoulders, streaming down her arms and back, falling to the wet cement.

Thunder rumbled again, closer this time, and the smell of rain was now in the air. "You can't swim when there's lightning. Let's go back over. Come on, I'll buy you a pop." The look in her eyes told me she did not like storms. She snatched up her bag, fins, and mask, and we walked quickly back to the lodge.

. . .

"I need to change," she said, as she walked past her father into the back room.

"I could use a towel," I said.

"Here. This is clean," Marty said, tossing me a fresh bar towel which I used to dry my hair and face. "Fell for the cannonball trick, huh?"

"I guess so. Where's my dad?"

"Your dad?" Marty ran his fingers through his thin, graying hair. "He said he was tired. He went back to your cabin."

"It's gonna storm," I said. "I should get back over there and close the windows."

"Your dad can do that, can't he? Why don't we ride out the storm here, in the lodge?" Marty pulled out his best grin. "You, me, and Josie can watch it rain, play some eight ball, listen to the jukebox. I love a good rainstorm."

"Don't you know my dad by now? I've got to get going."

"He'll be all right, Eddie." Marty let his grin fade.

"See you later, Marty."

...

I walked outside. The wind had picked up. Oak and birch leaves fluttered along the ground, and the tops of the pine trees by the lake lurched the way my fishing pole had under the weight of the northern. When I got to our cabin, my father was sitting at the kitchen table, the now half-empty vodka bottle on the place mat in front of him. He held the small white bottle cap in his right hand.

"We'll go fishing in the morning," he said, staring at the cap, twisting it in his fingers. "Rent a little boat. Catch our limit." With a groan, he stood up. He picked up the bottle, replaced the cap, and walked into the bedroom.

...

I changed out of my soaked shirt and swimming trunks into a gray sweater and jeans. I turned on the little black-and-white TV. There were only two channels, "The Muppet Show" on one and "Mary Tyler Moore" on the other. I chose "The Muppet Show." It was just beginning as Kermit, flailing his frog arms in the air, introduced the special guest, Sandy Duncan. After a minute or so, I turned the sound down and just watched, listening instead to the rustling leaves. The rain began to fall, the droplets sounding off the sheet metal of our car like clear notes in perfect tune. Just then, words began to scroll across the bottom of the screen. WEATHER ALERT. SEVERE STORM WARNING, OTTER TAIL COUNTY. I was sure my mother would have hated this. She hated storms more than anyone. Her timing was impeccable. I turned the sound back up.

I got up and looked in at my father. He was passed out on the bed, the nearly empty bottle next to him on the sheet. Rain was already collecting on the sill of the bedroom window. I closed the window, closed the door on him, then closed the rest of the windows throughout the cabin, ending with the small kitchen window, the only one with a view of the lake. The sun, which would not be setting for another half an hour, was no match for these storm clouds; it was nearly dark as night already. Out on the lake, I saw the indigo silhouette of a small boat pulling up to the dock in the choppy gray water. A family of four jumped out. They tied the boat off quickly, hauled in their water skis and life vests, and ran to their cabin. They were just boaters, I thought. Real *fishermen* could handle a little storm.

A knock at the cabin door startled me. I opened it to see Josie propping back the screen door with her foot. She held an umbrella in one hand, a bottle of Pepsi in the other. "You forgot about your pop," she said, handing me the glass bottle. "My dad sent me over with it, that is." She rolled her eyes. "He thinks storms are *so* much fun." Still barefoot, she had changed into a pair of faded blue jeans and a green sweatshirt with a crude drawing of the lake and *Four Seasons Resort* printed in yellow.

"I like storms too," I told her, "but my mom hated them."

"So does mine." She pointed at the bottle. "My mom knows a guy in Fargo who puts empty pop bottles in a big oven and stretches them out like taffy. He sells them at flea markets. They're really cool." She looked down at her feet. "Well, anyway, I gotta get back."

"Thanks for the pop." I looked out past Josie at the rain hitting the asphalt parking lot. "Better hurry," I said. "It's starting to pour."

Just then the TV beeped several times, and I turned to see the weather alert still scrolling across the screen. "What's this?" Josie closed her umbrella and stepped in past me.

The scrolling words continued. *TORNADO WARNING, OTTER TAIL COUNTY.* The warning named the cities in the line of the storm—*DETROIT LAKES, FRAZEE, PELICAN RAPIDS, PERHAM.*

Josie looked back at me. "This is bad. I gotta get back."

"All right. But hurry. Be careful."

As she headed for the door, the wind surged, pulling the screen door wide open, then blowing it shut again. Rain began to fall in sheets, bouncing off the cement doorstep, splashing in through the screen door.

"Josie, you shouldn't go out in this." I wanted her to stay.

"My dad will be worried," she said, looking out toward the lodge.

Thunderbolts clapped in quick succession. The lightning became almost constant, illuminating the cabins and trees in strobelike pulses.

"You can call your dad on the phone, tell him you're stuck over here." I set the bottle down next to the phone and picked up the receiver. "What's the number?"

The TV beeped again. I looked at the screen. The Muppets were dancing, playing instruments, laughing. *TORNADO WARNING, OTTER TAIL*

*COUNTY. RESIDENTS ADVISED TO TAKE COVER IMMEDI-
ATELY.* Then, with a high-pitched pop, the power went out and the image disappeared. The screen glowed a ghoulish white, leaving the cabin in near darkness. I hung up the phone.

Josie dropped her umbrella and put her hands over her ears. "What's that noise?"

From outside the cabin came a deep, rumbling howl that shook the ground with the weight of a diesel locomotive, but it was wilder, chaotic, the sound of a machine from before there were machines.

"It's a tornado!" Josie shrieked. "These cabins don't have basements! What should we do?"

I could feel Josie's fear as I had felt my own fear that spring, the evening when I came home late from a bike ride to find exhaust fumes churning from the tailpipe of our Volvo, filling our dark, locked garage with carbon monoxide.

I grabbed Josie's arm. I pulled her toward the closet and quickly inside, slamming the door shut. We crouched down against the wall and held each other. Josie buried her face in my sweatshirt. The telephone began to ring.

"Don't let go!" She forced the words through tears.

The cabin lurched, the windows rattled, and rain lashed against the cabin's siding like buckshot. We had done all we could do. We held on, the tornado still sounding like a train at full speed. I counted eight rings of the telephone, the storm nearly drowning them out. Another ring, a broken window, another ring, an object hitting the cabin, the final ring. I closed my eyes. I could see my mother, could see her slumped behind the wheel in our dark garage, the windows down, the radio on, me shaking her. I could see my father passed out on the couch in our basement, an empty vodka bottle on the floor, me trembling, me shaking him, everything spinning, everything ending.

Josie shivered in my arms, her hair still wet from the pool and smelling of chlorine. We didn't move and we didn't speak. Then, as quickly as it had risen, the rumbling faded. The tornado spun itself out onto the lake, maybe, or just lifted back up into the sky. Josie held on to me for another full minute. Finally, in the relative quiet, she let go. She stood and opened the closet door. When we emerged, the cabin seemed illuminated. Every surface reflected a dim bluish light from an unknown source.

Water covered the linoleum in front of the cabin door. I picked up the phone. The line was dead. Through the wet screen door, I could see it was calm outside—little wind, little rain now. Josie picked up her umbrella. Without a word to me, without even looking back, she pushed out the door and ran home. There was a faint, shifting beam of light shining from the lodge window. Her father. I leaned out the door and counted each of the other six cabins—all were intact. The worst, it seemed, was over.

. . .

In the morning I heard the Ford Bronco roar to life. I got up from the couch and warily stepped outside. An aluminum fishing boat had been tossed on top of a speedboat near the dock and in the parking lot a car sat upside-down, its roof torn and twisted. Our Volvo was covered in asphalt shingles and tar paper, and had taken a dent in the fender, but was otherwise undamaged. Several tall pines were toppled, their roots exposed like innards, the ground mostly mud and pools of water.

Marty stepped out of the idling truck and plodded over to me. "You all right?" He put his hand on my shoulder.

"Yeah."

"You did a good thing last night. Stayed calm. Your dad okay?"

"I guess. He slept through it all." I met Marty's gaze, then looked away. I left him there and walked toward the lodge. The fieldstone chimney had cracked and toppled to the ground. The neon signs lay shattered below the blown-out windows. An uprooted pine that just missed crushing the lodge had torn a hole in the ground so deep and wide it could have held our car. The bottom of the hole was so wet, the mud so soft and penetrable, I imagined diving in head first and never coming up.

Just then, Josie's voice came from behind me. "Don't fall in."

I turned to see her trudging toward me, her shoes caked with mud. "I won't," I said.

She glanced around. "I can't believe all the cabins made it. So much other stuff is gone or wrecked. I can't find the new bike. The tandem. It's not in that hole, is it?"

"No." I shook my head and put my hands in my pockets. "But I can help you look for it."

"It's gotta be around here somewhere. I want to ride up the highway a little. See what's what. You wanna come?"

"Sure. But my dad and I are leaving today. I can't be gone long."

"We won't be." Josie took a step backward. "Whoever finds it gets to ride in front. I'll check around the lakeshore."

"Okay," I said. "I'll check over by the pool." As Josie turned to walk away, I looked back down in the hole. I felt a chill at the thought of being trapped, buried in that muddy grave.

I walked across the spongy wet grass to the pool. All the deck chairs but one had been blown away. Hundreds of oak and birch leaves covered the surface of the water. I brushed a few leaves aside with my hand and scanned the bottom of the pool for any sign of the bike. There were a few sunken deck chairs, nothing else. I thought about Josie's graceful back dive. I wondered what she might look like diving into this pool of leaves, her red hair and white swimsuit disappearing under a blanket of green. I imagined her paddling slowly, trailing leaves behind her, then cutting across the water in brisk strokes, splashing and sending leaves in all directions.

"I'm driving!" Josie called as she rode up to the pool. She stopped and signaled me onto the back of the bike.

"Where was it?"

"Where the gazebo used to be."

"Is it okay to ride?"

"One pedal is bent, and the basket is gone, but the rest seems fine." She gripped the handlebars, her right foot on the bent pedal. "Come on, let's go."

We coasted across the parking lot and Josie aimed the bike north onto Highway 108. After half a mile or so, she turned to the right, down a dirt road marked "Private." The road was muddy and puddled and at times we almost slowed to a stop, struggling to keep the bike moving forward on the soft surface. The road curved gently to the left. As we came around the bend, a fallen oak blocked our way. Josie squeezed the hand brakes and we stopped.

"There's no way around," she said, looking left then right. "It's too muddy in the ditch. We've got to lift the bike over." The wide trunk of the tree lay across the road, a hurdle as high as my waist. We stepped off the bike. Josie lifted up on the handlebars and rolled the front wheel over the tree. "Now your end," she said, looking over to me. I grasped the rear seat and frame, swinging the long, heavy bike up on its left side across the trunk. I vaulted myself over the tree. As I landed, my feet made deep impressions in the wet road.

Josie looked at me across the trunk of the tree. "Eddie," she said. Her eyes became glassy. She pulled her arms in front of her chest, embracing herself. "I was really scared last night, Eddie."

"I was too." I didn't lie.

"I mean scared like I've never been."

I stepped out of the footprints. "Well, it's okay now. We made it. Everybody made it."

"Eddie?" Her voice was hushed and delicate. She drew a deep breath and carved a line in the wet road with her foot. "I'm sorry about your mom."

I looked past her up the road, rejecting her grace. "What do you know about it?"

"Your dad told my dad yesterday while we were at the pool." She looked down and retraced the line she had drawn. "And my dad told me. I'm really sorry."

"I'm not sorry." My voice shook. "Not for her."

Josie looked back up at me, then reached her hand across the tree. "Here," she said, "help me climb over." I took her hand. She planted her foot on the tree, glided up and over, and stepped down next to me.

"Eddie, if you hadn't pulled me in that closet, I might have tried to run home, been caught in the storm, and . . ." She kept hold of my hand as her voice trailed off.

I wanted to tell her everything right there. Tell her things my father didn't even know, things he would never know. That he was so drunk I couldn't wake him the night my mother died. That I knew I couldn't call for help or they might have taken *him* from me, too. That I pretended to be asleep when he found her the next morning. But I kept quiet.

"There's something up the road I want to show you, Eddie," she said, her voice regaining its composure.

"What is it?"

"First the bike." She let go of my hand, and I helped her pull the bike down. We got on and continued up the road, our path gently wavering from side to side. Trees along the road waded in vast puddles, almost lakes in their own right. Squirrels, still shaken from the storm, flung themselves nervously from branch to branch, surveying the damage. We rode in silence until the northern shore of Rush Lake came into view. Near the shore stood a small red structure.

"It's still standing," she said. "I was worried."

"What is it?"

"It's an ice house."

"For ice fishing?"

"Of course. What else?"

My father had always hated winter. We never left town when it was cold, and I had never seen an ice house in person. It looked like a grounded tree house to me, with its tiny windows and narrow door. We pulled up to it and stopped, leaning the bike against its back wall. "Whose is it?" I asked.

"My dad's. We haul it out onto the lake in December and fish."

"You come up this road in *winter?*"

Her eyes narrowed. "This isn't the moon, you know. People live here."

"Winter's bad enough at home. I don't think I could stand it up here."

"You don't know what you're missing. You and your dad should come back up after Christmas this year. We could ice fish all day. It's fun. Really. It gets so warm inside the ice house you don't even need a jacket." She stepped past me and opened the door. The wood made a wet moan. She turned to me. "Look."

I leaned inside the door. "It's dark."

"That's winter up here," she said. "But I know you're not scared of the dark. You can't be. Not anymore."

She was wrong. In my mind it was still dark, our Volvo was still running, the exhaust still choking me.

"Go inside," she said. "I know you're not scared."

I stepped inside the ice house. The torrent of the previous night had left it wet throughout. As my eyes adjusted to the darkness, I could see a stack of swollen newspapers and magazines on a bench across the back wall and a small wood-burning stove with a round metal duct leading straight up to the flat roof. I felt claustrophobic, the ice house not much bigger than the closet had been. Josie stepped inside.

"It's so small," I said.

"Just like last night." And with that she closed the door. I could hear her force something into the door handle. The darkness was endless, darker even than it had been with the tornado bearing down on us. I took one step toward the door and caught my foot in the fish hole. I fell onto the wet, cold carpet.

So this is it, I thought. This is what my mother had wanted. This darkness, this abyss. When I had stood by her casket that spring, I thought about closing it on her, right in front of everyone, shutting her away. *She looks so peaceful,* they all said. *Your mother was very ill, but she loved you just the same,* they all said. *Tell her you love her, Eddie, before it's too late.* But I kept quiet. I knew she wanted this darkness, a place where fear didn't matter anymore.

I stood up. "Let me out."

"First," Josie said, blocking the door, "I want you to tell me something."

"Just let me out."

"I'll let you out. But first, tell me."

"Tell you what?" I pleaded.

"That you love me."

I said nothing. It would have been so easy to tell her. But I kept quiet.

"Tell me, Eddie, please."

Water seeped through the roof and walls; the smell of rot consumed me. Cracks of light around the door cut through, and I could hear birds singing and a speedboat out on the water. I closed my eyes. I could feel her in front of me, could feel the tornado still shaking the ground, my eyes shut tight, in my mind Josie still diving into the pool, netting the northern, running back to her father after the storm. The fallen trees, the puddles of water, the tandem bicycle, the ice house. The Volvo, the exhaust, my mother, the casket. It would have been so easy to tell her. But I kept quiet.

She reached for me and I pushed past her. I kicked the door and it flew open. The twig that had held it shut fell in pieces to the ground. Daylight poured in. Josie slipped past me and immediately onto the bicycle. She rode off on her own, standing up on the pedals, driving hard through the gravel and mud. The tire tracks of our coming and her leaving marked the road as clearly as a signature on a contract.

Sketchbook: Atmospheric Conditions

Anastasia Faunce

Camouflage is the blending of the animal into the pattern, the environment; it is a search for invisibility. To attain this objective it is essential for the animal to lose its identity, that is to say to efface its outline, to assume one even color. . . . Above all, it must remain still: every movement will give it away unless such movement is one in keeping with the surroundings.

—Roger Caillois, *The Mask of Medusa*

1

I will begin by telling you what he told her—she being X, a physicist, and he being Y, the lover who left her, left her with all this new knowledge and longing, left her, is long gone, only his sketchbook left behind: *"In any good drawing, the subject drawn must reflect its yearning."*

He was an artist constantly seeking ideals and balance, creating what was not from what was. She knew he had been disappointed in her inability to see into things, to rearrange them, to make impressions. He continually explained to her that the sentiment, and consequently, the appearance of something was an entirely arbitrary choice on the part of the viewer.

"It's the color of the light that falls," he would say as he pointed to the work of Monet, a series of paintings with the same subject, in order to illustrate how Monet would work a number of canvases at a time, moving from one

to another as the circumstance of light changed. *"The light, or even the lack of light, changes everything. Don't you see?"* But she didn't see. She pretended to understand why this was so important.

See her here, deserted, alone, as she contemplates lovers with insatiable desires—Tristan and Isolde, Heloïse and Abélard, Heathcliff and Kathy, Kelly and Caron—this yearning he once impressed upon her, the words like small birds flying from the warm nest of his mouth. She understands it now—longing that will not yield—it is just like he said. This is what happened.

2

But this is not exactly what happened. Who knows what happened, really? It is certain that he, the artist, is gone, long gone, and that yearning is now the thing she knows best. It has the openness and freedom of a sketch, moves like a delicate, deceitful breeze through the apartment, rattles the heavy wooden doors with its true weight, then tears through the moorish room like the brute-force wind it really is.

The view from here is familiar. The landscape, decidedly midwestern, is hot with the fiery bite of late winter. See the view from her fourth-story window as she looks out over the park and the city's abundant skyline. The weather, uncertain, is caught in the great divide between winter gust and vernal blossom. A light snow moves through the air with restless, circular flakes, the dizzying waltz of Anna and Count Vronsky; it rides the wind in preordained patterns like the elegant wave of some beautiful float queen.

It is decidedly unscientific. She watches it for hours, which is why it appears before you now—this small picture of her at the window watching the weather—so you will know what it is like to live here with her. But who is to say what it is like, really, least of all you, least of all her.

3

At least she has her cat, her books and her cat. Observe them together, blanket wrapped in this cold room, Seamus' nocturnal bel canto purr coming from beneath the tight knit of the cover. The phone rings (brother, best friend, banker, landlord, lab supervisor, and on) and she flinches, knocking over three piles of books (almanacs, atlases, dictionaries, encyclopedias, flow charts, natural history guides, the periodic table, any and all volumes that contain the answers to questions), their solid forms once stacked like a smorgasbord of sandwiches atop the carpet's dull platter. In total: a demanding nineteen volumes and twenty-one voice-mail messages in thirteen days.

She no longer wonders who is calling, just rearranges the pillow on her bed, stares out at the city, and ignores the phone's persistent plea. See her hand perch at her mouth and the words she tries to comprehend. See her pull on the puckering skin of her lips as she traces the tiny trails of his speaking.

"*I'm going away,*" *he says, head tucked deep into his chest—unable, unwilling to look at her as she stands incredulous before him.*

"*Away?*"

Away? Away. Now her fingers are quick as claws, small talons scratching through the dictionary to get at the meat of his mantra, to produce a definition, an exacting strand of words.

Away: from this or that place; in another direction; a game to play on an opponent's grounds; a manner, fashion, style. A passage, a means. Also: far, distant, gone, moving, taken, parting from one's possession, without hesitation or delay. Or: out of existence, to an end, as in, the distance we have to go; as in, I cannot bear to be; as in, if there's a will there's. . . .

"Yes, away. As in, I'm leaving. I need some time, space."

She had wanted to be witty, brimming with Audrey-Hepburn-like ease and savoir faire but, "*Are you taking your drawings?*" was all she had been able to muster.

4

She spies on herself in his memory, hoping to better manage a mistake, reverse an attitude, admit a failing, so she can make it all right. But she can't locate herself there; she can only see him draw.

When he draws birds it takes all the strength he can muster. His hands ignite like fireflies released from a jar into a darkened room—white fingers fanning like feathers as small graphite starlings land softly on paper. His sketchbooks are filled with birds and insects, ornithological and entomological studies—a cacophony of locust, cicada, quail and shrike—ethereal images drawn side by side in heroic proportions.

Watch as she turns the page of the sketchbook to reveal a loose-leaf drawing of a giant snowy owl inserted randomly into the book; how, before she can turn another page, Seamus bounds from his perch at the open window to pounce on the owl, tawny cat fur flying through the air like molting. Seamus is gregarious, rolls like an acrobat across the book, pausing only for a moment to appease her, so that she may rub the white lichen of his belly.

She knows that as the weather turns he will yearn for the park, its infant birds, spindly trees, and long grassy stretches. He has been inside too long and has taken to pacing the sill and wailing whenever he hears the soft croon of Chief Nels, the neighborhood homeless man who she is certain is Norwegian but who wears a traditional Indian headdress and sleeps in the small alcove in the back of the building.

For Seamus, for Chief Nels, she welcomes spring. For herself, she wants nothing more than for the weather to remain cold, for winter to sit tight in its unsociable, dark shroud, for the room to remain in shadow as if lit only with the strange property of fireflies. She straightens the page and traces a talon with her finger, invokes this bird whose wings can spread as wide as the breadth of water.

He bends down and looks at the cover of the book that is concealing her research paper, "Curie's Law: The Coefficients of Magnetic Attraction," and teases, "Ah, Jane Eyre. Good for you!"

"It's about attics and the women who love them."

"Seriously, you need to get out of the lab."

"I am out of the lab," she says, doing her best c'est la vie flourish into the air.

"No, you're not," he says, pulling Curie from Eyre and tossing it aside, mock flourish. "You need," he says—flourish, flourish—"to get out of the lab."

Hear the quick snap of the paper as it flies from the carpet, the result of another Seamus pounce. See the giant snowy owl as it crumples into three dimensions and is batted about the room between cat paws—flutter to flight, like one desperate to rise.

5

Friday morning: *Breakfast at Tiffany's.* She stares out the window and looks for something strong to rise in the changing winter landscape, unable to watch the TV as Holly Golightly throws Cat from the taxi and into the pouring rain—a wingless creature abandoned, deserted, alone—a sight more dark, more forlorn than Pound's black bough.

She looks for Seamus and finds him sitting on the sill, licking moisture from the window with long, fluid lines. It is four a.m.: the streets are quiet with morning as she wipes the night's foggy breath from the windows to create a portal to the outside, a place she does not go.

Though she knows the answer, has seen the movie one hundred times before, she frets over how long it will take Audrey Hepburn to go back for Cat. She stops the movie and listens to the veristic sounds of winter: the radiator's deep growl and drip—like something just barely alive; the harsh scraping of a shovel on ice and pavement; car tires spinning across slushy streets; the droning moan of church bells; the absence of wind; the whisper of a lone car engine moving slowly toward somewhere that is not here. In her isolation, she is, has become, a small town where the train goes through and never stops.

She ponders: if Y leaves Chicago for an unknown destination on a cold day in February, and X remains forever in the place of Y's leaving, how long before X and Y again intersect?

And what exactly does Holly Golightly want? This, she cannot comprehend. Holly has it all: a New York flat, a steady income from Sally Tomato's prison cell, and George Peppard, who is mad for her. The thought of Cat having to seek refuge in a cardboard box hits her with its full, poignant weight so she cannot bear to look at Seamus, whose nose is still pressed to the glass when he should be sleeping, sleeping soundly in this small, tortured room.

6

She tortures herself in small sketches. It is her consolation—the way she makes herself feel worse, a giving in to the grieving—her most extravagant necessity, her most necessary extravagance.

See her fingers as they riffle through the abandoned book, assault its pages like surefire bullets. Watch her face as she stares at two naked figures, roughly sketched—a woman on the left page, a man on the right—their backs fused on the pages that come together at the book's inner spine. It seems to her a message, a maddening code, a small hint of sorcery.

She thinks of the Greek symbol for God: a man, a woman, standing back to back in precisely this manner. Perhaps they are leaning against one another for support, or defense, or in defense? Or perhaps the symbol refers to the moment in Genesis when the disputed rib was cut free? Divine or divided symmetry? Or perhaps they share muscle, hair, skin, as Siamese twins? Or perhaps they share an even deeper organ—a communal heart, the same metronomic beating?

But the beauty of the metaphor falters in the face of the truth before her: joined, yes, but for how long, and why are they facing in opposite directions? Why have they turned? The phone rings and she does not move. Turn on a dime; turn on one's heel; turn on a friend.

She kisses his cheek, starts toward the bedroom and says, "I'm turning in."

"Turning into what?" he asks. He calls her Jane Err.

She conjures his spirit, a riddle that is lasting.

7

His sketches carry a spirit, are riddled with a precise lyric that rivals even the most beautifully crafted phrases. She examines the sketchbook as if it were an elemental chart, a periodic table, a key to the things that quicken his heart: antennae, wing, and eye; talon and beak; breast, arm, and thigh— stable isotopes rendered in small, manageable portions.

Here is a Comet Moth, or scientifically, *Argema mittrei*. She reads: *The Comet Moth navigates by starlight. Night-flying males locate mates by following a trail of female pheromones. But still, the males need a reference point, so they fix on a star or the moon and fly toward it, keeping themselves oriented always to the light.*

She wonders about a moth's capacity to determine latitude, longitude, the moon's vast distance, and if a moth ever believes it can fly beyond its given talents, the power of pheromones propelling its wings beyond the bony whiteness of a star.

She thinks of the tabular arrangement of elements in the periodic table, then counts, tries to chart the number of times she has wept in her lifetime. She calculates her propensity for misunderstanding.

8

Her sleep is calculated, chimerical, teeming with misconstrued words and images, senses and theories—the silence of Cage, the white of Rauschenberg, the dangerous mimicry of an insect.

Here is a mackerel skilled in its vanishing: its back, indigo, the color of the sea; its belly, white, the color of the surface water or a clouded sky. Two colors, two sides, simultaneously melting into two backgrounds as it courses through the water, its energy first loud and surging, then dulling, its frantic fins slowing to wings, its full and fleshy form turning delicate, paper thin.

Now we are in a forest with Nabokov. He and his wife are carrying large nets as they search for rare moths and butterflies. He wears a tan suit, his wife, a blousy white dress. Both are outfitted in ridiculously large hats that sag with graceful swoops of mesh. They come upon a sluggish moth remarkable only for its seeming exhaustion, the strange white of its wing.

"*Euglyphis braganza*," Mrs. Nabokov announces, pointing to her guidebook. She reads: "The white pattern on the costa of the hind wing is intelligible only when the insect is seen alive at rest. In common with others of the same genus, this moth has a habit of passing the day motionless on tree trunks."

Nabokov nods, says nothing. He places the moth in his specimen jar and writes in his notebook: *The eternal nocturnal.* He walks ahead, motions to his wife, begins to whistle.

She wakes to the chanting of Chief Nels, the responding cry of Seamus, then returns to the ease of sleep: nature's quiet, perfect undoing.

9

In the mornings, she can feel the returning heat, the ease of sleep on the tiny buds of her tongue. The weather has turned, signaled by the damp of Eos, the taste and smell of things buried too long underground: feathers, fruit, and shells—rotting twigs and tubers. From the window, the topsoil looks damp and stony. See her as she turns an ear to spring's cabaletta—the birds' frantic aria, vocal pyrotechnics, and the sustained high note that drives the audience wild with apoplectic desire.

Seamus is sluggish, no longer entertained by hiding in baskets, cupboards, drawers—the thrill of concealment gone. From the bath, she can hear him cry at the window's sill; the faint "Here kitty, kitty," swoon of Chief Nels in return.

She maneuvers her body, concentrates on the wall's endless white tiles, the faint smell of caulk that is overtaking the squares' yellowing creases. She moves and water swells from the tub onto the floor, drenching the towel she is using for a bath mat. She does not care—is too tired to care—sinks deeper into the tub, causing another small wave and considers the mating probabilities of birds of passage and homing pigeons.

The heat of the water reminds her of blood coursing through veins at rapid speed, pumping life into the body's fleshy vessel like synaptic firings, uncontrollable urges and failings, the incredible ache for love—its tiny, tricky kiss.

She studies the red swell of her body, the winglike sag of skin beneath her arm, then swirls the bath to integrate the water's dark pools of cool and warm, winter and spring. Her white breasts break through the bath's quiet eddies like the belly of a mackerel and she thinks of his kiss, deep and unexpected, their two tongues darting like fish in water.

When she steps from the tub, Seamus rubs against her wet legs, uncertain what is floor or ceiling, earth or sky, in the thick fog of the bathroom. Watch as she blows on the mirror's warm frost, draws a small circle with her finger, peers in with only one eye.

10

She knows from him, the lover who is gone, long gone, that it is bad luck to remove a page from an otherwise complete sketchbook. This is why you see her here, still unwilling to believe this was something he would have done intentionally. She runs her finger along the splice in the book's solid center—the Exacto cut chlorine clean, sharp as winter. There is nothing to navigate on this pure plane, no stain of a bird or winged creature taking flight. The page is ether, air, ozone—its atmosphere empty, unproven. Her mind reels with what may have once been here, what was once, what may have been.

On the next page, a Brazilian moth with windowlike wings whose pencil-line veins and white scales give the illusion of a moldy leaf infected by fungus or gnawed by caterpillars. Next to the moth, his notes read: *A change of color to that of the environment can often be enough, but in the most extraordinary cases, the entire structure of the being is modified—down to the most minute detail—in order to achieve a deceptive appearance.*

She considers camouflage, an insect's capacity to change and conceal. She sees these insects as spies, spellbinders, deceitful agents in tiny-winged trench coats. She thinks of Columbo, returns to the mark of the missing page, and allows her mind to reel with invisibilities: *The Emperor's New Clothes, Harvey,* so many Shakespearean heroes disguised.

She imagines the Curies, Madame Marie and Pierre, in their delirium of proof and perfection: blood racing—alpha, beta, gamma, alpha, beta, gamma—as they search for radium. She feels the white heat, imagines the sixteen isotopes of Y's tongue as it slices the page from the book.

See her here as she runs her finger, again and again, along the severed seam of the page, and longs for DNA, blood type, muscle, the rigid rib cage press of a lover—something strong and reliable—something proven, something seen.

11

She sees herself at the end of seven years of memory, yearning, and desire, and knows that to rebuild, she must move slowly and that pleasures must come simply.

Today: the faint cream and flutter of a moth where the wall meets the ceiling. She wonders if the moth became lost in its search for light and has now reached a decisive end to some long stretch of sky, the ultimate despair.

Seamus stares with salmon-tinted eyes as they both concentrate on the furious dance of the moth—no tendons, no taut muscles, just the quick, fluid movements—the white-light movements of something inexplicably strong.

Why I tell you this, I do not know. It is part of the moment and, if he were here, he would surely remark on it. And if he were here, she would tell him that she is not unlike an insect, a bird, the creamy moth hovering in the corner—at once here and not here—trapped and longing, flitting about the room with imaginary wings, wandering its way toward the proven light of a seemingly reachable star.

12

She wakens to the predictable ring of the phone, a wild banging of fist against the other side of her door. Listen as she calls for Seamus, again and again until she hears Chief Nels wailing below. See her spy the white curtain as it flies out the screenless window, the riot of soil from the overturned planter by the outer edge of the sill. Four stories below, Seamus' fur shines like sun against the pitted gray of the sidewalk.

Watch as she races out of her apartment, down the stairs, and, with a dramatic push of the door, enters a world of warm air and blinding light, where she can smell a faint compost of lilac, lily, coffee grounds, and shell, and hear the chaotic chirping of nameless birds, seasonal pleasures she can just barely recall.

A crowd of people has gathered, but she sees only Chief Nels, who has gone from wail to song, something reminiscent of a hymn. He strokes the cat as it rolls in pleasure atop a modest nest of feathers that just a few minutes earlier had been a headdress. Nels gives her a thumbs up and smiles.

Seamus' whiskers shine with the brightness of morning, and she leans in to press the cat's sweet flesh, to feel his whitefish belly for movement—a steady rise and fall of breath.

Chief Nels puts his arm on her shoulder and shakes his head. "It's a miracle," he says. He looks older, and a rogue swoop of blond hair covers most of his weathered face, the face of a believer.

Everyone else remains in their close-knit circle telling stories about the other falling cats they have known, their uncanny abilities, the scientific theories that can substantiate such remarkable feats.

X does not think of Darwin. She does not think of cloning, entropy, or biotic potential. She does not consider the undisputed percentage of cats who fall from great heights and land on their feet.

Instead, she stares at Seamus in his costume of wings, marvels at how he has taken on crown, crest, wing, and covert—and appeals to whatever masked force has given him the ability to adapt and survive.

Four stories up, she marks the scene, sees her apartment on the vast window-checkerboard of the building, her curtain still flapping its surrendering white.

She wants to go there, to remove herself from this flock of people, but instead is compelled to lower her body to the ground, get on all fours, and stroke the cat, nuzzle her face in his, so feathers and fur and hair blend to create a resilient, unidentifiable creature.

See her here as she lies beside Seamus on the pavement—in front of everyone, all of them—not caring who is watching, who sees. See her.

Remains of Life

Kirk Wisland

Tommy came home today. Drawn, quartered, reconstituted and reconfigured, Tommy stared silently as I winched the wheels of his chariot to the bed of his pickup truck and slid a pillow under the stumps of his legs.

Tommy came home today, riding a wave of melancholy that drowned our words. In this little Iron Range town, where gossip flourishes in the stagnant boredom, it is now graveyard silent.

I drive Tommy to my family's lake cabin, where we'd spent so many similar summer days when he was whole. This is where Tommy wanted to come first, to see one of those lake sunsets.

Tommy struggles to control the wheelchair with his one remaining arm, bumping hazardously down the hard, sun-baked slope toward the lake. He grunts his displeasure at me when I try to help, but acquiesces when he comes to the simple plank ramp I rigged up to get him up the final step to the dock.

Tommy takes up a position facing west, where the sun sinks slowly over the trees that outline the far shore. A pair of Jet Skiers weave like mating snakes in the glare of the shimmering waters.

"I should be dead, you know." Tommy says.

"That's not true . . . you're lucky to be alive." I manage a weak smile.

Tommy laughs. "Still can't lie to save your life."

"Shit, Tommy." I struggle with the words. "What can you . . . I mean, what still . . ."

"What works?" He laughs again, rubbing the patchy beard that sprouts up between scars on his face. "Let's see."

"Tommy, don't—"

"Legs!" He bellows, cutting me off. "Gone at the knees! Right arm, MIA and presumed irretrievable, sir!" Tommy raises his left arm and snaps a salute to an imaginary officer at the end of the dock. I stare, mute, while Tommy traces the naked lines of the scars with his fingers. "The sunset feels good." He smiles and puts his hand up as if to tan his palm.

"Does it . . . work?" I ask.

"I think so." Tommy sighs, scratching his beard again. "It's been almost two years. I tried a visit to Rosy Palm, but I'm not a lefty." He laughs, clenching his hand. "Besides, there were always nurses around. After my first attempt they tucked me in with my hand tied to the bed." We laugh about this until Tommy notices my tears. "Don't," he says, reaching out and clasping my arm in his hand. "It doesn't work." He smiles, his grip gentle but firm, and listens to the waves lapping at the shore until the sun disappears in a final kaleidoscope of pink and orange across the water.

. . .

Tommy used to be beautiful—deep blue eyes, granite jawline, sandy blond hair. He was a man in high school, growing a full beard in ninth grade. Not because it looked good, but just to show us he could. He strutted through school, bearded Adonis man-child, and that night a half dozen of our classmates went home and shaved off their scraggly toothbrush-bristle mustaches.

Tommy played quarterback; one of the best Minnesota had ever produced. People made all kinds of comparisons—Favre, Brady, Manning. By our junior year Tommy had to pick up his mail at the post office because the flood of recruiting letters overwhelmed his mother's mailbox.

Tommy was a natural with the girls. "If you're a rock star or an athlete, you don't have to be pretty," he would say with a smirk, knowing full well that he was both. Around here boyfriends still lived with a healthy fear of angry brothers or fathers. My grandfather knocked out his future son-in-law with a vicious left hook when he found out my dad had gotten his only daughter pregnant before their wedding day. After they were married and I came along, all was forgotten.

Tommy never had these problems. All the fathers, uncles, brothers, and grandfathers in town rooted for him, even though he'd been with enough girls to deserve a whipping from all of them.

I gave up trying to compete with Tommy when I was twelve. Not because he was my best friend; sometimes you know you can't win. With sports, girls, and the other gauges of teenage popularity, we were all a distant second, vainly trying to carve out space in his shadow. Sometimes I wished he wasn't so good looking, such a natural star, such a lady-killer.

Especially after Irene.

. . .

"Jake! Jake! C'mere!" Tommy's waving me over from the corner of his mother's deck.

It's been a week since he came home. When I see him I feel a weight of guilt, remembering that petty teenage envy. I'd give anything to play runner-up again.

"Jake!"

"I'm comin'! Hold on."

Tommy's mom has thrown a welcome back/late birthday party for Tommy, his twenty-second birthday having been spent at the Walter Reed Medical Center. Tommy's propped up on a La-Z-Boy throne that's been moved onto the deck for the occasion. His mother bought a brand new white dress shirt, which Tommy has managed to stain twice already, struggling to balance food and drink.

The shirt was the one concession his mother had wrung from Tommy. She'd been on him to cut his hair and shave since he got back, not being a fan of the Jesus look, his shaggy mop and beard combo. When I showed up early to help with the preparations for the party, she tried to enlist me in her crusade. I wanted to tell her that after all Tommy had lost, he should be able to do what he wanted with what was left. But I just smiled and said that I liked the new look.

The backyard is packed with a herd of well-wishers come to pay their respects. They're unsure of how to deal with their wounded legend, leaving a buffer zone around Tommy. Those outside the zone mill about somberly, talking in hushed funeral tones. "Such a shame . . . he could've gone pro . . . so unfair." Each of them takes a turn leaving the gloomy herd to enter Tommy's domain. When they cross the invisible boundary, they erupt into smiles and back-slapping good cheer. They reminisce and share funny stories. Nobody talks about the present.

. . .

The last time I'd seen Tommy, three weeks before his second deployment, he still *looked* like Tommy. The Marine Corps buzz cut was a little shorter than his hair had been in high school, but otherwise he still outwardly appeared the same when I picked him up from the airport.

But the previous year in Anbar had clearly left a residue under his skin. His old joviality was absent, replaced by a humor that was dark edged, cynical, occasionally cruel. He sneered at a "Support the Troops—Bring Them Home" bumper sticker on the car next to us as he threw his duffel bag in my trunk. He caught me wincing at his derision, and while he didn't say anything, he kept his guard up around me afterward.

Tommy was quick to anger and hell behind the wheel. When another pickup truck crept too close to his one day on the interstate, he unleashed a horn-honking, profanity-laced tirade at the distracted driver, leaving me in stunned silence as he raced to the next off-ramp, two exits ahead of our scheduled destination.

On his last night in town I tried to draw him out, drinking whisky around the fire pit at the cabin. It was a tradition dating back to junior high, sitting in ageless lawn chairs, adding wood until the loons went quiet with the approaching dawn, sending our secrets and future plans into the dying embers like missives to God.

But the whisky, rather than loosening Tommy's tongue, had just hardened him. I knew his unit had seen bad shit during their first deployment, and I wanted Tommy to know that he could unburden himself, that I was ready to listen to my friend. But Tommy saw an agenda.

"I'm not going to be a poster boy for your fucking surrender-hippies club." He'd said quietly, face illuminated by dancing flames, the low volume of his voice failing to mask the venom.

We didn't speak for several months after that, until I received a brief Christmas e-mail from Fallujah, well into Tommy's second tour.

. . .

"Jake! JAKE GET YOUR ASS OVER HERE!" Tommy bellows at me, gesturing with his left hand, teetering perilously over the arm of the La-Z-Boy.

"Tommy. Language!" Tommy's mother registers her disapproval.

"Sorry, Ma," Tommy grins. "Hey lead foot, move your BUTT!" I make my way through the yard and up to the deck. People pat me on the shoulder and give me their *you're a good friend* looks as they part for me. *Go to hell*, I think, smiling back at them. *You idiots think he doesn't notice the relief on your faces after you've paid your respects and can scurry back to the pack of mourners?*

"How's Irene doing?" Tommy's mom asks without looking up, intent on brushing crumbs off the chair. "Is she still out in California?"

"Yeah, I got an e-mail from her a couple weeks ago," I say, trying to untangle the instant knot in my stomach. "She's doing fine. Getting married in October."

"Really? Oh, that's great. I always liked that one." Tommy's mom, having unknowingly and casually gutted me, scurries away to greet a newcomer to the party.

"Hey, sorry to hear that, man," Tommy says, offering me a can of Pig's Eye from his personal ice bucket next to the chair.

"Yeah, well. . . ."

"It's not too late, right?" Tommy asks, trying to lighten the moment with a mischievously raised eyebrow.

"Yeah, Tommy, yeah it is." I smile with the tepid force of winter sunshine, trying to banish the vision of my last trip to California, an awkward week punctuated with the news that she'd been seeing someone else. I crack open the beer, taking a long, cold sip, trying to focus on the simple pleasure of the moment, steadying myself before turning my attention back to Tommy. "We having fun yet?"

"Loads," Tommy smiles, watching his mother until she moves out of earshot. He drops his smile and grabs my arm. "Get me *out* of here."

"Your mom would kill me. Not everyone has shown up yet."

"Let's go get a drink."

"Later." I catch Tommy's mother at the other end of the deck, eyeballing us with that look that says we're going to be in trouble before we even start.

"Let's go *now*." Tommy is getting frustrated with me.

"Wait 'til sundown. Everybody who's coming will have made it by then."

"Sundown. You swear?"

"I swear. We'll leave at the first hint of dusk."

"If you don't, I swear to God I will hunt you down and run your ass over in my wheelchair. It's military issue, combat ready!" Tommy finishes with a laugh, maniacally shifting imaginary gears with his left hand. Heads turn in the pack of mourners. Tommy looks to the west, where the sun hangs above the tree line. I look at my watch. Four-thirty.

. . .

I met Irene in ninth grade. She was my first girlfriend, and we were in-separable for our four years of high school. I was drawn to her because she was brilliant, with a breadth of interests far more cosmopolitan than our redneck town. By the time we were in tenth grade we both knew that we were destined for bigger things. We took special college prep courses and planned to go off to school together.

Irene was pretty, too. Not beautiful, but with a subtle grace camouflaged by studious glasses. It didn't hurt either that Irene seemed immune to Tommy's spell. The three of us hung out all the time, along with whoever was Tommy's girl of the month. In the frequent aftermaths we were damage control and therapy, providing excuses for Tommy and a shoulder to cry on for the teary-eyed jilted. This teamwork made us that much closer. The future seemed clear.

But on the second Tuesday of our junior year, they flew planes into New York skyscrapers, shattering that future clarity.

. . .

Tommy leans his head into the wind as we cruise down the highway, eyes closed, smiling. He looks truly relaxed for the first time all day.

We didn't wait for dark. Over the protests of Tommy's mother, we left when half the sun still glared over the trees. She admonished us not to drink too much, demanding promises we both knew we wouldn't keep.

"Let's get drunk," Tommy says, pulling his head in from the window. He tucks long strands of wind-whipped hair behind his ears, clearing his face.

"Okay."

"I mean *really* drunk."

"I hear you. We'll get drunk."

"Smashed." Tommy pulls a pack of cigarettes from the pocket of his T-shirt and, with practiced single-hand precision, gets one out of the box and lit before I can even think to offer help.

"Yeah, smashed," I say, trying to muster enthusiasm. "Where do you want to go?"

"Out of town." Tommy exhales a cloud of smoke toward the open window, which is promptly blown back in. "I don't care where, just as long as we're beyond the reach of my mother's circle of gossip."

"Cotton?"

"Nah, my mom goes to the flea market there every Saturday." Tommy catches a grin spreading across my face. "What's so funny?" he asks, punctuating his inquiry with a quick punch to my shoulder.

"You did two tours, man. You still afraid of your mom?"

"Yeah, screw you, buddy. You're lucky; your mom doesn't give a rat's ass."

I feel my hands tighten on the steering wheel. "My mom hasn't had a drink in two years."

"I'm sorry, man." Tommy puts his hand on my shoulder, talking through the cigarette dangling from his lips. "Seriously. That was uncalled for."

"That's all right." I gun the motor toward a group of crows feasting on a lump of roadkill straddling the center line. Tommy's right. My mom fell in love with the bottle after my dad left. At my high-school graduation party, Tommy spent the whole night fending off her slobbery drunk kisses.

"Two years, huh? That's great."

"Yeah, it is." The crows take flight at the last second, parting like a black sea as I pass through. Tommy stares out at the lush July green racing past, his hand coming to rest on the stump of what used to be his left knee. His mom has meticulously sewn up his old jeans to fit the new, reduced Tommy, the closed ends forming the toes of two denim socks. As if putting Tommy back into his old Levis might somehow make him whole again. Tommy rubs the stump while whispering something lost in the rush of the wind.

"What?" I ask.

"Huh? Oh, nothing. Just thinking . . . not quite two tours," Tommy says, looking straight ahead. Tommy got extended at the end of his second tour—"*fucking surged!*" was how he'd put it in one of his terse, infrequent e-mails. He'd had less than forty days left. I feel a rise of bile. I want to curse my country, but I stop short.

"Anyway, it's not like she doesn't know what's up. I just want to spare her the details," Tommy says, switching the focus back to his mother.

"Probably a good plan."

"Besides, she's bigger than me now." Tommy laughs, but all I can manage is a sickly grin. I don't know how he can laugh about it, or why I can't.

"How about Makinen?" I offer.

"Makinen . . . Makinen." Tommy repeats the name of the town, his eyes closed, searching for connections. "Makinen has security clearance." He grins at me and then points to an exit sign rapidly approaching.

"Okay. Makinen it is," I say, taking my foot off the gas and easing onto the ramp.

"Look out Makinen!" Tommy slaps the dashboard and sticks his head out the window.

"Lock up your daughters!" he bellows into the wind, his hair whipping crazily behind him.

...

A part of Tommy died on 9/11.

We all suffered, we all mourned. But as we sat glued to the television in our study hall, watching one, then another tower disintegrate, the care-free, easy Tommy who had been my best friend died with those icons of Manhattan.

Tommy was probably destined to be military. He was born on the Marine base at Camp Pendleton, his dad a career soldier who'd been decorated re-peatedly during his tours in Vietnam. I met Tommy's dad once and under-stood immediately why Tommy's mom had fled back home to Minnesota when Tommy was just two years old. Most of the Vietnam vets split after the war into two camps—those who thought it had been a tragic waste of fifty-eight thousand lives, and those, like Tommy's dad, who carried a bitter chip on their shoulder, the certainty that we *could have won*, if not for the national weakness manifested by those back-stabbing hippies.

My father fell into the first camp, coming back from Vietnam with a pathological hatred of guns born from seeing his best friend cut down only five feet from where he stood. A hunter since childhood, my father sold his rifles and never put his finger on a trigger again. Listening to the anger and sorrow in my father's voice on those rare occasions when he would talk about his time in the jungle instilled a healthy skepticism in me toward my government, and a natural aversion to people whose impulses were quick to war.

Like Tommy's father, whom I met when he came to town for Tommy's ninth birthday. We held a disastrous party at our cabin, which quickly dis-integrated into a drunken argument over Vietnam and ended with Tommy's dad and mine nearly coming to blows.

Tommy went out to California to see his dad after that. I was never invited along.

So maybe it was in Tommy's blood, a genetic predisposition to milita-ristic bluster. As we turned our gaze to Iraq after that quick, clean invasion of Afghanistan, Tommy became increasingly belligerent and impossible to reason with.

I'm no pacifist. I would have gone to Afghanistan in a heartbeat. To the dismay of my father, I even talked about enlisting with Tommy, surfing the patriotic wave of those short months of unity after 9/11.

Of course Tommy, like so many idealistic patriots, didn't go to Afghanistan.

Some of us smelled manipulation in the drumbeat to Iraq. Irene was gung ho about a future in journalism, and as editor of the school paper she became a lightning rod because of her early and outspoken stance against the looming invasion. What began simply as a defense of my girlfriend from the barbs of the simple minded—*Support OUR Troops!*—became my own full-blown certainty of impending disaster. This made Irene and I popular targets in the flag-waving fever of 2002.

Although Tommy never publicly antagonized me, he wasn't shy about his belief that I was becoming a deluded, weak-kneed *librul*. I heard his dad's voice coming through, and I hoped I could wait him out, but as our arguments got more heated it became harder to see past the political caricatures we were becoming. Yet we managed to navigate this turbulence with the stored goodwill of our decade of friendship. Tommy even used his clout around school to take some of the heat off of Irene and me when we stoked up the resentments of our classmates.

Tommy's dad, who was blustering about reenlisting for active duty, flew Tommy out to San Diego in October of our senior year, a week before the Iraq authorization vote, and took him to meet the Marine recruiter on base.

When I tried to share my apprehensions with Tommy upon his return, he turned on me publicly for the first time, cursing me as a coward at the senior homecoming party.

Two weeks later, Senator Wellstone's plane crashed in an ice storm thirty miles from our high school. And I didn't even think to ask Tommy if he wanted to come with when Irene and I drove down to Minneapolis to shed our tears at the memorial service.

. . .

At dusk we stop at the Front Street Bar and Grill in Makinen. It goes quiet when I open the door and try to get Tommy's wheelchair up the steps. I can't get him in by myself, and a couple of sunburned farmers come over to lend a hand. They're both wearing baseball hats advertising herbicides, so after the three of us get Tommy up and through the door, he thanks them as "Mr. Roundup" and "Mr. Banvel."

"No problem, buddy," they grunt and return to the bar. I wheel Tommy toward an empty corner, ignoring the eyes of all the people following our progress. As soon as we get settled in, the din of the bar starts up again.

. . .

During Christmas break of our senior year, I spent a weekend in Minneapolis touring the University of Minnesota. I'd been accepted into the honors program there, and my subsequent refusal to commit to going to school out of state with Irene had led to some harsh recriminations about my commitment to our relationship.

I worried about it all weekend, barely taking note of my surroundings, and then rushed back, driving perilously fast through a near blizzard.

Irene came out onto the porch of her parents' house as I pulled up. I knew something was wrong the moment I saw her. I couldn't figure out her expression as I clambered up the steps to the porch, although later I realized it was probably fear. I'd barely said "hello" when she told me she had slept with Tommy.

She might as well have slugged me with a baseball bat. I stumbled around the porch in disbelief. She cried, pleading with me, telling me she was sorry, it just happened. There was a party and they'd been drinking. I didn't want to know, I didn't care, I couldn't breathe. I headed down the steps and Irene grabbed my arm. "Let go of me!" I yelled, losing my balance as I jerked away, tumbling into the fresh snow.

"Are you okay?" Irene asked, coming down to help me.

"Stop! Don't come *near* me!" I sputtered through clenched teeth as I jumped up and dusted myself off.

"I'm sorry, Jake. . . . I love you."

"Shut up! Shut up! Shut your goddamn lying whore mouth!" I yelled, jabbing my index finger toward her face. She flinched, thinking that I was going to hit her. Which I might have. She sagged against the railing, and I stood statue still, pointing my accusations at her with my quaking arm.

"Jake . . ."

I turned away, boots crunching angrily. I reached my car and threw up violently next to it, a little cloud of steam rising as my vomit sank into the snow. I got in the car and sped off, shaking so hard I could barely stay on the road. I wanted to hurt someone. I wanted to hurt Tommy.

. . .

The good people of the Front Street Bar have finally stopped staring at Tommy as we finish our first beers. We're reminiscing about the many loves of his high-school era when a guy I vaguely remember, a linebacker Tommy used to play against, comes over to our table. He says he heard what happened to Tommy and he's sorry, and that his cousin is over there now with the "Red Bulls" of the Minnesota National Guard. Tommy thanks him and the guy returns to his table, stopping along the way to order us a pitcher of beer. We raise our glasses to him, and from the other side of the room he does the same. Each time we're just about done with the last one, a fresh pitcher appears, and with every new round we raise our glasses in silent salute across the bar. Each time he returns the gesture from his end, and we carry on with getting drunk.

. . .

The day after Irene told me about her and Tommy, I stayed in bed until noon, unable to sleep, unwilling to rise. I just lay there, juggling different scenarios in my head, trying to find some way to undo what had been done. Eventually I gave up and headed for school.

I arrived during lunch break. Maybe that was my plan all along. It was gray and snowing, big flakes settling like a blanket of wet cotton over the landscape. Tommy was in the parking lot with the other football guys, and as I parked and got out of the car, I tried to stop the telltale trembling of my hands. A flurry of snowballs greeted me. "Hey Poindexter, how's life in the big city?" one of the guys yelled as a snowball exploded in my chest. My face felt like stone, and I had to concentrate to keep my feet moving forward. "Why so glum?" someone yelled, followed by laughter as another snowball detonated on my jacket.

Tommy was the only one not joining in the fun. He held my gaze with a poker face, but I thought I saw pain in his eyes. I stopped a couple feet in front of him, feeling the heat rising from my stomach into my face.

"Hey Jake," Tommy said, his voice barely a whisper.

"Hey Tommy," I returned, trying to still my hands. Tommy dropped his gaze to my shoes and exhaled loudly, his shoulders slumping with the expelled breath. "Look, Jake," he began, keeping his eyes on the ground, "I'm sorry. I don't know—"

That's when I hit him. He never saw it coming. I hadn't thrown a punch since third grade, but I put my whole body into it and felt an explosion of pain in my hand as it slammed into his cheek. Caught off guard, Tommy staggered and almost fell, leaving a snowless smear as he caught himself on the side of a car. "What the hell, Jake?" Three of the guys moved toward me menacingly. Tommy waved them off as he came forward. I braced myself, but Tommy didn't try to hit me back. He rubbed his face where I'd punched him, smearing a little dot of blood. I was breathing heavy, my heart pounding, adrenaline surging through me.

"Jake."

"What?" I growled.

"I didn't mean for it to happen."

"Fuck you, Tommy."

"I know you're mad, Jake, and you've got every right to be."

I punched him again. He barely flinched, and this time a sickening crunch accompanied the pain in my hand as I connected with his nose. Tommy went down, teetering on his heels before finally falling awkwardly on the seat of his jeans. The football guys bowled me over, smothering me in the snow. "What the hell is going on with you?" The fat offensive lineman who had me pinned barked at me.

"Get off of him!" I heard Tommy's voice behind me.

"Tommy, for Christ's sake!" the guys pleaded in their confusion.

"I said get *off* him!" Muttering profanities, they let me up. Tommy had his hand over his nose and blood trickled out from between his fingers. "I'm sorry, Jake," Tommy continued, "she started, she started kissing me—"

"No!" I yelled, shaking my head, trying to dispel the images. Couldn't be Irene. Not her lips kissing him, her hands . . . his hands on her naked body.

"I'm sorry Jake, she started—"

"Nooo!!!" I erupted into a guttural roar and hit him again. He staggered backward and I attacked him savagely, raining punches on him. I wanted to beat the beauty out of him, to rip off that pretty face. "C'mon! C'mon!!" I screamed at him. I'd hit him, he'd stumble, and I'd wait for him to regain his balance, to return the punches.

But he never even tried—just waited for the next punch. Finally he fell, and I leaned in to land one last grazing blow as his head was halfway to the ground. Then I was being dragged off, kicking and flailing maniacally, screaming at Tommy, who was crumpled in the snow.

"You bastard! You could've had any girl you wanted! You goddamned backstabbing *snake!*" I was shoved into my car by a phalanx of angry letter jackets. I sped off, careening down the street, clutching the wheel with my left hand because my right was too battered and bloody to help.

After three weeks of ignoring each other at close range, we all made an uncomfortable peace. Tommy and Irene were the most important people in my world. Even though I could barely look them in the eye those first couple months, I couldn't bring myself to turn my back on either of them.

My individual reconciliations with Tommy and Irene held tenuously through vigilant separation, which made navigating the high-school social circuit extremely difficult. It was a winter of abruptly ending conversations and awkward silences when the three of us ended up in the same vicinity.

Irene and I stayed together, and I forgave her, but as hard as I tried I couldn't forget. Our affection would have its rebirth as the sting of winter receded into spring, but in the early going it was a hands-off reconciliation, as if I were blaming her body rather than its operator.

As it turned out, we'd get used to infrequent lovemaking, because Irene was the only one who got into Berkeley. Besides, my father left the week after Christmas, and my mother started drinking heavily in his absence. After finding her passed out in our driveway for the second time, her car still running, I decided that I didn't want to go too far from home. So the fall after our graduation Irene went out to California and I headed down to Minneapolis.

Irene and I managed to hold on, against the odds of the long-distance relationship, for almost three full years.

Tommy passed on several scholarship offers, including a full ride at the University of Minnesota, and instead enlisted in the Marines. He left town two weeks before I did, headed for boot camp in South Carolina. Five months after basic training he was on the road to Baghdad.

I forgave Tommy for Irene, because I couldn't really blame him. I knew he just did whatever he could get away with, like a lovable but poorly trained puppy.

But I never could forgive him for not hitting me back.

. . .

Tommy and I are drunk. I know I shouldn't be driving, but I don't care. It feels great, tearing down the highway at eighty miles an hour, the wind screaming past the windows, the trunk, tied down haphazardly over Tommy's wheelchair, clanking rhythmically behind us. I've got Springsteen blaring at top volume, the speakers shuddering and threatening to give out. In the dark of the car all I can see is Tommy's profile and his left hand slapping the dashboard in time with the music. For the first time since he's come home it feels right. Just Tommy and Jake, on the prowl. Nothing else matters. Nothing else exists.

We're singing along at the top of our lungs. We're connected with the Boss, singing his heart out about America. All the right and wrong, heroes and villains.

"Glory DAY-YAYYS! Yeah they're PASSIN' BY!" Tommy bellows, slurring along off-key.

"Glory days! In a young girrlll'sss eye!" I jump in, feeling the blood rushing to my head.

"I WENT down to that WEELLL tonight and I DRANK 'til I got my FIILLL!" Tommy takes lead vocals again, slurred, out of sync. The way it should be when you really mean it. I watch him fumble for a cigarette with drunken fingers that have lost their touch. I want to tell him that everything's going to be okay, he's my friend and I love him. I'll help him make it.

"Deer!" Tommy screams. I slam on the brakes and look back to the road. The tires screech as I swerve to avoid it, but the bumper catches the tail end of the deer with a sickening thud. We skid to a stop halfway into the gravel shoulder of the highway, my hands locked onto the steering wheel, my foot crushing the brake pedal to the floor. Tommy reaches over and turns the key with his left hand, killing the engine. It's silent except for the sound of our breathing.

"You okay?" Tommy whispers.

"Yeah, yeah, I'm okay," I lie. The shakes begin, starting in my feet and hands. They travel along my limbs, converging in the middle in waves until my whole body is trembling. "I-I never saw him."

"Nothing you could do."

"I know." I unlock the door and get out, making my way unsteadily to the front of the car. The corner is crumpled metal, the headlight shattered from impact, a tuft of fur sprouting from broken glass.

I get back in, gingerly pulling the door shut after me. Tommy's staring out his window, tracing the scars on his face with his fingers. I've noticed that it's a habit of his when he's thinking. I take a deep breath, forcing calm as the trembling subsides to a faint buzzing under my skin. I start the car, and the sound of the engine breaks Tommy from his reverie. "We've got to make sure it's off the road," he says, turning to look at me. His eyes look wide and tired and I suddenly feel painfully sober.

"I know." I ease my foot onto the gas and turn the car around. The deer is about thirty yards down the road. A young buck, with little sprouts of antlers barely six inches high. I stop about twenty feet away.

The buck is shattered, splayed awkwardly on the road, struggling to rise. In six years of high-speed cruising past "deer crossing" signs, I'd never come close to actually hitting one. I look down at the dashboard, hoping that when I look back up the deer will have disappeared.

"Do you still keep that .22 in the trunk?" Tommy asks.

"What?"

"We've got to put it out of its misery." Tommy's looking directly at the deer, his face placid.

"I can't, Tommy."

"Dammit, Jake! Look at it! For God's sake, go and put it out of its misery."

"I can't," I plead with him. "I've only shot cans and targets." I feel shrunken and weak, tears welling up in my eyes. I want to be a kid again, to have someone here to take care of the situation.

"I'll do it," Tommy whispers.

"You?" I ask incredulously, regretting it immediately. Tommy turns his head slowly toward me. Although his face is tight, his eyes are strangely gentle.

"I'm sorry Tommy, I didn't—"

"I know. I'll pull the trigger, but you're going to have to get me out there."

I stare silently, unfocused eyes blurring the deer to just a shade of tan.

"Jake?"

"Yeah, okay." I get out and grab the .22. I put it on the hood and open Tommy's door. He's turned himself around so that his back rests against the dash and his left arm faces the door. I get him out of the car, his arm angled at the back of my neck, my arm under the stumps of his legs, cradling him like a child. With great difficulty I grab the rifle with my free hand and head toward the deer.

The buck is still, and I hope for a moment that it's already dead, but when we approach he bursts into frenzied action, trying in vain to flee, his broken body unwilling. "You're gonna have to hold him still," Tommy says, but there is no need. The buck collapses onto its side, its head propped up by the antlers. His chest heaves with rasping breath, his shiny black eye staring up at us.

I lower Tommy gently to the pavement, my back screaming in protest. Using his left arm he shifts himself a few inches. "Give me the gun," he says, holding up his hand without looking away from the deer. He grabs the middle of the barrel and gently brings the end to rest against the buck's head, a couple inches below the antlers. I flinch, expecting the buck to start flailing again, but he stays motionless. "Okay, Jake. Grab it right where I've got it." I wrap my left hand around the barrel, trying not to look at the deer.

Tommy wiggles the rifle, testing my grip. "Hold it tight."

"Yeah, I got it." My voice is a hoarse whisper. The deer snorts loudly, its nostrils flaring.

"Ssshhh. It's okay, boy. It's okay." Tommy intones, his voice a soothing hum. "Ready?" he asks without looking up.

"Yeah," I turn my head, staring up at the stars and the bright low moon, which bathes the pines that line the highway in an ethereal bluish tint. Tommy pulls the trigger, and, with a loud crack, it's over. The deer is still. The shot repeats itself in the empty night a half-dozen times before fading into the woods.

...

We drive home without words, the stereo silent, the low growl of the engine the only sound. I stare at the empty road, watching the yellow dashes in the middle zip by in a steady rhythm. I had managed to drag the deer off the road and get Tommy back in the car without making eye contact with either one of them. I'd never seen death up close. I feel ashamed at my weakness, making Tommy pull the trigger.

I look at Tommy. He's staring straight ahead, his hand resting in his lap. In the faint interior glow of the car, his face is peaceful and still. Beneath the beard and the scars, he's still beautiful.

A question lodges in my mind as I turn into his mother's driveway. I wonder if he's killed a man. "Tommy?"

"Yeah, Jake," he says turning to look at me as I pull to a stop. Maybe he knows what's coming next. Maybe he doesn't. Either way, there's something in his eyes that tells me not to ask.

Zamboni Blues

Robert Voedisch

I notice them the second I come out of the break room: two teenage dirt balls—grimy jeans, leather jackets, tendrils of peroxide-yellow hair—sitting up at the top of the bleachers during girls' figure-skating practice. They seem cagey, kind of half watching the girls, half watching the other people in the stands. Now, just because I drive the Zamboni doesn't mean I get off playing Rink Security Guard, nor am I big on jumping to conclusions about people, but it doesn't take a genius to know nothing good could come from this.

"Can I help you two with something?" I say, and plant my boot on the bleacher right next to them, my heel coming down so hard there's a clanging sound.

They start a little, their eyes going wide then dropping to their laps. They look so guilty I almost feel sorry for them.

I repeat my question, and when they don't answer I say, "Listen, it's not open skate right now, so unless you know somebody here, I'm going to have to ask you to leave."

The one with purple polish on the nail of his middle finger raises his head to look me in the face. "You're Danny Fulson."

His friend pipes up, "We heard you were working here. We were walking by and decided to come in to, you know, say thanks. Like, seriously, thanks for the music. It's meant a lot."

The first guy nods at this. "Totally. Absolutely. *Lay Off* is a classic. You smoke on that."

"Your lead's hotter than rug burn."

"Yeah, rug burn. Totally."

I take my foot down, a little stunned, although I guess I should have seen this coming. A couple buttrockers in this skating rink on a weekday afternoon? Of course they're waiting for me. "Well, thank you," I say. "That's nice to hear."

There's a lull, so I fill it by asking the obvious question. "You guys in a band?"

"Über-whore," says the one wearing nail polish. "I'm Matt, lead vocals and rhythm guitar."

The other one holds up his index finger. "Jim, lead guitar." It's like they're being interviewed by MTV or something.

"Been playing out?" I ask.

"Here and there," says Matt. "But it's hard getting gigs."

"Well, there's a lot of good bands out there. Minneapolis is kind of a music town."

He smiles. "Because of you guys."

"You set the bar pretty high," says Jim.

"Oh, I don't know," I say. "We'd get high at the bar. Does that count?"

They laugh, way too loud, the skating moms turning to look our way. I pretend to check my watch. "Hate to be a party pooper, but I should really go get the machine ready."

"That's cool," says Matt.

"Yeah, no problem," says Jim.

They push themselves to their feet and the three of us move down the bleachers, me taking up the rear as if trying to herd them. At the bottom I say the obligatory, "Good luck," and am just about to start toward the Zamboni when Matt pulls something from his jacket and holds it out to me. It's a tape.

"Any feedback," he says, "would be *super* great." Then he gives me these kind of puppy-dog eyes. Bloodshot, sure, with last night's mascara still clumped in the corners, but puppy dog nonetheless. I take the tape.

. . .

We called ourselves The Next. I guess you could say we were something of a cult band. Other musicians liked us. The critics *loved* us, *Rolling Stone* once proclaiming, "And they really are!" Well, that should've been it, right? That should've made us. Of course, what they loved about us—besides the music, and yes, we could play—was that we were a bunch of beer-guzzlin' blowhounds with a penchant for drag. It became a kind of legend.

After a particularly chaotic tour, we decided to take some time off, a two-week break to clear our heads. But the two weeks turned into a month, and the month into eight. And that was that. We didn't break up so much as we just never got back together. Chuck, our lead singer, went out and formed a new band. The bass player got a job running sound down at the Entry. The drummer married and found God, and has since been quoted as saying we were the devil, which I must admit I find a little flattering. As for me, I tried my hand at lead guitar player for hire, but it never really took off because most of the bands sucked, and because by this time I was using coke pretty hard.

Without the free and easy access touring provides, I was forced to buy my own drugs. Just like a normal person. So out went my guitars, my amps, some memorabilia, a few of my more extravagant outfits. My royalty checks, what little money they were, started going that way too, until one day I found myself at our old manager's house, begging for an advance. At three in the morning. The story is I threatened him with a screwdriver, but I don't remember there being any screwdriver. Somehow, he was able to talk me down. Years of practice, no doubt. He let me in, I spent the night on the couch, and the next morning he made me breakfast. There were no big lectures, nothing like that. Instead, what he said to me as I sat in his kitchen, drinking his coffee, was, "You know you could always go back to music, but for right now, you might want to think about getting a job. A *real* job. Just until you figure things out. I'd even try and help you find one. But it's all up to you. It's your call, Daniel."

Daniel. What could I do?

The hunt began right away, me sitting at the kitchen table with my hands between my knees, him at the phone, dialing up everyone he knew who could maybe get me a job. Restaurant owners. Bowling-alley supervisors. Garbagemen. People said things like, "Danny Fulson? The Next was my *favorite* band back in college. You know, I once saw him take a bottle on the chin without missing a note!" Or, "Does he still have that pink dress?" But no job offers were forthcoming, even though most of them knew who I was. Especially because they knew who I was.

And then a friend of a friend told him about a job driving the Zamboni at the Riverside Ice Arena. I didn't know the first thing about Zambonis, but the friend of a friend, a secretary, seemed to think it was something I could try for. "They'll teach you how to run it, of course," she said. "J.T.'s looking for a 'motivated person with good hand-eye coordination,' but between you and me he's desperate to fill shifts and will probably take just about anybody." I went down the next day.

I still remember walking into the arena that first time: the light, blinding as it ricocheted off the white walls and even whiter ice. The slap of cold. (It was August, and going from muggy midwestern heat into that thin, airtight coolness was enough to make me shiver.) The electric, almost mediciney tang of the Freon mixing with those sour locker-room smells. The noise of buzzers, of people shouting, of skates clawing the ice dry. But even with all that commotion, the place had an odd stillness to it—the temperature, the lights, even the sounds, clear and sharp, like I was inside this giant crystal. I was standing there, watching some hockey players lace up their skates, when a guy who looked like he'd once played a little hockey himself came up and asked if he could help me. I said I was looking for J.T, he said, "You found him," and just like that I was being trained in.

It was difficult in the beginning, especially for a person like me. I mean, I wasn't someone you looked at and said, "Oh yeah, let's get this dude up on some heavy machinery asap." But a few goofs notwithstanding (a chipped board here, a cracked piece of Safe-T-Glass there), I made it through those first weeks and soon found, much to my surprise, that I liked it. A lot. There's just something about it: the buzzer rings, the skaters hurry off, and you open the doors, the rink stretched out before you like some empty ballroom. You climb onto the machine and turn the key, fiddling with the choke until it coughs to life, then you shift into reverse and jockey through the doors. Which is a lot harder than it looks. It's as if you're trying to parallel park a salad bar.

As soon as you're out on the ice, you shift into forward and step on the gas (not gasoline, but real gas, propane) and drive up alongside the white-paneled boards. There you flip one of the little metal levers on the dash, the Zamboni whirring loudly, slowing from the transference of power as a hydraulic arm swings from its side. On the end of the arm a spinning brush, this blurred circle of blue angling into where the ice meets the wall. The edger. It looks like something that'd come shooting out of the Jetsons' robot maid.

Another lever, another whirring sound, and down goes the resurfacer (the coffin-shaped metal box on the back of the machine), everything caught up in a violent shudder as the blade digs in. You give it a little more gas (stalling out's a definite possibility with this much drag on glare ice) then hit the jets, the resurfacer steaming like a laundry press as it lays down a sheet of water, this swath of light in your wake. And you're making ice.

That's what I've been doing with myself, anyway, for going on nine years now. Fourteen times a day, Saturdays and every other Sunday off.

. . .

The very next afternoon Matt and Jim come in asking if I've listened to their tape yet. They come in the next day, too, and the one after that—and the one after that—until I finally have to tell them, "Look, I'll get to it when I get to it."

And I do, about a week later. It's after work and I'm up in my apartment, rubbing at my red, wrinkled feet, sipping a greyhound. And I do still have the occasional drink, if only to help me relax. I know that may sound sacrilegious, dangerous. Stupid. Anyway, there I am, and I get to wanting to hear some music. So it's up, across the room, and over to the stereo. I'm flipping through my records, but then I see the tape on the little end table where I throw my keys and loose change. I pick it up, slide it out of the case. Tape's so cheap there's not even a label, just the words WHORE: DEMO written with a Sharpie in a looping, childish scrawl. I jam it into the deck and hit play.

The first song's nothing to cable home about. Same with the second, just typical proto-garage-punk. (I take it then the Iggy-Pop-circa-'71 hairdos are *not* an accident.) About to give it the heave-ho when the third song kicks in, and bam, I'm sitting up, hooked on this riff. All loud and scrappy, yet melodic too. Warm. I can *feel* the heat breathing out from old, dusty Marshall tubes. I mean, it's a *hook*. A Keith Richards hook. Or Johnny Thunders, more likely. With a good first line to boot: "The papers read, *Local Boy Makes Bad.*" And as much as I like the riff, the chorus is a stone killer, this explosion of sound, of brightness, like my room's opening up all around me. Before I know it, I'm keeping time with my glass, humming along, even though I can only catch about half the words. It's not until the second time through the chorus I'm able to figure out what he's singing: *Where'd you go, man? Where'd you go? You were just here a minute ago. So where'd you go?*

I jerk my head to the side, my ear aiming right at the speakers. What was that? I sit there a few seconds, then—because of the lyrics, his voice, *something*—I get up and grab the cassette case, and, for the first time, actually read the names of the songs. At the third one, my heart grabs. "Zamboni Blues." Well. You cheeky little shit.

It goes into a guitar solo then, usually my favorite part of any song, but I just can't get into it, still hung up on that title. Seriously, what the hell?

Is this some kind of joke? Whatever it is, it's giving me this weird, self-conscious feeling, like I'm on display or something. Like there's people hiding behind my furniture, watching me. I put the case back down, sip at my drink. Again. Then I gulp at it.

After the solo, it's back to the chorus. Only this time I answer it. "Fuck you," I say. But it's too late, the song already done, the guitars crashing to a stutter-stop.

. . .

They don't have to come find me: I pounce the second they're through the door. "Well, I listened to it last night, and I have to say, that's quite a batch of songs you got there."

"Yeah?" Matt says. They're both positively beaming.

"Uh huh. Especially that third one."

Still smiling. Then they get it. "Yeah," he says, his face closing down into itself.

I wait for him to continue, but he doesn't. "Well, Jesus," I say. "How am I supposed to feel? That's me that song's about, right?"

"We didn't mean any disrespect."

"It was done *out* of respect," says Jim.

"*Where'd you go?*" I say.

"It's because we miss you," Matt says. "A lot of people do."

I wasn't expecting that, and it throws me a little. "Okay," I say. "Okay, but just promise me the next time you write a song about somebody you won't give it to them as a demo. Or at least obscure it first. I mean, we're not exactly talking *veiled* here."

"Sorry," says Matt.

And then we all just stand there looking at one another, this awkward little group in front of the trophy case. I finally break the silence. "Anyway, you're here. Come on. I'll buy you a cup of coffee."

A figure of speech, of course: it's just over to the break room, where I splash some of the flat company coffee into a pair of Styrofoam cups. I fill my own mug (a holdover from the day, this heavy white stoneware thing with the words *Uptown Bar* on the side), then shake open a few folding chairs, arranging them by the window that looks out onto the rink. We sit down, the two of them right back to beaming, perched on the edge of their chairs as if they think they're going to win something. I have to admit, they are kind of cute in a way. My little punk chipmunks. "First thing," I say. "Could you think about maybe changing the name of that song? For me?"

They nod.

"Thanks. Oh, and put it at the front of the tape. Make it your lead off."

"Yeah?" says Matt.

"Yeah. Weird as it is for me to say this, it's your best tune. You got about thirty seconds to convince someone to keep listening, otherwise, ka-ploonk. In the trash."

"First song," he says. "Gotcha."

I give them the rest of my spiel, about how you should never have two songs in the same key back to back. About how your songs should never get too busy, too complicated, too long. How you should always leave people wanting more. They're all ears at first, but then they start to get antsy, like there's something they want to say. I cross my arms. "All right, what?"

"Nothing," says Matt. "It's just, we wanted to tell you we're playing out Thursday."

"Where?"

"Down the street. The 400. Headlining."

"Headlining? Good for you."

"You should come. Stop by after work. We'll put you on the list." They exchange glances. "In fact, if you wanted to, you could sit in on a song."

"Yeah," says Jim. "Nothing big, just like a cover or something. You wouldn't even have to bring anything. I'll let you use my guitar."

I wince. Another thing I should've seen coming. "I'm flattered you guys want me to do that. Honestly, that's cool. But I'm going to have to say no."

"You sure?"

"Yeah. Kind of a policy with me."

They nod again, slower this time. Then they stand up. "Let us know if you change your mind," says Matt.

I raise my mug into the air, lower it, and they're gone.

Leaning back in my chair, the break room now suddenly quiet, it dawns on me that I was perhaps a little harsh, telling them I have a "policy" about playing with people. I mean, I *do* have one. When news got out I was working here, it seemed every band in town stopped by trying to get me to join them on stage or play on their album. But still, I shouldn't have said it. It was arrogant. And unnecessary, come to think of it. After all, it's been a while since someone actually came in here. I take a drink of my coffee, set my jaw. Really, what's it been anyway? Two years? Three? Four? I count it back: that group called Donkeypunch-n-Judy, who wanted me to play with them during First Avenue's twentieth-anniversary concert. And this fall's the twenty-fifth.

I get myself a refill and head back to my spot by the window. Kids in oversized hockey gear are circling the rink. Today is Tuesday, so it must be North-Central Pee Wee. I watch them for a long time, although from where I'm sitting I can barely even see them, just their little orange helmets gliding along the top of the boards like toy cars on a track.

. . .

Home, one boot off, I glance down at the end table, and lying right where I left it the night before is the cassette case. I sweep it into my hand, turn it this way, that, until I find what I'm looking for: near the bottom edge of the foldout it reads in big black letters, "*?'s about Über-whore? Don't fret! Your brand-new favorite band can be reached at . . .*" followed by the number.

I tap the case against the heel of my palm. Then I peg-leg it over to the phone. Okay. So if—*if*—we're going to do this, it can't be an Über-whore song. Especially not "Zamboni Blues." That'd be way too lame. Nor one by The Next. Even lamer. No, Jim's right, it's got to be a cover. Neutral ground.

"Baby Strange" by T. Rex, I decide, is as good a candidate as any. A great tune, and one they probably know, given their apparent love of all things glam. I take the phone off the wall and dial the number, then reach over and grab my old JCPenney Harmony, my first guitar, the one I wouldn't sell. When Matt finally answers, I set the phone down on the kitchen table and start playing right into the receiver. But the guitar's a little out of tune, and I'm having trouble remembering how the riff goes.

"Hello? Hello?" he says. "Goddamn it, who is this?" Then he hangs up.

I wait an hour before calling him back.

. . .

The bartender's handing me my greyhound as the first band takes the stage, a bunch of skater kids who introduce themselves as Obi-Wan Chernobyl. They play for about a half hour, then it's Über-whore's turn. Next to Obi-Wan, the Whores come off like elder statesmen of Rock. Tight (but not too tight), and damn good at working the crowd, who by now are banging their heads in unison like some multimulleted beast. I'm starting to think I may've undersold my little chipmunks.

Grooving to the music, drink in hand, I nose about the club, just to see if it's changed at all since the last time I was in. It has: a new sound booth, new tables, one of those electronic dartboards. On the back wall, they've hung a bunch of thick, arty-looking picture frames. I go for a closer look. There's this live shot of Gertrude's Excuses, the singer Kurt "Kurt" Wiley, microphone clenched between teeth, crawling around on what has to be the stage of the old Longhorn. Below that, a faded handbill for Eel Pout, a band we used to tour with. My eyes drift to the next one.

Yup. Me, smiling out at me. More hair. Fatter too, which doesn't seem quite right, but yeah, it's me. All of us, as a matter of fact. In front of a gray brick wall (our practice space?), Chuck spitting beer into the air, a broken line of white and brown arcing above our heads, my face laid open in mock terror as I try to get away. Did I, or was I drenched? Can't recall. I'm laughing at any rate. I mean, I can see that I am, right there. And yet the frame, the glass, the dust glazing both, makes everything seem closed off, silent. Sealed. I give the thing a friendly tap right on my face, then head back to the bar for another greyhound. And, just because, a quick shot of Jäger.

Sometime during the second encore (or maybe it's the third, I've kind of lost track), Matt calls me up. I actually have to push my way to the stage because no one's moving to let me through. They probably just think Matt was making a joke, that I'm not even in the club. But as soon as I climb the stairs and into the lights, they know. A round of applause, and only getting louder now that I'm blowing these giant, Miss-America-sized kisses.

A woman shouts, "We love you, Danny."

I press my fingertips together and bow a swami bow in the direction of her voice. Then I stand up, straight, and undo the buttons of my trench coat. A few of them stick for some reason, but after a bit of yanking they come loose, the coat slipping from my shoulders to reveal a pink, low-cut prom formal held up with spaghetti straps. On my feet are a pair of dyed-white triple-E pumps, and around my neck a string of pearls. I raise my arms into the air, hands tucked demurely, two white swans above my head. The place goes wild.

Jim hands over his Stratocaster, hurries offstage, clapping and pointing at me as he goes. I slip the guitar on and nod at the other guys in the band. The drummer clicks out a four-count and they're into it, chunking through the riff. I follow, soloing. Tentative at first, these long notes, bending my way into each one (a half step, a whole, then two) as if trying to sneak up on something. When I finally start to relax, I tick off this little run.

Another, longer this time, a full phrase. Then I'm there. Playing the melody straight—almost too straight—then changing it, shading it, disguising it, leaving it far behind in a rain of sour notes, and, just when it can't get any worse, falling back into it, prettier than ever. Faster now, chasing down a bumblebee, then a bumblebee on coke, and still faster, and the audience is screaming, and I'm playing, and someone is yelling, and I keep playing, and the person that's yelling is the bass player (do I even know his name?), and what he's yelling is, "Verse! Verse!"

I snap my head up, blinking. Just how long have I been going at it? Felt like only a few seconds, yet Matt's already at the *I'm shadowed under / You're like some thunder* part of the song, so I must've been soloing way, *way* past the intro, right over his vocals. A little embarrassed, I mute my strings and settle into the verse. We go through the chorus, into the turnaround, and there I decide to redeem myself. Nothing fancy, a quick fill. Something's wrong though, like I can't get my fingers to work. I mean, I'm hitting the right notes (most of them anyway), but it's not music. It's not Danny Fulson.

A smudge out of the corner of my eye. Matt has backed away from the microphone and is now standing right next to me, his guitar held high in the air, the fretboard almost touching my nose. I know what this means: he wants me to look at his fingers. I shake my head at him, then hunch over my guitar for another go. What comes out of the amplifier is little more than a long, groaning squeal, the sound of a building collapsing into itself. I turn back toward Matt, only he's no longer there. He's over by the drum riser, mouthing something to the drummer, then the bass player. Then somebody offstage. "No, come on!" I yell. I wrench at the strings, leap into the air, my feet splaying apart as I land, a sudden coolness on my hip. Air. I popped a seam. "Come on, come on, *please.*"

But the guitar is lifted off me. Jim. I watch him fit the strap around his neck. Watch him watch his own fingers as they fall, effortlessly, into the riff. To their credit, the boys keep it classy, wrapping up "Baby Strange" and then immediately launching into this impromptu blues vamp, Matt shouting over it, "Danny Fulson, ladies and gentlemen. Give it up for him. Danny Fulson. Local legend, right there." It takes me a moment to realize that's my cue to leave. I walk across the stage and down the stairs, necklace swinging, hitting my chin, teeth, so that I have to clutch it to my throat, and like that, I lumber into the crowd. This time, everyone moves.

. . .

I flip a switch and the giant lights hanging above the rink come on one by one, the darkness falling away in sections. Standing there, a little wobbly in my high heels, I gaze about the arena: the bleachers, the large banner-style pennants for the local hockey teams, the Zamboni parked front first in its concrete bay. I walk to the glass and look at the ice. It's a mess, dull and powder dry, the red lines and face-off circles blurred by the crosscut of skates. I usually do a final run at the end of each shift, but tonight I'd ducked out early to go to the club. The idea was to come in and clean the ice before we open. And I know that's just what I should do. I should keep moving, get to the break room, grab my clothes, a quick cup of coffee, then head home to sleep it off. I should leave all this for tomorrow.

But I don't. Instead, I walk over to the rink doors, pop the latch, swing them open. I step out of my pumps and up onto the machine. A few seconds later I'm out on the ice making for the boards, cold wind pushing past my bare shoulders, lifting the dress off my legs. I start pulling levers—the edger, the resurfacer. I turn on the jets and a soft tumble rises up from the ice.

The Broken Group

Ethan Rutherford

On the fourth day of their time together—their vacation within a vacation, his father called it—Robert let the anchor chain slip through his hands before he'd been able to secure it, and it plunged back into the bay. The chain at his feet uncoiled up and over the bow with startling violence as he stood, frozen to the moment, and watched. The sound of the chain paying out was like playing cards on spokes, but deafening. Within five seconds the anchor was back on the sea floor. "Dumb," he said to himself. In three weeks, he would be twelve years old. "Idiot," he said.

His father came forward from the cockpit and stood beside him. "What happened?" he said. The engine was idling.

"It slipped," Robert said. "I couldn't stop it."

His father kneeled down and ran his hand over the toe-rail. The chain had jumped its track and gouged the wood on its descent. "Jesus," he said, picking at splinters. He looked at his son. "You all right?"

The boy nodded.

"This could've been wrapped around your legs."

"I know," he said. "It wasn't, though."

His father ran his hand one more time over the rail, then stood and grabbed the line. "We'll do it together," he said. The bay was empty. They hauled the anchor and his father went back to the cockpit and put the engine in forward. When Robert was done washing the deck with the pole brush, he sat down next to his father. "I don't want you to worry about that," his father said.

"What's Craig going to say?"

"Craig's just going to be happy to get the boat back."

The boat was a Valiant 32 they had borrowed from one of his father's friends, a sailboat built for cruising, a solid and friendly vessel. But, as his father had said at the beginning of the trip, this was the ocean; anything could happen. Inattention had consequences at sea, so it was important to be careful. He'd said it in a funny voice, a captain conjured from a long-lost comic book, but he'd also made it known he was serious. When his mother and sister had been with them, they wore life jackets at all times unless safely below deck. They were to keep one hand on the boat when walking bow to stern, no matter how calm the water looked. Still, with all this preparation, the boom had skimmed the top of the Robert's head on a violent jibe, drawing blood, and sent everyone into a silent funk. The propane stove whommed upon ignition. His sister, before she and Robert's mother had left, had been terrified of the propeller.

They glided out of their anchorage into the strait, which was calm, and powered for a time in silence. The sun was out and hot, and the wind blew divots in the water. They were heading south, back to Seattle. To the west of them was the mainland, tree-thick hills balded at their tops from clearcutting. To the east, a view of the unbroken ocean. Robert knew his father wanted to sail, but his father remained silent at the helm as the breeze moved across the cockpit.

"Where are we going?" he finally asked.

"You tell me. We've got three islands to choose from." His father spread the chart on the divan and set his binoculars on it for weight. They were in the Broken Group, a cluster of islands on the outside of Vancouver. He circled a spot on the chart with his calipers. "Those three."

Robert studied the chart. One of the islands was shaped like a jagged crescent moon. The other had a cove. "Wower," he said.

"Are you looking at this day?" his father said. "Look at this day!"

...

They made it to Wower as the sun was going down. His father looked at the chart and lowered his speed as they entered the cove. He kept his eyes on the digitized depth reader, whose numbers jumped wildly as they passed over rocks and shoals. Robert stood at the bow, watching the water for rocks and kelp clumps that could muck up the propeller. "Okay," his father called from the stern, and he dropped the anchor, and his father backed it down.

Theirs was the only boat in the cove, which was, perhaps, unsurprising given the recent weather. There had been a storm, and it had caught them, unprepared, seven days earlier. Since it had passed, they had seen only a few other vessels trolling in the distance, and they'd grown accustomed to the isolation, reveling in it even. No more crowded anchorages. No more foreign voices carrying over the water, puncturing their sleep. No one watching them except for sea birds and the occasional seal. The feeling, as far as Robert could pin it, was akin to being outside of time.

When his father cut the engine, Robert felt relief in the silence. The two of them got into the dinghy, and while his father rowed toward shore Robert paid line over the stern. "Life jacket?" his father said.

"I forgot it."

His father looked at him. "This water's fifty degrees," he said.

Robert nodded.

Ashore, they secured the first line to a birch tree and then hopped over the rocks and looped a second stern anchor around a large piece of driftwood his father said must've rolled from a log boom offshore. Maybe on its way from Alaska. It looked like it'd been there for years, sunk deep, near its base, in the sand. It was secure.

On the way back to the dinghy, Robert caught the toe of his heavy shore boot on the lip of a rock and fell on his hands. Barnacles dug into his palm, but he kept from crying. His father put a hand on his back and led him down to the shore, and the boy put his hands in the salt water until the sting was gone. "Cold, huh?" his father said. Back aboard *Pamier* his father rummaged a drawer by the stove and came topside with some Band-Aids.

The stern anchors were perhaps an unnecessary precaution. For the last four days the weather had been beautiful and calm—the barometer had climbed and plateaued, and the voice on the ship-to-shore radio mounted over the instrument panel droned on and on about pleasant conditions. There was no mention of the storm, nothing of the shipwrecks Robert, before going to sleep, imagined. No distress signals. No calls for help.

"How's the hand?" his father said.

"It's okay," he said.

Later that afternoon Robert went by himself in the dinghy to set the crab trap, and then rowed over to a kelp bed and leaned over the side with the look box. Under the water he could see starfish, orange and deep purple, some with too many legs to count, and crabgrass. He watched an anemone contract its bluish suckers and then release them to wave gently in the current.

Ashore, his father showed him how to fillet the salmon they'd caught the day before, which made him squeamish but also, as he put one gloved hand on the body of the fish and with his other made his first cut, exhilarated. As he felt for the spine with the knife, he remembered how his father had brought the club down on the fish's head, three whacks, until it stopped flipping around and lay in the cockpit, stunned at its own suffocation, its gills clapping open and shut. Robert had never seen his father hit anything, and watching this he'd felt his own weight to be less than the fish's. He had caught it. He had hooked and reeled it in. His father had been at his shoulder, excitedly shouting instructions about line tension and angle, finally grabbing the fish with one hand while the other reached for the club. The wet blows sounded like a cabinet shutting. "That's *your* fish!" his father had said, holding it up for appraisal before dropping it on the deck. Robert had smiled, but then had felt ashamed. He wanted to throw it back, or at least part of him did, but the blood was dark, and its scales, like small mirrors in the sun, had flecked off onto his shoe. It could not be undone. He was relieved when the fish stopped moving at his feet.

After they'd collected enough wood for a fire, Robert walked on the beach below the tide line, picking up sand dollars and skipping them back into the water so they wouldn't dry in the sun. He flipped rocks and watched tiny crabs scuttle over each other in the sand. He delicately carried a crab in the basin of his shirt to a tide pool, crouched down, and dropped the crab into a sea anemone, which closed around the crab. It looked to him like a hug, a greeting. He didn't know whether or not anemones ate crabs, but eventually the crab stopped moving, and the anemone opened itself again.

They cooked and ate the salmon ashore, and after dinner they sat facing the water as the sun went down. As the light flattened, they saw an eagle, and watched it dive and swoop just beyond *Pamier*. Soon it was dark. When Robert began to get sleepy, he and his father stood and peed on the fire side by side and then his father kicked sand over the remaining embers. On board, they slept in the main cabin, together. It had been this way since his mother and sister had left, the two of them bunking up, and it was a comfort to Robert. He would not have admitted it, would not have said it aloud, but he was unable to sleep in the unfamiliar boat, with its stays and halyards constantly adjusting in the wind, knocking into the mast, without knowing his father was two feet away from him, in a matching and old-smelling sleeping bag. .

. . .

The storm had come up suddenly, and had been more severe than the man on the weather channel had predicted. When the wind picked up, his father jokingly announced it was time to batten the hatches and get out the board games. "I don't think this is funny, Joshua," his mother had said. His father looked at her and shrugged. He went topside to check the anchor and returned to say there was nothing to worry about. Robert's sister was two years younger and scared of the wind. When they were in their sleeping bags in the bow cabin that first night, the cabin the two of them had decided to call "the cave," he'd let her sleep on his bunk between him and the hull.

The next morning a front rolled in, bringing with it a gale-force warning. His parents discussed trying to make it to Ucluelet, but by the time they'd decided to leave, the wind had already arrived, and his father said it was too late. It would be safer to stern tie to shore and hunker down than to attempt an open-water crossing.

"There are no other boats here," his mother said.

"We'll be fine," his father said.

"You think, or you *know?*"

His father didn't answer but turned to Robert and told him to put on his foul-weather gear.

"You must be joking," his mother said. Robert had never seen her so angry. "He's not going out there with you." Outside, through the hatch, it was dark.

"I need someone to help with the stern tie."

"Well, not him."

Robert already had his slicker, but his mother told him to put it away. "How could you do this to us?" she said to his father, almost under her breath.

"What do you want me to say? I'm sorry."

"You knew it was late in the season to be out here. You told me." She opened the closet near the galley and pulled out a pair of rain pants and slammed the door shut. "Unbelievable, Joshua."

His father watched her stomp rain boots on. When she stood, he was still watching her.

She turned to Robert and his sister and told them not to worry, and then she climbed topside after her husband.

The two of them watched the storm and their parents' progress through the oval-shaped cabin windows. The trees on shore whipped and swayed. The rain was coming down sideways and in sheets, and looked at times to be billowing in the wind. He could hear his parents shouting, but it sounded like a combination of directional advice and nonsense.

"What if they don't come back?" his sister said. She was nine and shorter than he was by a foot, with her mother's brown hair.

"That's stupid."

"What if?"

After a while they heard their parents scrambling back aboard, and Robert turned to his sister, who was crying, and said, "See?"

That night his sister whimpered until their mother brought her sleeping bag into the forward cabin and slept with the two of them. In the morning the storm seemed to have passed over them at least partially, but the voice on the radio said that in the north, hurricane winds were being reported and an all-craft advisory was issued. They spent the day in the cabin playing cards and board games. When the wind kicked up again, Robert's father went topside to check the anchor and returned wet and angry. "We're dragging," he said.

"What can we do?" his mother said. It was the first time they'd spoken to each other all day.

"I don't know," he said.

Robert's sister began crying again. "That helps," his father said. "The crying helps."

...

At some point, Robert fell asleep, and when he woke up he was surprised at how quiet it was in the main cabin. The storm had stopped. Morning light was streaming in through the hatches, which were now open. His father sat at the chart table with the radio on low volume.

"We're taking your mother and sister to Ucluelet," he said. "They'll catch a bus and then a ferry home."

"What about me?"

"I need you," he said. "The boat has to come down. I can't do it by myself. The storm's over. It'll be fun." He stood and stretched. "We can poke around the islands for a few days before heading down. Me and you. It'll be fun. I promise."

It took six hours under power to get to Ucluelet. As they pulled past the breakwater, his sister pointed to the shore abutting the marina, where a number of the boats that had been free anchored were stacked almost on top of each other, as if they'd been swept into a corner by a large broom.

Robert hugged his mother and said good-bye to his sister at the bus station. His sister was crying for no reason. She gave him a drawing of a tree, and he thanked her for it. They waited for the bus to pull out, and then he and his father returned to *Pamier*.

Later, they talked about Robert's mother. "She thinks I put us in danger," his father said. Robert nodded. "I don't know what she told you and your sister. But I want to tell you I didn't do that. She's wrong about that. I was maybe not as careful as I could've been. But look, I got us out of it, right?" Robert nodded again. "No one's hurt. No need to summon a fugue state." They were playing Rummy-Block on the foldout table in the main cabin. The wick on the kerosene lamp was low, and the light was soft.

"I figure as long as we avoid the pirates, we'll be fine from here on out," his father said. He cocked an eyebrow.

"That's lame, dad," Robert said, putting his tiles on the board.

"Not true!" his father said. "I heard them, just last night. Rowing around the boat, singing yo-ho-ho. I didn't want to wake you. I didn't want to scare you."

"I wouldn't be scared of *that*."

"Oh yeah, tough guy? What would scare you?"

Robert felt like he'd been kicked, caught by surprise. He wasn't ready for this. He'd thought about it, but thinking wasn't the problem. He wanted to say, being alone. He wanted to say the kids at camp this summer, so sure of themselves, scared him. But he couldn't. What could his father possibly say? These kids, they had hated him for no reason he could think of except that he was there by himself and hadn't, like them, signed up with a group of friends. He wanted to tell his father that when these kids had lured him deep in the woods, and tied him to a tremendous oak and left him, he'd been scared. That he'd been driven into himself, and it was like a desert. When he'd finally untied the knots, it was getting dark, and he didn't know which direction the camp was; he'd sat at the base of the tree and cried until a counselor had come to find him. He hadn't moved, just like he'd been instructed to do. No one apologized, but he hadn't wanted anyone to apologize. He'd wanted to disappear. He'd wanted to just be blown to the ground and stepped on as if he wasn't there. He'd told no one. Not his father. Not his mother when she came to pick him up at the end of the week. He kept it to himself, hardening his memory until it was diamond sharp. It had happened to him, and it couldn't be changed. That was the important part. No one had been there to help.

"Not pirates," Robert said.

His father let him win the game, and then they turned in.

...

The next day, Robert woke early. He'd slept in his clothes, which made him aware of his mother's absence and also made him feel older somehow. His father wasn't in the opposite bunk. He went topside, rubbing the crust from his eyes and squinting at the morning sun. The air smelled fresh. His father sat in the cockpit, reading Louis L'Amour and drinking coffee.

"Want some?" he said. Robert nodded, and his father poured coffee from a thermos into a cup. The cup was made from red plastic, and across the front *Bosun* was written in maritime font. His father drank from the *First Mate* cup. Robert never drank coffee at home, and having it this morning with his father felt like a secret between them. He went below and came back with his own book, a Gary Paulsen novel he'd already read, and sat next to his father until the sun was high enough that it didn't feel like morning anymore.

When his mother and sister had been aboard, the days had been crowded with shore exploration and card games and elaborate hunts for pirate treasure, but the four days with his father had been punctuated only by occasional conversation and eagle spottings. The hours unraveled, and then it was time to eat. Or time to pull up the anchor and brush the deck down. Robert preferred it this way. It wasn't that he didn't miss his mother and sister. It was just different without them. Quieter. Grown up.

His father stood. "You want to help me wash her down?" he said. Robert shrugged. "Get your stuff, then," his father said.

After he changed his clothes and put on his life jacket, he handed the bucket of soap water to his father who was sitting in the dinghy, holding on to the rail. Then he turned and climbed backward into the dinghy, searching blindly with his foot for the seat. He felt his father's hand on his back, felt the seat with his toe, and let himself down.

They spent a good half hour washing the port side, his father inspecting every scratch and wondering aloud if it had been there before the storm. It was hot, and his father pulled his shirt over his head and threw it on deck. When they got to the bow, his father told him to sit down and then grabbed ahold of the anchor chain and pulled them under. As they moved under the chain, Robert looked up from the bottom of the dinghy, where he'd been watching sand swish back and forth in an inch of sea water, and toward shore. Standing at the tide line was a man in a red flannel shirt. His arms were crossed, and though he was more than fifty yards away, Robert could feel he was staring at them.

"Dad," he said.

His father turned. At first, the man did nothing. Then his father cupped his hands and said, "Hello?"

The man slowly raised his hand. He was the first person they'd seen in the islands since the storm.

Robert's father stood still in the boat, watching the man. He reached for the taffrail and missed it, reached again and grabbed it to keep them from drifting.

"Thank god you came!" the man said. He didn't shout. His voice carried over the water. It sounded like his voice was coming from behind them. The man's hair was brown and disheveled. Something about the way he stood struck Robert as odd, as if one leg were longer than the other.

Robert's father looked over his shoulder, scanning the bay to see if he'd missed a boat. He laughed. "We came?"

"I'm wrecked," the man said. "On the other side. Of the island. You're the first boat I've seen."

His father asked him if he was all right. The man said yes.

"Do you have a radio?" his father said. "Did you radio it in?"

The man said nothing. Then he said, "Yes, it's a little frazzled now, though. I never got a time, but they said they'd be coming."

"The coast guard?"

"The coast guard."

His father turned and put his hand on the rail and then turned back to the man. "You need help?"

The man dug his boot into the sand. Then he laughed. "Clearly," he said.

Robert's father looked at his son, and then back to the man. "Okay," he said. "Hold on. We'll be right there."

His father told Robert to climb aboard and tie the dinghy. Then he heaved himself aboard as well. Robert tried a buoy knot his father had taught him, but it didn't take, so he tied a square knot. He looked at the man, who was standing perfectly still, and then followed his father below.

"Are we going?" he said.

His father was looking at the ship-to-shore radio. He sat for a while not saying anything. Then, finally, he told Robert to get some food from the cabinet and put it in a paper bag. He packed some Doritos and crackers. Some cottage cheese. As he was reaching for the soda, his father said, "Sort of came out of nowhere, didn't he?"

Robert nodded. "Maybe we could call someone," he said.

His father didn't respond. Robert looked out one of the cabin windows but couldn't see the man. He went farther aft and looked out another window and then saw the man standing near one of their stern ties, inspecting it. "Well, let's go," his father said.

...

Robert sat in the stern of the dinghy as his father rowed toward shore. The dinghy pulled left, and every five strokes or so his father glanced over his shoulder and corrected their path with a few port strokes. Robert held the stern line in his lap and practiced tying bowlines so he wouldn't have to look at the man, who was waiting for them on the beach, standing almost perfectly still. When they landed, he made no move to help them.

"Father-son thing, huh?" the man said.

Robert climbed over the bow, and he and his father pulled the boat over the sand until it was above the tide line. They found a rock and looped the bowline around it.

"You got it," the father said.

The man looked at Robert. "I think it's okay to take your life jacket off now," he said. Robert flushed and fumbled the clasps. The life jacket was too big for him and made him feel like a child. He dropped it in the dinghy. "What's your name, my man?" the man said.

Robert looked at his father. "Robert," he said.

The man smiled. "Robert," he said. His eyes were deep brown. His face was like bark. "Robert." He took a breath. "Like the poet."

Robert said nothing.

"Like his uncle," his father said.

"Like, his, uncle," the man said. Then he turned to Robert's father. "You can put the Doritos down. I have food. You get caught in the storm?"

Robert's father set the bag down at his feet. "Yup. Alma Russell."

"No shit."

Robert looked at his father, who was shifting his weight around like he couldn't get comfortable. The man's forearms, crossed on his chest, were gigantic. "Well, didn't that wind come out of nowhere? One minute, sky's clear to Japan. Next minute the furies. Least you were in a nice boat, though. Those Valiants. Nice boats."

"We were lucky."

The man ran one of his hands through his hair, got stuck halfway through, and tugged it out. "Well like I said. I got wrecked on the other side here. Just been waiting for someone to swing by. You're the first boat I seen."

"Four days ago?"

"I suppose so. I suppose that's what it would be."

The boy's father looked over his shoulder at *Pamier*. They'd left the hatches open. "You need us to take you somewhere?" he said. "We're heading south. We could tell someone."

The man shook his head. "I just gotta move some stuff ship to shore, if you know what . . . two people could do the job, easy. It's a," the man paused to watch something in the distance, "portable generator. Some food. That's all. The boat's wedged on a shoal. Just can't do it by myself. Half an hour, tops."

"We're on a tight schedule."

"Half an hour," the man said. "Tops."

. . .

The path into the woods was obscured by dead branches, and they followed the man over driftwood until they came to the opening. It was less than ten feet from where they'd had their fire the night before, a small, almost invisible seam in the growth. The man bent over, picked up a desiccated buoy in their path, and hulked it into the woods before continuing up the dirt trail.

He led them at a slow pace, stopping now and again to kick a branch out of their way or sometimes for no reason at all. They stayed close behind him. Sunlight filtered through the oak canopy and mottled the ground at their feet. It was at least ten degrees colder inland. Robert felt like he was now walking through a Gary Paulsen novel.

After ten minutes of silent hiking, the man suddenly stopped and turned. He put his hands on his hips and looked at them as if he were considering something. The he grabbed Robert's shoulder and said, "If you look up, you can see an eagle's nest."

Startled, Robert stepped back but was held in place. He looked up. He didn't see anything but trees. "Right there," the man said.

"Where?" his father said.

"In the trees," the man said, pointing. "Top of that one, there."

Neither Robert nor his father saw anything that looked like a nest. The man shrugged. "Take my word for it," he said. "Eagle nest."

"Okay," Robert said. "Okay."

The man turned back up the path. "You ever see an eagle catch a salmon?" he said after a few minutes. He seemed interested only in talking to Robert. His father stayed close. He had fallen behind them a number of times as they weaved through the woods, but now he stayed close.

"Yeah," Robert said, even though he hadn't. He'd seen eagles, plenty of them, flying while gripping salmon, but hadn't seen an actual catch.

"Water, then air," the man said. "Imagine it. Just imagine."

"Something else," his father said. "For sure."

On the map, the island hadn't looked large enough for a forest this size. They walked for fifteen minutes, scrambling over debris felled by the storm, Robert's father helping him by keeping a hand on his back. They walked through ferns and over moss. They passed fishing buoys lodged in the crotches of trees. Robert pointed out to his father what looked like a flannel shirt and a pair of pants draped over a bush, as if hung there to dry. His father nodded, and then looked at it like he was working something around in his head. Finally they broke through the other side into the sun, and Robert was filled with relief. In front of them was a huge cropping of rocks, and below that the water. The beach itself was piled with driftwood, sun-stained logs rolled tightly together like bleachers.

The man turned to them. "Down this way," he said.

"What way?" his father said.

"Around."

His father stood there. "Four days?"

The man looked at him. "About," he said. He pulled himself up to his full height and smiled. "About."

Robert's father was quiet. Then he said, "Let's do this, then. My wife's waiting for us."

"On the boat?" the man said.

"On the boat."

The man laughed, and looked at his shoes and then looked at the sky like he was checking the weather. "No, she's not," he said. "Why would you say something like that?"

. . .

Robert followed his father, who followed the man over the rocks. They walked with their backs to the forest, moving slowly, the man not looking at them. From behind it looked to Robert like the man was covering his mouth. He picked up his pace, and as they approached the end of the outcropping he was almost at a run. Then the man suddenly stopped and turned. "It's," he stumbled. "I'm down here," he said.

Robert's father put his hand on his shoulder, stopping him. "There's no easier way down?"

"Swim," the man said. His eyes were wild. "I swimmed."

Robert noticed the man's mouth was bleeding slightly. The man looked at Robert like he'd just remembered him and smiled. One of his front teeth was smeared brown. He looked like he was trying to keep from laughing. "I swum to be here with you today," he said.

"You all right?" Robert's father said.

The man shrugged and looked over his shoulder at the ocean.

"We're leaving," Robert's father said to his son. Then he turned to the man. "We're leaving now."

"You can't," he said. "I'm just down there."

Robert was aware of something passing between his father and the man but couldn't place it.

Robert's father was kneading his shoulder, pressing him into his body. "It's just us. Us two," he said.

"Come down here," the man said. "Two's enough."

"No," his father said. Robert felt his stomach tighten. He was getting dizzy. He thought he might throw up. "We're leaving."

...

Robert walked quickly with his father behind him toward where they had come out of the woods. "Move." He was worried they wouldn't be able to see the trailhead, but it was clear, as if everything were pointing them in the right direction. At the edge of the forest, he looked back and saw nothing but the windswept shore, debris littering the beach. Seaweed above the tide line, dry and cracked and fly buzzing.

When they were twenty yards up the path, his father said, "I need you to run." He said it in an almost unrecognizable register, and it was this that frightened Robert. More than the size of the man. More than his dead tooth. His father's voice. It seemed conjured from the earth, something from the soil. He ran.

They ran for what seemed like half an hour, but, though Robert was exhausted, he didn't slow. Twigs snapped across his face. His father's breathing was loud in his ear.

Robert felt his father's hands on him and felt himself being lifted off the ground. He held tight to his father around his rib cage and his father held tight to him, carrying him over the ground. He seemed to lose his hearing and his sight and became overwhelmed by the fact of his father's body, cradling his own while careening through growth. He felt his father's breathing. He felt his father's heart. He felt his father's arm around him, iron and unbending. They were a tree themselves, moving through other trees.

...

They were pushing the dinghy and had it halfway down to the water when the man came barreling into the sunlight. Robert saw his father reach for the fish club in the bottom of their dinghy, grab it, and turn. The man stopped briefly at the mouth of the trail, snorted, then resumed his charge. Arms outstretched, like wings.

...

The man collapsed. Robert's father exhaled what sounded like an animal whine and then hit him again with the club, this time on the back of the head. Then again, pushing his features into the sand. The man was motionless, but his father hit him one more time and then, sweating, looked at his son. Robert was on his knees, watching a crab. In both hands he had fistfuls of sand. His father took him quickly in his arms and then the two of them pushed the dinghy into the water and began rowing toward *Pamier*, his father grunting with each stroke, Robert in the bow, as far away from his father as possible.

...

On the boat, they sat in the cockpit. The man, still on the beach, wasn't moving. Someone his size, Robert imagined, would, in a few minutes, rise. But they watched for a few minutes, and nothing.

...

"Is he dead?" Robert asked. He'd searched for and found the fillet knife they'd left in the cockpit and was now holding it in his lap.

"I don't know," his father said. "I don't think so."

Robert wanted to say the man needed help, but was afraid.

"Give me your knife," his father said.

Robert shook his head.

"I need to cut the stern ties. Please."

Robert handed his father the knife, and he leaned over the stern and began sawing the lines. Then he gave up. "Just untie them," Robert said. His father looked at him and then at the cleats that held the lines, reached down, and freed them. They dropped into the water with a tiny splash and sank.

. . .

On the beach Robert could see the bag of food they'd brought for the man, tipped over, not six feet from him. The orange of the Doritos bag. The soda can catching the light. It looked like the man, carrying a bag of groceries, had suffered a heart attack and fallen. Not in the sand. Not on a desolate beach in the Broken Group on the outside of Vancouver Island. But in an asphalt parking lot, where someone would find him, tell whoever needed to be told, and be on their way.

His father stayed in the cockpit. He did not go below for the radio. He did not reach for his son.

Finally he asked his son if he was hungry. Robert shook his head. "Thirsty?" he said.

"No."

. . .

He said, "Your mother loves you very much," and Robert started crying.

. . .

The sun was high over the mast, and the dodger didn't provide much shade. Robert's father was sweating when he stood. He looked at the beach and then told Robert he was going.

"Where?"

"I'll be right back," he said. "I'll be right where you can see me, the whole time. I'll be back."

"He needs help," Robert said.

His father didn't say anything.

"He needed our help."

His father coughed and then asked him if he remembered how to use the radio. "I'm coming with you," Robert said.

"No."

His father climbed down over the lifeline and into the dinghy. Robert followed him and stood at the rail.

"Do you want the knife?" he said.

The father looked at the boy. "This is not your fault," he said, and then pushed off the boat and began rowing to shore.

. . .

"Why can't we just leave him?" he said. He knew his father, thirty feet away in the dinghy, could hear him, but there was no response.

. . .

From *Pamier*, he watched his father beach the dinghy. He stepped onto the sand and, holding the fish club close to his leg, approached the fallen man. At his side he bent over the man, as if whispering. Then he stood. He turned to face the woods and then lobbed the club underhand toward the dinghy. A few rotations, and then it landed inaudibly in the sand. His father stood with his hands on his hips over the man, and when he saw Robert watching him he raised one hand in a wave. Robert waved back. Then he saw his father bend again over the man, put his hands on his shirt, and pull. The man was enormous, and Robert watched as his father began to drag the man up the beach, above the tide line.

It was not easy going. He could hear his father strain with the load, heaves that sounded like tiny yelps as he jerked and tugged. The man's shirt ripped, and his father fell backward. He stood, wiped the back of his pants, and then clasped the man's hands in his and pulled him that way. His father, from this distance, struck him as small. The toes of the man's boots carved parallel grooves in the wet sand.

Robert saw where his father was going and wanted to tell him to stop. He watched him and gripped the halyard until it cut his hand. His father, at the mouth of the woods, paused for breath, and then bent again and disappeared into the growth. The man's trailing legs jerked incremental progress, as if there were all the time in the world, until he too disappeared into the woods, and then there was silence. Robert thought of his sister, at home, and then thought of the radio. He imagined an issued distress signal, moving out from his boat and pulsing under the waves, washing up across the ocean. He imagined someone who looked like his father, but older, removing the receiver and answering. Lighthouses rhythmically sweeping the bay. He unsheathed the fillet knife and lay it across his lap. He listened in their gentle anchorage to the wavelets sucking against the hull, and waited for his father. Come back, he imagined saying. *Come back.* He promised himself he wouldn't move until he saw what he wanted to see. Someone—perhaps many—would come. They had to.

The King of Marvin Gardens

Miriam Karmel

On the days when he came whistling through the door, I knew that I was about to be roped into what my mother called, "One of your grandfather's cockamamie schemes."

"Come on, bubeleh," he'd say, dangling the car keys. "I've got a job for you."

He never let on where we were going. "Just sit back and enjoy the ride," he'd say, as if he were a Buddhist monk counseling me to be in the moment, and not the president of the men's club at Congregation B'Nai Emuneh on Chicago's Near North Side.

We drove with the top down, the hot summer air caressing my face, my frizzy braids flying. I liked to think we were plummeting down the Bobs, the fastest roller coaster at Riverview Park, one that in my twelve years I had never worked up the nerve to try.

I remember the way my grandfather's straw hat stayed on his head, as if he had willed it to obey, just as he must have willed his Olds to propel forward with the gas gauge hovering near empty. He never put in more than a dollar's worth of gas at a time. Mother said he didn't want to die with a full tank.

Sometimes we drove downtown, where grandfather paid a visit to his stockbroker, Muzzy, a stringy, nervous man who kept several rolls of Tums on his desk and a toothpick tucked in the corner of his mouth. I understood nothing about the nature of their business, except that on days when my grandfather walked out of Muzzy's office whistling Broadway show tunes the market was up.

Most of the time we drove to the apartment building my grandfather had bought three weeks into retirement. The family called the place "Juneway," as if it were a beloved pet, or an English country manor. But it was neither beloved nor grand. Juneway, a three-story yellow-brick structure that had aged the color of tobacco spit, stood in the middle of a street named Juneway Terrace, three blocks west of Lake Michigan, just over the city line from Evanston. Grandfather's plan was to rent the eighteen units for easy retirement income. "Prime real estate," he boasted, as if he were the owner of a yellow or green Monopoly property. "Baltic Avenue," my mother sniffed.

My grandfather must have imagined that he would fill the apartments with families where the women bought the kinds of garments he'd once sold in his ladies' apparel shop: fur-collared jackets, knitted dresses with cinched waists and knife-pleated skirts, blue velvet hats with veils and ostrich feathers. Before he retired, I loved stopping by his shop for a piece of the candy he set out in cut-glass bowls. Sometimes I'd hang around and watch as his fragrant clients swept out of the dressing room in stocking feet, coyly circling him. "You don't think the hemline is a little long, Mr. Rosner?" pronouncing his name with a long *o*, as if he hailed from a family of rose gardeners. "Not too tight across here?" they'd ask, brushing manicured hands across full bottoms and breasts.

Even then, I knew he was handsome, though I didn't understand that he exuded an easy sexual energy that women are naturally drawn to. He had the kind of craggy good looks one associates with aging southern senators. He was what was called in those days a snappy dresser. In summer, he wore cream-colored linen suits; in winter he favored dark wool slacks and a herringbone jacket. His silver hair, curling above the collar of his broadcloth shirts, never looked unkempt.

Like my grandfather's sister, my Aunt Edith, the family's "Queen Bee," the women who patronized his shop lived in solid buildings with doormen and awnings that extended all the way to the curb so that when they stepped from a taxi the rain or snow wouldn't dampen their newly minted hairdos. The brass on the heavy glass doors of Edith's building was so lustrous I couldn't pass it without checking my reflection.

Juneway lacked such refinements. It was strictly utilitarian, a building with a sense of purpose. Its rooms were large and square, its ceilings high. It had solid doors and concrete lintels and window frames. If Juneway were a car, it would have been a four-door Chevrolet.

By the time my grandfather took over, most of the original tenants—closeted bachelors, aging widows living on small pensions, and the kind of spinsters who bequeath small fortunes to cats—had died off or joined the great suburban migration. The city was changing. Shortly after my grandfather bought the building, Martin Luther King was assassinated and riots broke out, destroying a three-mile swath of the city's west side. Hundreds of families were left homeless. At the urging of my Nonna, a big-hearted woman, my grandfather let these families in. He did so knowing that they couldn't afford the modest rent, but he was an optimist who believed that somehow they'd find a way. After all, hadn't he, an immigrant who barely spoke the language, managed to parlay his meager earnings from peddling day-old bread into a dress shop that allowed him to retire young enough to dabble in the stock market and buy a building three blocks west of a Great Lake? "America!" he'd exclaim, as if his astonishing success required no further explanation.

But his tenants didn't find a way, and my grandfather's easy retirement became a full-time headache. He got no sympathy from my Nonna. Big-hearted one minute, disapproving the next, she took to calling her husband "the King of Marvin Gardens."

The King and I fell into a routine that summer. Starting at the top, we worked our way down the three flights, knocking on the doors of those tenants who were behind in the rent. Along the way, my grandfather swept cigarette butts and candy wrappers from the stairs and noted anything that needed fixing—burned-out lightbulbs, loose hinges, broken window panes.

It was after the graffiti appeared that my grandfather started carrying a baseball bat in the trunk of his car. I swear he never used it, but from time to time he'd pick it up, slap it against the palm of his hand, and say, "Believe you me. If I ever catch one of those gonifs."

Then I'd imagine him running after one of those punks the way he once chased our cat down the street with a salami, after he caught it nibbling at the bat-sized sausage that hung by a string from the hinge of a kitchen cabinet. But my grandfather wasn't a fighter, which explains how he wound up in Chicago, far from his native Eastern European land of ever-changing borders.

His decision to leave the place he called "Poland Russia" took hold the day a group of thugs attacked him while he stood waiting for a train to Warsaw, where he was to arrange for a shipment of pelts for his uncle's coat factory. He tried hiding behind his newspaper, pretending not to notice them, when one of the louts grabbed the paper out of his hands, threw it to the ground, and stomped on it. Then the bullies circled him, pointed to the other end of the platform, and shouted, "Jews over there!" My grandfather, a young married man with a child on the way and a considerable amount of cash sewed into the lining of his coat, didn't want any trouble. He moved. And they followed. Circling him again, they pointed back toward the spot he'd just vacated, shouting, "Jews there!" After several rounds of their cruel game, they left my grandfather alone with his soiled newspaper. Then just as the train was pulling into the station the thugs reappeared. This time they knocked him down and kicked him, breaking two of his front teeth and shattering his left ankle. Within the year, my grandfather, my Nonna, and their infant daughter, my mother's older sister, were on a ship to America.

For the rest of his life, whenever it rained, my grandfather walked as if he was favoring a foot with a blistered heel, and he'd say, "Thanks God for those gonifs." Then he'd turn to me. "Remember, Ceely, always to be looking on the brighter side." My grandfather could find the silver lining even in a mugging. It was years before I understood that if he hadn't been assaulted, he would have shared the fate of his parents and three of his siblings who, a few years later, were sent to the death camps.

So the baseball bat stayed in the trunk, while we looked on the brighter side and changed lightbulbs and glazed windows. We scattered grass seed on the tiny patch of dirt between the sidewalk and the curb. We placed a concrete birdbath beside the statue of Saint Francis that a former tenant had generously set in the courtyard. We filled huge flowerpots with gera- niums and ivy, and after setting them outside the three entryways in the U-shaped courtyard, my grandfather stood back and beamed, as if he'd just created the heavens and earth. Soon enough, the pots and birdbath became receptacles for whatever cigarette butts and candy wrappers hadn't been cast aside in the stairwells.

One afternoon, after collecting the rents and cleaning up the flowerpots, my grandfather stuck a Polaroid in my hand and instructed me to take pic- tures of the graffiti splattered bricks. Somebody had gone wild with a can of spray paint, covering the building with slogans concerning the liberation of a Black Panther who was on trial for the murder of a Brink's driver during a holdup that went awry. *Free Fred! Fred Lives! Off the Pig! Smash the State!* My grandfather intended to send the pictures to his insurance company, though Mother predicted he wouldn't collect a nickel.

We had just finished taking the pictures when an imposing woman stepped boldly into the courtyard and stopped, the way I imagined my grandfather's car would halt the moment it ran out of gas. She appeared self-assured, standing tall in open-toed high heels, which she wore with obvious disregard to her height. Her dress was well cut, though like the shoes a few years out of fashion. She removed a slip of paper from her purse, studied it, and looked up with a puzzled expression at the three entryways.

"You are maybe looking for someone?" My grandfather—who had long ago honed an easy way with women, especially the good-looking ones—swooped in with a slight bow and a tip of his straw hat. Though this woman was, as Nonna would say, no spring chicken, it was possible to discern in her face traces of former beauty, which had settled into a pleasant composition that some would call handsome.

"The super," she said. "I'm looking for the super." She had an accent, distinct from my grandfather's, who had just been telling me that he wasn't going to let "a few bad epples spoil the bunch." Dapper as he was, his accent betrayed him as an outsider, an Old World misfit. His speech was a sepia-toned picture compared to the slick Polaroids I was clutching. The woman standing beside him in the open-toed shoes had a lush accent that reminded me of mangoes, though there was nothing languid or tropical in her demeanor. On stage, she might have portrayed a countess from a small Eastern European duchy. She sounded, in fact, like one of the Gabor sisters.

"The super is on vacation," my grandfather lied.

The truth is there hadn't been a super on the premises for nearly a year. Prior to that, the building had been managed by a string of hapless men who had neither the aptitude nor stomach for housekeeping and tended to decamp without notice. Thinking he'd have better luck with a woman, my grandfather hired a middle-aged Polish woman named Bertha Wozniak, whom my Nonna called "the Valkyrie." Bertha managed to hold things together until her boyfriend, Turk, moved in, at which point the two of them spent their days chain-smoking and playing gin rummy. When my grandfather finally asked them to leave, they refused until he threatened legal action, which meant that he dictated a letter that I typed on stationery he filched from my uncle's law office. Bertha and Turk took with them the whistling teakettle and what had been my Nonna's "everyday" dishes, until she replaced them with something better.

With another bow to the imposing woman, my grandfather repeated the lie that the super was on vacation, adding, "Perhaps I can be of assistance?"

He assured her that the building was his and anything that a super might do he could do better. He was back in his dress shop with the preening ladies. He was *Mr. Rose-ner*, purveyor of silk and fur and fine woolen goods, not the landlord of an aging building riddled with liberation slogans and a swastika, which I'd secretly photographed when he'd gone back to the car for another pack of film.

"In that case," the woman said, handing him a yellowed newspaper clipping. It was so old that I thought it might crumble in his hands like the wings of a dead moth. He read it to himself, his lips moving, as they did when he mumbled his morning prayers. Then, either to hide his confusion or to buy time, he read it aloud. "The nicest 1 BR apartment around! Clean, lots of windows & morning sun. HW flrs, coin op lndry on site, convenient bus line."

An awkward silence followed. The woman looked at my grandfather, as if waiting for the oracle to speak. My grandfather looked at me, a twelve-year-old foundling whose mother was holed up in her room behind a Do Not Disturb sign, reading Jane Austen, waiting for Mr. Darcy to come tap, tap, tapping on her door. And I looked at the strange woman, wondering how she'd acquired hair the color of a bright penny, and whether she knew that her fuchsia lipstick had strayed outside the lip line.

Breaking the silence, she introduced herself as Magda Rothstein, and said, "I don't suppose it's still available. Silly of me." Then she returned the crumbling ad to her handbag and apologized for taking my grandfather's time.

"Dond be silly." He dismissed her concern with the wave of a manicured hand, his diamond pinky ring winking in the sun. "In fact." His face brightened. "In fact! Ah hah! I've got just the nicest place for you."

"You do?" I blurted.

He shot me a look, but I knew that ad had run long before he'd acquired the building. Besides, we'd just made the rounds collecting the rent. There weren't any vacancies.

"You have a place?" I repeated, at which point he stepped on my foot. The blow was so unexpected that I dropped the pictures.

"Gutten Himmel, Ceely! Now look what you've done."

As I bent to retrieve the pictures, the woman named Magda Rothstein said, "Ceely. That was my sister's name. I always wanted that name."

I didn't tell her that I'd always wanted any other name. Sally. Caroline. Jane. Instead, I was named for my grandfather's sister, the one who died shortly after being liberated from Auschwitz. People were always telling me that I had Ceely's pale skin, frizzy black hair, generous bone structure. Even when I wolfed my food Ceely was invoked, with a warning that if I didn't slow down my stomach would burst. "Just like Ceely," my mother would say, and tell me again the story of the young girl who, after months of starvation, ate her first meal too quickly and died. Before the war, my grandfather had tried sending for Ceely, but visas were impossible to get. Only now do I think that on some subconscious level he regarded me as his lost sister, especially that summer when I was the age she was when he last saw her.

I was on the ground gathering the pictures when my grandfather told Mrs. Rothstein, "You've come to exactly the right place!"

I considered asking her to excuse us for a moment while I took him aside to ask why a woman in a well-cut dress and high heels would want to move into a crummy old building with a bunch of deadbeats for neighbors. And where would she live? I knew he wouldn't evict anyone, not even the woman in 2B who'd answered the door in a kimono that had fallen open to expose her generous breasts so that my grandfather had to look at his shoes while explaining that he'd come for the rent. She nodded, pulled a pack of cigarettes from her pocket, and after lighting one let the match drop to the floor as she leaned into the doorway and exhaled. Through a haze of smoke, she offered him three books of S&H green stamps.

As we headed down the stairs, she called out that she'd been saving up for a bathroom scale, as if somehow that enhanced the value of those books. Ignoring her, my grandfather turned to me and said, "Ach, Ceely. It's hard to be a Jew." That's when the man who could find the silver lining in a mugging handed me the Polaroid and said we had work to do.

With the appearance of Mrs. Rothstein my grandfather's mood brightened, the way it did when the market was up, only instead of whistling Broadway show tunes he appeared taller and somehow almost debonair. He insisted that Mrs. Rothstein, who had bent down to help me pick up the pictures, get up. "Ceely will see to that. I dond want you should trouble yourself."

She smelled of lemon and cloves, and I wanted her to stay.

"It's no trouble. Really. Mr.—"

"Rosner," he said, with a long *o*, like the ladies who'd once bought dresses from him. "Get up, please. I insist." Then he stuck his foot between our hands. Undeterred, Mrs. Rothstein reached across his foot and picked up one of the pictures, which is when I saw the blue-black numbers tattooed on the inside of her right arm. I knew what they were, because my grandfather's cousin Anya had numbers on her arm, though I was never allowed to ask about them. Before Mrs. Rothstein could hand the picture to me, my grandfather bent down and snatched it away. Perhaps he thought that she hadn't already noticed the graffiti, and only now, in a grainy, slightly out-of-focus Polaroid, would she discern the truth about the *nicest 1 BR apartment around!*

By the time I was back on my feet, my grandfather was leading Mrs. Rothstein toward the super's apartment. If she was disappointed that it didn't correspond to whatever crumbling fantasy she'd been harboring in her handbag for who knows how many years, she didn't let on. Instead, she beamed as if she'd just toured one of the Seven Wonders of the World. Turning to my grandfather, she said, "Mr. Rosner, from now on you won't have to lift a finger. I'll keep this place spic and span. Even the hallway stairs. I guarantee, you'll be able to eat off them." Then they shook hands, though it seemed they held on longer than necessary.

On the drive home, my grandfather called Mrs. Rothstein a mechaieh, a real joy, a miracle, the answer to his prayers. Had Elijah himself come sailing through the door and drunk from his appointed glass on the Seder table, my grandfather couldn't have been more delighted.

When I reminded him that he hadn't placed the ad, he said, "You dond know vat you're speaking." Then he told me to pipe down because he had to pay attention to the road.

"But you didn't, did you?" I demanded. Besides, what did he know about Mrs. Rothstein, except that she had a sister named Ceely, information she offered only after hearing my name? "You didn't, did you?" I persisted. "Tell me the truth."

"Dond talk nonsense." And again, he pleaded with me to just let him drive.

. . .

I didn't get asked along much after Mrs. Rothstein moved in. Instead, it was I who did the asking. Most of the time my grandfather said no, that I would be bored, that I should hang out with kids my own age. But I noticed that if I asked in front of Nonna, he'd shrug and say, "Vy not?"

Mrs. Rothstein always had something for me: perfume samples that she picked up at the fragrance counter at Marshall Fields, or pencils from the oculist or dry cleaner. She even sewed a corduroy jumper for me. Nonna had one of her dizzy spells when I modeled it for her, though it wasn't until

Mrs. Rothstein gave me a box of Dutch chocolates in the shape of wooden clogs that I thought I understood why.

That's when I made the connection to an assortment of pastel jellies and raspberry buttercreams that I'd received the previous summer at the end of a visit to family friends in Memphis. As I was leaving to return home, a neighbor stopped by and made a fuss of presenting the candy to me, which I figured was a local custom, the way my mother had pressed a dime in my hand when she took me to the airport for my flight to Memphis. "In case you need to make a phone call," she'd said. So when I received the candy, I thought that I'd divined a difference between the South and the North as significant as speech patterns or attitudes toward slavery. A southern send-off was marked by sweetness and light; in the North, an impending journey was marked by visions of catastrophe that could only be remedied or, who knows, warded off, by one thin dime. I preferred the southern way.

My mother saw right through that one-pound summer assortment, which she spotted the minute I got off the plane. "Where'd you get that?"

"Gloria Brody." I clutched the box to my chest. "The Weitz's neighbor."

"Very interesting."

"That's how they do things in the South," I insisted, clutching the box even tighter.

"I see."

I didn't know what she saw, yet looking back I recognize that as the moment I crossed some line into a world of comprehending and knowing. By the end of that year, Sam Weitz left his wife and three children for Gloria Brody, who had a husband and three children of her own.

I never understood how mother could predict the breakup of two marriages, two families, and the shattering of eleven lives on the basis of a one-pound summer assortment of candy. But I understood enough to keep the Dutch chocolate under wraps. I didn't want mother divining anything about Mrs. Rothstein. And I certainly didn't want my Nonna to have another one of her dizzy spells.

Progress Center

Clean Laundry

Michael Walsh

I couldn't have been happier that summer. Tyler, my best friend, had dumped his girlfriend and come back to me. It wasn't the first time, and he wouldn't admit that he liked guys better, but he revived our much-discussed plan to get an apartment together. Even though I had the money for my share of the deposit from my high-school graduation party, I still needed my share of two months' rent. If I didn't have it really soon, Tyler might change his mind again. Out of twelve job applications, only work as a farmhand fit my cashier's schedule at the gas station, and a dairy farmer named Glenn Amundson hired me.

At a glance, Glenn's farm looked like any other. Cornfields stood on each side of his driveway. His house was white, his barn red, and his cows black-and-white. On the first day of the job when he shook my hand, I compared my new blue jeans and white T-shirt to his farm wear: a sun-faded hat emblazoned with a winged corncob, a dingy white T-shirt, Levis with a hole forming in the right knee, and scuffed brown boots. I tried to guess his age and decided on late twenties. Even though it was early June, his arms and neck were already tan. Glenn didn't seem different than any of the single guys I'd seen doing shots and flirting with the nineteen-year-old waitresses at the VFW. I wondered if I could pass long enough to make my cash.

Before he started showing me the ropes, Glenn wanted a photocopy of my driver's license for his records. He led me inside his house. In passing I glimpsed the living room—green carpet, a coffee table with stacked copies

of *Northern Gardener,* and framed drawings of penguins on the walls, different from the scattered tractor magazines and pictures of mallards hanging
crooked in black plastic frames that I expected. In his office there were white
packets of seeds all over a table and small plants in black plastic pots near
a window. Behind his desk he kept a small photocopier and a fax machine.
When I handed him my driver's license, he held it up to the light and then
looked back and forth between it and my face, as though I was a suspect.

Finally he said, "Yeah, that's you, Jake."

"Who else would it be?"

"I don't know—your brother?"

"I don't have one."

"Hey, don't take it personal. I hired a fifteen-year-old once—a middle-
school kid—who stole his older brother's ID. Even opened a bank account.
The family really screwed me over in the end."

"I'm not fifteen. And I don't have an older brother."

"I know. Like I said, it's you."

He walked behind his desk to the photocopier. The machine hummed,
and its light moved under the glass. The photocopy in one hand, he handed
me my license with the other. As he set the copy on the desk next to the ap-
plication I had filled out and mailed to him last week, I opened my billfold
and inserted my driver's license into a flap, behind which I kept my fake
ID. Standing in the doorway, Glenn motioned for me to follow. He led me
down a short hallway and stopped at the open door of a bathroom. At the
hall's end under a window sat his washer and dryer.

"You can shower here after chores if you want. Some people don't like
the barn smell in their cars. And if you want, you can leave your barn clothes
here." He pointed to an empty blue basket. "I wash a load every night."

I looked from Glenn to the basket and must have had a strange look
on my face because he responded, "Either way's okay. I always offer that to
anyone who works here. I have to mention something else, but you might
not like it." He examined my beat-up blue tennis shoes. "Those shoes won't
cut it. Why don't you try on some of my old boots and see if a pair fits? You
have to get your own—something with a steel toe."

Now that he mentioned it, I remembered his emphasis on heavy foot-
wear. Glenn brought me to a closet near the front door and pulled out a
bunch of boots, some of which were incomplete pairs. I squatted on the
linoleum and tried on a few sets, but Glenn had smaller feet than mine.
Nothing fit, and I changed back into my tennis shoes. He shrugged and

said, "Watch your step then." As he and I walked the wet slope to the barn, I carefully chose my steps to keep my balance.

At the door my shoes were so caked with mud that I had to scrape them off on the doorjamb. I started breathing through my mouth right away. In two long rows the cows lay in straw or stood flicking their tails. Behind each row was a two-foot-deep gutter. As I followed Glenn past the cows to the walkway that divided the barn down the middle, one cow arched her back and peed, a huge yellow splash against the concrete. Droplets landed on my bare arm, which I shook vigorously.

We arrived at a big metal door, open just enough that I could see the pasture, but Glenn didn't take me there. He led me to the milking room with its stainless-steel tank. He lifted the lid to reveal a propeller-like blade stirring the milk. On hooks, the milkers, full of tubes, hung like steel and rubber spiders. At Glenn's instruction, I filled a gray pail with hot, soapy water and brown paper towels. He carried three milkers with one arm and a pail of iodine with his spare hand. I followed him to the first cow, and he placed the machines on hooks while I waited for him to tell me what I should do. The cow's legs, stomach, and udder were coated in mud. As I pondered the task ahead of me, I doubted this work was worth the minimum wage Glenn would pay me.

Because there was no space between this first cow and her neighbor, Glenn pushed the second cow to the side and made room in the middle, where we crouched with the bucket. The first few towels turned black from the cow's dirt, and Glenn instructed me to throw them in the gutter. I kept wiping until she seemed clean, but on inspection, gunk remained. Three of my soapy towels later, Glenn deemed her udder sanitary, and he attached the milker.

He continued to lead me through his routine, and the next two hours were the worst first day on the job I've ever had. I couldn't get the cows' udders clean enough, and Glenn had to wash some. A cow hit the side of my head with her tail, which made the hair above my left ear damp and sticky. When I approached an ornery cow on her left side (she preferred being milked on her right side), she kicked my thigh. Limping, I started to wonder whether Tyler would bring girls home to spend the night. It seemed likely. While I contemplated my future betrayal, a black cow with a white forehead stepped onto my left foot and stood there, all two thousand pounds of her.

My toes felt like twigs under a tire. Oblivious, she chewed her cud and swung her tail at flies. Instead of making any noise, I held my breath and gave her a shove. She was too content to notice how hard I elbowed her ribs. I couldn't back up and really make it count, so I yelled for Glenn to help. A tear was trickling from my right eye. I could feel it, but he couldn't see it.

"Kid, I told you, you need boots."

Normally I would have said something about the kid comment, but I was clenching my teeth. From the wall Glenn grabbed what looked like a two-foot-long plastic ruler and smacked the stupid cow's flank. By the sound, it really stung. She raised her hoof to kick Glenn, and he smacked her leg. When I jumped back across the gutter, I slipped. My good foot sunk up to the shin. I reminded myself that for the chance to have a place with Tyler I had to be willing to do mostly anything. While I limped away and dripped, he smacked her twice more. She went still, and Glenn followed me to the door. As he started to speak, I hoped he wouldn't mention my choice of shoes.

"Chores are pretty much done, Jake. You didn't do too bad. Why don't you hose off your leg and shower? I'll finish up. But before you go, you should meet the slapper." He handed me the plastic ruler, warm from his grip. "If one of them kicks you again, use it. If you let them get away with too much, they won't respect you."

But I didn't care about earning the cows' respect. After soaking my gross foot with a garden hose, I grabbed my duffel bag from the car. It had my change of clothes and my good shoes, which I needed to find a different job doing anything but getting kicked and crushed by cows. I took off my shoes and socks on his porch and hiked up my jeans. There was still crap on my ankle.

Leaving my duffel bag, I walked back to the garden hose for a final rinse. Glenn emerged from the barn, and, seeing me, walked in my direction instead of toward the house. "Is your foot all right?" he asked.

"It's all right."

"Diamond, the one who stood on your foot, she's kind of dumb. I should mention I usually pay on the first day, just to let people know I'm for real, and sometimes because it doesn't work out. So let me know what you're thinking."

"A check would be good."

"Oh," he said with a disappointed shrug. "Sure then. You know where the shower is, so I'll find my checkbook."

I waited for him to turn away before I reached down, wiped away the last trace with my fingers, and rubbed my hand on the grass. Then I rinsed my hand, too. It still smelled like cow. I didn't know how that was possible. Afterward I grabbed my bag from the porch and knocked on the door.

"You don't need to knock," Glenn said, check in hand.

Walking in, I took the check he extended. He didn't meet my gaze, and I didn't look at the amount, which I thought might be rude.

"You look like you want to clean up," he said, pointing down his hallway.

In the bathroom I stripped and noticed too late that Glenn's porcelain was better than clean, not even a hair in the sink, and I was about to stain either the white of his countertop or his linoleum. I hadn't thought to bring a garbage bag with me, and I didn't want to get dressed just to walk through his house and look for one. Then I saw the magazine rack in front of the toilet. Holding my jeans in one hand, I pulled loose some newspaper. Several magazines fell, too. I spread a few layers of newspaper on the floor and dropped my jeans there.

The edge of the check was poking from my pocket. I looked at the amount of payment, which was fair; at the bottom of the check in bold print appeared the statement THIS IS GAY MONEY.

I hadn't locked the door, so I did. I had been ready to leave Glenn's farm and not return, but getting into the shower, I thought about all the different people who must read his checks. By the time I finished my shower, I had changed my mind again. I quickly dried off and dressed. Steam coated the mirror. I hadn't turned on the fan, so I clicked the switch. Except for the pants, which I rolled up in the newspaper, I threw my dirty clothes into the bag. Leaving the bathroom, I found Glenn on his couch.

Having changed into his bathrobe, he was resting his heels on a *Northern Gardener* magazine. His head tilted back, mouth open slightly, eyes closed, and arms limp on the cushions. He hadn't mentioned how long he'd been without help, but it looked like too long. I dropped the duffel bag. Eyes open now, Glenn turned his head to look at me. He sat up and, placing his feet back on the floor, said, "I'm sorry it didn't work out. If you hear of anybody who's looking for a job, I'd appreciate a mention."

"Actually, I'll take the job."

Glenn raised his hands, palms halting the moment, and said, "I thought you just wanted the check."

"No, I'm trying to get a place. With a friend. I need the money. That's all. I should have said something."

He lowered his hands to his sides. "Oh. Great! I misunderstood. You did fine with the cows. Better than a lot of kids I've had help me. It takes time."

"I should've had boots. I'll get used to it."

He nodded and said, "If you want to leave your barn clothes here, just let me know. That way you don't have to bring the stink home with you."

Taking steps toward the door, I said, "Maybe I'll take you up on that tomorrow. My friend's expecting me to go make some trouble."

Glenn walked me to his front door and offered another handshake, which I took. "I'm glad to have you here. I really need the help," he said with his best smile. "Now don't get caught in any trouble with that friend of yours."

. . .

Siren, the town where I lived with my father, was a half-hour drive from Glenn's farm. I didn't live in Siren proper, but in Siren's equivalent of a suburb—a little cluster of town houses outside the edge of town. The houses were brown rectangles with identical windows, and at Christmas, with all the snow and the flashing lights, they looked like a gated community for gingerbread men and their elite offspring.

At home I bundled the newspapers under my arm, grabbed my duffel bag, lifted my jeans by the waistband, and sped up to my room before my father could sidetrack me with conversation. He always had questions, but at least he respected my privacy. I trotted downstairs to the laundry room in the basement, but my father heard my feet on the wooden stairs, and, calling my name, he followed. As I dumped my barn clothes into a washer, he stepped alongside it and closed the lid. I hoisted the heavy blue jug of laundry soap, but he kept his palm atop the lid.

"Take these filthy clothes out of my washer."

"They're dirty."

"I'm not going to have shit-covered clothes stinking up my house."

Widening my nostrils, I sniffed the air in mockery.

"I smelled you the moment you walked in. The community theatre called you for an audition in that play you mentioned. If you get it, I'll pay you to go to rehearsals. We can't have you working for some farmer. You can hate me all you want, but I'm going to be resolute about being unreasonable." He smiled at his clever phrasing. "If you're going to work in some barn, you can keep your dirty clothes in your car and take them to the laundromat."

I threw the washer lid open to make it clang. "Rehearsals wouldn't start for weeks, and I need the money now. I'm moving out, remember? Me and Tyler and the apartment?"

"I'm not giving you money for that apartment. That kid can't tell whether he's coming or going, and the two of you were so busy making your last
plan to move in together, you didn't apply for college last year." My father,
unchanging in his belief in the power of higher education to transform my
life, had been unable to conceive of any different, legitimate choice I could
make as a high-school graduate. His father had never been to college and
made more money as a truck driver than my father did as an accountant, but
I decided against mentioning it right then.

"Why don't you go back to college and study acting if you want to live
through me so much?" I pulled the clothes out of the washer and watery shit
smeared my palm. After two armfuls, the dirty clothes, including the previ-
ously quarantined jeans, were mixed with formerly clean ones in my bag.

"You should be studying Shakespeare, not driving a tractor."

I tried to zip the bag shut too fast and jammed the zipper. As I wrestled it
loose, he closed the lid of the washer again. I lifted the bag, and before I reached
the stairs, he said, "Even your mother says you're falling asleep at the wheel,
Jake, and it's been a long time since she and I saw eye to eye on anything."

"Oh, blow me. Both of you."

On the wall of the stairway I wiped my palm. It left a brown streak
on the white paint. My father followed me upstairs and recited everything
he wouldn't help me with anymore—laundry, college applications, favors,
move-in money—but he didn't notice the mark. After getting quarters from
my room, I called Tyler and asked him to meet me at the Fast Spin on the
main drag.

. . .

By the time he arrived in his beater, I was pulling my clothes from the dryer.
His Twins ball cap had rumpled and warped his blonde hair. Between his
blue eyes his nose twisted slightly to the left if you looked really close. When
he was a kid, he fell off a tractor and snapped his nose. Sometimes it made
him seem cross-eyed. He took a seat next to the dryer at the end of the row.
Most were empty, but in a few, buttons clacked against the glass doors and
metal chambers. While I tried to concentrate on folding laundry, I told him
everything about my day except for the statement on Glenn's check.

"You're going to be pissed at me, but your dad has a point." I noticed that
so far, I had only folded three T-shirts. Under the fluorescent light, the white
undershirts were strangely pale. I picked up a fourth and shook it to smooth
the wrinkles. "You're not cut out for farm work," Tyler said. He stood and,

to my surprise, reached for the pile. For a few minutes he and I folded the clothes. He lifted blue jeans, but not any underwear, and only at moments when my hands didn't touch any nearby clothes. Each time he took another pair, I wanted to touch his timid hand, but I just kept folding my briefs.

"You're not really going back there tomorrow, are you?"

"Tyler, I've been in school all my life. I don't want to be anybody's robot. I don't want to learn what I'm supposed to learn anymore."

I said that a lot louder than necessary. An elderly woman wearing sunglasses and two young moms with hyperactive kids gave me looks. Tyler lowered his voice and said, "Dude, keep your voice down. I'm just saying you're so smart, you should be in school."

I kept folding laundry. Only pairs of underwear were left, and Tyler wouldn't touch them. Through the glass doors of the washers, I watched other people's laundry slosh and tumble, endless as hamsters in wheels. "Hey," Tyler said to get my attention, "here's some good news. I'll have the rent money in a week. We're selling some pigs this weekend, and my dad said I could take my share of the rent from what we make."

"The sooner we move, the better."

"You don't have to keep that barn job, Jake. I know you don't really want it."

"It wasn't so bad. I kind of like it."

"Are you trying to get on your dad's bad side permanently?"

"No, the cows need me, Tyler. It's my calling."

"If you say so," he said. "Hey—let's get some beer tonight. I've got the money if that ID you bought still looks enough like you."

. . .

That night we drove around with a twelve pack. My fake ID said I was Michael Thompson, and while I had a few despite my distaste for beer, Tyler drank way too many. I stopped my car on a dirt road so he could puke in the weeds. Afterward, he wouldn't stop talking about Lisa, the girlfriend he recently dumped. "She was too good for a schmuck like me," he kept saying. I let him jabber and tuned him out.

Back at my place, Tyler could barely walk. I led him from my car, through the side door of the house, and up the stairs to my room, where he flopped onto my bed instead of the old green futon. He started unbuttoning his shirt but stopped halfway. Then he sat up to untie his shoes, started giggling, and whispered my name until I said, "What?"

"I can't do the shoes," he laughed. He removed his shirt and I saw that perfect line of hair traveling from his groin to his belly, dividing him. I turned off the light, undressed down to my boxers, slipped under the covers, and set my alarm. Eventually Tyler got his shoes and pants off and lay there on the comforter, chuckling to himself. A deep sleeper, he passed out fast. I listened to him breathe for a long time.

Later I woke up on my left side with Tyler's arm around my waist, his hand limp across my stomach, which meant that tonight he wanted comfort. I didn't know when he'd gotten under the blanket. I turned onto my back, which disturbed him a little, and once he settled again, I reached for his dick. It was hard under his boxers, but unlike most other nights, he flinched and pulled away from my touch. He sat upright in bed in the dark. I remained on my side and looked past him toward the wall as he leaned close to my ear and whispered, "We keep doing this, we're going to end up homos. You said so yourself."

I couldn't deny what I'd said to Tyler almost two years ago. He repeated it whenever he got jittery in bed, but instead of sinking into a disgruntled sleep, I yanked the pillow from between his back and the headboard, threw it against the futon, and moved my face close to his. I whispered, "Go sleep with Lisa if you like girls so much," but my attempt at an insult was half-hearted.

I closed my eyes. A branch outside was scraping against the siding. I tried to count myself back to sleep according to its rhythm, but I couldn't focus on anything but Tyler. I didn't know how long it was before he slipped from the covers, but I heard the futon creak when he moved there. By the time the alarm rang at 7:00, he had gone.

I went downstairs to the living room, where my father was sitting on the carpet to stretch his legs before his morning run. As I tried to walk through the room to the kitchen, he asked, "Is Tyler all right?"

I stopped to answer and noticed his left hand reaching for his right foot and touching the toe of his shoe. He held his trembling fingers there.

"Yeah, Tyler's all right."

His stretch faltered, and he redoubled his effort to touch his toes.

"Are you okay then?" He exhaled a pained breath.

"Yeah, I'm all right, too," I said with annoyance.

His fingers let go of the shoe, and his arm relaxed. "Tyler was crying in the bathroom last night. Real loud." My father's right hand reached for his left foot.

"Oh that," I lied. "It wasn't a *big* deal, it was just, well, he gets really sad sometimes."

Remembering to breathe, he took a breath and said, "He gets pretty talk-ative when he's sad. He says stuff I don't think he'd ever normally say."

"What did he say?"

"Nothing that surprised me."

"What did he say?"

My father braced one palm on the floor, gripped the toes of his left shoe, and exhaled deeply. Walking away, I called Tyler, who didn't answer, and left a message asking him the same question.

. . .

Hours later, I still had no answer. I kept imagining what Tyler might have said as I worked the midmorning to midafternoon shift, bought a pair of boots at Fleet Farm, and then drove toward Glenn's. On the road I called Tyler for the fourth unsuccessful time and got his brother, who said that Tyler was too busy to talk. When I parked, Glenn didn't emerge from his house, so after I put on my work boots and slid my cell phone in my pocket, I knocked on his door, my duffle bag in hand. I waited. His truck was in the driveway. I raised my voice and asked, "Are you here somewhere?"

I heard my question echo against the sheds and barn and double back, as though someone else were asking. After waiting a respectable minute, I let myself into his unlocked house, made my way to the bathroom, and closed the door. I changed into my barn clothes, transferred my cell phone to my loose-fitting jeans, and folded my good clothes before placing them back in-side the bag. Then I heard Glenn's faint voice call my name. I went outside. Glenn was opening the pasture's gate to let himself into the yard. When he was near enough to speak, he said, "How's my troublemaker today?"

"I'm—I'm fine," I stammered.

"Well, I hope so," he said. "You said you were expecting to make some trouble with that friend."

My wits returning, I managed to keep my face from going red. "No, I had fun instead."

After Glenn made a polite laugh, he gave me the overview of today's work while he and I walked to the pasture. A cow had busted the fence earlier that afternoon. He'd chased most of the escapees back inside to their stalls for milking, but a few adventurous heifers and their feisty ringleader were far and gone. At the pasture gate, he lifted a red plastic handle attached to the fence wire, and after I walked through, he closed the gate. I found the stout, smooth broken handle of a tool in the dirt, which Glenn approved of as a weapon.

He brought me to the break in the fence. The wires, stripped from their plastic insulators, lay loose on the ground. After passing through, I scanned the corn and alfalfa fields for a minute before I saw a small, black-and-white shape near the edge of Glenn's western field. To the east and north were more cows, each imperceptible until Glenn pointed to one in relation to trees and roads. Upon reaching a point further north than the cow had gone, he and I stopped. "You spook her back toward the barn," he said, "and I'll stay a few rows to her side and keep her from wandering off another direction."

The stick under my arm, I gathered a few rocks from the field. First I threw the small ones, which startled her enough to take a few steps. But Glenn said, "Use bigger rocks," so I pried two hefty rocks from the field and chucked one. When it hit the cow's back, she made a strange, baffled sound and ran. Stick in hand, I ran after her. In my pocket the cell phone started vibrating, but I couldn't answer. Glenn kept pace with her in the corn row. Then she stopped to chew on a cornstalk.

Reaching her side, I yelled, "No, you keep going," but she didn't move. Why was I trying to talk to a cow? I hit her ribs. She started running, but Glenn and I herded her back through the fence and into her stall, where he locked her down. Checking my caller ID, I saw Tyler's number but no red message light. I returned his call but hung up at the ding of his voice mail.

. . .

After chasing the remaining cows to the barn, Glenn and I milked the herd. Afterward, I reached into my pocket for the cell phone, which I hadn't checked for hours. It was gone. Glenn helped me search his barn and pasture, but by the time we stopped, the farm was dark except the yard light. Glenn said, "I'm feeling bad about your phone and keeping you here so late. Let me put something on the grill for you."

"Sure, I'll have some grub."

"Grub? Have I turned you country already?"

He and I walked to his house. On the porch, I was a step ahead when he undid his belt and dropped his dirty jeans. Hearing his belt buckle hit the planks, I looked back. He was standing there in his tighty-whities and his work T-shirt. Gripping the jeans, he followed me down the hallway and tossed them into the blue laundry basket. I closed the bathroom door. As I undressed, I heard water pipes hum in the walls and a shower start upstairs. I showered, changed clothes, threw my clothes in the washer with Glenn's, and started the wash cycle.

By the time I went outside, Glenn had started the grill and molded raw hamburger into patties. Waiting for the charcoal to heat up, he sat at the picnic table and drank a beer. Just in case I had forgotten that I put my cell phone in my car, I decided to look there. When I closed the door in disgust, Glenn held up a beer.

I approached the picnic table and took the beer from his hand. It was cool but not cold. Popping the tab, I asked, "You don't get all your farm-hands drunk, do you?"

Giving me a serious look, he shook his head no and took a swig from his can. I sat down across from him and set the beer on a crooked plank. "You might think I'm a crazy farmer for what I'm going to say, but a few of my cows are pretty good at judging character." By the look on my face, he knew he had to explain, and he continued. "I've got three smart cows—Sassy, Daffodil, and Mitzi. They know who they shouldn't trust, so I just watch how they behave around my new help. Sassy hasn't kicked you, Daffodil hasn't stripped off her milker when you weren't paying attention, and Mitzi hasn't laid down in her stall on top of you while you tried to wash her. Now, I've gotten a better sense of you since yesterday, and those three have gone two milkings without trying to get rid of you. I think I can give you a beer. Don't worry. I won't let you drive on too many." He guzzled the dregs and opened another can.

"You must be talking about someone specific. Who worked here before me?"

"Right before you it was Billy Forester. I'll never forget that twerp. After the first check, he asked for cash only. I told him I couldn't do that. Those cows I mentioned were acting up every day, even though he came from a dairy family. Then I started to notice how much gas was going missing from my tanks." Glenn carried the plate from the picnic table to the grill and started cooking. "Usually I don't hire high-school guys. Only if I have to—no offense. A lot of them have a problem working for a queer. I don't see what the problem is with gay money. It's still money, no matter who's got it."

An ant bumbled across the picnic table. It climbed the side of Glenn's empty can. When it reached the top, two more ants started to ascend.

"I don't have any problem with that kind of money."

"Oh really?" He flipped the burgers onto their pink sides.

"I wouldn't ask for cash."

He turned to look at me. "That friend of yours, what was his name?"

"Tyler."

"He's your boyfriend?" Glenn flipped the burgers again.

"I guess. He'd say we're friends. But it's been more than that. We've been talking for a long time about getting an apartment together. We almost have one right now. But he gets cold feet. Then later, he's all gung ho. I don't think it's going to work out."

"So who's in love with who?"

"Me with him. Him with me, I think. Him with whatever girl. At least he thinks he loves them."

Glenn transferred the burgers to plates. He and I added fixings and each ate two. His forehead was creased, as though he were thinking very hard. Waiting for him to say something, I noticed the thick and slightly raised scar that ran across his right wrist.

"Are you really moving in with this Tyler guy who's probably gonna keep having girlfriends on the side and wants you around for those couple of days each year when he admits he really wants a man?" Glenn asked. "He sounds like a mess." Then he rested his elbows on the table, a posture that revealed the scar. It seemed composed of many smaller lines. I remembered how Glenn kept mentioning staying out of trouble.

"You didn't get that from a handcuff, did you?"

He laid his palm flat on the table so that I could see his forearm. Even slighter, less noticeable white lines crisscrossed his arm from the elbow to the blue veins of his wrist. Looking at his arm, he shook his head no, and I reached across the table. Glenn flinched but let my index finger trace the main scar. While he watched my hand, I watched his stoic expression. I moved my single finger to the other marks. When I had touched those, I spread out my hand and tried to touch the more tender skin near his elbow, where there were fewer scars, but Glenn withdrew his arms from the surface of the table. He hid his hands and forearms underneath. Now he was looking at me, but I didn't want to look at him. A cluster of ants had gathered on top of that empty beer can. I watched them swarm over each other.

Then he stood. Walking away from the table, he started to speak. "Listen, you're a nice kid, and you're good with the cows. You're easy on the eyes, too, so don't start thinking nobody's ever gonna love you. Just don't—

don't let that take charge of you. I guess I'm trying to say you have to mind your manners."

He stopped where the tree line began, and I heard him unzip. As he started to piss, I noticed a red, flashing light on the darkening gravel near the barn, and when I reached its location, I saw that Tyler had called seventeen times. I accessed my voice mail and pressed my cell phone to my ear. There were four new messages recorded during the last three hours.

In the first he said, "Come on, I know you're just milking cows," but in the second his voice turned vindictive when he said, "Hey, I just got off the phone with Lisa. I wanted to tell you about it." In the third he sounded choked up when he said, "I'm sorry about that last message. Really. Call me." In the final message he sounded completely composed when he said, "As soon as you get this, we got to talk about the apartment."

. . .

After leaving Glenn's, I called Tyler, but when he answered, he said he couldn't hear. Just in case he was playing me, I said, "I'm going to tell Lisa you're a cocksucker." He asked me to call back. To the dead air I said, "I'm going to give your parents the love letter you wrote me." Each time I remembered another great way to out him, I called and asked if he could hear me. I was rehearsing what to say loudly in person.

Down the road from his family's farm, the reception improved enough for Tyler to hear me say hello. I held the phone to my left ear while I drove with my right hand and my knees. He said, "You jerk, you've been calling me every couple minutes for a half hour."

Watching his yard light grow larger and brighter, I said, "You were the one who called me seventeen times."

"Listen, I don't know what your dad said, but he took it the wrong way. It's like this. I love you, man. But I don't love you. I'll live with you, but it's separate bedrooms."

I was ready to walk into his house and begin the loud, incriminating conversation I imagined. But, turning into his driveway, I parked my car. I looked at the house he still shared with his parents. Dim light was visible through the white shade of his bedroom window, but I couldn't see his silhouette.

"No, Tyler," I said, despite my uncertainty. "No separate bedrooms and no apartment. I don't want it that way anymore."

"Don't talk to me like that," he said. "I'm not your girlfriend."

"Yeah, you're my boyfriend. My ex-boyfriend."

"I'm not your boyfriend, I'm your friend. Your best friend. Sometimes this kind of stuff happens between best friends. I've been reading about it."

"I don't need to read about it to understand what's going on."

"Fine by me, Jake. Be gay. More girls for me. We can do double dates. But the apartment. That's what we've got to talk about."

"Are you deaf?"

"We got to move out. I can't afford that place by myself."

"Good luck finding someone," I said as I hung up. Turning off the phone, I set it on the passenger seat and drove. I wasn't lost, but I didn't know the roads well. They led me between sloughs, past small cemeteries where people rarely buried anyone now, and onto unmarked gravel. Slowing for a sharp bend, I recognized the field rocks piled above the embankment of the curve. Tyler and I had driven here last night. I noticed my phone's red light starting to flash.

Starting down the first bend of Snake Road, which would soon curve sharply downhill, I slowed further. I knew I would hear a plea when I listened to that message, and part of me wanted to pretend I'd never told Tyler no, but another part of me was willing to keep saying it. My headlights lit up the ditch. In the weeds bloomed wild roses, their white and pink buds closed for the night, and atop the rock pile, empty, glittering beer bottles. Appearing then in my peripheral vision, a buck trotted calmly out of the ditch. My foot hit the brake, and the car skid ninety degrees but stayed on the gravel. He hadn't even turned his head in my direction. He just kept walking, totally confident or utterly reckless, I couldn't tell. He looked like he knew he wouldn't be hit.

The Second Wife's Daughter

May Lee-Yang

I know they will hate me before I even see them.

It is inevitable, I know that much.

He tells me I will be happy. He tells me that he has a daughter just my age. We will become best friends, he assures me, but I already know she, too, will hate me.

I don't hate them though. I can't, for there is a heavy guilt in my heart. My mother doesn't say anything, but I know she is anxious too. And maybe, like me, ashamed.

When we arrive at their house, my mother and I stand in the doorway. His wife opens the door and nods to us. She is still young, in her midthirties like my mother. And she is beautiful. His daughter, Kalia, who peers at us from behind her mother, is beautiful too. As we take in their beauty, they must take in our plainness, our forgettable features. It makes me wonder why he has betrayed them.

He ushers us into the house, and even though we enter, we remain on our own sides, looking at each other. Kalia forces a smile, probably something her father requested. We stand there, women and children, holding in our pride and pretending everything is fine while he smiles and does introductions.

He tells Kalia to show me my room, and she takes me to the basement, a small, carpeted room with two beds. On one side, I see pictures of Korean movie stars, boy bands, and collages of friends. On the other side, there is only an empty wall. My wall.

"Where will my mother sleep?" I ask.

"My old bedroom," she says. "Upstairs."

"Oh."

I want so much to say to her, "I'm sorry. We didn't mean to hurt you or your mom. I want to go home." But I can't, so I pretend everything is okay too.

. . .

My father died on August sixteenth of last year. By October, my mother had at least five boyfriends. Well, boyfriends might not be a good word for them; it wasn't like she was dating them. She didn't even like them, but they kept coming to our house.

At my dad's funeral, all of the old women said to my mother, "Nyab, now that your husband is gone, why not go back to live with your in-laws?" She smiled and nodded, but she didn't give them an answer. My mother hadn't lived with my grandparents since I was five, and I'm almost fifteen now. Besides, we already had our own house.

I don't know how the men got our phone number, but somehow they did and called a lot. It got so bad, my brother Joey and I just stopped answering. My mother didn't answer the phone either. After two weeks, she changed our number.

Once, when Aunt Kia was over, a man came by. Aunt Kia wasn't really my mom's sister, just an older relative that we called "Aunt." She and my mom were talking when someone knocked on the door. My mother told me to look out the window.

"It's some old guy," I said. Quickly, she whispered to Aunt Kia then ran into the bedroom. Aunt Kia answered the door, and I stood there wondering who he was.

"Nyob zoo," he said.

"Nyob zoo," Aunt Kia returned. "Who are you here to see?"

"My name is Paoze Thao. I come from California. Is the housewife here?" He kept looking past Aunt Kia and into the house. I turned and saw no one but Joey and Timmy.

"No, she is not home right now," Aunt Kia told him.

"Will she be returning soon?"

Aunt Kia looked like she was thinking hard about this question, but something made me feel like she was putting on an act. When she finally answered him, she said, "Hmmm . . . I don't know. I think she'll be coming back late. Yes, maybe late."

By now, I'm smart enough not to say, "She's in the bedroom." It's good the other kids can't hear us. When we're at the buffet and my mother tries to pass Timmy off as six, he'll embarrass her by telling the truth, "Nuh-uh. I'm nine."

The man kept looking behind our heads as though he didn't believe Aunt Kia, but he didn't try to budge in either. He asked again, "You're sure you don't know when she'll be home?"

"No."

"Well, then, maybe I will return tomorrow."

"All right then," Aunt Kia said politely.

As soon as she closed the door, she swore, then told my mother to come out of the bedroom. That was the last time we ever saw Paoze Thao, but more came, and my mother didn't always have Aunt Kia to open the door for her.

...

This is how things work: My mother and Kalia's mom work first shift. My mother works at a factory that makes hospital supplies, and Kalia's mom works for one of the Hmong organizations in Saint Paul. He works second shift at a machinery place. During the day, only he is home. When all of the kids come home from school, he leaves for work.

One day, Kalia and I get home around the same time and see her mom's car parked in the driveway.

"What are you doing here?" she asks her mom. "Aren't you supposed to be at work?"

"I'm on my lunch break," her mom replies. Kalia and I both look at the clock. It's almost three in the afternoon. "I eat my lunch late now," her mom explains.

So now, we always see her mom when we get home from school. She cooks lunch for both of them, packs him a dinner, then leaves at the same time as he does.

Most of the time, I don't see him. He doesn't come home until nearly one in the morning. We only see him on Fridays when the adults let us stay up and on the weekends when he doesn't work. On weeknights, Kalia's mom cooks dinner for us while my mother and I linger in the doorway.

"Kalia Niam-ah, what do you want me to do?" my mother will ask.

"I'm okay," Kalia's mom will answer. "Maybe later you can do the dishes."

Sometimes my mother cooks a side dish. Sometimes she makes the pepper sauce. Kalia's mom usually lets her make at least one thing. Then, every night, my mother does the dishes while Kalia and I clear the table and sweep the floor.

On weekends, when he is there, it is different. He likes to see both of them cook. Once, he smiles at them. "You look like twin sisters working together." I see them smile wryly. They must be thinking the same thing I am: *No matching dresses please!*

...

I try to make up for us by cooking and cleaning. I make rice before they tell me to. I do the dishes before they tell me to. Kalia helps me in the evenings, but, when her friends come over, they disappear into the basement. She doesn't introduce me to them. Only once, when one of her friends asks who I am, she tells them my name but doesn't say, "This is my stepsister." They probably still wonder who I am or, if they *really* know who I am, they must sit in the basement living room and say bad things about me.

When I was younger, one of our cousins married a second wife whose daughter, Pachia, was the same age as me, and we became best friends. Pachia's mom was the type who would take you shopping for clothes during the Fourth of July Tournament and who cooked sweet rice cakes for us for no reason at all. I liked her a lot. But one day, when we were at an ua neeb ceremony for one of our relatives, I heard the other women, my mother included, say to Pachia's mom, "How can we keep our husbands if women like you keep flirting with them?" They were smiling when they said it. It seemed almost like a joke, but Pachia's mom wasn't smiling. Even at the age of twelve, I knew enough to feel bad. She had been married into our clan for nearly five years, but they still didn't like her.

It makes me scared for my mother and me.

...

Kalia's house looks small on the outside, like it is just one story, but inside there are actually two stories. Upstairs are three bedrooms: one for my mom, one for Kalia's mom, and one for her two brothers. Downstairs in the remodeled basement is a living room, complete with an entertainment center and a couch set that looks like it is recycled from upstairs. There are other rooms, too: second bathroom, laundry room, storage room, our room.

We kids stay downstairs, where we can watch MTV, play on the Game Cube, or just sit around without being bossed. Upstairs, the adults are always watching Thai movies, listening to khwv txhiaj, or giving each other bad looks. They never come downstairs unless they need to do the laundry.

When I first meet everyone in his family, I am shocked. Kalia is my age. Her brothers, Seng and Jordan, are seven and ten, about the same ages as my brothers. I look at his family and it looks just like ours. I wonder why he needs a second family.

"He doesn't need a second wife," I overhear Kalia's friend, Mai Yer, saying once. "He's just a dick like every other Hmong man. He's just doing it because he can."

They don't know that I have just come downstairs, that I can hear them through the thin door that separates our bedroom from the basement hallway. Another person speaks. I think it's her friend Jessica.

"Is her mom pregnant or something? 'Cuz I heard that when old dudes get caught, they still gotta get married just like teenagers."

"I don't know," Kalia mutters. "We'll see in a couple of months."

My mother pregnant? I don't even want to think about it.

...

I think I hate my grandparents. I am afraid to say it, but I feel it. Even on that last day that I saw them, I couldn't look at Grandma or Grandpa. I felt like they betrayed us. A few weeks before, they came to our house. Grandma kept saying to my mother, "You should marry him. He will protect you."

Marry who? I wondered. There were so many of them.

"We'll be okay," my mother said.

"Don't you know? They're starting to say things about you."

I wanted to say, "What kind of things?" but Mother didn't ask so I just sat there. I wished then that Aunt Kia was there. She wasn't afraid of anyone. She was so old now she didn't care what people thought of her, and so she did something I rarely saw adults do: told the truth. She could have said to Grandma, "They're okay. They don't need a man. Your daughter-in-law has been a good wife and mother. She isn't doing anything bad." But Aunt Kia wasn't there.

And so a few weeks later when my mother agreed to marry him, Grandma and Grandpa intervened. They wanted the boys. They wanted the boys to remain Xiongs, but they said nothing about me. I did not think this could happen. They were my brothers. They were my mother's sons. They were our family. But, before the wedding took place, Joey and Timmy were sent away, and then it was just Mom and me.

...

I know that, because we have moved, I will have to transfer to a new school in the fall, Kalia's school. For now, though, my mother and he decide it's okay for me to stay at my same high school since there is a bus stop a few blocks away.

I am grateful because I don't want to lose the few friends I have. Even though my mother sometimes picks up my friends and drops us off at the mall, I know that can't last forever. If you stop seeing people almost every day, eventually, you won't see them at all.

Though my best friend is Michelle Vang, we haven't talked to each other for a while. A few months ago, my mother and I drove to Michelle's house to pick her up. We were supposed to go see a movie at Rosedale Mall, but when I got to Michelle's house, she didn't come out right away like usual. My mother honked the horn, but still no one came out.

"Why don't you go knock?" my mother suggested.

I knocked on the door but no one opened right away. I put my ear to the door. I could hear voices, so I waited. Finally, the door opened and Michelle was there. But she had no shoes on.

"Didn't you remember I was coming?" I asked.

"I tried to call you . . ." she started saying.

"What's wrong?"

"I can't go out today." She didn't look at me but kept her eyes on the ground.

"Why not?"

"My mom says I gotta stay home and cook."

"Can't someone else cook?" I didn't want to be pushy, but I didn't want to go to the movies alone either.

In the back, I heard Michelle's mom call out, "Who's there? Who are you talking to?"

"No one," Michelle yelled to the back of the house. When she turned back to me, she said, "I'll call you later, okay? I gotta go now."

Then she closed the door. Just like that. As if I didn't matter.

When I returned to the car, my mother asked what happened.

"I don't know," I said. "I don't know."

. . .

That night, I called Michelle's house but her brothers said she wasn't home. I could tell that they were lying; the only thing I didn't know was why they would lie to me. I wondered if maybe she was sick. Or maybe she had a boyfriend and wanted to hang out with him instead. I began to think that she wouldn't call me, but at 10:30 p.m., the phone rang, and it was her.

"Do you have a boyfriend I don't know about?" I asked.

"I wish," she said.

"Then why were you acting so weird today? Why didn't you just call my house before we came to pick you up?"

"Listen, I don't know how to say this . . ."

"Yes?"

"Umm. . ."

"Just say it."

"My mom doesn't want me to hang out with you anymore."

I became silent. Michelle and I had been friends since the fifth grade. Her mother was always nice to me. Now, though, I wondered if it was fake nice, when someone smiled and said hi to you even though they hated your guts. But her mother had once said to me, "You're a good girl, aren't you? See, Michelle, you should be more like your friend here. She has such nice long, black hair." I didn't think the color of your hair showed whether you were a good girl or not, but her mother had liked me enough to let us be friends for five years.

Into the silence, Michelle asked, "Are you still there?"

"Yeah," I muttered.

"It's nothing against you."

How could it be nothing against me? Maybe Michelle heard my question because she kept explaining things anyway.

"She says it's your mom."

My mom?

"She says your mom is a . . . a . . . I can't say it."

Say it!

"She says your mom is a slut."

Now I understood.

"And she thinks that your mom is taking us to go see guys and that. . ."

. . . and that she will turn us into sluts, too.

"I'm sorry." I heard Michelle's voice tremble on the other end. "I didn't want to tell you."

I didn't say anything to Michelle for a long time. When I finally did, I said, "My mother is not a slut" and hung up.

...

Before I came to this house, I never kept secrets. There was nothing to hide, no one asking me to keep my mouth shut.

But here, in Kalia's house, I have become another person. I've become one of those quiet girls. I wonder if this is how they were born or if, like me, they learned to hide their voices.

No one has said I have to keep secrets, but I know instinctively what we can say and what we cannot. So does Kalia. In public, we don't speak to each other. If we do, we look in front of us, at the sky, but rarely make eye contact. Perhaps she might say, "I wonder what we're having for dinner?" or I might say, "How was school today?" but we could be strangers, merely making small talk.

I have learned to become quiet. It is much easier not to speak than to tell lies.

I don't talk about my dad to anyone because no one wants to hear. I don't call Michelle, my ex-best friend. I've even kept myself a secret. It's hard to remember now how life was before Dad died.

I'm always hiding. In the basement. In my room.

But at night, when I go to bed, my bed speaks, crinkling, letting Kalia know my every move. I want to hide here in the darkness, but the bed will not be quiet. There is plastic underneath the sheets.

"Can I take the plastic off?" I ask Kalia.

"Ask my mom. She left the plastic on because Jordan used to pee on the bed when he was a kid."

She must have seen the grimace on my face because she adds, "Don't worry. The bed's clean. The plastic protected it."

I want to get rid of the plastic but don't want to talk to Kalia's mom. Kalia's bed doesn't make noises, but at night, you can hear every move I make.

. . .

I wake up in darkness, crying. I dreamt about my father, but that's all I can remember. Before I can go back to sleep, I hear Kalia's voice in the darkness. "Are you okay?"

I'm embarrassed. "I'm sorry," I say. "I didn't mean to wake you."

"It doesn't matter," she says. "What were you crying about?"

I don't want to tell her about my father, afraid she will laugh at me and say something mean like, "If you love him so much, why don't you leave my dad alone!" She asks again, "What made you cry?"

Before I can stop myself, the words come out. "My father."

"Do you miss him?"

"Uh-huh."

"Where is he?"

"Dead."

"Oh." Doesn't she know? But then I realize we barely talk, and she ignores my mother if she can. Then she says, "I'm sorry. I really am."

We have not said much, but perhaps because it is dark or because she is actually talking to me, I feel bold enough to ask, "Kalia, do you hate me?"

There is a long pause before she says, "No. But I hate my dad. I hate him so much, I wish he were dead."

We don't say anything else after that. We just lay there in the dark, thinking about our fathers.

...

One day, we have early release from school, so I get home around noon. I see his car parked in the driveway. I also see the Corolla that belongs to Kalia's mom parked on the sidewalk. Maybe she is having three-hour-long lunch breaks now.

I enter through the back door using my house key. As soon as the door is opened, I hear voices in one of the bedrooms. I lock the kitchen door and tiptoe toward the basement, hoping they won't hear me.

I don't want to hear what they are saying, but the house is small. Their words carry to the kitchen.

"If you love me," she says, "then get her out of my house!"

"Wife," he says, "Be patient. Ua siab thev."

"Be patient!? I let that whore move into my house. I let her eat my food. I take care of her daughter. Who is more patient than me?"

"What is done is done," he says. I can imagine him standing in front of her with both his arms raised in the air, as if to say, "Oh, well."

"If you truly love me," she repeats, "you will get her out of this house right now!"

I don't want to hear any more, so I begin walking downstairs. I try to be quiet, but the stairs squeak loudly and I freeze. In the distance, the voices stop, too.

"Is someone in the house?" she asks.

"There's no one," he says.

"I heard something," she insists.

"I'll go check." As I hear his footsteps approach the basement door, I walk quickly to my room. When I reach the bottom, the door above me opens, letting in a stream of light. Against the door, I see his shadowy frame peer down at me. I wait, expecting him to say something. When he finally does, his voice is so soft I barely hear him.

"Don't think anything of it." Then he closes the door, leaving me in darkness. Above me, I hear him say to his wife, "It was no one."

. . .

"How did he do it?" Kalia asks me in the dark. "How did they meet?"

I think back, trying to remember everything. I was there but many things are still blurry, mostly because I didn't understand them to begin with. I always remember Grandma and Grandpa's words to her: "They're starting to say things about you."

But then I did I hear and see a lot of things, mostly because I don't matter. Adults think that because we are American kids, we don't understand Hmong. Because we are quiet, we aren't listening. And so they open their mouths when I'm there. They will say things like, "Niam Xue"—my dad's name was Txiv Xue—"should get married. It won't look good with all of these men around."

It was never good with those men around. No one saw the dinners that were interrupted when a Tong Pao or a Leng Xiong would come knocking. They sometimes brought flowers—"like the Americans," they said to her, or they brought candy for us kids. While Joey and Timmy always ate the candy right away, I would never touch it because, in some way, I knew we would have to eventually pay for it. There were men who would say to us kids when it was ten o'clock, "Why don't you go to bed? Don't you have school tomorrow?"

My mother would always have me stay up with them. Or she would say that she needed to get up early to drive us to a school event the next day. After a while, she wouldn't even open the door, wouldn't even let them in. But it was hard to do that when some of the uncles brought over men. Then, you couldn't *not* open the door.

When I think about it now, I don't quite remember Kalia's dad. He was just one of many men whose faces blurred together. He was only memorable because he came with one of my uncles, Uncle Long. Uncle Long is the oldest of my father's four brothers, my father being the youngest. At first, my mother let them in. We didn't think anything of it because Kalia's dad never came with flowers or candy or anything. He was just Uncle Long's friend.

Another time I remember Uncle Long and someone—probably Kalia's dad—coming to the house. This time, it was strange because my mother didn't open the door. In fact, she whispered to me: "Get your brothers inside the house. Now!"

I ran to the backyard to get them, but before I could say anything, I saw Uncle Long's head peeking over the wooden fence: "Joey, open the door for your uncle!" And then they were in.

...

The next day, I go to my mother's room. It is much smaller than the other two bedrooms. A new full-sized bed is tucked in the corner. The bed sheets and blankets are new, wedding gifts for my mother and him. A small, pink-colored dresser sits beside the bed. It is not ours. There is no closet, so what clothes my mother cannot stuff into the dresser are stacked in laundry baskets that line the third wall. There are light, clean squares on the dull yellow walls where I suspect the boy-band posters must have been. None of these things are ours. I remember his words to her:

"You don't need to bring anything to your new life. What will people say if you bring all of your furniture here? That I can't take care of my own wife?"

And so we leave everything behind. I don't know what happened to it. Maybe it has been sold. Maybe Grandma and Grandpa have it. We have nothing but our clothes and my mother's Camry.

I wait for my mother to come to her room. Her bed is made, covered with a Korean blanket, red with images of soaring birds. I know it is soft, but I don't sit down. I just wait.

When she enters the room, I close the door.

"What did you want to talk about?" she asks.

"Why did you marry him?" I say the words quickly before my courage fails me.

"Why not?" she asks, as if it's not a big deal.

"People get married when they're in love. Do you love him?"

"Sure, I love him." But the words sound fake to my ears.

"Are you pregnant?"

This time, she gets angry. "Why are you asking all these questions? Kids don't need to know these things."

But I'm feeling bold today, so I ask again, "Are you pregnant?"

"No!" I feel a little relieved, but I still don't know why we are here, living this life that is not our own.

"Why did you marry him? Don't you miss Dad? Don't you miss the boys?"

Instead of answering me, my mother sits on the bed and begins to cry. I have only seen her cry twice before: when my father died and when the boys went to live with Grandma. Now, her hands cover her face as if she's embarrassed. I want to hold her, but I am embarrassed too. We never did much of that: holding and hugging. As I stand there ashamed that I have caused this, she says, "How can you think I don't miss your dad? I think of him every day. Do you think my heart is so cold I don't remember where my children are?"

"I'm sorry," I say. The words sound flat and meaningless.

"You are my own daughter and here you are thinking the worst things of me. You think I have forgotten your dad, sent your brothers away, and now this: that I let another man use me? Mis ntxhais, you don't know how hard life is."

I think she will tell me to leave or lecture me on being a more respectful daughter or just put me off. But then, as I wait, not knowing what to do, she begins to tell me what happened.

I want to hear that he forced her, that he just took her. But she says it was she who agreed to the marriage. And it is all because of the house.

"When your dad died," she says, "I couldn't afford to pay the mortgage anymore. Even though we had some money saved, it wasn't enough, not with my job."

So Uncle Long told her to sell the house.

"But I knew that, even though we would have some extra money from the house, where would we live? Who would take care of us?"

"Why couldn't Grandma and Grandpa take care of us?"

"Mis ntxhais, don't you know? How can they take care of us when they depend on Uncle Long and his wife?"

"Why couldn't we just go live in a small apartment? I'll be sixteen next year. I could get a job."

My mother shakes her head. Her face is filled with a sadness I don't understand. "And what about you and your brothers? Don't you remember when your friend Michelle said she couldn't be friends with you anymore?"

I nod my head, not understanding. "Her mother didn't want you to be friends anymore because of me. Because they think that, now that we don't have a father anymore, I am a slut and that I will turn all of you girls into sluts, too. How could I go on knowing that, everywhere, people would ridicule me and my children just because I have no husband? I know you don't understand this, but when you get older, you will learn the value of having a man's name."

"But why him? Why couldn't you marry someone who didn't have another wife?"

She then tells me something I don't wish to hear. He was one of the younger men. He had agreed to let her keep most of the money from the house sale. And he was Uncle Long's friend, meaning we would still see my brothers.

But then I remind her, "It's been over a month, and Joey's birthday is in two weeks."

"I know," she says. I wait for her to ease my mind by saying, "Let's go see them next weekend," but she doesn't. Instead, she just holds me.

. . .

That night, I can't sleep. I want to toss and turn, but the rustling of the plastic makes me self-conscious.

I get up and turn on the light.

"What are you doing?" asks Kalia, but I'm already out the door, heading upstairs to the kitchen. I return with a knife.

Kalia doesn't say anything but her eyes freeze, and I want to laugh because I can tell she thinks I mean to do her harm. Instead, I throw my blanket and sheet to the ground and make a slit through the plastic, careful not to cut the bed.

"What are you doing?" Kalia asks again.

"I'm tired of the plastic. The noise it makes is annoying."

I set the knife aside and rip the plastic apart. I almost want to ask if her mom will get mad I have cut open the plastic, but I don't care. Her mom probably doesn't care. She has not come into our room since I've come to live here.

"You need some help?" Kalia asks.

And I do, because we have to lift the bed to one side so I can slide the plastic sheath off the mattress.

I bunch up the plastic, pick up the knife, and start to leave the room.

"You can just leave that here until tomorrow. It's not going to go anywhere."

"I know," I say. But I want to get rid of it. I want to throw it in the trash can, away from this room, my room.

Later, when the darkness has found its place again in our room, I move around my bed, able to toss and turn, to flip on my belly without worrying what these sounds might give away.

It is getting late, and I know we should go to sleep. But Kalia and I talk anyway. It seems this is the only time we can speak together, when the darkness hides our faces.

"Did your mom know?" I ask.

"At first I didn't think so. I certainly didn't know. He just came home one day and said, 'I'm bringing a new wife home.' My mom didn't say anything then. She just sat there and looked at the ground, but I could see she was so mad." Kalia pauses then she says, "But I think she knew he was playing around. She was kind of sad before your mom came here, and they fought more than usual."

Playing around. What they say when men go fishing, gambling, or flirting.

He had been laid off, Kalia said, which was why he had time to come see my mother. He would say that he was hanging out with his friends, which was probably true. He was with Uncle Long a lot. But no one thought anything of it.

"All my mom ever yelled at him about," Kalia says, "was to find a new job. I don't ever remember them fighting over the other woman."

The other woman.

There is a question that hangs in the air, a question I know she wants answered but is afraid to ask. So I answer it for her, not because I want to be her friend but because I want her to hate my mother a little less.

"She didn't go after him," I say. "He just came over one day with my uncle."

Kalia's silence makes me uncomfortable because her unuttered questions still hang over my head, beckoning me to answer them. "She said she married him so he could help us out."

"How could he help you out when he couldn't even help out his own family?"

"We sold our old house," I say. "My mother agreed to give him some of the money."

That night, Kalia doesn't say "good-night" to me like usual, even though I know her past ones were said only to be nice. Instead, tonight, I hear her turning in her bed until I imagine that she is facing the wall, her back to me. Tonight, it is she that I hear crying quietly in the darkness.

...

Today, I ride my old school bus. Without thinking about it, I begin to walk the familiar paths to my old house. I pass the black church that is always empty on the weekdays. I pass the corner candy store with the

Arabic owner we called bin Laden because he always jokes about sending money to the Middle East. I pass all these until I come to our old house on Edmund Avenue. I expect it to be worn down, the grass to be unmowed, a "SOLD" sign on the front, the house empty. But there are cars in the street. Flowers decorate the front. The grass is cleanly cut. And my mother's wind chimes are still there, barely moving today because the air is calm.

I walk toward the house and peer in through the front window. I see them sitting there: Grandma and Grandpa watching TV. I think about turning back, returning to Kalia's house, but before I can stop myself, my hands knock on the door.

"Oh, it's you," Grandma says when she opens it. "Where's your mother?"

"At work," I say. "I came by myself." I stand there and wait for her to let me in. When she finally does, I feel strange in this home that was my own. Nothing has changed much about it. Our old couch set is still there. Beyond the living room, the dinette table is still the same. About the only thing that has changed are the pictures. My mother used to have pictures of our family hanging alongside the staircase. Now the pictures are of my grandparents, my uncles, and their families. I don't see one single photo of my mother or me.

"Look who came to visit us," Grandma says as we enter the living room.

Grandpa, who is watching a Hmong videotape of buffalo fights, turns to me. "Oh, mis ntxhais, you're here." Their voices seem happy to see me, but I know they are wondering why I am here.

"Where are Joey and Timmy?" I ask.

"They're not home from school yet," Grandma answers. I look at the clock. It is barely 3:00 p.m.

"I'll just wait," I say and take a seat on the couch.

I see that Grandpa is watching calmly as two water buffalos fight amidst a crowd of people. At the end of the fight, the loser buffalo sways as if drunk. Some men string it up while other men cut off its horns. Underneath, there is smaller, naked, white, horn-shaped skin covered with slivers of blood. People crowd around the dying buffalo, and all they want to see is the size of its horns, the gashes on its body, the blood everywhere. All of a sudden, the video changes to shots in which one of the men goes around and tries to flirt with girls, telling each how beautiful she is. *Tell us your name*, the person holding the camera says. *Tell all the people in America how old you are.* I want to roll my eyes, but who would notice? Who would care?

I sit through four buffalo fights before the boys come home. I hear their footsteps on the front porch, and Grandma is already opening the door.

"Look who's come to visit you," Grandma says to them. They turn to the living room and see me. We run to each other then stop. In the movies, this is the part where you hug and cry, but we're embarrassed. So we stand there, blocking Grandpa's view of the TV, and just stare at each other.

Timmy is still wearing one of his Dragon Ball Z T-shirts and Joey is wearing the Gap shirt my mother bought him last year, the one he thought made him look cool. Only one month has passed, yet we seem like strangers, afraid to talk to one another.

Then they both ask at the same time: "Where's Mom?" "Why didn't you come to see us before?"

"We've been busy," I say, because I don't know the true answer to that question. "How come you guys are still here? I thought Mother sold the house already?"

"She did," says Timmy. "Uncle Long bought it, don't you know? Grandma and Grandpa are just staying here until Uncle Long and his family can move their things here."

I didn't know.

Suddenly, I remember the loser buffalo, swaying, strung up, stripped of its horns. The way people crowded around but didn't care that it was in pain. When I think of the men trying to mack on the girls, telling each of them how beautiful she is, I start to cry.

In the background, I hear Timmy ask what's wrong. I hear Grandpa ask us to move out of the way. I hear Grandma calling me a stupid girl. And I see Joey's silence, his quiet eyes somehow accusing.

"I'm going to call your mother," Grandma says. "What's your new phone number?"

"I'm not going anywhere," I hear myself say.

"Joey, what's their phone number?" But he doesn't know either.

"I'm not going anywhere," I repeat. "These are my brothers. This is my house." Then, as two more buffalos are set loose on each other, I go to the VCR, take out the videotape, and pull out the film.

"Whoa!" Grandpa's voice is shrill, like I am committing the biggest crime. "Stupid girl, why did you do that?"

"Get out!" I yell at them. "Get out! We can take care of ourselves. Get out of our house!"

I see Grandma already dialing the phone. She is calling Uncle Long, probably to get *his* number. Grandpa gets up, raises his hand like he is about to hit me, then sits back down. I notice that he has the cover to the buffalo-fighting video in his hand. Now he looks at it sadly, like I've taken something precious away from him.

When Grandma gets off the phone, she looks straight at me and says, "I knew this would happen. As soon as your dad died, I knew your mother would not be able to raise anything better than a pack of wild dogs."

. . .

I know my mother will come to take me away. She will whisper reassurances in my ears and say we must accept our new life, that there isn't much we can do. She will say I must be obedient. So I prepare myself to fight.

Timmy and I hold hands on the couch, the only contact we feel okay to make. Joey sits in a separate chair, not looking at me. When a knock sounds at the door, I hold my breath and ready myself.

"There," Grandma says. "Everything will be fine now. Your mother has come to pick you up. Now aren't you embarrassed at yourself?"

But when the door opens, I see my mother with *him*. He should be at work, I think.

Grandma and Grandpa greet them, saying how long it's been since they've seen my mother and joking about how I came to the house on my own and went a little crazy. They invite my mother and him to sit down. Before my mother can move, Timmy bolts from the couch and runs toward her. He hugs her leg fiercely and begins to cry. He keeps telling her, "I miss you," while she lowers herself and hides her face beneath his shoulder, concealing tears I know are coming.

Then I hear him say to Grandma and Grandpa, "My wife misses the boys. She cries for them every night."

Grandpa says, "The boys like it here. Right, Joey? Right, Timmy? And in two weeks, Long and his children will move in too. They will have plenty of children to play with."

He continues, "We've been thinking that maybe we should take the boys back." For the first time, I look at him. At Kalia's house, he is always smiling, like he knows some inside joke he won't share with us. Here, he looks different, nervous. He doesn't sit back in the chair like usual, but he sits forward, alert.

Grandpa says, "We can't do that. These boys are my grandchildren, my youngest son's children. We can't let them go into another family. They need to carry on our name."

"I want to go with Mommy," Timmy says, still holding on to her.

"And you, Joey? Do you want to go with her, too, and abandon your grandparents?"

Joey has been silent all this time, but tears have streamed down his face.

Grandpa continues, "You kids don't love your grandparents anymore, do you?"

"Don't think like that," he tells Grandpa. "They still love you. We all do. But the kids miss their mom and their mom misses them."

Grandma finally finds her voice again. "But can you take care of them? Long said you have your own children to take care of too. Do you have space? Money?"

"We are Hmong," he says. "We can make it work."

Grandpa is about to say something again when my mom finally speaks up. "Mom and Dad"—I am surprised she can still call them that—"I love your son. I still honor his memory, but we have a new life now. Even though these children may have lost their father, they still have their mother. Would you rather have them live like orphans?"

"Nyab, we already talked about this. You agreed to leave them with us."

"I never—"

"They said you didn't want us anymore." Joey's voice is quiet but I hear every word. "That all you wanted was to be with your new boyfriend."

"My son, I never wanted to leave you."

"Then why did you leave us behind?"

"Because I didn't know I could take you with me."

"Mom and Dad,"—he says this to be polite—"Tonight we'll take the boys home. This weekend we'll return to talk things through. It's getting late, and the kids have school the next day." Grandma and Grandpa begin talking at the same time, but I don't hear a single thing they say. All I hear are the words he says to me, "Take your brothers upstairs to go pack up some clothes, okay?"

...

That night, as we drive home, he tells Joey and Timmy that he has sons just their age, that they will be happy. And, somewhere in my heart, I have hope that it might be true.

We Are Each the Seventh Generation

Marcie Rendon

We are each the seventh generation. Seven generations back someone put tobacco out, praying for the seventh generation ahead, a generation yet to be born.

A grandmother, standing in a grove of maple trees, hungry after a lean winter. A winter made leaner by the lack of promised government rations. This grandmother leaned against a maple tree, her moccasined feet numbed by the damp winter chill, the damp that was warm enough to send the sap running but cold enough to keep the snow frozen on the ground. Tears ran down her cheeks. Salty drops mixed with the sugary maple sap collecting in a birch-bark bucket.

In the distance, back where they were boiling the sap, she heard a baby cry in hunger. And in the silence that followed, in the silence when she knew the child's mother had put the baby to her breast, in that silence, the grandmother sank to the ground. Her hands covered her face as her body shook with sobs.

Through her sobs, she prayed to the creator. "Creator, have pity on me. I held my hand over my child's mouth. My husband said, 'That child will get us all killed. Keep her quiet.' And he left us, half-buried under a fallen tree, in an abandoned fox den. He shouldered his gun, checked his gunpowder before leaving to join the other men.

I hid with my child, day and night, my hand silencing my child's fear, her hunger, her love, her anger. My whole palm covered her mouth. Tender lips pressed flat against the white nubs of her first teeth. Her eyes frantically searched my face. I breathed in shallow gasps. Pretended I was a fish under-water. I could feel my air brush the tiny hairs on my upper lip. I removed my hand. My baby gasped, sucking air. I could see only the whites of her eyes skittering back and forth, searching my face. My milk let down as my body read her fear. Her lips moved toward the lifeline/love line of my future. She sucked and gasped, my breast silencing her in a way my palm couldn't. She nuzzled life.

Over her sucking, I heard the soldiers come. I thought we would die. I pulled her off the breast and covered her mouth once again with my palm. Again, her eyes skittered with fear across my face. The soldiers passed with-in feet of the downed tree my husband had laid the two of us under. My thighs shook, rattling dead leaves. Cold sweat ran in thick rivulets between my breasts, thicker than the milk my daughter drank. The soldiers passed. My husband would have never missed our hiding place. But these soldiers did not know our world, and they passed us by.

When my husband came back in the middle of the night, he knew right were to find us. He said, 'Don't let her cry. Let's go.' We traveled all night. He took us to a cove on a lake I had never been to. My brother and mother were there. We stayed there until the fighting stopped, then moved west. When the government promised us peace, our band never signed. But we were given allotments anyways. My husband took his allotment and a name I can't pronounce.

The child that I stopped from crying, she was taken, torn from me, and sent to boarding school. She returned without a language, without the knowledge of how to comfort, laugh, smile, and tap a maple tree for syrup. This child that I had almost killed to save our people was stolen from me. She never laughed. Whatever they did to her at that school took more life from her than my palm over her tiny lips.

Creator, my heart is broken in as many pieces as there are dead leaves in this forest.

Where once life flowed from my body, now tears that scorch the ground with salt are all that fall. Creator, I thought the worst had happened, and yet I dream of harder times to come. And so I pray for another daughter, who will be born seven generations from now. I see her standing alone, not even the memory of belonging to hold her to this earth. I sing my songs for her and pray her into being."

That is how grandmother prayed. She sang a prayer for a granddaughter, seven generations ahead, so she would be protected, blessed, watched over.

She sang a song for when the nights were too cold. Too long. Too alone. She sent her spirit seven generations ahead.

...

I remember the bed as clearly as if it were yesterday. An old metal bed frame. At one end, thick round posts arched on either side from floor to floor. At the other end, a shorter version. Each leg resting on a hard rubber wheel. Smaller, vertical metal poles evenly spaced between the straight of the arch. A sagging mattress, covered with gray and white ticking held in place by thick strands of white cotton yarn. The mattress laid across bedsprings intricately hooked like the metalworking of spring clothespins. Everyone slept in this bed.

This night I was sleeping alone. My ears had scanned the house and heard no other movement, no voices, no creaking floorboards, no coffee cup being set down after each drink onto the kitchen table. Alone and cold, I rolled into the center of the bed. Bedsprings creaked with each motion as I tried to slide the woolen squares of the cotton-backed quilt off of me so that only the cotton side was touching skin not covered by my white cotton panties and undershirt I was wearing. Cold, alone. Outside the second story window, tree branches bare of leaves shifted in the breeze carried up from the riverbank. If I lay still enough, I could hear the Red River flowing and the occasional car passing by on the main road into town.

I started listening for the cars, hoping one would turn down the quarter-mile dirt road to our house. Scared that one would and someone would find me, cold and alone. The longer I listened, the more scared and colder I got. I wrapped myself tighter in the quilt, reached out to touch the bare mattress, feeling until I found a piece of cotton yard to tug at. There was no comfort in the cotton strand. I watched the wall at the head of the bed, hoping for headlights, knowing this meant someone was coming. Fearing the headlights, knowing this meant someone was coming. What was I doing here all alone?

I rolled. The bed creaked. I couldn't hear over the creak, so I determined not to roll again. I pulled my legs to my chest, hoping for a little warmth. I remembered the baby chicks. The sweet, yellow baby chicks. Daddy had brought them home from town, had let me hold one. As I cupped one in my hand, I could feel its aliveness on my palm, its tiny heart beating. That night, Daddy put them in a cardboard box filled with old rags and tucked it behind the oil heater in the living room. The next morning we woke to a freezing house: the oil heater had run out of fuel during the night. The sweet, yellow chicks lay stiff among the rags. My daddy didn't cry, but I read the heartache on his face, even as he tried to assure me all was well. Only years later did I understand how poor we were, and how a piece of hope died for him that night along with the yellow chicks that might have fed us twice that year—first in eggs and then in meat.

As I thought of the chicks, I shivered. Creak, creak. Wrap the blanket tighter. I felt across the mattress, searching for the shredded yarn. I found it and rolled it back and forth between my thumb and forefinger in the dark. I listened for the river and heard her still running on the muddy banks. I heard the tree outside the window bend in the breeze, tires on the gravel as another car drove past a quarter of a mile away. Did I even know what a quarter mile away was? I had heard the words so many times; it's a quarter mile to get the mail; a quarter mile to the road to town; that's a long quarter mile of mud in the spring. I rolled. Creak, creak. And then I heard a song. Hey ya hey ya hey ya hey ai ya ay ya. . . . The singing came closer. I rolled uphill enough for my elbow to catch purchase on the mattress and propped myself up. A woman stood there. Alone. Long dark hair, a long skirt and billowy blouse. She kept singing, ai ya ay ya, and reached out a hand to pull me up from the bed. When my bare feet touched the wooden floor, my small hand clasped in hers, she walked me toward the window and out through the wall—singing ai ya, hey ya ai ya hey. We walked across air, twelve feet up, until we reached the tree. She sank into a crook of branches and pulled me onto her lap, her blouse and skirt sheltering me from the nighttime breeze. She reached into the folds of her skirt, brought out a handful of cooked wild rice, and fed it to me—kernel by kernel, all the while singing softly under her breath. When the rice was gone, she rocked me, her hair brushing on my cheek, singing ai ya hey ya ai ya hey, and I slept.

. . .

After that night, the nights when my mother left me alone were the nights this woman would sing me into the tree with her, and reach into the folds of her dress and bring out a handful of rice for me to eat while she sang me back to sleep. A soft burst of turquoise light always preceded her appearance. As a child I would be playing and I would see her in the trees, or on the riverbank, or even sitting in my dad's car. She was as real to me as my brother and sisters. As real as my mom and dad. Her long black hair fell below her waist and was pulled back in a loose ponytail. Sometimes in winter she would wrap her hair around me like a blanket to keep me warm. Her clothing was long and flowing, a floral cotton print on top, a gray or faded blue skirt with deep folds and hidden pockets. She was thin and strong, with a voice that shone; sometimes when she sang, I could see her voice, could see the song. Pure, clear light emanated from her mouth and wove among the branches of the trees.

As a child, I assumed that everyone saw her, talked with her, knew her. I remember talking to my dad about her. He asked me what her name was, and I, not knowing her name, and not wanting to appear dumb, answered, "Sam."

He said, "But that's a boy's name."

So then I said, "Maybe it's Ben."

He said, "That's a boy's name too."

...

We lived three miles out of town. Two and three-quarter miles of gravel road north, then a left turn west down an even smaller dirt road. A quarter of a mile later, on the banks of the Red River of the North, stood our home. For the first three years of my life, home was a tar-paper shack. No electricity. No running water. During the day, the sun provided light; at night the oil lamps were lit. A wood stove was used for cooking and heat.

I remember my second birthday. My mother asked me what color frosting I wanted on my cake. I said yellow. She sent my dad into town to buy her real butter, butter that was dyed yellow, not the white butter she made at home. She made me a cake with yellow frosting. Some neighbors came and gave me a small windup doll that crawled. One of the kids teased me, saying it wasn't mine, and I cried. My mother held me on her lap and softly brushed my hair behind my ear as she smoked a cigarette. I loved to watch her smoke. She held the filterless Pall Mall between her lips and talked while the ash grew longer and longer. It never failed, she always removed the cigarette in time to flick the ash before it fell on its own. When she finished the cigarette, she put me back on the floor to play with my windup doll. It had a blue diaper painted on it.

The Christmas when I was two, going on three in March of the coming year, my father got us a Christmas tree. A church from town also brought over a tree, decorated with white stars. My father, who never yelled or raised his voice, was angry. As the church people left laughing and singing, I watched my father's eyes and saw anger and hurt. I didn't understand. I was happy with two Christmas trees. I remember matching outfits for my sisters and I, and a bride doll for me.

The bride doll was my treasure. My younger sister and I would play under the kitchen table while my mother smoked her cigarettes, read her *True Love* magazines, or did the washing and ironing. On a day like that in March of the year I turned three, my younger sister and I were under the table playing with my bride doll, dressing and undressing her. It was laundry day, and the room was hot because my mother had the wood stove burning steady; my sister and I wore only cotton panties and thin-strapped undershirts. The ironing board was set up midway between the table and the wood stove. My mother would set one of her two heavy metal irons on the stove to heat it up while ironing with the second until it cooled off. Then she would switch irons, licking her finger and tapping the bottom of the iron from the stove to see if it would hiss. Her ever-present ashtray sat on the wide end of the ironing board.

"Mom," I peeked up from under the table, "I smell smoke."

"It's just my cigarette," she said. "I'll put it out in a minute."

My sister and I played a bit longer.

I said, "Mom, I still smell smoke."

"I'll check the kerosene stove on the porch," she said.

The next thing I knew, my mother reached under the table and grabbed my sister and me, throwing each of us under an arm like a laundry basket. She ran us out the door, through a wall of orange-red flames, across the narrow drive, and into the small cove of brush that held our chicken-coop dollhouse. She tossed us in there and yelled, "Stay." She ran back through the wall of flames and rushed out carrying a basket of clothes. She knelt down and grabbed my upper arms. "I have to run into town to get your dad," she said. "Stay right here. Do NOT go back into the house. Do NOT let your sister go back in. Do you understand?"

Without waiting for an answer, she took off running down the dirt road. She was wearing a white blouse, black pants, and no shoes. It was a Minnesota March day. Snow still lay on the ground. I watched my mother run out of sight, my arms wrapped around my baby sister. I saw flames licking the walls of the house, orange against black tar paper. The house didn't stand a chance.

My sister cried. I told her it would be okay, that our mom would come home, that Daddy would be here soon. We shook with cold in our mostly nakedness. Our bare feet turned red on frozen dirt.

Eventually, the town firemen arrived. So did our parents. My mom wanted them to get her sewing machine out. The firemen crawled in and out of the back window, trying to find her machine, but not allowing my mom to help. Finally, in desperation, she rushed around the opposite side of the burning house, leaned in the window, and pulled out the sewing machine the men had been crawling on and over to get into the room.

...

A downed tree stretched out over the Red River at the bottom of the riverbank that sloped behind our house. It was on that dead tree that my dad placed a gunny sack filled with rabid cats and shot them with a shotgun until the bag toppled into the river. The bag floated north before sinking.

It was on that downed tree the summer I was four that I had my first discussion about God. As you might have guessed, we were not a church-going family. I did not know what a church was or who God was.

...

My brother, four years older, was a magnet for the boys in town. With no adults to supervise, we could have some wild times on our little bend of the riverbank. My brother would walk the three miles into town and come back with a handful of boys ready to play. Cowboys and Indians was always a favorite, and given that it was our farm, and my brother an Indian, the Indians always won. War was another favorite. My brother also thought it was great fun to have me climb to the top of the chokecherry trees. He would climb up after me. Beneath both of our weight, the chokecherry tree would lean toward the ground. At a given point he would holler, "Hold on!" And he would jump off. Holding on for dear life, I would go swishing up, and back and forth, and back and forth. He built some rafts and I was sent riding on muddy red water, clinging to a rope as he ran the along the shore. When I didn't sink, he would then try the raft. I remember being the guinea pig for a team of paratroopers, too. My brother tied the four corners of an old army blanket together, then told me to hold on tight and jump off the barn roof. It was quite a ride down. Maybe the army blanket weighed more than I did, because it went down first and I landed on it. No bones broken.

...

Whether it was that day, or another, a small group of young boys and I sat on the dead log lying out across the river. We watched the sun glint on the water. We watched the water bugs make trails. We laughed about the size of the bullfrogs we could only hear croaking, imagining giant green legs and who would actually eat them. It was warm. It was summer. As usual, there were no adults to question why five or six children were sitting on a fallen tree out over the muddy, red, swirling water.

. . .

I suppose the conversation was bound to turn to talk of water. Talk of water turned to baptism. One kid asked, "Are you baptized?" I asked him what he was talking about. He rambled on in a theological discourse, as only a five year old can I imagine, about baptism and souls and God and children and sin. These were all brand-new words and concepts to my four-year-old mind. I looked at him as if he were nuts. At that point, he said with perfect solemnity, "You're going to go to hell."

I asked, "What's hell?"

The group of boys whooped and hollered, causing the fallen tree to sway dangerously. "She doesn't know what hell is," they hollered to the catfish swimming below us.

Then junior minister explained hell to me in vivid detail. How God would be angry with me for not being baptized, and if I died without being baptized, I would burn in a fiery hell for eternity, which according to him was longer than my daddy was old.

I had seen my house burn to the ground. I had watched my mother run, barefoot, into town for my dad and the fire truck. To my memory I had never been hit by an adult, nor seen another child hit by an adult.

I remember walking down the road to the neighboring farm. There were older children there, and they talked of getting a spanking. This was as foreign a concept to me as hell. I remember their mother putting one of the older girls over her lap and demonstrating for me what a spanking was. As she softly paddled her daughter's behind with her bare hand, they were both giggling. So I really couldn't understand the purpose of that particular activity, although the mother said she spanked her kids when they were bad. I wasn't exactly sure what bad was, either, but decided not to show my ignorance further that day. My mother beat up grown men who were mean, or ugly, or stupid. "Bad" was not a term I was familiar with.

So when this boy told me if I died without being baptized, I would go to hell, I would burn in fire forever, I knew he was lying.

I said, "I don't know who God is, but everybody loves me. Everybody. No one would ever be that mean to me. No one would ever leave me to burn in a fire."

I walked off the tree that day confident in my goodness, confident that God, whoever he was, could never not love me. Confident that adults, big people, did not treat little people badly. And I knew that everyone loved me. Those boys did not know what they were talking about.

...

Today this young girl, now a grown woman, put tobacco out and prayed for a grandchild, seven generations ahead. Maybe the oil will run out. Maybe there will be no drinking water. Maybe the earth will be parched or covered with ice. But our people will live, and they need our prayers and songs sent ahead to comfort them. To hold them close. To give them hope. To give them a knowing that they belong. That they belong to us.

There are young people today living away from us. They see spirits. They hear songs. They dream dreams. And someone needs to tell them, "Those are your ancestors speaking to you across the generations. You are not alone. You are never forgotten. We remember you in our prayers. We pray ahead for those yet to come. We knew you would be here. We knew times would be hard. We knew that sometimes all that would keep you moving forward, sometimes all that would help you get up tomorrow would be a dream. And in that dream, someone would give you a gift, someone would sing you a song, someone would hold you close or run across open fields, or fly into a night sky. We know you are here. We know more are coming. And so we pray."

...

Two women stand side by side. One can see the other. The other cannot. One is tapping maple trees. Dressed in jeans and a down jacket. Leather gloves keep her hands slightly warm. The other, dressed in a long, flowing skirt with deep pockets, has long hair, long hair that flows on the wind and becomes the wind. She hums, hey ya ay ya. . . . Watching. Waiting. The woman in jeans has tears streaming down her cheeks. She leans against a maple tree and begs, "Creator, tell me what to do. How am I going to raise these children by myself?" In the turquoise-colored flash of a second, the woman singing appears and says, "I Stand Alone."

Knowing You in Snow

Dominic Saucedo

Sometimes I wake to the crashing. I have this dream of snow rushing down on this city, a furious storm of softly drifting flakes. Flakes that echo when they touch the ground. I wake and follow the noise out into the hallway to discover my brother at the radiator with one of his barbells, beating away at the valve. He turns to me and mutters—it's so cold. And before he can turn away I marvel at the scar that runs the length of his beautiful face. How it is shiny and smooth, almost reflecting the faint light of the moon. I wander back to my bed in the front room. It is these times that I think of you.

. . .

I could hear movement in the next room. It was low, guttural, a cry almost, and I was embarrassed to hear my brother. But the moan rose, continued on up into the sound of a woman, and I knew that he had brought someone home. I pulled on my jeans and a sweater, ran water through my hair, and crept out of the apartment between their heavy breaths.

It was blue outside, the color of early morning, and I stood watching my breath curl into the cold. I could never remember a coat, remember to skip the water in the hair, which dripped down my scalp in icy rivulets. I headed for the coffee shop across the street.

I used to make coffee back home, but one of Omar's girls came out of his room one time and that was enough for me. I was standing at the counter watching the drips when I heard her ask if there were two cups. She was in the doorway, a brunette in my brother's robe, and she had the sash untied, like curtains drawn open on a window. My skin jumped as she came toward me, poured coffee, and ran her hand down my chest.

—Guapo like your brother, she said.

Since then I would head out of the apartment when people began to stir.

I opened the door of the coffee shop to the morning rush. People standing in line, rustling newspapers, still talking in their sleep. You said nothing to me, but smiled. I sat by the window and watched the snow begin to fall.

. . .

The first night in Saint Paul, my brother picked me up from the airport. My mother had taken my father back. Sent me to Omar to finish high school. We drove through the city, the tall buildings crouched together, each of their sides a back turned to the cold. I marveled at the cramped space, the maze of streetlights—the kind that didn't hang over you in a looping arch but stood planted, firm, like torches in the dirt. These were not LA streets.

. . .

People took their jackets off and threw them onto the dining-room table. They unburdened themselves of the heat. The sound of zippers opening, the laughter, and the scent of bodies rushing out and pushing against each other. No windows open.

I stood at the back of the room watching my brother get over on the girls. He had this kind of dance that moved him around the room from girl to girl, in a circle, and for five seconds of his rotation each one could fantasize about him. He'd smile. Wink. They ate it up. Every time.

I saw you watching him too. Standing against the wall. Omar made his way over to you and peeled you from where you stood. Some kind of mambo played and your body stiffened, your feet confused. He danced you over to me and pulled me onto the small dance floor. You kept dancing, momentum, and I put my hand in the small of your back, trying to get our feet straight, the rhythm right. We were both too scared to stop. This is how we met. Do I have it right?

. . .

When you were done with your shift, you came to my table and sat down. You worked from seven to nine, filling in the first two hours of a friend's

shift, a friend too lazy to get up that early. I don't know if I would have gotten up for ten bucks, but you did.

—I gotta get to work, you said.

I raised my head at the coffee you pushed toward me.

—You just got off work.

—You know what I mean. I have to be downtown by ten. But first I have
to stop off at home. Come with me?

Your house was a large apartment a few blocks from mine. A mess of
gray cinder-block squares crisscrossed by sidewalks and muddy patches of
grass not even the snow could make clean. You unlocked the door and asked
me to wait. I leaned against the wall. The curtains to the living room moved
back and I caught your sister's eyes. Her hair curly black, a little nose, smiling mouth. She had a doll's face. One of those kind you see late at night on
TV that sell for a hundred bucks. Painted features and a pretty dress. In a
second she let the curtains fall back and I could hear her scamper away on
the other side of the thin door.

You came out, grabbed my hand, and headed for the bus.

—My sister. Lea, you said.

. . .

Two things have made me a writer. I'd come home late sometimes from walking the neighborhood and Omar would be waiting. If he was in the front room
watching TV, I knew I was all right. But if he was in the tiny kitchen, crouched
over the table, it was time for me to write. He'd sip on a beer, lean back in his
chair, his stained dress shirt open to the T-shirt below. Omar would start by
telling me a story of a woman. The ones he liked were mostly blond. Blond
women that he'd meet at the restaurant. He'd get their numbers, slyly if they
were with other men. Drinks later on that night and other stuff. I'd write it all
down because his Spanish was worse than mine. Besides, he'd tell me:

—I like the way you make it sound.

. . .

That first night we danced you told me where you worked, and I showed up
the next day. Hair wet. The cold electric in my skin. I tried to play it down,
but you noticed the shivering and brought me coffee. I didn't have winter
clothes yet. November in LA was a heavy sweater, a nylon jacket for the rain.
I'd doubled up on the sweaters and put on two pairs of socks underneath
my tennis shoes.

We walked through the neighborhood talking. The houses big, run down. I told you that my house back in LA was off a busy street and that you could hear the cars swishing by at all hours, echoing off the walls of the freeway. But here. Here they crept up on you, moving silently in the snow. They reminded me of how dogs loose in the neighborhood could surprise you from behind, their noses suddenly at your feet. You told me that when you were eleven you were stuck walking home with your mother in a storm. The snow so thick that when you slipped, losing her hand, you were nowhere, her body invisible, her voice faint in the cold. Even your voice, you said, seemed to fall back inside.

. . .

We walked in the quiet along the nighttime streets. The snow drifted in large flakes. Everything was a careful step over slippery sidewalks and snowbanks. At the corner of your street, a Buick turned toward us, and we stepped back to let it pass. It moved with all the weight of a large ship, its exhaust a cloud in the air. Its tires spit, and we turned our backs to the spray. I noticed that even as we moved to avoid the ship, trudging into the snowbank itself, you didn't lean into me, reach for my hand, or even my sleeve.

At the front door of your house we stood awkwardly. You smiled, shy in the yellow light. I took this as a sign and moved my hand up to touch your arm. I let it run from your wrist to your elbow. Slowly. Lightly. You let the three feet between us remain, a gap filled by our breath. And then the click of your key as you turned to leave.

When I got home I headed for bed. The apartment was quiet but I knew Omar was there—his apron hanging from the corner of the hallway door. The first thing was his voice.

—Can you write?

I knew he was leaning there against the kitchen wall. Sitting at a tilt with the chewed stub of a pencil clenched between his teeth. I moved into the hallway toward the kitchen, a slow drag, hoping that he would forget by the time he reached the table. When I peeked around the corner, he smiled at me, a deep, broad smile. He shook his head and laughed, pointing to the crossed-out lines.

—It's always easier for you, he said.

I sat down at the table, picked up the scarred pencil. Omar studied me for a moment, pensive eyes, then asked.

—Well?

I knew what he wanted to know. How far? How much? I told him I got nothing, and he shrugged.

—All these long walks for nothing?

—I like to walk, I told him.

He wasn't believing it.

—Maybe you got her out in the cold too much. Probably too frozen to know what to do. Take her to the movies. It's dark.

He started to say something more, but I nodded him into quiet. We sat there for a moment in silence until he leaned in his chair.

—Well, Mama wants to know how the studying's going, he said.

I frowned.

—I told her that it was going good but that you needed money for books. Maybe you wanna start looking at schools. Get a job while you check around.

I told him that I'd check and then motioned to the paper.

—She was blond, right?

He smiled.

. . .

I watched Omar from the bus-stop bench across the street. The restaurant's dining room was a long glass window facing the avenue. I could see him in his apron, twisting and turning through the tables, moving toward each raised hand. I wondered where they would hide me in there—probably washing dishes. I wouldn't be able to see the street. He had told me to show up after the lunch-hour rush and see if the manager would get me in.

No car. A small apartment. I asked him a few nights after I arrived how he got them. The women. These were the first nights, when he still came home early with a few beers smuggled from the back of the restaurant. Happy to have me there. I promised him over the first beer not to tell Mama that he wasn't in school. He told me that he'd gone a few weeks but that it wasn't right. And the women weren't much to look at. He pushed away from the table, and when he came back he had his apron on. He gathered the empty bottles and balanced them on a plate, palm flat but wavering.

—It's all in the back, bro. Everything's got to be straight.

Omar ran his right hand up the line of his back while he balanced the beer.

—I wait on them, but I never bend down with the plates. Never let a girl see you bend. They have to look up to catch my eyes. See?

He motioned to me and pointed to my tilted head.

I nodded.

—Then you smile.

And he gave me a slow grin.

He clanked the dishes down into the sink. The bottles crashing.

—At first it's about the back. But later it's about the hips. You know?

He swiveled his hips against the sink. His back to me.

—Sure, I know.

It was getting cold, and my feet were wet from the snow. I watched my brother clearing a table, cars cutting here and there into my view. I stood up and headed down the street. Off to find you.

. . .

I was always dragging you into the skyways. Looking for places where we were alone. Long deserted stretches where the shops were closed and there was nothing but the fluorescent lights and the wire gates pulled across the faces of stores. Come here. C'mon, I'd tell you, and the minute we left the busy corridors you would go quiet, ready to fend off my hands. You'd kiss me sometimes, a tentativeness buzzing through your body, and then pull me off in the direction of some busy store. Something I have to buy, you'd say.

I suppose you felt the urgency in the way I touched. Knew that hurried hands were dangerous things.

Outside we'd be strange. Your smell gone. Your warmth gone. Both of us quiet as we waited for the bus.

. . .

It was always this way. Eventually he'd just get tired of me. I thought that maybe he resented the job I'd turned down. There was a summer we worked at the same restaurant in LA. When I was excited by the newness of a job. Even the exhaustion with him was fun. The way we'd float home late at night, me talking to keep him awake.

We just bumped heads in the apartment now. The only sounds I heard were women in his room—or the clink of his free weights.

. . .

We'd meet at the corner of my building. Take the city bus to where you worked. It was always crowded, with only the bar to hang on to. I told you how when I was little Omar and me had looted an abandoned building and sold everyone's stuff out on the street. The time my mom piled us into a Volkswagen and drove from Los Angeles to Chicago, and we all got food poisoning from the sandwiches she made. We spent three days in an Ohio motel, her so scared she almost turned back. She finally did go back to my father. Omar and me ended up here.

I liked the telling of all this. How I could inch closer, as you listened, and along the cold bar I would find your hand. This was the nearest, it seemed, I could get to you. Standing tall. My back straight.

. . .

By the second month, we were awkward. He never came home until late, and I was out walking, talked my way out of the job. I was in the kitchen that afternoon when the lock tumbled, coats fell to the floor. He knew I was there. Shoes in the hallway. For a while it was quiet, and I considered staying, forgoing the cold gray outside. The first moan was Omar's, and I stood. Before I reached the door I heard her voice, soft and pleading: Elias. She let my name out at a crawl, followed by stifled laughter. My brother roaring on the other side of the door.

. . .

Your mother thought you were safer with your sister around, another pair of eyes to watch you. She'd walk along behind us, mostly quiet, every now and then running to take your hand. But she spent more time watching me. Her coal black eyes peering up when she stepped between us.

The night I took you back to my place I turned on the small TV in the kitchen and hoisted her up onto a chair. She melted into the screen, and I pulled you off toward the front room.

You resisted right away.

I wrapped my arms around your waist and forced my lips on you. I'd seen it done so many times in movies, in TV. How men could make women want them with quick hands; if you could just touch them long enough, the struggle would fade away.

I had my lips on your neck, your hand on my chest. You twisted out of reach, and when I opened my eyes, I saw your sister's face there in the doorway.

She stood quietly.

—Elias, you said. Angry.

—I just wanted some time alone, I told you.

You shook your head and pushed Lea toward the front door.

. . .

When Omar came home, he kicked off his shoes and headed to the kitchen for a beer. I was lying on the couch when he came in and tossed a small blue coat to me.

—Oh, I told him, it's her sister's. They left in a hurry.

He took a long swallow from the beer and threw me a fresh, slippery one. It was the first time I'd seen him smile in days.

—Don't worry, he said. She'll come back. Even the difficult ones do.

. . .

I came home from a walk one night to see Omar sitting in the kitchen, only the dim light over the sink lit. He held a beer but put it down over and over again to touch his face. There was thick gauze taped to one cheek, and the jawline looked swollen, like maybe there was cotton under the skin. The tape covering the gauze was speckled with red.

He looked up at me sheepishly.

—I didn't even see the guy coming, really. I was heading for the bus and there he was. He even pulled his girl's number out of my pocket after he cut me.

—Does it hurt? I asked him.

He put his beer down again to touch his cheek.

—It hurts. But I got a lot of pills.

—Maybe you shouldn't drink, then.

—Maybe you could just kick me in the head and I could pass out.

He winced as he said this, the sting in his voice fading.

I helped him up out of the chair, but he waved me off, steadying himself against the wall all the way to his bed.

I left the door open so I could hear him if he called.

. . .

And then, hours later, there was you.

You stood at the door of the apartment shifting awkwardly on your feet.

—I thought that maybe I could come in, you told me.

I led you into the front room and pulled you toward the couch where I slept. You asked me where my brother was, your only resistance. I said that he was working late and would be out drinking.

I'd never seen a girl pull a shirt over her head.

Or the way breasts fell when the bra was undone.

I ran my face against your stomach, buried it in your thigh. You pulled your underwear down and wobbled out of them, dropping them into a pile of your things. I stood up and took off my own pants, shirt.

You lay down on the couch and slid underneath me.

—Go slow, you said, I've only done this once.

I held still for a moment, just feeling the warmth of a bare chest pressed against a bare chest. Then you guided me, pulling in a quick breath. I thought about my brother and the women I'd heard on the other side of the wall. What had he done to make them loud, for the noise to carry? I pushed in harder and crashed around, even though you tried to bind me there with your ankles.

I didn't stop until you cried out—and not until the second, long cry.

. . .

When I walked you home, the snow began to fall. Heavy flakes that wet the skin. You murmured to me:

—We're all right now, right?

Your voice muted in cold and half sleep.

—Yeah, I told you, it's all right.

But did you know we were lying to each other? Was it just my lie?

We came to your street, and I saw the light to your living room, wondered how you would explain being out so late, almost twelve-thirty.

You asked me to leave you there so that your mother wouldn't see.

—Besides, you said. You've only got on a sweater. Go back inside.

I nodded, and you turned to leave.

How would we talk about tonight? I wondered. When I picked you up at work? Would we linger in the skyways, the touching still reticent, a collection of awkward grabs? Would you pull close on the bus just for the story?

I followed at a distance behind you, my feet soft in the snow. When you got to your front door, your mother opened it. She stood there for a moment looking at you, and in a second her eyes, angry, traveled to me, standing off in the street. And then you turned—your eyes, wide and deceived.

. . .

When I got home Omar stood in the hall, leaning in his doorway.

—So you finally did it, bro.

He tried to smile, but the bandage covered his face, and I imagined a thin line of flesh opening just a little on the cheek. He winced. I wanted to reach out and grab him, throw him up against every wall in the hallway. Tear the bandage from his face and slap him over and over again across the torn cheek. Put my knee into his slouching back, to the softness between the shoulder blades. Instead I just pulled him by the wrist toward the door, toward the parking lot outside. And I was surprised at how easy the fever made him, how I could drag him out like a child.

We stood there between two cars, the snow falling deeper now, a constant hush, like the echo of distant traffic off the freeway. The sky was heavy with it, and I stared up wondering how much would fall between then and the morning.

—What are we doing? Omar asked.

I looked at him, standing in his socks in the snow.

—It'll help your fever, I told him, the cold.

—Doesn't sound like something Mama would say. And he looked out vacantly at the neighborhood, the roofs feeling their own weight, the cars sunk deep.

I pointed to the sky, to the sliver of snow shown by the streetlights.

—It's so quiet here, I told him. Like if there was more in the air I wouldn't hear you. Like maybe there's enough of this stuff so that I wouldn't know you. Enough to separate you and me.

Omar turned to look at me. The flecks of ice melting on his eyebrows, mixing there with the fever and sweat. He shivered. The teeth just chattering, even though the smooth muscles of his neck tried to hold them still.

—Can we go inside, Elias?

Almost pleading. And he reached over and tugged at my sleeve.

. . .

In the end this is a story with an epilogue—at least it seems this is the only way it can be.

I stayed on in that front room for a year. Went to school. Got a job. Omar went back to LA, and I kept the apartment, kept on with the writing, not his letters, but my own stuff this time.

I saw Lea, when she was maybe fifteen.

After work I'd still walk the skyway. Walk from my cubicle in the Norwest building, cross Seventh Street above the fading traffic, to the Mann's movie. She stood there outside the theater with another boy. Still had the doll's face, still the big, dark eyes. I wondered if I stood there long enough, just watching, whether she'd recognize me. But they were too busy feeling each other out, the alternate touching, almost too intimate in public. She, it seemed, less interested in him. More resigned to it all.

The counter worker called out that the movie was starting, and the boy pulled her toward the two double doors thrown wide open, the light shifting between bright and dim inside.

I watched them both hand in hand. His feral eyes, and her willingness to go.

It was like knowing you in sleep.

It was like knowing you in snow.

Some Advice on Arranged Marriage

Pallavi Sharma Dixit

You must understand immediately, arranged marriages are not what they used to be. If you intend to plunge yourself into this age-old tradition, you must forget the story of how your mother wore a pink sari, a lovely silk one, not too flashy, and sat, stiff and awkward, with her parents, three sisters, two brothers, grandparents—both sets—and two pairs of aunts and uncles, across from your father, also attended by a retinue of relatives. You might've heard that the relatives of your father interrogated your mother, and hers him, and that your mother and father never actually spoke with each other that day, but that your mother did a splendid job of serving the snacks and respecting the parents. You must forget this. There will be no tea trays or touching of elders' feet here.

If you are in love with someone already, this will not work. Take my case. How could I be sitting at Bombay Chaat House waiting for someone named Arun if I still loved Jack? It's not possible. I spent three years with him, then it was over, and I was an old maid. In the New Jersey Indian community, at least. Note: if you are an Indian girl not married by thirty, you will be the scandal of your parents' community. You will not be able to show your face at weddings of those younger than you. When you find yourself at an Indian function—a college graduation, perhaps, or a Diwali party—always try to mention in conversation with the aunties the news of the latest divorce in the community. If there isn't one, make it up.

Two months ago Jack and I broke up, and a month ago I gave in to my parents' vigorous nagging about launching me on a series of dates. That's all it is, really. Arranged dating. It's been translated into American. It's just the same as normal dating except the men are handpicked and thoroughly researched by your parents, who deliver the numbers or e-mail addresses directly to you and your potential life partner to do with as you like. No saris or star charts necessary.

Now, you may be concerned about where these eligible bachelors are being unearthed by your parents. This is not a cause for concern. Mine, as I'm sure yours will, provided me with a variety of options:

1) The matrimonials from the *India Abroad*. Other papers have sprouted up in recent years, which also may lead to marital bliss. *India in New York, Desi Talk*, etc.
2) Your local cultural association. You know, the conventions and potlucks you were forced to attend, ages three through fourteen. For instance, the Bengali Samaj, the Gujarati Society, and the Bihari Alliance of North America.
3) The Internet. Indiamatch.com, Shaadi.com. Sites with photos are best.
4) Friends, relatives, and acquaintances. Your parents will use this network to send out a nationwide call for eligible boys. Like the Bat Signal.
5) Strangers at parties.
6) Religious institutions. The local Jain Mandir, Gurudwara, Ved Mandir, etc. have lists for this sort of thing. Pandits are surprisingly resourceful people.

...

Personally, I chose to dismiss options 1 and 3. But it's up to you. When placing my order, I also specified that I would not consider F.O.B.'s. Those straight-from-the-motherland guys are not for me. But that's not to say they are not for you. My friend Sunil found the girl of his dreams in India. Through a matrimonial magazine, I think it was. Glorious Bollywood-style love is possible with someone from India met through an advertisement. I repeat, it is possible.

Before you begin, it may be wise to draw up a pros and cons list. Many are doubtful about this whole arranged dating thing. Some hesitance is understandable. A list can really help in making such a life-altering decision. Here's mine for your reference:

PROS	CONS
Background check	Questionable level of romance
Parental preapproval	
Steady income	
No commitment necessary	
Steady stream of dates	
No more Indian singles' happy hours	
Good family values, probably	
No religion or language dilemmas	
Free dinners	

As you can see, the decision wasn't hard. Although the lonely item on the cons side did carry a lot of weight. But I accept that this method of meeting my mate will not be like when I met Jack. Like in a movie, I was drawn to him from across a crowded party. Backward baseball cap, hands tucked into his butt pockets. Orange-striped shirt. Conversation was easy, yet sprinkled with those hopeful pauses you get when two people know they'll probably be in love in one to two months. I liked his optimism and blue eyes; he said later he liked my smile and baby blue toenail polish. I teased him for the duration of our relationship for not remembering what I wore that night. (Blue jeans, lavender tank top.)

But that's all beside the point.

When an attractive man (business suit, plenty of hair) comes through the door of the restaurant, I know it's Arun because he appears to be in his early thirties and he furrows his brow and searches the room. He seems overjoyed to see me and says, "I'm so sorry I'm late. The hospital, you know," and I smile my sweetest smile and reply, "Don't worry about it, I just got here." He walks past me and kisses a girl (too skinny, slutty clothes) and turns to me, now facing him and the girl, and says, "I'm sorry, did you say something? No, I mean, not to you, I was on my cell."

The waiter accosts me a second time, and I promise to order as soon as my friend arrives. I pour water into a murky plastic glass. I decide the management should really think about repainting the pink walls a more appealing color, like almond or écru. The next guy to come in is certainly

Arun. Though he is short, possibly two inches shorter than I am, and has an utterly large nose, I determine to keep an open mind. Note: Personality and sense of humor are extremely important factors to consider in this business of arranged marriage.

"Anjali? You're more beautiful in person," he says and sits down across from me. He perches at the edge of the seat, and it is clear to me that he does this to create the illusion of height. And his comment, I'm not sure, but I think it could be an insult, to my photograph at least, but I decide to let it slide because, after all, he must be nervous. And, let's be honest, I've been nervous in first conversations, too. I smile and say, "Thank you. It's so nice to meet you," and we exchange the usual questions and answers. I've listed some questions below for your future use:

1) What kind of work do you do?
2) Are you close to your family? Any siblings?
3) What do you enjoy doing in your spare time?

These are, of course, basic queries to be followed by others and inter-spersed with colorful and humorous anecdotes. Arun is a management consultant who lives in the city, like me, and who is home for the weekend visiting his parents and two brothers with whom he is quite close. He likes to skydive and read books by Fortune 500 CEOs. His nostrils flare and his eyes blink excessively when he talks. I could find these things endearing in ten years, perhaps, when we throw a small but elegant dinner party in our New York City brownstone apartment on the Upper East Side. "You know, we should probably order," I say.

He has masala dosa and I have bhel puri, and he asks if I like to cook. "I do, I love it," I say, and he leans in close, as if to share an intimate secret, and says, "I like that in a girl." I ask him about his own skills in the kitchen, and he says, "No, no way, haven't got the time."

It's generally not a good idea to raise the issue of previous relationships during a first meeting. Arun is not familiar with this rule. He does not even wait until the food arrives to bring up the question. I tell him I got out of a relationship pretty recently but I'm over it now, and he asks why we broke up, and then, thankfully, the waiter arrives with two orange trays with plates of steaming food and I avoid answering.

He says the dosa is great and I did a great job picking the place.

"Did you know this place used to be an ice-cream parlor? And over there," I point out the window, "Gokul Vegetarian Restaurant used to be a Pizza

Hut, you can tell from the overbearing red roof, and down the road there's a diner that's now Delhi Darbar and a Delhi Express that was once a Boston Market. They have Chinese food, too."

He laughs, a little too loudly, and says, "So, do you want to know my history?" I don't, but I say, "Yes, so what's your story?" It seems the polite thing to do. Note: Politeness on a first meeting goes a long way.

It turns out that Arun dated a non-Indian, too, and he left her because she lacked family values. "These white girls," he says. "No moral fiber. Not like our desi kuddis." As he says this he reaches his hand, in a bold maneuver, across the table to touch my wrist briefly with a chuckle, and I am horrified, partially by the gesture, partially by the comment.

"My ex, Jack, has excellent family values, I might add, more than some desi men I've known. He talks to his mom every other day, and he organizes a family picnic every year, and he let his sister move in with him when she needed a place to stay. You really shouldn't go around making such generalizations." Arun's enthusiasm has faded, and he leans back in his seat.

"I didn't mean to attack you," I say. I feel suddenly ridiculous eating my bhel puri across from this tiny, unpleasant man. On my first date with Jack, he asked me to name what I thought were the top five most important historical moments. We filled out the list together, combing through centuries, debating the meaning of "important." In three years we must have completed more than fifty lists over dinners. Top five songs of the 80s. Top five reasons not to wear velour.

I make less controversial small talk with Arun as we finish our food. I tell him about the recent string of robberies targeting Indian homes. "It's for the jewelry," he says, then tells me he loves kung-fu films. I have nothing to say to this.

When we're finished, he returns both of our trays to the counter. It's chivalrous, in a way. I offer to pay, and he says he won't hear of it. As he commends the cashier on the excellent food, I realize he isn't as short as I had initially thought.

We smile, not fully and generously, but with our mouths closed, the corners turned up just enough to qualify as a smile, and shake hands. "You know, I have nothing against white people," he says and sort of laughs, as if he's told a joke.

"I'm sure," I say. "It was nice meeting you."

...

The thing to keep in mind throughout this process is that you're not going to meet your soul mate on the first try. You might, but probably not. It's of the utmost importance that you keep a positive attitude. You should arrange a series of dates, a gauntlet of sorts, which will lead to your Prince Charming. You must believe me, the success rates for arranged marriage are staggering.

I call Sunita after the disaster with Arun. She met her husband through her parents after summarily dismissing seventeen prior candidates. I must confess, I was skeptical when she was going on all of these dates—she's a picky one, Sunita—but in the end she found the perfect guy. Tall, funny, good nose. They've been married a year now and are on a perpetual honeymoon. You'd never guess they were arranged.

"Don't sweat it, Anj," she says. "Just remember what I had to go through."

"I know, you're right."

"It's totally worth the effort," she says. "So, he was racist?"

. . .

I have a date lined up for tonight. I can tell from his voice he's handsome. We spoke for almost an hour, so the formal questions are done with. Vikram is a medical resident—my mom put a star next to his name on the list—and enjoys traveling and dancing. His sister is his best friend.

We've decided to meet for dinner at Dimple Vegetarian Restaurant— we both love their papdi chaat. I arrive early and stroll down Oak Tree. I go into Khazana, which has the most stylish outfits on the whole street, just to take a quick look. But I can't buy anything new. There aren't as many weddings to attend this year.

A young girl, giggling and lovely, emerges from the dressing room clad in a magenta sari, heavily sequined and embroidered with gold. It's clearly a bridal outfit. She spins round and round, too many times, before the mirror, sweeps her hair into a pile on top of her head, holding it there with one hand. "It's perfect, isn't it?" she asks her mother. "I think it's perfection," she says. I pretend to browse the racks, but I take a good look at the outfit. It's not at all what I would call perfection. For one thing, it's too sparkly. In a wedding, the attention should be on the bride—her delicate expressions, the suggestion of tears in her eyes—not on what she's wearing. Yet the outfit should compliment her, support her innate beauty. Mine will be a light shade of pink with fine embroidery that twinkles, but only when the light hits it just so.

It's true, I've had a wedding outfit in mind for months now. I have also imagined my sangeet and reception lehengas. I haven't been able to find these in any stores in Edison, so a trip to Delhi after the engagement is a must. Note: On an arranged date, you can never admit to having already selected bridal attire. Some other things not to mention:

1) That you've looked at wedding venues and narrowed it down to two.
2) That you've selected a mandap: gold-and cream-colored with a crystal chandelier hanging from the center.
3) That you're thinking Bali for the honeymoon.

I can't stand watching this foolish little girl any longer, so I leave Khazana and step back into the commotion that is always Friday evening on Oak Tree Road. I inspect the curve of my eyebrows in the window of Payal's Beauty Salon and decide that I can hold off another week before getting them threaded. Besides, the waiting area in the salon is standing room only at this time, and I have a date.

Dimple is jammed with Indians shoving and squirming about each other like at a Macy's One-Day Sale. Through a tangle of elbows and silky black hair I spot a thirtyish man trying to hold down a table. Sharp jaw, sharp nose, no unibrow. He is wearing a light blue shirt and yellow tie. It is obvious he works out. I admit, I'm startled by his good looks. I run my fingers quick through my hair and take a deep breath.

"Anjali?" He stands up as he says this, kisses my cheek.

"Yes, Vikram, hi!" I smile my widest smile, and I think he does too.

"You look like one of these actresses from a Bollywood movie I just saw, but I can't remember her name."

I sit down and so does he, and I ask, "Do you watch a lot of them?" and he says, "Just the ones I hear are good," and we are soon immersed in a dialogue on the recent films compared with the Amitabh Bachchan classics of the 70s. At the same time, we both remark that the music is not like it used to be, and then we laugh, together. He puts me at ease yet stirs up butterflies. Kind of like Jack on our first date, actually.

"Even though I live out in New Brunswick, I try to come down here once a week to eat," he says. "There's something about the chaos. The smells."

"Like India, right?"

He looks up from his menu and smiles. We fall into conversation about summers spent in India. Camel rides and Campa Cola. His favorite place is Jaipur, too.

This is not something I could ever share with Jack. I told him stories and he soaked them up—he loved India without having ever gone. He made plans, constantly, to take a vacation there, read the entire *Lonely Planet India* guide. But he hadn't grown up visiting there. This didn't bother me, at first, but then it did.

Vikram says, "We've been here an hour and haven't even ordered yet!" We both have papdi chaat, and the conversation is never awkward. I notice him studying my face when I talk, and it makes me giddy.

At the next table, a couple sits down and holds hands across the table as they read a menu. Vikram says, "How about meeting me in the city tomorrow night for a drink?" I try not to seem too ecstatic when I say, "I'd love to. Where should we go?"

. . .

When a first date goes well and you have a second date pending, it is imperative that you do not compare him to previous men you've been involved with. Do not pull out old love notes scribbled on napkins or photographs from your trip to Aruba that your parents never knew about. Do not replay in your head that first kiss on his front porch when it suddenly poured rain. Do not recall omelets he cooked, with spinach and cheese, just the way you like them, and the way he made your bed meticulously every morning without your asking. And—now this is crucial—do not question the validity of the arranged marriage process. You must remain focused. True love may be lurking three dates away.

. . .

I get back to my place in the city on Saturday afternoon, throw open my closet, and call Sunita. She arrives within an hour, and we pluck skirts and shirts from my wardrobe, holding them up then letting them accumulate in a pile around our feet. The winner is a sleeveless red top and standard black skirt. My hair will be down.

"So, you have a good feeling about this guy?"

"Yeah, yes, he was wonderful," I say. I feel vaguely like I do when I have just told a lie.

. . .

I enter the lounge near my place where we had agreed to meet, and I don't see him anywhere. I sit at the bar, which makes me feel seductive, and order a martini, which achieves the same effect. The room is barely lit yet, bright with red velvet couches and red walls and rugs. I've been here many times, but I survey the room because, of course, I want to appear occupied when he walks in.

Vikram looks striking as he walks toward me. He holds a pink rose. This can be considered cliché or adorable. I determine to consider it adorable.

He kisses my cheek, lingering longer than the first time, and gives me the rose. "I hope you won't think I'm cheesy," he says.

"Of course not. You're so sweet."

He orders a drink and slides onto the stool next to mine, swivels to face me. Our knees touch, but we do nothing to change this.

"So, the thing I don't understand is why a girl like you agreed to getting set up," he says. I don't see any suspicion in his eyes. Just curiosity.

"I used to be a man," I say and order another drink. He laughs and I am glad. A sense of humor rates high on my checklist.

"Really, how can you be single?"

"I was wondering the same thing about you," I say, and I mean it. There doesn't seem to be anything wrong with him. He is disturbingly flawless. He tells me he has no time to meet anyone, and even when he does it's never anyone with potential. "Like just last week, I met this girl at a party who said it's hard being the prettiest in the room. I couldn't believe her arrogance. There was another time when a girl, after ten minutes of conversation, asked if I wanted kids—"

"After ten minutes?"

"Yeah, and when I said probably, she said she hated kids and then puked on my shoes!"

I am struck by his animation while he tells these stories. An image of him in a tuxedo flashes in my head, and I wouldn't mind if he kissed me right there, but it's probably just the martini playing tricks.

His story leads us into an exchange of drinking-related college stories and away from the topic of my own history. This is good. I don't want to talk about Jack. And I have some fantastic drinking stories.

It is probably an hour that we sit and chat, sometimes touching knees, wrists, arms in our laughter. He buys us another round, maybe two, and our silly tales of Harvard and Princeton evolve into a thoughtful discussion of our majors, our work, our aspirations. I am relaxed and unfettered. If his intelligence and charm are not a façade, I could marry this guy, I think.

He asks, "What are your top five favorite movies of all time?"

I stare at him for perhaps too long. His smile fades and he asks, "Are you okay? Do you want some water?"

"I'm fine," I say. "I just can't answer that question." He asks the bartender for a glass of water and then holds it up to my mouth as if I need help drinking it. "I'm not drunk," I say and push the glass away. I take a sip of my martini.

"What was wrong with my question?"

"Can you just let it go, please? I just need you to let it go."

"I don't see what the big deal is," he says, almost to himself, but I must have spoken too loudly because everyone around us is silent and watching. Like they were in that moment when Jack and I knew it was over. In our favorite little Italian restaurant we thought we were fine. And then he pressed me to talk about our future and I said, unthinking, "You are not the future I planned," and then the light had gone from his eyes, and I'd said these words that could not be taken back. A wrinkled woman with bright red hair at the next table stared, I thought contemptuously, at me, and I felt like saying, "You don't know how complicated the situation is, you don't know the things that have to matter to me," but instead I wiped my nose and cheeks on my napkin, and I stood up and left.

I realize I must seem crazy to Vikram. I need to explain. I want so much to like him and for him to like me, so I need to explain. "The thing is that my ex-boyfriend always asked top five questions. Top five most embarrassing moments. Top five novels about World War II. It was our thing."

"Ah, so now I'm finally learning something about your mysterious past." He smiles a half smile and nods an all-knowing nod. I suddenly hate him.

"You don't understand anything," I say and down the rest of my drink.

"Well, why don't you tell me?"

"I can't. That's not how it's supposed to go."

"If you're over him, then it shouldn't matter," he says. He is snide and uncaring. Things Jack never was. Jack, who knew just how to calm me down when spiders would crawl into my bedroom. Who would capture the spiders in a glass then let them go outside. Jack, who took off from work when I had mono. Who would sing to me at night as I recovered, who sang out of tune, always.

My head feels heavy now and nods forward. Vikram offers me water, and I take it, and he offers to take me home, and I accept that too.

. . .

The cab seems to be swerving significantly, and I say I'm feeling sick. Vikram rubs my back then holds my hand. He's kind, this man I barely know. He could have the cab drop me off in front of my building and then push on to his friend's place where he is crashing, but he pays the driver and gets out with me. I tell him there's no need, but he insists.

In my apartment he finds a glass and fills it with water, leaves it on the nightstand next to my bed. I am lying down; I will be asleep very soon. Vikram is a hazy figure looming above me.

"Thank you," I say. "I'm sorry," I say.

He says, "Don't worry about it," and holds up a slightly crinkled picture he found on my desk. "Is this the guy?" But I am falling asleep now, I just want to sleep. I hear the door shut, and he is gone.

Authors' Biographies

Ann Bauer is the author of *A Wild Ride Up the Cupboards*, a novel published by Scribner in 2005. She lives in Minneapolis with her husband and daughter.

Jacey Choy lives in Minnesota although she was born and raised in Hawaii. Jacey writes fiction and poetry and teaches in Saint Paul, Minnesota. She lives with her artist husband while their two daughters seek the meaning of life in New York City.

Pallavi Sharma Dixit was born in India and raised in New Jersey; she currently lives in Minneapolis. She received an MFA in creative writing from the University of Massachusetts, Amherst, and recently participated in the Loft Literary Center's Mentor Series. She is at work on a novel.

Anastasia Faunce is a poet and writer of short fiction whose work has appeared in *Communication Arts, HOW, Print*, and *Water~Stone: A National Review of Literature*. She received an MFA in creative writing from Hamline University, as well as scholarships or residencies from the Blacklock Nature Sanctuary, Cranbrook Academy of Art, Inside Books Publishing Institute, Norcroft Writing Retreat for Women, and the *Utne Reader*. A former editor and publicist, Faunce is currently the director of the Split Rock Arts Program's two entities: Summer Workshops and Online Mentoring for Writers, at the University of Minnesota, Twin Cities.

Shannon Gibney is a creative writer, educator, journalist, and activist. Her poetry has appeared in *Black Renaissance Noire, Wicked Alice, The Bellingham Review,* and *PMS.* You can find her nonfiction in *Essence Magazine* and *Outsiders Within* (South End Press, 2006). Gibney was awarded a 2005 Bush Artist Fellowship and the 2002 Hurston/Wright Award in fiction. Her short fiction has appeared in *Tea Party* and *Brilliant Corners.* She is a 2002 graduate of Indiana University's MFA program in fiction and also holds an MA in twentieth century African American literature from that institution. Gibney recently returned from a research trip to Liberia where she gathered information for her new novel, excerpted in "Norfolk, 1827." She is also currently at work on *BROWN ON BROWN,* an anthology of essays on building coalition between communities of color.

Linda LeGarde Grover is a professor of American Indian studies at the University of Minnesota, Duluth. Her research articles have been published in *Minnesota History* and *Bimaadizing,* and her prose and poetry anthologized in *Sister Nations* (Minnesota Historical Society Press, 2002) as well as in the collection *Nitaawichige: Selected Poetry and Prose by Four Anishinaabe Writers* (Poetry Harbor, 2002). She is a member of the Bois Forte Band of Ojibwe.

Miriam Karmel's fiction and nonfiction have appeared in numerous publications, including *Bellevue Literary Review, Dust & Fire, The Talking Stick, Sidewalks, Passager, Jewish Women's Literary Annual,* and *Water~Stone Review.* She is the recipient of *Minnesota Monthly's* Tamarack Award for her short story "The Queen of Love." In 2007 she received the Kate Braverman Short Story Prize and the Arthur Edelstein Prize for Short Fiction. She received the Carol Bly Nonfiction Award in 2007 and 2008. *Nora's Story,* a novel in stories, was the May 2007 selection at www.bookwise.com.

Chrissy Kolaya is a poet and fiction writer from Chicago living in Morris, Minnesota. Her stories and poems have appeared in *New Sudden Fiction* (Norton, 2007) and the literary journals *Crazyhorse, North American Review, Iron Horse, Salt Hill, Birmingham Poetry Review,* and *PoemMemoirStory.*

Steven Lang, born and raised in Saint Paul, Minnesota, received his BFA in studio arts from the University of Minnesota, Twin Cities. Both a writer and a visual artist, his first published work of fiction appears in this volume. Lang has been a working artist and freelance writer since 1995. He lives in Minneapolis. (www.stevenlang.net)

May Lee-Yang is a writer, poet, playwright, and performance artist living in Saint Paul, Minnesota. Her writing has been published in *Bamboo Among the Oaks: Contemporary Writing by Hmong Americans, Water~Stone Review, To Sing Along the Way: Minnesota Women Poets from Pre-Territorial Days to the Present,* and other journals and magazines. Her plays include *Stir-Fried Pop Culture, Sia(b),* and *The Child's House.* She is the past recipient of a Minnesota State Arts Board grant, a Playwright Center Many Voices fellowship, and a participant in the Loft Literary Center's Mentor Series in Creative Nonfiction and Intermedia Arts' Naked Stages Program.

Éireann Lorsung grew up in Minneapolis, Minnesota. She received her MFA in writing and her BAs in English and Japanese from the University of Minnesota. Her previous work includes *Music for Landing Planes By* (Milkweed Editions, 2007). Her writing has appeared in *The Rake, Diode, Caffeine Destiny, MO, Barrelhouse,* and *Prairie Schooner.*

John Reimringer is a novelist and short fiction writer. A Fargo, North Dakota, native, he grew up in Kansas and moved to his father's hometown of Saint Paul in 2001. He is the recipient of two Minnesota State Arts Board grants, and his work can be found in *Carolina Quarterly, Colorado Review, Gulf Stream Magazine,* and *Louisiana Literature.*

Marcie Rendon is a member of the White Earth Anishinaabe Nation. She has received The Loft's Inroads Writers of Color Award for Native Americans and the Saint Paul Company's Leadership in Neighborhoods grant. She is author of *Farmer's Market: Families Working Together* (Carolrhoda Books, 2001) and *Powwow Summer: A Family Celebration of the Circle of Life* (Carolrhoda Books, 1996). She was also featured in *Nitaawichige: Selected Poetry and Prose by Four Anishinaabe Writers* (Poetry Harbor, 2002).

Ethan Rutherford's work has appeared in *Esopus, The New York Tyrant, Verb, Faultline, American Short Fiction,* and the Minneapolis *Star Tribune.* His fiction has been nominated for the Pushcart Prize and for inclusion in the *Best New American Voices* anthology. He is pursuing his MFA in creative writing from the University of Minnesota.

Dominic Saucedo, a native of Los Angeles, now happily resides in Minneapolis. He has received fellowships from the Minnesota State Arts Board, SASE/Jerome Foundation, and the Fine Arts Work Center.

Kaethe Schwehn earned a BA from Gustavus Adolphus College and an MFA from the Iowa Writers' Workshop. Her work has appeared in *jubilat, Flim Forum, Crazyhorse, Forklift, Ohio, Sojourners, Faultline,* and *The Literary Review.* She has been the recipient of an Academy of American Poets Prize and the Donald Justice Poetry Prize. She currently teaches at St. Olaf College in Northfield, Minnesota, where she lives with her husband, Peder, and their dog, Luxy.

Sun Yung Shin is the author of *Skirt Full of Black* (Coffee House Press, 2007), co-editor of *Outsiders Within: Writing on Transracial Adoption* (South End Press, 2006), and author of *Cooper's Lesson* (Korean/English, Children's Book Press, 2004). Her poems and prose can be found in journals and anthologies such as *Five Fingers Review, Court Green, Mid-American Review, Indiana Review, Encyclopedia A – E, Xcp: Cross-Cultural Poetics, Transforming a Rape Culture* (second edition), *To Sing Along the Way: Minnesota Women Poets From Pre-Territorial Days to the Present, Riding Shotgun: Women Writing About Their Mothers, The Praeger Handbook of Adoption,* and elsewhere. She co-edits WinteRed press, which has published chaplets by Fanny Howe, Rodrigo Toscano, Thomas Sayers Ellis, and many others. She is a 2007 Bush Artists Fellow for Literature and has also received grants from the Jerome Foundation and the Minnesota State Arts Board. She lives in Minneapolis.

Sarah Stonich's bestselling novels *These Granite Islands* and *The Ice Chorus* have been translated into eight languages. Her honors include the Loft McKnight award for fiction and numerous fellowships and residencies. Her work has appeared in anthologies and magazines here and abroad. "Assimilation" is from her collection *Vacationland,* sixteen connected stories recounting experiences of guests at the same resort. She lives in Minneapolis with her husband Jon Ware. (www.sarahstonich.com)

Josiah Titus grew up in a south Minneapolis home where books lined every wall and the dining-room table was the classroom. Every day started with bowls of cereal and his mother reading from novels and biographies. It was a childhood imbued with stories, so it came as no wonder that Josiah soon began to dream of writing his own. Now, with a degree in writing from Metropolitan State University, and currently at work on his MFA in writing at Hamline University, Josiah is doing just that. His stories have appeared in online literary journals and in print in *The Rake* magazine. Josiah lives in South Minneapolis with his wife of six years; their walls are lined with books.

Diego Vázquez wrote stories in *Twelve Branches* (Coffee House Press), and his novels include *Growing Through the Ugly* (W.W. Norton) and *The Fat-Brush Painter* (forthcoming). Recently, he was selected as a Saint Paul *Everyday Sidewalks* poet. He is proud to have his poem stuck in cement.

Robert Voedisch was raised on a farm outside of Forest Lake. He has earned a BA in English from Augsburg College and an MFA in Creative Writing from the University of Washington, as well as a Loft Mentor Series award. His fiction has appeared in *The Greensboro Review* and *North American Review*. He teaches at the Loft Literary Center and lives in the Longfellow neighborhood of Minneapolis.

Michael Walsh is the author of *Adam Walking in the Garden*, a chapbook published by Red Dragonfly Press, which will also publish his second chapbook, *Sleepwalks*. He has been the recipient of a Minnesota State Arts Board fellowship and a residency for emerging artists at the Anderson Center for Interdisciplinary Studies, sponsored by the Jerome Foundation. His poems have appeared in *Alaska Quarterly Review, Blue Mesa Review, Chattahoochee Review, DIAGRAM, The Fourth River, Great River Review, Meridian, The Midwest Quarterly, The New York Quarterly, Permafrost*, and *Southern Poetry Review*.

Diane Wilson is a creative nonfiction writer whose first book *Spirit Car: Journey to a Dakota Past* (Borealis Books, 2006) won the 2006 Minnesota Book Award in the category of Memoir, Autobiography, and Creative Nonfiction. Her work has been featured in *The American Indian Quarterly, The Reader, A View from the Loft, The Wolf Head Quarterly, Minnesota Women's Press*, and the *Pioneer Press*. She is a past editor for *Minnesota Literature*, former board chair and member of SASE: The Write Place, and the founder and editor of *The Artist's Voice*.

Kirk Wisland is a Minnesota native who received his studio arts degree at the University of Minnesota in 1999. He currently resides in Tucson, where he is pursuing his creative writing MFA at the University of Arizona.

Editor's Acknowledgments

Many people had a hand in shaping this anthology. In the early stages, libraries, colleges, and universities around the state posted our call for submissions, as did such organizations as Springboard for the Arts, MNArtists.org, and our neighbor in Open Book, the Loft Literary Center. The quantity and quality of the resulting submissions would have been much diminished without their efforts. Many of our authors, colleagues, and friends—too many to name—also provided leads, encouragement, and consultation along the way. The Jerome Foundation merits special thanks for its longstanding support of emerging artists in Minnesota, and of this publication in particular. I would also like to extend particularly effusive thanks to editors Ben Barnhart and Jim Cihlar, without whose invaluable assistance this book never would have progressed to publication.

About the Editor

Prior to moving to Minneapolis in 2005, Daniel Slager worked in New York as an editor at Harcourt Trade Publishers and at *Grand Street*, a leading quarterly magazine of literature and fine art. He is currently the Publisher of Milkweed Editions.

Milkweed Editions, a nonprofit publisher, gratefully acknowledges generous support for *Fiction on a Stick* from the Jerome Foundation and an anonymous donor.

Milkweed Editions also gratefully acknowledges sustaining support from Anonymous; Emilie and Henry Buchwald; the Patrick and Aimee Butler Family Foundation; the Dougherty Family Foundation; the Ecolab Foundation; the General Mills Foundation; the Claire Giannini Fund; John and Joanne Gordon; William and Jeanne Grandy; the Jerome Foundation; the Lerner Foundation; the McKnight Foundation; Mid-Continent Engineering; a grant from the Minnesota State Arts Board, through an appropriation by the Minnesota State Legislature, a grant from the National Endowment for the Arts, and private funders; Kelly Morrison and John Willoughby; an award from the National Endowment for the Arts, which believes that a great nation deserves great art; the Navarre Corporation; Ellen and Sheldon Sturgis; Target; the James R. Thorpe Foundation; the Travelers Foundation; Moira and John Turner; U. S. Trust Company; Joanne and Phil Von Blon; Kathleen and Bill Wanner; Serene and Christopher Warren; and the W. M. Foundation.

Interior design by Connie Kuhnz, Bookmobile

Typeset in Adobe Jenson Pro by Bookmobile Design and Publishing Services, Minneapolis, Minnesota

Printed on acid-free Enviro Rolland (100 percent postconsumer waste) paper by Friesens Corporation